PRAISE FOR GATHERING STORM

'A bit of a Heart of Darkness/Apocalypse Now tale. It is part thriller, part hippie road story and part rite-of-passage trip in search of identity. Above all it is a compelling, stylish and well-paced read. Frightening at times and searching in its awareness of landscape and family secrets, this is a fine debut.'

Weekend Australian

'A deeply moving fiction debut in which Dub examines the virtue of truth, the harm of lies, the pain of secrets, the desire for belonging and the difficulty of confronting ones past to ensure the future.'

Weekend Gold Coast Bulletin

'A gritty sandblown kind of story that once begun gets into your consciousness with compelling insistence. Yes, it's a page-turner and yes, it's a thriller-cum-rite-of-passage tale… It is a book of many pathways to the heart and soul, of not only a country but families who deny the truth of who they are and what they strive to protect …'

Sunday Tasmanian

'Here we have a Tasmanian writer with a first novel that grabs you from the very first page. Well written, it is a compelling story that takes the protagonist on a journey of self discovery… We will hear more from Rosie Dub; well done.'

Tasmanian Life

'A fascinating story of discovery, generations, Romany lore, Australia, and of Storm herself.'

Cairns Post

* * * * *

Adelaide Advertiser

'An absorbing first novel.'

Women's Day

'A tale of mystery, personal growth and discovery, this wonderfully crafted novel is uncompromising in dealing with challenging issues and exploring the life of a motherless child who has grown into a disaffected, directionless young woman.'

M/C Reviews

OTHER WORKS BY ROSIE DUB

FICTION
Flight
Between Worlds

Dr Rosie Dub is a novelist, and her short fiction and creative non-fiction articles are published internationally. Her writing, teaching and mentoring are deeply rooted in the role story plays as a vehicle for psychological and spiritual transformation. This was the subject of her PhD, and her *Alchemy of Story* newsletter on Substack continues this journey into the heart of story. She also runs a range of *Alchemy of Story* workshops in Australia and the UK, which fuse big ideas with practical techniques for creating stories that reimagine ourselves and our world. Rosie lives in Hobart, Tasmania.

Alchemy of Story
www.rosiedub.substack.com

Rosie Dub
www.rosiedub.com

First published in Australia by Penguin, 2008
Second edition, published by New Mill, 2017
Third edition published by Alchemy of Story, 2025

Copyright: © Rosie Dub 2008, 2017, 2025

The moral right of the author, Rosie Dub has been asserted

All rights reserved. No part of this publication may be reproduced, stored in a retrieval system, or transmitted, in any form or by any means (electronic, mechanical, photocopying, recording or otherwise), without the prior written permission of the copyright owner.

All characters and events in this publication are fictitious and any resemblance to real persons, living or dead, is purely coincidental.

Cover design by Jason Anscomb
Formatting by Streetlight Graphics

ISBN: 978-0-6481227-6-0

GATHERING STORM

ROSIE DUB

For Tim, Nikita, Freda and Harry

CHAPTER ONE

My hands are shaking as I put down the phone. They look bloody, splattered with the deep red ochre I've been using. I take up my brush and try to push the dizziness away. It's useless, but I try anyway, going back to my painting, concentrating on the bottom corner, the bit I can't get right. Going over and over. Trying to refocus. Trying to steady my hand and lose myself inside the process again. Usually it's easy to slip outside of time and into my painting space. But today the phone call keeps intruding, making a loop inside my head. The stranger's voice, regretful and soft. First the slow reluctant words, then a swish of speed at the end to get the cold hard facts over with. A gentle 'I'm sorry' followed by a silence that left me stupefied. All those words and only one of them mine. 'Is this Storm Cizekova?' 'Yes,' I said. That's all. Just yes. What else could I say?

I'm holding my breath, trying to keep his words at bay, trying to keep the questions from forming and jostling about inside my head. I keep holding, feeling the panicky need to gasp, but I don't because I'm trying to hold onto time. I don't want it to move on and away from here, into a different future with a space in it that can't ever be filled. The blood is thumping in the side of my head and the vein in my neck is almost bursting but I keep holding until it's impossible and my breath comes out in a rush. My hand slips and the brush sends a blood-red line right across the canvas.

Cutting it in half. Something snaps then and I'm moving. Fast. Coat... bag... heater... lights... door.

I pause in the doorway for a moment, letting the panic subside and my head adjust to the organised bustle of the crowd out here. It's strangely disorienting to be suddenly one of many. The rain is a soft slow drizzle and there's just a hint of green in the sky. A sure sign, Nan would say, but it won't snow, it hardly ever does in London. Not anymore. It's cold though and people's faces are pinched up tight and ugly against it. Mine too, probably. I button up my coat, stuff my hands deep into my pockets and step out into the crowd, walking briskly towards the Underground, heading for Paddington and a train out to Malvern. There will be snow on the hills though. And ice. I flinch as a picture of Nan fills my head. It's so vivid my body almost buckles under the pressure, as if someone's hit me hard in the stomach and I need to stop right here in the middle of the street and curl up into a little ball against the weight of it. But instead I run, pushing through the crowd, breathing steamy dragon breaths, heavy clumps of brittle hair slapping at my face, the icy wind stinging my eyes. As if speed would change anything.

The District line to Paddington is full. And too hot. The atmosphere is heavy with the stale manufactured smells of deodorant, perfume and aftershave, none of which manages to camouflage the smell of unwashed bodies, greasy hair, and damp woollen coats. It's noisy too: clanking doors, loud speakers, rustling papers and voices talking into mobiles. All these people, linked somehow to the outside world. I imagine lines joining them, a great intricate webbing. I'd like to paint that, see if I can draw together all those connections and find a pattern. It would make a change from the minimalist wastelands I've got stuck on.

The train stops and starts, sometimes at stations, sometimes between them. I hate the between-stations bits, when it's dark out there, and the carriage falls into a sneaky uncomfortable silence because we're all checking out the exits. There's no guarantee that we'll ever start again and it's not how any of us want to die, not together, that's for sure. Not squeezed up tight between the greasy window and my wheezy neighbour. It seems worse today because I'm heavy with the news. Singled out somehow. It's tempting to shout it out. Hard not to stamp my foot with frustration. Anything to ease the tension of all these stops and starts. I don't suppose the outside of me shows how inside I'm speeding way ahead. I can't, I won't believe this, until I get there and see for myself.

It's only just after three, too early for the commuters, so the Malvern train is nearly empty. My seat is ribbed with knife slashes: the ceiling, the walls, everywhere, all covered with signatures and messages, the whole thing lit by the cruel glare of flickering white fluoros. I read the messages: 'I was here', names and dates and too many fuck this's. I flick through a section of the newspaper someone's left behind: a race riot up north; suicide bombers; government corruption... hate and greed, and more hate, and they're all missing the point. I turn away from the bold headlines and desperate faces. Today my own drama has taken the power from the news.

Outside are the suburbs, rows of grimy houses and tiny yards backing onto the train line. It's appalling, the smallness of everything and the sameness, the arbitrary fences dividing people's lives. Everything seems shabby and ugly and hopeless. Not long ago, Christmas was lighting up the winter, but now all that's left are dying pine trees, thrown into back yards, sad-looking forgotten decorations strung around windows, and too much rubbish.

Further out, the open fields are better. The sky is low and grey. A dreary colourless scene with muted tones, blurred at the edges. There are painters who could make something of these scenes, add romance, even a tragic pathos, and I envy them that. Because I need hard edges and lines that hurt. I need the glare of sunlight… somewhere else. People keep asking about the light in my paintings. It's not European, they say accusingly, as if I should be able to pin it down on a map.

'It's from here,' I tell them pointing at my head. I'm worried though, that now I've moved into a bare kind of minimalism, I might get stuck. Max says not to worry, that my style will evolve. Anyway, he keeps telling me there's a place for minimalism. People like it. It's easy to hang on their walls. Easy to live with. I guess he's right, my paintings do sell. But I'm not so sure. I don't want people buying my paintings to blend in with their designer furniture. That's not why I paint. For me minimalism is more like the next to last stop on a late night bus route. I mean where do you go from there? A blank canvas? A frame? A bare wall? I feel like I'm backing myself into a corner. And I don't know why it's happening.

It's a relief when the rain starts again and the drops against the window make everything run, washing away the world out there. I reach into my bag for the phone and then hesitate. I need to talk to Max, but don't want to ring him at work. I couldn't bear that preoccupied efficiency Max gets in the office, listening with one ear while he's thinking about something else entirely, or even worse, the patient tone he assumes when I go 'all emotional' as he puts it, which I will do if I speak to him. But worst of all, I might have to talk to his personal assistant, Fi, with her 'You're not good enough for my Max' voice, and her awful, greedy-for-gossip sympathy.

None of this is fair on Max, who needs to know, not least because we're supposed to be meeting at the opening of Petra's show later on. My fingers are shaking again as I push the numbers. It rings and rings and then switches over to his voicemail. He must be in a meeting or out with a client. I try his mobile, but he doesn't answer, so I leave a message in a voice that's shaking as much as my fingers.

'Hi', I say after the beep, 'it's me. I'm on my way to Nan's.' I pause for a moment, reluctant to say the words... Then: 'She's dead.'

It's the first time I've said this out loud and the short sharp drama of it is like an electric shock. I recoil from the awful excitement that's surging about in my belly and blink away the swirling tears. I was going to visit Nan next weekend. Only four more days. And now she's gone. We didn't tidy things up between us the way you should before someone dies. We didn't even get to say good bye. It isn't fair.

I briefly consider ringing Alison. We went to school together and she knows Nan, so I wouldn't have to explain anything or fill in the blanks. She's also a social worker and is used to listening. But she'll still be at work, listening to someone else whose life has unravelled. I should probably ring Petra too, but she won't miss me tonight, she'll be too busy scoffing cheap red, smiling a lot and not speaking properly to anyone, which is what we all do at our openings.

I switch off the phone. There's a lump growing in my throat and I have to keep swallowing to hold it down, so I probably couldn't talk anyway. I don't want to cry here amongst the slashed seats and the graffiti and the people I'll never know. It feels like I'm teetering on the edge of an abyss. All it would take is someone to ask: 'Are you alright, dear?' Then I'd howl and howl.

Leaning back against the seat, I close my eyes and concentrate on my breathing, After a while I settle into the clickety-clack rhythm of the train, letting it slow me down until I'm not ahead of myself any more, not even in a hurry. I don't know how many times I've made this journey from London to Malvern, but I've never tired of it. Two and a half hours outside time and space and the whole tangled mass of connections between everything. Usually I dream, or sketch, but today all I do is sit and feel the awfulness settling inside. Nan is gone. The words go over and over in my head. She's dead. She's gone. Forever. I'm alone. And every time I think it, the world seems bigger and my connection to it more tenuous.

Enough. I try to shake myself free of the fear and consider the practicalities: newspaper notices, a coffin, a funeral… things I know nothing about. Things that Nan does well. Not me. I don't know where to begin and I feel a flicker of resentment at being forced into this new role, which is stupid because I'm twenty-eight years old and should be able to handle this sort of thing. Grow up Storm, I growl to myself.

The rain has stolen the last of the daylight and now, looking out, I am faced with myself. I look startled, as if I've been caught out at something. The double-glazed windows give my face two edges. One hollow and gaunt, almost a skeleton, the other more fleshy, more like the real me, but it's scary to see just how little there is between one me and the other. I realise too, with another shock, what a mess I am, dark hair frizzing and fanning about all over the place and paint splodges on my cheek and chin. It's me all right, a messy me, that only an hour or so ago was in a different space, painting and not caring. Underneath my coat I'm still wearing my work clothes: paint-splattered jeans torn at the knee, and an old jumper of Max's that's unravelling at the elbows, with its loose strands of wool that dangle in the paint and add their own interpretation to things. Max says it's not professional, but I like the way their little intrusions take my work down paths I wouldn't normally go. They make me adventurous.

I tug at my hair, spit on a tissue and wipe my face, trying to fudge the cross over between then and now, that space and this. For a moment I'm back in my studio, with the unwashed brushes, the sharp smell of turps, the insipid, hopeful glimmer of the rusty bar heater, my coffee, cold on the bench, with its ugly thick skin… and my canvas, almost filling an entire wall - two blocks of colour sliced horizontally, one white-blue light, one deep-red dark. A self-portrait, I'd called it when Max asked. He laughed and said I was a blockhead, but I was only half joking and so was he and somehow the name has stuck. A self-portrait and I couldn't begin to explain why.

The eyes and the skin in the window are darker than mine. It's me, but not me, and for the first time I see the truth of my likeness to Great Gran Milada. I wonder if I'll end up with Millie's ferocious thick black eyebrows and the perfect white hair that was once perfectly black. Probably. Without the help of black henna, my hair is already speckled with white. Millie's hair was glossy and smooth, its waves reaching all the way down to the small of her back. Mine is shoulder length and has its own messy mind. I loved brushing Millie's hair, listening to it crackle with electricity, but I hardly ever remember to brush mine.

Millie and Pop and Nan were the only family I had. They brought me up between them. Nan was Millie and Pop's only child. She was also my grandmother and my reluctant surrogate mother. It was Nan who fed and clothed me and taught me her version of the world. And now she's dead. With no warning, and I'm not ready to be left alone like this. The thought of it makes me dizzy. There's no one else. That's it. No one except Max. Suddenly I'm swamped with an irrational fear. What if I lose him too?

Poor Pop was the only man in a house full of women. He was Millie's long suffering husband, Nan's patient father and my ancient great-grandad. Pop was also the closest thing I've ever had to a father, but he died when I was ten. He was tall and thin, with a curved-in chest and a curved-out back, and when he got old and sick the curves got curvier and he got shorter, or so it seemed. Perhaps I was simply growing up. He had a slow kind of gentleness and huge square hands. They were black in the cracks and under the nails too, because he always had them in the soil, and they smelt of earth and the sap of living things. Millie told me once she thought it a wonder they never blossomed.

I was twelve when Millie died. It was probably throat cancer that took her, but we never knew for certain because she wouldn't go to the hospital for tests. Even though Nan begged, Millie wouldn't do it. She hated hospitals, like all Romany people once did. Hospitals are for death. The sheets, uniforms, walls, operating gowns... all glaring white. And for Millie white represented death. It was the colour of pain, the colour of mourning. She wouldn't see a doctor either. Nan even snuck one in for a home visit once, but Millie had him out the door in a second, waving her skirts at him and shouting that he was a filthy devil Gadje.

Right up to the end she spent every afternoon sitting out the front on an old tree stump, with her skirts spread wide around her. Most days Pop would sit with her, raising his cap to passersby while Millie puffed on her pipe. They hardly ever spoke which bothered me a bit, because I was the sort of child who liked to fill in spaces, but it seemed a companiable silence, not a hostile one. I'd wonder if they'd been married so long their minds had welded together somehow and the messages just went straight through without words.

After Pop died, Millie kept on with her sitting ritual and most days after school I would sit with her for a while. We'd both try to ignore Nan, hovering busily behind us in the kitchen, sending out regular glares of shame and disapproval.

'What are you doing Millie?' I'd ask.

'Watching the world pass, girl.'

I'd try to copy her, sitting as still as I could on an upturned bucket and chewing a soursob or a piece of grass in place of a pipe. But there was always something to distract me: a line of ants, a ladybird, people passing... Millie would hardly move, just spread her mouth into a great toothless grin, revealing her obscenely pink gums. One of the things I learned from sitting out there with Millie was that people look away from toothlessness. I once asked Nan how much of your face you could lose before nobody would see you at all. 'Silly billy,' she said and tugged at my fly-away hair, trying to keep me in order. That's the problem with being a kid. Nobody takes you seriously.

Then the Thomson kids moved in down the road and started tormenting Millie. They'd hide behind the wall, chanting stupid songs: *My mother said, I never should, play with the gypsies, in the wood ...*

At first Millie roared at them and they'd run off squealing. 'Like pigs having their throats cut,' Millie said, laughing in big gasps. When her voice dried up she took to spitting globs of black and green muck that I'd poke at cautiously with a stick. But when the Thomson kids turned on me, I abandoned my upside down bucket and went inside. I was eleven and my loyalties were already turning away from family. Millie was sixty-seven, and dying. I wonder if she ever knew I was ashamed of her.

And now Nan is dead. I don't know why or how, but suddenly I'm struck by the coincidence. She was sixty-seven too.

CHAPTER TWO

It's nearly 6 p.m. when the train pulls in to Greater Malvern station. Snow falls in thick flurries around me. The hills are a heavy brooding silhouette against the glowing orange of a snowy sky. I climb into a waiting taxi but the driver shakes his head. He looks tired, with great folding bags under his eyes, as if he's been working for days on end.

'I don't know lassie, it's icy up there.'

'Please, just up to the Cutting.'

There's an edge to my voice that gets to him.

He nods, fatherly now. 'Come on then, we'll have a go.'

He drives in low gear, winding carefully up the hill, up and up, into the fairytale land of my childhood. I love these hills, all nine miles of them, laced with paths and ley lines, weaving through woods and scrub and wide open grassy patches, from North Hill to Chase End Hill. For all their magic, the hills are solid. And so is the cottage. They are part of my childhood. Real evidence. But the rest of my childhood lies only in the foggy realms of memory, frustratingly elusive. I guess it's only nostalgia, but the past has a power over me that I can't explain.

In a way it was this yearning for an ungraspable past that made me an artist. Perhaps I'd already lost too much, because even as a child I tried to capture and hold on to everything. At first with stories and then sketches, because they came more easily to me. Art was my anchor, a way of ignoring the fleeting, transitory nature of life. And because of that, my painting is not what it should be. I remember once reading about the Moors, how they wore silk and rode their horses lightly. When an arrow pierced them, the silk came with it into the body, penetrating but protecting. In contrast, the English wore armour so heavy it exhausted them. They sweated and stank and could hardly move in it. I want my paintings to be light and strong, like the dance of a warrior in a silk vest, but they're becoming more like a suit of armour, heavy and constricted.

As we near the top, the snow gets thicker. A snow-plough has been through, piling up the snow on either side, but the road is already covered with a fresh layer and the taxi's wipers are feebly trying to keep the windscreen clear.

The driver stops at Wyche Cutting. He looks anxious and beaten and I see that it isn't just the bags under his eyes. The rest of him seems to have folded into the shape of his seat.

'Sorry love, I can't get any further.'

'That's fine,' I tell him, digging out my wallet. 'I can walk from here.'

I step out carefully, but it's not slippery yet. The snow is powdery and deep and my feet sink a long way down. It's impossible to tell where the path is, so I lift my feet and knees high, feeling silly, as if I'm on parade. When I was little that's what I pretended when the snow was deep like this. I was a marching girl, or more often an explorer, wading through Arctic snow in my wellies.

There's no wind, so the snow falls gracefully, almost floating. It feels as if someone has turned gravity down, as if any moment I might float too, in a gentle dance with the snow. I lift up my face to the sky and let the flakes settle. They're soft, almost caressing, but within seconds I can feel the cold creeping into my skin and taking over. By the time I step across the invisible line that runs along the hilltops, separating Worcestershire from Herefordshire, I have a fine coating of snow on my head and shoulders.

When I turn up the little lane to the cottage, I'm shocked to find it shrouded in darkness. Nan always left a light on. Just in case. I have to push the gate hard against the snow and the hinges squeak, obscenely breaking the padded silence of the night. As I fumble about in my bag for the key I've never needed before, a cat darts swiftly past, making me jump. It's absurd that I'm this nervous.

I half expect to see Nan standing at the door, her hair cut neatly to just below her ears, practical, the way she always liked it. She inherited Pop's hair: tame and fine mouse brown. But she got Millie's hips, wider than wide and sitting awkwardly on her thin top half. Nan would swear that her big bottom was the only thing she ever got from Millie and maybe she was right. They were so different. Millie spilling out everywhere, Nan holding herself in. Millie in her long flowing skirts and Nan always in trousers, the stretchy sort with elastic around the waist and ironed-in pleats up the front.

If Nan were here now she'd call out to me as I walk up the path.

'Bless your legs,' she'd say and then she'd almost smile, just a twitch at the corners of her mouth and a softening around her eyes, so subtle most people would miss it. But not me. I was always studying Nan's face, looking for the softening that hardly ever came.

Then Nan would look me up and down as if I was a starved chicken that wanted fattening. 'Still too thin. Doesn't Max look after you?'

I would frown. As if Max was my keeper. As if I wasn't old enough to look after myself. But she'd ignore it.

'Come on,' she'd say, 'come and eat some proper food.'

Cooking was Nan's way of loving. The whole process was so important for her: planning meals, buying ingredients, preparing, cooking, feeding… she poured into it a part of herself that had no other way of connecting with the world. When I ate Nan's food I accepted her love in the only way she could give it. To refuse her cooking would have been a betrayal so deep, neither of us would have recovered.

If Nan were here now, I would meekly follow her inside to the heart of the cottage, her kitchen, so different from the one in Max's apartment, with its smooth stainless-steel finishes, empty surfaces and lingering smell of disinfectant. Or my studio, with its paint-splodged trestle table and two-burner stove wearing the thick stains of a long history of overflows and oversights. Nan must be one of the last people in Britain not to have a fitted kitchen. Instead there's a motley assortment of furniture: dark wood dressers; benches; a rough stone sink in which hundreds of dishes must have chipped, cracked and smashed over the years; and a heavy wooden table scored with history. I'd sit at this table while Nan chopped and stirred and clattered, and study its surface, a zigzag of chopping marks and messages, my favourite written by my mother: 'Kita was here,' and the date '1965'. That's all. I've read and reread this short message countless times, running my fingers across its contours, as if by doing this I could know something about her.

But Nan isn't here and I resist the temptation to call out for her, knowing that my voice will be too loud. Instead I concentrate on detail, shaking the snow off my shoulders and out of my hair, unlacing my boots and wincing as my feet absorb the shock of the cold stone floor. I keep my coat on because there's no warmth in the house. The smell is already wrong and I wonder that a person can be wiped away just like that. It's better with the light switched on, but still cold and there's nothing cooking. No rich smell of ground coffee either. The only sign that the police have been here are the little puddles of melted snow from their boots. I hate the thought of them traipsing about the house.

In a moment I'm busy, as if movement will dispel the emptiness. I go back out into the swirling snow to fill the coal bucket, then build a fire in the tiny olive-green room off the kitchen where we all used to sit on those long silent nights, reading or just staring dreamily at the fire. When I was really young I loved these evenings, staying up after dark, comfortable and safe with the grown-ups. I loved the darkness outside and the way the warm yellow light from the flames made patterns on the walls, and I loved the bookshelves that reached all the way to the ceiling and were filled with mysterious words I would read one day. But as I got older I felt the resentments simmering under the surface and sensed the harsh unspoken words, the tension drawn tight through the air: Nan reading with a fierce concentration; Pop sighing over his book, only half reading; and Millie staring at the fire with a wild kind of wanting in her eyes. Then later, when Millie and Pop were dead, the room was still too full: Nan blocking me out with her books, me filled with impatient teenage energy, and the desperate feeling of being stuck.

While the fire takes, I grind coffee beans, put the percolator on the stove and check the fridge. There's rhubarb pie and leftover lamb casserole that I sniff at cautiously. I'm not sure I want to eat anything. There's a sense that this food is tainted in some way. The food of the dead. Still, I haven't eaten since breakfast. I never eat when I'm painting. For me it's always better to work with an empty growling stomach, a prickly unsatisfied need. I get absorbed, losing track of time in a way that I rarely do in my other life.

Now my stomach wages a short battle with my mind and wins. I grab a spoon from the drawer and eat the pie straight out of its dish before there's time to change my mind. In a sense it seems fitting that Nan is reaching out from the dead and still feeding her hungry little bird. But it's weird too. Just yesterday she was clattering about here in this kitchen and now she's cold and stiff and covered up, laid out on a slab somewhere in Worcester and this is the last time I'll ever eat her rhubarb pie. At the thought of this, the pie sticks in my throat and a chill makes its way down my spine. Nan never showed me how to cook, never passed that part of herself down to me. I wish she had. I wish I could conjure Nan: in the tart sweetness of her rhubarb pie; in *shax shuklo*, the chicken and cabbage stew Millie loved so much; or the minted lamb casserole Audrey showed her how to make; or in my favourite, *galushki*, sugar and almond dumplings boiled in milk. Romany and Gadje, two halves of Nan split right down the middle, and I can conjure neither.

The fire's crackling, the coffee's ground and bubbling on the stove and the casserole's heating in the oven, sending out a warm meaty aroma. I have almost succeeded in banishing the cold emptiness of death. But when the phone rings, it's still too loud and I hesitate, half expecting Nan to answer it. It's Max; he must have been trying the mobile, but I forgot to switch it back on.

'Storm? Are you okay?'

As soon as I hear Max's voice, I'm not okay. I nod, because I don't trust my voice, but of course he can't hear that.

Storm? Are you there?

And now I'm sobbing and trying to tell him about Nan but all I can say is 'She's dead' but he already knows that. Max out of his depth. He doesn't know how to deal with the immeasurables of life, and emotions are in that category.

After a while the sobbing slows of its own accord. 'Sorry,' I say, wiping my eyes with my coat sleeve and taking big shuddering breaths.

'How did it happen?' Max asks gently.

'Someone found her up on the hills… they think she froze to death.'

'Jesus! How? I mean… Why?'

'I don't know, maybe she slipped. They're doing an autopsy.'

'Jesus!… I would have come with you,' he says, then pauses. 'Do you want me to drive up now?'

I hesitate. There's a big part of me that wants Max here, the part that wants to lean on him and let him take over, the way he usually does. But there's also a seed of a feeling that's growing and it's telling me not to let anyone intrude on the sacredness of this night. Not even Max.

'The weather's foul,' I say, 'and I bet the M40's gridlocked. It would take hours. Can you come up tomorrow?'

There's a silence and when Max finally speaks, I can hear the relief in his voice and the control. He's back on track.

'Okay,' he says, 'That's probably best. I've got a meeting I can't get out of in the morning, but I'll get Fi to reorganise everything else… Will you be okay up there by yourself, *chiriko*?'

Max picked up my pet name from Nan, but Millie gave me the name years ago. It started as *chirikillo*, which means little bird, and then when I got older Nan dropped the 'little' part and just called me *chiriko*. Max would call me *chirikillo* if he could pronounce it, because I am little, only up to his shoulders and he's not that tall himself. Flighty and fast, Millie used to call me, and that's how I got the name.

'I'm fine, Max, honestly. See you tomorrow,' I say trying to sound brave, but when I put the phone down, the silence is suddenly too loud and the atmosphere poised, as if it's waiting for something. For just a moment I wish Max *was* coming and I even feel a flash of resentment. Why didn't he insist?

I'm sitting up close to the fire, eating the casserole when there's a banging on the door. I sigh. So much for keeping tonight sacred. It's the police. I half expected them to visit. But even so, my palms break out into a sweat and I don't know what to do with the piece of chewed-up lamb still in my mouth. The older one has three chins and gives me a reassuring smile, but the younger one's face is hard and suspicious. His eyes rove about the room behind me and then fix on the plate I'm holding. Suddenly I'm ashamed to be eating at a time like this.

The older one introduces himself as Police Constable Dutton and asks if I'm a relative of Mrs Cizekova. I have to think for a second before I realise he's talking about Nan who was never married. I manage to nod and give him a weak smile. But I can't look him in the eye.

'I'm Storm,' I say. 'Her granddaughter... I'm her only...' The words get stuck in my throat as the full impact of my isolation hits me.

'I'm sorry,' he says and I wish he wouldn't because it makes me want to cry all over again. 'A neighbour,' he pauses and consults his notebook, 'a Mrs Audrey Woods, has identified your grandmother.'

I nod, relieved. But poor, poor Audrey, having to do that. She and Nan were so close. Even though they were from such different worlds: Audrey so posh, with roots stretching right back; and Nan, well read, but not grounded, with no sense of certainty about where she belonged. Audrey loved cooking, which must have helped open Nan's heart to her. How often I came home from school to find them with their heads together, studying a recipe, or drinking coffee at the table, while a cinnamon teacake or scones sat baking in the oven. If anyone knew Nan's secrets it would be Audrey.

'But if you'd like to see the body...' Constable Dutton must see the horrified expression on my face. 'There's no visible sign of injury,' he adds quickly. 'It could've been a heart attack, but we'll have a better idea once they've done the autopsy.'

I shouldn't be surprised. I knew they were doing an autopsy. But there's a huge difference between the word and the things that are behind it. I feel sick at the thought of some stranger in a white coat cutting open my Nan.

'Was she depressed?'

The young one speaks too quickly and I don't think I've heard him properly.

'Pardon?'

'Did she seem depressed at all?'

I'm shocked. If it had been Millie I would have said yes. Millie had wild swinging moods, working herself into a swirling ecstasy that caught everybody up with it, and then plummeting down into a hellish low. Nan and Pop had to gently draw her back out. Sometimes it took weeks or even months. Once they almost gave up and talked about sending her away somewhere, though nothing ever came of it. But not Nan. She was always so level. So steady. *Steadily unhappy*, I think, and once the thought is there I can't push it away. Perhaps the worst sort of depression is the one that stays on and on, banishing you to a shadow land, a world of monotones, with no highs and lows. Maybe Nan *was* depressed but I never saw it because I never saw past my idea of Nan and into Irene Cizekova. I wasn't there for her, not the way she was for Millie. I was never loyal to the Romany way.

'Did she?' the young one asks again, jolting me back into the ugly reality of now.

'I don't think so,' I eventually stutter. 'I talked to her a few days ago and she sounded fine.'

PC Dutton nods and I get the feeling I've confirmed something for him. But the young one thinks I'm hiding a vital piece of information. I can tell.

'We didn't find any evidence of a note,' he tells me.

Suddenly I'm angry and this sweeps away the paranoia. 'Hang on a minute. What are you insinuating?'

'I'm sorry,' says PC Dutton, 'but we have to check all possibilities.'

At the gate he turns back as if he's just remembered something. 'By the way, she wasn't wearing a coat when they found her.'

I shut the door quickly to hide the shock. Sure enough, Nan's Barbour, with its pungent smell of damp earth and oil, is hanging on the hook near the front door, the sleeves still creased at the elbows as if she's just slipped it off. For a moment I can almost see Nan coming in from one of her walks, her cream woollen beanie pulled down low over her ears, her cheeks and nose red from the cold air, the light fading from her eyes as she shuts the door behind her. No one in their right mind would go out on the hills without a coat. Not at this time of year. I turn away, not ready to tackle the implications of that.

Restless now, I wander from one room to the next. The dining room is cluttered with the potted plants Nan brought in for the winter. The soil is still wet. She must have watered them yesterday. Do people water plants if they're planning to die? I can't imagine it.

Upstairs the air is cold and still, already musty, and my breath comes out in billowing clouds. Nan's bed is perfectly made. The dirty-washing basket in the bathroom is empty and the bathroom is spotless. But that's not unusual. Aside from Max, Nan is the tidiest person I know.

I move on. Millie and Pop's old room is full of junk: Nan's things, and all my things that Nan never could bring herself to throw out, but nothing of Kita's or Pop's because Millie was around when they died and she burnt some and tossed the rest. It's the Romany way she said, and that was that. Nan only managed to salvage a few bits and pieces: a school exercise book of Kita's, full of doodles and bad spelling, and an old pair of her leather sandals, Indian style. There's nothing of Millie's, because when she died Nan did as she was told, burning the bedding and her nightdress and throwing out the rest. I guess she didn't want Millie's *mula* coming back to haunt her.

My room was Kita's once. My bed was Kita's. And yet there's nothing of my mother in this room. Not even the bedding. Millie saw to that.

'The dead live on in our heads and our hearts,' she told me when I asked. For her everything else was just clutter. But this made it worse for me. I didn't remember my mother. How could I? And no one ever wanted to talk about her even though I nagged and nagged.

'She's not in my head or my heart,' I said, sobbing. 'She's nowhere.'

Millie hugged me tight and tried to make me safe, but she couldn't bring back my mother. Nothing could. Kita was dead and there was never any doubt that it was my fault.

Leaving isn't the same as dying and Nan liked to keep everything, so she's left my room pretty much how it was when I moved to London to go to the Royal College of Arts, ten years ago. Even though London was only 120 miles away, leaving was one of the hardest things I ever did. I took very little with me, just my painting equipment, a few clothes, a large apple pie, Nan's blessing, and the awful knowledge that, like my mother, I was breaking Romany tradition, and breaking Nan's heart.

I look around. It's all here: the bed with the pingy mattress, the scruffy old Peggy doll that I've had forever. Nan called it a hygiene risk and wanted to throw it out, but I loved it so much she couldn't, so she washed it and patched it again and again. And six gold ribbons for running. I was good at that. Could run like the wind, Nan said.

Some of my paintings are on the walls: a realistic watercolour of Malvern Priory, with the brown rut of ploughed fields behind it; an abstracted study of bluebells on Midsummer Hill; and that final painting I did for my A levels, when I'd just discovered oils and loved squeezing them straight and thick onto the canvas, playing with texture and adding new dimensions. I was so proud of it then, but now I see it for what it is, a self-conscious, self-portrait, melodramatic and overly serious.

It's all still here as if a part of me has never moved on and my childhood is a separate entity, stored in this room for safe keeping. But tonight I'm not tempted to enter into it. Instead I'm drawn back to Nan's room.

I go in tentatively, lose my footing and stumble onto the bed. I'd forgotten how bowed the floor is, how it tilts the bed towards the window, and props the rest of the furniture at all different angles. One day the floor will fall right in and everything will land in a pile in the little green room downstairs. I look about Nan's room, at the big deep cracks that run right along the wall and the small square panes on the window, the glass so old that it's thicker at the bottom and makes funny shapes of the trees outside.

It's so long since I was last on this bed and now I'm too big and it's too small. After a bad dream I sometimes used to climb in with Nan and lie there soaking up her comforting warmth until the shaking stopped. She hardly ever let me stay in her bed all night though, only sometimes when I was sick and delirious and everything was fast and grainy and I was afraid of the shadows in the corners of my room. I'd convalesce in her bed too, spreading my miniature dolls and farm animals across its vast hilly expanse. But usually Nan's room was out of bounds. Every year I would sneak in to search for Christmas presents and once I stole a few pence out of her purse. I can even remember the sweets I bought with her money - raspberries and milk bottles - and how they tasted different, sort of guilt-flavoured. I never owned up and now it's too late.

I feel like a child again, trespassing in Nan's private space. But I'll have to get used to this. Soon I'll be expected to go through everything, making impossible judgments about what's valuable and what isn't. Or should I do it Millie's way and burn the lot? I don't know. Nan didn't leave instructions.

I open the wardrobe, and am dismayed to find it absolutely overflowing. The mustiness makes me sneeze. There's a trunk too, and a chest of drawers, both stuffed full. It's strange how tidy this room is on the outside, but inside it's crammed and chaotic, everything squeezed in tight and threatening to explode. A bit like Nan.

As soon as I spot the envelope I know it's important. Even before I see my name on it, I know it's for me. It's sitting on the bedside table asking to be found. It's not been sealed and there's no doubt the police will already have looked in it, so it can't be a suicide note. I turn it over in my hands, feeling it, looking for clues, but not opening it, because there's a part of me that's afraid of what I will find. This must be the way Pandora felt when she looked at that forbidden box – fear and desire all mixed up together. Of course she opened it. And of course nothing was ever the same again. Because you can't undo knowing.

I steady myself, take a deep breath and open the envelope. Inside is a photograph. I pull it out and for a few seconds stare at it blankly, trying to decipher the image. There's something about the colour of it that makes it look old, even though it's in good condition and not tattered or faded, not even fingered much. Then the whole thing clicks into place. It's the seventies. It's my mother. And she's holding a child. I turn the photograph over. On the back it says quite clearly: 'Kita and Storm, 1978'.

All at once I'm overcome with vertigo. Suddenly the ground has given way beneath me, taking all my certainties with it and rewriting my history. My heart is pumping loudly inside my ears, drowning everything out, except Nan's voice.

'Your mother died having you... It happens... A complication.'

I believed her. Of course I did. I never questioned it. She was my Nan.

'A life for a life,' she said, and I still remember the heavy lead-like weight settling inside me. I was only nine or ten, too young to understand, but when she told me that, I felt a kind of instinctive recognition. It was almost a relief. I finally had an explanation for the thing that was missing between me and Nan.

I look at the photograph again, at my smiling mother holding me in her arms. What a monumental thing this is, and yet there's a part of me that isn't surprised. I've always known there are secrets. This house is full of them. But why did Nan lie to me about this? And why leave the photograph here, now, when it's too late to ask questions?

I fumble blindly back down the stairs and rummage through the cupboards until I find a bottle of Nan's elderflower wine. With the first mouthful I realise how cold I've become. My whole body is shaking and oozing a thick, unhealthy sweat. It's a sweat of fear and revelation. I stoke up the fire and sit close to it, letting the warmth slowly make its way into me before I dare look at the photograph again.

I already have a photograph of my mother. Just the one. I've had it ever since I can remember. It's a head and shoulders picture, so I could never tell what her body was like. In it she's laughing, her mouth big and wide, her teeth white and even. She has an expressive mouth, built for a language other than English. Her hair is shoulder length, thick, and shiny black, almost blue, and her eyes are black like her hair. I keep the photograph in a silver frame next to my bed. Max says we're alike, that like me her eyes have a spark in them, something irrepressible. But aside from her hair, I can't see it. Who can ever see their own likenesses?

This photograph is different. She's older. Still smiling, but her eyes are hooded, maybe even a bit vacant. The spark is gone or been replaced by something else, a brooding sadness. Her hair is long this time and parted in the middle. She looks thin, almost gaunt, in a silky cream lace top and an ankle-length wrap-around skirt with one of those busy Indian patterns in ochre-toned reds and yellows. Around her neck is an amulet like the one Millie used to wear, a gold coin threaded onto leather.

Kita has changed. She's a mother. Maybe the new look in her eyes is the weight of responsibility. Or could it be disappointment? Did I fail to make her happy? I stare hard at my toddler self, fascinated. We didn't have cupboards full of family albums, like the kids I went to school with. There aren't many pictures of me as a child and none as a baby. I must be about two. I'm smiling, but my eyes are anxious. There's muck around my mouth and a smear of something down my right cheek. My outfit is clean though, as if I've been dressed up for this photograph, but my mother has forgotten to wipe my face. I stare at her face and then mine. We are alike, but I still can't pinpoint the similarities. I have tight black curls, her hair is longer, wavy but without the lustre of the earlier photograph. There's something else too, one edge of the photograph is slightly crooked. It's been cut and if I look really closely, I can make out the shoulder of the missing person.

The questions come all in a rush. Where was this photograph taken? And why? Where is my mother now? Why did she leave me? Is she still alive? If not, then how did she die? Who cut the photograph in two? And why? Is that my father's shoulder? Questions, questions and no one left to ask. My father's name is listed on my birth certificate: Michael William Harding. But that's all I know about him. Whenever I asked, Nan and Millie only ever met my questions with blank stares. I sensed there was more, that uneasy glances were being passed over the top of my head.

'I never met him,' Nan would say, but she did tell me he was dead. 'Long gone,' she told me. 'Don't worry about him.'

And all Millie would say was, 'Leave well alone'.

I have a sense that the questions themselves might hold the answers, if only I could look hard enough at them. Maybe then I could see a pattern, some sort of repetition through the generations, something that might explain why there are so many secrets. But right now I can't look at anything too closely because Nan's lethal elderflower wine has sent the room into a spin. An overwhelming weariness comes over me. This day has already gone on too long. I don't want to sleep upstairs tonight, so I take a cushion and blankets from the linen cupboard and curl up downstairs, on the floor in front of the fire. Knees tucked high into my chest, too drunk to care how hard the floor is under this square of carpet.

A knocking sound drifts into my consciousness. Someone is at the front door. I lie still and quiet, waiting for whoever it is to go away. There's a battle raging between two sides of me - one to understand, the other to step back to a time when I didn't know. This lie has made all the losses seem bigger somehow: my mother and father, then Pop, Millie and now Nan. All gone. There's no one left to demand the truth from. They've taken it with them. And left me all alone. A surge of self-pity rushes through me as the knock comes again, louder this time. I've left all the lights on, but I'm still going to pretend I'm not here. There's a long tight pause before the gate creaks shut behind the intruder.

My sleep is punctuated by dreams. I'm trapped in my painting, immersed in vast dazzling blue and dark burning red. For a while nothing happens, but I know it will soon and I'm filled with an absolute terror. Suddenly there's a dreadful whoosh of wings, so large they obliterate the blue and fill the space in front of me. I see cold round eyes and a darty round head, and then a curved sharp beak appears, pecking viciously at my eyes. I'm there and not there, seeing it from somewhere else, feeling the burning pain. Nan is standing nearby, watching and waiting and I'm clinging to her, begging for help, but she's turned into a lump of rough granite that strips the skin off my fingers. All night I keep waking, but I can't get out for long, the dream draws me back in.

In the morning the fire has gone out. I am stiff and sore and filled with a new clarity. I've been betrayed.

CHAPTER THREE

There's a saucepan sitting on the doorstep. It's soup, frozen hard. Audrey must have left it there last night. Her kindness makes me want to cry and the brittle cold makes my nose run. The ice is melting from around the eaves, drilling a border of little holes in the snow. A drip lands on my head and another finds its way down the back of my neck, sending goose bumps all over me. I try breaking the ice on the bird bath, but it's frozen solid, so I go inside and get hot water. When I pour it in, the ice makes a loud cracking noise and steam rises into the air. I sprinkle some seed about and the birds come straight away, even though I've never had a way with them. For a few minutes the front garden is filled with a busy twittering. They're sparrows mostly, but there's also a resident pair of blackbirds and a pair of robins, so tame they'll sit on Nan's hand, the way they used to with Pop, but never Millie, with all her fiery fury.

At the gate I turn right, walking up through the thick snow, past the little row of terraces, heading towards the Beacon. I tread carefully because overnight the sky has cleared and in some places the snow has turned to ice. The trees are sagging under the weight of snow, and around each leaf, blade of grass, berry, is a delicate transparent frosting that makes the world look like a glittering jewel. Normally I would stop and wonder at these things, but not this morning. I'm too focused on my furry unscrubbed teeth, my aching dry eyeballs and making sure I stay upright. And anyway, I'm looking for the spot Nan died.

To the east are the plains of the Midlands: motorways, crowded cities, historic villages and the ugly brown smudge of a fume-filled sky. Then there's the Channel and the Continent, the Czech Republic, and somewhere in there, Bohemia. To the west are the gently rolling hills of Herefordshire, the mist sitting low in the valleys, the occasional pillar of smoke rising from chimneys, uncertain without the wind to direct it. Then further, the dark mystery of the Black Mountains of Wales. On again to the rugged, bitten Welsh coast and then Ireland. The whole scene made mysterious by the shadows of the low winter sun, sitting near the horizon and flushing the colour from the clear sky.

I remember times when I'd find Nan staring out to the east. She never went back though, always insisted there was no need. She was only three when they left and didn't remember anything, not in her own right, only from the things Millie and Pop told her. But Nan never went anywhere really, not in the last twenty-eight years anyway. She visited me in London twice, that's all. And every year she went to Aberdovey for her seaside holiday. Never further. As a teenager I came to see this as a failure of sorts. And I guess I was hard on her, condemning her homeliness as cowardice, believing she was denying a part of herself.

'There's no higher point between here and the Urals,' she'd say when the chilling easterlies blew. Then she'd take deep satisfied breaths as if the air held Bohemia within it. As a little girl I was enchanted by the idea of breathing in a country. But when I got older it seemed stupidly sentimental and I was irritated. Maybe it was her nostalgia that bothered me, or maybe the unformed yearning. At an age where the world is full of possibilities, it seemed impossibly weak not to follow your dreams. I was too young then to see that Nan's choice could be a resolution of sorts.

'It's just air,' I'd say.

'No it's not, it's the air of our homeland.'

And then we'd argue because back then I was a stickler for facts and the Urals were not Bohemia. Poor Nan probably hated taking me for walks.

I'm halfway up the hill when the wind picks up, knocking the tranquility out of the morning and the snow from the trees. I draw my coat tight around me and tuck my chin into the collar. It's a bitter easterly blowing the past back at me. And it isn't even my past, it's theirs: Millie's and Nan's. I resent them both because they never let me have it and they never let me leave it. As a teenager I used to shout at Nan. She was all I had left by then, the only one I could vent my frustrations on.

'I don't want your past. I want a future. I want to look ahead.'

'You can't run away from yourself,' Nan always called after me as I turned my back again and again, stomping furiously away from her. I didn't understand that there are lots of ways of running, and that our family were connoisseurs of them all.

But as a child my appetite for the past was insatiable. I would stand on the hills, sometimes with Nan, but usually it was Millie, and I would dig for stories. Stories of the Bohemian Mountains, of my wild mother, of Millie, of Nan, of before. These were my fairy tales, along with Hans Christian Anderson and the Brothers Grimm. I didn't distinguish between them. Harsh tales of horror and fear, wolves and poverty and unrequited love, magic helpers, talking birds, and frogs that turned into princes. I romanticised Romany life, choosing not to hear Millie's stories of frost bitten toes and growling empty bellies, the stones gadje children threw as they passed and the worse things grown-ups did to them. Instead I imagined freedom and travel and music and colour and laughter and big families. All the things that were missing from my grey and solitary little world.

I knew right from the beginning that there were secrets too, embedded in the spaces between the stories, filling me up with fears and uncertainties. Nan's 'Never you mind' and Millie's 'Leave well alone' left me grappling with the maddening sense of never quite getting to the centre of things. I threw my whole weight against these secrets again and again, trying to shake them out of the silences.

'Tell me another story Millie,' I would beg, hopping from one foot to another, imploring her. And Millie would shake her head sadly and look into me, her dark black eyes framed by the even darker hollows underneath.

'It's the curse,' she'd say, 'sitting there, heavy like a broody chicken, waiting. If you don't watch out it will get you too, girl.'

'What curse?'

Millie would look around nervously, then lower her voice to a whisper. 'My own mother threw it down on me, for my sins. There's no escaping a curse girl, we've all had it... one way or another.'

I would shudder and glance over my shoulder, uncertain how I'd recognise something as abstract as a curse. I couldn't quite believe in the dangers of a brooding chicken, so eventually I settled on an image I'd seen in a vampire movie: a bat, with huge wings and dripping bloody teeth, that would swoop in one night and get me. But even then it was too late. Looking back, I can see that the curse had already claimed me. It was there, in my blood, tearing me in two, one part floating off and away, whilst the other part desperately searched for something to ground it. And that's why I needed the stories so much. I consumed them as if there were a great hollow inside me that needed filling and that once filled, their weight, the weight of my ancestors would act as an anchor. I never even considered that these stories might also be great billowing sails. Or worse, ways of evading the truth.

The wind is blowing in heavy gusts, blasting its iciness through my coat, looking for cracks and openings and turning my fingers stiff and blue. *Like Nan*, I think and then try to stop the thought because it's too awful. No matter how angry I am, it's simply too awful. But I am angry. If Nan lied about one thing, maybe she lied about others. Lies breed lies, that's what she taught me. Maybe there are so many lies cobbled together to construct my history that if you pull one thread the whole thing will unravel. I don't know what's real and what isn't anymore. There's nothing solid to hang on to. Only Max and a mother who might be alive somewhere after all, but not here. Where she should be.

Before Millie got sick she walked the hills every day. I went with her, when she let me and when Nan ran out of excuses to keep me by her side. Nan hated my dumb unquestioning love of Millie. Hated to see Millie filling me with her wildness, the way she had with Kita. Sometimes they would argue over me and I'd feel like the rope in a tug of war, Nan shouting at Millie to leave me be and Millie shouting back that I was hers too, while Pop quietly slipped out to his roses and I tried so hard to be two people at once.

Millie had long legs. When I was six or seven it took three steps of mine for every one of Millie's. Later it took only two, but she died before I could match her, stride for stride. She walked fast in the sensible brown lace-ups that did for every occasion. That's how I remember her, tall and straight, with sturdy ankles and great long strides, her full skirt slapping the air, wrapping and unwrapping itself around her legs. Formidable, according to the mothers of my friends. Scary, according to my friends. And she was. I could never predict her moods but I loved her to bits, right through my fear. If I was lucky she told me stories and sometimes she hugged me so tight it would squeeze the breath right out of me and crush my ribs. But I didn't struggle because

I never wanted it to end. I loved Nan too. She seemed safe and grounded in a way Millie never was. Safe in a way that let me take her for granted. She looked after me the most, doing all the things mothers are supposed to do. But it was different. Nan was all shut down like a stunned bird. With her I was careful. Millie was like a swift, darting and ducking, reveling in the acrobatics of flight, the sheer joy of movement. With Millie I could be wild.

So when Millie let me, I'd run along by her side, half afraid of her fierceness, but eager for a story. Between breaths I'd probe and probe, asking questions: 'What was Bohemia like?' 'Where did you live?' 'Did you have any brothers and sisters?' Sometimes she would talk, but not often. Much of the past was taboo for her.

'Too much death,' she'd say, drawing her lips tight shut and building more walls between me and the past. Back then I always wanted things to be black and white. I spent years trying to work out if Millie had turned her back on her homeland or if it had turned its back on her. I didn't understand that there were grey areas too, endless shades of them, and that the answer could possibly be both.

One summer morning we were walking through buttercups, down into the farmer's fields, following the rights of way that had been in place for centuries, and collecting nettles and yarrow for Pop's arthritis. The grass was still covered in a thick dew that seeped through my running shoes and soaked the bottom of Millie's skirt, making a jagged dark line. We stopped and leaned over a fence to pat a pretty piebald mare. I held my hand out and fed it a crab apple, savouring the warm, velvety feel of its tongue on my palm.

'I was suckled by a mare,' Millie said.

Immediately I held my breath and fought down the questions, knowing that patience was the only way to get more.

'Every night we'd set up camp, unharness Beng.' Millie stopped and laughed loud, remembering something I couldn't share. 'You know what Beng means? Devil! She was a devil. Stubborn too, like a mule. So she got many whippings. But she was gentle with me …'

I waited, hoping for more, but Millie had already moved away, leaving me to imagine her snuggled up against Beng's hot chest, guzzling the rich warm milk, the close smell of hay and dung, the heavy horse's breath, the swirling Milky Way and the hypnotic glowing embers of the camp fire. I had never slept outside. I had never suckled. Or so I thought back then.

With a sudden shock I realise that I probably was breastfed, that my mother would have held me close to her warm skin, that I must know her smell and the sound of her voice and the way she comforted me when I cried. The thought brings tears to my eyes, but in seconds they're dried by the icy wind. The paths to these memories have been closed for so long, I'm not sure I can find them, or even if I want to. I turn my face away from the wind and struggle up the hill, wondering if my mother had also walked these hills with Millie, begging for stories and being fed only snippets.

Millie and I often stood up here together, staring out over Worcestershire towards her childhood, because unlike Nan, Millie wanted to go back. From the moment Pop took her away, she ached to return. But it wasn't a home Millie missed, it was *o lungo drom*, the long road, with no place to go and no turning back. She yearned to return home, but there was no home to return to, and this was the tug, the contradiction that made her want to keep moving.

'Where did you travel every day Millie?'

'Here and there?'

'But where?'

'Over the mountains… by the side of a vast lake… through thick forests… sometimes towns.'

'But *where* Millie?'

'There's no good in names.'

'It must have a name.'

She sighed. 'The gadje called it Bohemia. The Bohemian mountains.'

I sighed too, a child replete with the satisfaction of a name. From then on, at school when the teacher asked about origins, I had something beautiful and mysterious to tell. 'Bohemia,' I would say proudly, savouring the word and the passport it gave me to another world.

Now there is no Bohemia, only the Czech Republic. Cartographers and politicians have changed the borders, removed some nations, merged others. It took me years to understand that I had it wrong. For Millie borders were like the walls of a prison. She was a Romany woman, not a Bohemian or a Czech citizen, or later an Englishwoman. She never kept a passport or papers, never valued identity in this way. Nan explained once that as a Romany child in Bohemia, it was safest for Millie to be stateless. This way, she couldn't be sent back to anywhere. But the authorities kept changing her world, drawing and tightening arbitrary rules, making her journeys smaller and smaller until they eventually came to a dead end. When Millie looked out to the east, it wasn't a country she was yearning for, but her family, her journey and the life she had lost. And when Nan stood on the hills staring out to the east, she was looking for her mother, for the part of Millie that was left behind in Bohemia.

I've found the spot. On Summer Hill where I expected. Nan came here often and sat on this little rock ledge, looking out to the west, over Herefordshire to the Black Mountains. Strange that in the end she chose to turn her back on the east and all that it represented. Shocking that the police have marked this place with glaring orange ribbons. And impossible to imagine Nan lying here dead.

It has snowed since yesterday, so there are no signs, no flattened grass or scuff marks, nothing but the orange ribbons to make this spot stand out from any other. There's no message either. Why would there be? Just the crossed sticks, coated in ice and frozen in place. Maybe these sticks are her message or more likely they mean nothing, like the doodles I make when I'm on the phone.

I step over the orange ribbons and sit down on Nan's ledge, which is sheltered from the wind. My feet sink right up to the ankles in the perfect snow. I watch them disappear, wondering vaguely if I'll get frostbite. Down below, the valleys are patchworked in a blanket of white and grey. The trees are thin grey skeletons tipped in white and casting long shadows across the fields. The early fog has gone, leaving just the occasional puff of smoke from the chimneys. It should be peaceful. But even here there's no peace from the traffic, with the constant humming of the M5 to the east. Perhaps it was the last thing Nan heard.

What was I doing when she died? Did I stop for a moment? Feel some sort of tug? It's already two nights ago and I have to think hard to remember. A takeaway from the local Indian, then chatting to Elise on the phone, while Max cleaned out the fridge and ironed his shirts and grumbled about me leaving globs of toothpaste in the bathroom sink. Then a bath and a book, but no sex because Max was grumpy. And all that time Nan was out here, waiting. After a while her eyes would have got used to the dark. She would have seen lights from the houses in the valley and she might even have made out the silhouette of the Black Mountains. I don't suppose she was scared. I read somewhere that dying from exposure isn't such a bad way to go. Just a slow sinking into unconsciousness.

The police didn't find Nan's letter and I'm pleased at that. There's no need for them to know. It was tucked in behind the toaster, not near the phone where she usually kept her mail. A booking for a mastectomy. Why didn't she tell me? Why didn't she ask me to help? Nan tried to send Millie to hospital, but when it came to the crunch she couldn't go there either. Maybe she had more of Millie's blood than she liked to think.

I'm trembling with the cold which has seeped up from my feet and turned my legs into aching blocks. But I can't move yet. The questions are going over and over in my head. How long had she known? When did she find the lump? She knew I was coming up this weekend. Why didn't she wait? Why didn't she say good bye? That's the one that hurts the most. Why didn't she say good bye?

There's nothing finished or satisfying about Nan's death. I can't even remember what our last conversation was. Did I miss some sort of cryptic message? I saw her for Christmas, a week and a half ago, and she didn't say anything. I rang four, maybe five days ago to tell her I was coming up on the weekend. Nan needed a new nightie and a dressing gown, so we agreed to go shopping in Worcester and maybe see a film. Shopping is something you do when you still have a future. Perhaps she was planning to have the mastectomy, but then changed her mind.

I don't know what else we talked about. It ought to be significant, but probably it wasn't. I didn't say, 'Nan, I love you.' I didn't ask, 'Are you well Nan?' And she didn't say, 'Storm dear, I'm sick …' Probably we talked about the weather.

When I cry it comes in a flood. Oh Nan. I could hate you.

CHAPTER FOUR

This is the first funeral I've been to since Millie's and Pop's and I don't remember much of either. Pop's funeral was so crowded there weren't enough seats and people had to stand in the aisle. The priest went on about what a wonderful man Tomas Cizek was, an 'asset to the community', which made Nan snort and everyone else dab their eyes with handkerchiefs. Millie wore white and wailed and everyone looked the other way, including Nan. Millie's funeral was almost empty and no one said Milada Cizekova was wonderful, though the priest did mention 'long suffering'. There should have been music, a band even, and the air should have been filled with the sobs of her family. She should have been buried, but she was burnt, and no one wore white, or even cried, though I could feel the despair inside Nan. Both times I had the burning need to giggle and had to blow my nose loudly on Nan's handkerchief, and both times I cried alone out on the hills the next day.

The only other funerals I've seen have been in movies, and they're always dignified affairs, with everyone in stylish black mourning clothes, holding immense black umbrellas and wearing dark sunglasses, even though it's raining. Aside from the persistently thick drizzle outside and Audrey's perfectly tailored black suit, this funeral is nothing like those. I hate everything about it. Hate it that I organised this nondescript semi-modern room with its ninety degree angles, tepid off-white walls and ugly beige vinyl floors. And Mr Russell, the stupid priest, or celebrant, or whatever he is, who's saying stuff that doesn't mean anything, in his ringing self righteous voice that bounces around the walls, making the chapel seem even emptier. But most of all I hate how distant I feel from all this, as if I'm sitting on the moon peering down at a bunch of aliens doing strange things in a square box. Only it's Nan we're talking about and that ought to mean something.

In movies, something mysterious almost always happens in the funeral scene. People find out unexpected things about the deceased. Maybe two wives turn up and fight over the coffin, or the murderer makes a discreet appearance, looking for his, or her, next victim. In Nan's case I've been hoping for a sight of one man - my grandfather, Kita's father and Nan's once upon a time lover. None of us know who he is. Except Nan, and that's one more secret she's taken with her.

I scan the room again, still half-hoping for a stranger in the back row. But there's just me and Max and Audrey, who is almost family, and a few other neighbours. There's Ed, the butcher with the red hands from down the hill, who always had a soft spot for Nan and made sure she got the best cuts. His suit jacket is too tight and makes him look as if he's going to explode. And there are two women I don't recognise. One's huge, all rolling chins, folded-over arms and smug certainties, and the other's little and fidgety, with thin empty bones and a twittery head. That's all. Nan has always kept pretty much to herself. She wasn't a member of anything I can think of. Not the Women's Institute or the local Baptist church, though she sometimes went. No knitting groups either, not even a gardening club. She didn't enrol in adult education courses and she didn't play bridge. Nan didn't go on demonstrations, though she felt injustice like it was her own and plagued MPs and newspapers with ranting letters about refugees and homelessness. The MPs wrote back conciliatory, evasive letters that drove her mad with their patronising tone.

Mr Russell drones on and on. Practised words in a practised voice and he's managing to look bored and reverent all at once. Nan didn't believe in any god, at least none she ever told me of. She didn't ask for anything. As far as I know she never even thought about it. She never left instructions, never said: 'Storm, when I die can you please give me a church service, or throw a party, or scatter my ashes on the hills …' But even so, I can't help the feeling that I've let her down by organising this pedestrian little gathering and a mediocre priest to send her on her way. He's got too much hair for his wrinkly face and it doesn't move with the rest of him, so I'm pretty sure he's got a hair piece glued on there somehow. Max would know, but he'll frown if I ask him now, so I'll have to save it for later. Then maybe he'll laugh despite himself and roll his eyes and say 'Stoooorrrmmm' in his deep gravelly voice.

Max is funeral perfect in a black suit and crisp thin black tie, his dark hair cut short, not a strand out of place. I study his freshly shaved face and feel a surge of pleasure. He's missed a bit, just below his ear. I have an almost irresistible desire to stroke his cheek. Max sees me looking and reaches for my hand. I love Max's hands with their long tapering fingers, clean, squared nails, the palms so soft, and on the back, the curl of black hair and the dark blue lines of his veins standing out against the white skin. My hand looks tiny, engulfed like this in Max's. I filed my nails for a change and they don't look too bad, but there's still paint under them, even though I scrubbed. We are so different, Max and I, and it makes me afraid. I turn his hand over and peer at the lines, trying to identify the heart line, the life line, the fate line… trying to see what the future holds and wishing I had Millie's gift.

Max pulls his hand away and nods fiercely at the front, meaning I should concentrate, but my mind keeps jumping about, determined to avoid this room and what's happening in it. Max's black shoes are so shiny I can see myself in them. I can also see a big run in my brand-new black tights. Unlike Max and Audrey, I've hobbled together an outfit. My skirt is too short for this sort of thing and my boots come up to mid-calf, which is an awkward place when you've got a skirt t. Last week his length I accidentally put my favourite black cashmere sweater in the dryer, so now it's three sizes too small and the sleeves keep riding halfway up my arms. All in all, I feel completely ridiculous and definitely not sad enough, just cynical and angry and distant. I've felt like this for three days now. Ever since I realised the depth of Nan's betrayal. How could she? What right did she have to keep my mother from me?

'Before we finish, I believe Irene's granddaughter, Storm, would like to say a few words.'

Straight away everyone is looking at me with dreadful compassionate smiles and I can't think whether I'm supposed to go to the front or just stand up here. Max gives me a push into the aisle, so I'm committed. I tug uselessly at my skirt as I make my way up to the front, frantically trying to remember what I wanted to say. There's a wail inside me, rising from somewhere deeper down than I knew existed. And I know that would do. A wail like this would say everything that needs saying. But I can't. I mustn't. It simply isn't done. Not here anyway, in contemporary middle England, where we all politely push death into the background over a cup of tea and talk about something else. Alison says that's why we're all so fucked up.

I swallow the wail back down and clear my throat.

'Um… ' I say, and that's come out too loud. 'I'd just like to say… '

Outside the next group are waiting for their turn. There's a general murmuring, sort of like a hum. Then someone laughs out loud.

'Good to see you again,' shouts a man in a ruddy voice.

Inside it's quiet. I look around at the empty seats. The few expectant faces are looking straight at me, waiting for me to say something profound and illuminating about Nan. And I wonder how I can sum up Nan's life in a few measly words. How can anyone do that?

'Um... Nan was... Nan was a good person.'

And I'm thinking - was she? Was she really? I don't know anymore. A suicidal neurotic who, unlike me, was good at keeping secrets. Irene Cizekova. What does that mean? Who was she? Lots of things probably. We all are.

'I'll miss her. We all will ...'

Audrey is nodding away encouragingly in the second row, so I must be on the right track.

'I keeping thinking about a Superman movie,' I say. 'I saw it years ago, when I was a kid. Where Lois really did die and Superman broke all the rules and meddled with history. He grabbed the whole of the earth and spun it backwards until just the moment before Lois died. And then he rescued her... '

Audrey's wiping her eyes now, so it can't be all bad.

'I wish I could do that for Nan,' I finish. 'Thank you for coming.'

Mr Russell dismisses me with a reverential nod of the head. Then he offers us the chance to join him in prayer. We're supposed to have bowed heads and shut eyes when the coffin disappears discreetly behind the curtains and drops into the furnace, but we all sneak a look as he presses the button. Somebody's forgotten to oil the conveyor belt. It squeaks reluctantly and then jolts the coffin forward all of a sudden. Then at the last moment the velvety curtains snag on the coffin and threaten to tear off the railing and the priest has to lunge over and fix it.

I'm not going to laugh. I'm absolutely not going to laugh. But it comes anyway, in a little burst that I try to make into a cough. Max squeezes my hand and glares at me, but it isn't enough. There's another laugh coming. A bigger one, and I have to look away and try to think of something else until Mr Russell eventually says 'Amen' and we all make our way out.

It's still raining, so we shelter awkwardly in the foyer, while the next group file into the chapel. The fat and skinny women come over and introduce themselves. Janice White and Bridget something, which I don't quite catch.

'Terribly sorry,' they say in plummy voices.

'Yes,' I say. 'So am I.'

'We're old school friends of Irene's,' says Janice. 'We lost touch with her years ago, but I like to keep up with the notices.'

Bridget waggles her head. 'She does you know. Every day.'

I nod and look around for Max. It's time we left.

'She was terribly bright,' they say shaking their heads sadly. 'Terribly bright …' Repeating it so I can't miss the subtext. 'And such a good education.'

Poor Pop. With a foreign accent and a suspect 'gypsy' wife, he couldn't get a teaching job anywhere in England. He'd had some training in carpentry from his father, so in the end he went back to that. He must have struggled to put money aside year after year to give Irene the best education he could. And then she went and had a baby at seventeen. It must have broken his heart. I wonder if it broke Nan's heart too, seeing all her hopes come to nothing, just like that. If it did, she never let on.

It's hard to imagine Nan pregnant and I can't begin to imagine her being seduced. What promises did he make? Maybe Nan thought it might help her escape from Millie. Or she might have known it wouldn't last and didn't much care. It's hard to picture

Nan sneaking out of the window at night. Maybe she made up some excuse - a night class or something. Or maybe at seventeen it was okay for girls to go out for a date. She might have just walked out, with her hair up and her lips painted pink, and left Millie pacing about, afraid of losing her only child. And Pop placating, telling Millie it was only natural, that she had to move away sometime. And later, Millie bursting to know, edgy and angry and nervous. And Nan, tormenting Millie with her silence.

They're looking at me curiously, obviously waiting for some response to their 'Terribly bright' or something they've said since, that I missed. I panic and invite them around for tea and biscuits, thinking they'll do the right thing and refuse, but they don't.

When we get back to the cottage the drizzle has turned the snow to muddy slush and everyone walks muck inside. Nan would have been appalled. Max leads the few guests into the green room and stands about making excellent small talk, while Audrey puts on one of Nan's aprons and does things in the kitchen. I still feel as if I'm on the moon and watch with a vacant interest while Audrey puts the kettle on to boil, hunts about for the teapot, swishes it with hot water and spoons in way too many tea leaves.

'One for the pot and one for each person,' she explains, seeing my look. She hands me three packets of biscuits. 'Mixed,' she says, 'We couldn't go wrong that way.'

Then she lays out the best cups and saucers on a tray, while I tip the biscuits onto a plate and make a half-hearted attempt at arranging them in a pattern.

I take a tray and plunge into the green room, smiling and nodding and handing out Audrey's horribly strong tea in the delicate floral-patterned cups and saucers none of us ever used. Then still smiling and nodding I walk about holding the plate of biscuits, feeling like an extra in a movie and waiting desperately for someone to shout, 'CUT!'.

When everyone seems satisfied, I put the plates on a side table and stand in the doorway sipping my tea, the thick tannin settling on my tongue as I watch moving mouths and animated faces. I'm overcome with the unreality of the scene. Any minute now, surely, Nan will walk in that door, pour herself a cup of tea and demand to know what the fuss is about. But I know she won't, because in the end I did go to see her in the funeral parlour. I didn't want to, but Alison told me it was important to see the body. She said I wouldn't believe in it properly until I did. And Max agreed with her, which is very unusual for him. So I went.

The funeral parlour was exactly how I expected it to be. The atmosphere heavy with quiet. Sounds magnified, and me thinking that the staff must wear mufflers on their shoes, because their feet made no noise and mine were a deafening clip-clop. The room they showed me into smelt of formaldehyde, and disinfectants, masked by perfumes, so heavy I could taste them. In the corners of the room were plinths with elaborate flower arrangements, and in the middle was a table with a coffin. I knew she was in there, but even so when the man lifted the lid it was a surprise to see Nan. I half expected her to open her eyes, smile and tell me it was all a joke, but Nan was never a jokey sort of person. She was wearing her slippers which seemed absurd. She couldn't have gone out onto the mountains wearing them.

Nan looked like Nan and that made it easier in a way, easier than relating to a pile of ashes. Her face was calm, her skin unlined as if her worries had been smoothed away, like a hand across velvet. I expected her to be pale, not all pink and warm looking. But when I reached out and tentatively touched her face, it was cold and this turned the fiction of her death into undeniable fact for me. She was dead. And she'd taken all her stories with her. I leaned down and brushed my lips on hers. But even that last kiss wasn't straight forward.

'Good bye Nan,' I whispered, but what I really wanted to do was grasp her shoulders and shake the truth out of her. *Why did you lie about my mother?*

Bridget grabs my elbow and makes my tea splash into the saucer.

'You know,' she says, 'it's been more years than I can remember since I've stepped foot in this house. Such a long time. And it's still the same. What a thing!'

'Doesn't it take you back, Bridget?' asks Janice as she joins us.

'Oh yes. Do you remember that last time? We came to see Irene, after the baby was born. What was her name? Kitty? Kita, that was it. Your mother?'

I nod.

'Yes of course. It must have been the late fifties, or thereabouts. She was rude wasn't she? Asking us what we wanted, as if we didn't have any right. But she didn't want people to talk, poor soul.'

'Your great-grandmother, Milada wasn't it? She said it was hers, and it could've been. I mean she was still only young. But it wasn't hers, we all knew that,' says Janice, smacking her lips together. 'After a while, she gave up the pretence and let Irene take over. The poor thing, looking after that wild daughter of hers.'

'And then her crazy mother,' adds Bridget and immediately clamps her hand over her mouth, glancing at me nervously.

Janice gives her a stern look.

'Tomas helped a bit. Your great-grandfather, you know. A good man, but it was all he could do to manage his wife, let alone a child.'

'More tea?' I ask. My voice is too high, but they don't seem to notice.

'Please,' says Janice, speaking for them both, and I retreat back to the kitchen for a fresh pot.

Audrey's still there doing all the things I should be doing. She refills the pot while I hunt about in Max's bag for the bottle of whiskey I saw him slip in earlier. I pour myself a big slug, then tip a little onto the floor. For Nan.

Audrey is watching.

'It's traditional,' I say, pouring her one too. 'Whiskey at wakes.'

We clink teacups and drink. It feels good, burning all the way down. Maybe it will melt some of the numbness that has taken me over.

I pour a shot into Max's tea, certain he could do with some help.

Back in the green room, Bridget and Janice have him cornered.

'Poor Irene,' Bridget is saying. 'They bullied her at school, you know. With a gypsy mum, striding about like that, looking all fierce and tall in those long skirts of hers. She must have been so ashamed, but she never let on.'

I don't suppose Bridget has any idea of how rude she's being. For a moment I feel like washing her foul mouth out with soap, the way Nan used to threaten when I was a kid. But there wouldn't be any point. She's only telling things the way she sees them and she's probably right. Most likely Nan was ashamed of Millie and envious of all the other kids with mums who made apple pie and ironed their underpants. Poor Nan, she only had Millie, wild caged Millie who'd lost almost everything and was beyond caring what people thought.

Max takes a sip of his tea and splutters it out all over the saucer. He glares at me and mutters excuse me's, with Janice looking down through her chins at him.

'Irene was quite a pretty girl,' she says. 'She had spirit. But over the years she got plainer and plainer. Do you remember Bridget? It was as if she was trying to disappear.'

Bridget nods eagerly and I try for a moment to imagine Nan pretty. It's not easy. The only picture I have of her is a school photograph and it's hard to distinguish Nan from all the others. She's not scruffy or neglected, her hair is neatly braided and her uniform has got all the pleats pressed in the right place. She told me once how much she loved Millie doing her hair each morning. The long ritual of tugging and twisting it into place. By then it was the only time when Millie was there, just for her. Pop did her uniform though, at least until she was old enough to manage it herself. Millie washed, scrubbing at clothes until they split, as if she were punishing them, but she never ironed. In my photograph Nan is neat and tidy, but she isn't smiling, her eyes are serious, looking at a point past the camera. Even all the way back then she was distant.

'Irene was top of the class every year,' says Janice.

I'm not surprised. I knew she did well at school. Unlike me. But despite all her lost opportunities, she never pushed me to do better. That was one of the good things about Nan, she always said I should do what I liked best. Though at the time I thought it was because she didn't care.

'And she was certainly an avid reader, wasn't she, Bridget?'

'Oh yes, she always had her nose in a book.'

I smile, remembering how Nan devoured books. Remembering her stirring the porridge, a book in one hand, or chopping vegetables, a book open on the table and her stopping now and then to turn a page. She hardly ever watched the television, just sat each night in her favourite saggy armchair, with a book, reading and reading and lost to me. If cooking was her way of loving, then reading was her escape.

'The teacher wanted her to go on to university. But it wasn't to be.'

'Never mind,' I say and mumble something stupid about fate and the paths we choose.

They nod gravely as if I've said something profound.

There's a picture emerging now. Of Nan at seventeen, denied the career everyone wanted for her and signing up for a lifetime of caring - Millie and Pop and Kita and me - though Millie did offer her a way out, saying Kita was hers. I wonder why she didn't take her up on it. If it's true that lives can be destroyed by children, then there's a pattern emerging in our family: Nan sending Millie into exile from her people and her country, Kita stealing Nan's future, and me... arriving just as Nan had finished with my mother. Another burden.

I leave them sipping lukewarm tea and go back to the kitchen for more whiskey. Audrey has already helped herself to another and her cheeks are glowing red. Max comes in for one too.

'Next time give me some warning,' he says drinking this one straight.

Max puts his arms around me, draws me close and kisses me on the forehead. I lean on him, feeling my legs giving way, my whole body sinking, and realise how tired I am. Underneath this numbness, is a raging anger that's wearing me down.

'You okay?'

'Fine,' I say and we both know I'm lying. All I want to do is stay here in his arms forever and shut out the world, but the world has other ideas.

'Come on then,' says Max, 'let's get rid of them.'

I plaster a smile on my face and take large sips of whiskey, while Audrey does the washing up and Max starts the shooing everyone out the door small talk that I'm so bad at.

We're already drunk by the time the guests leave. It's almost dark and outside the rain has turned to sleet. Max is lying on the couch. His eyes are shut and a glass of whiskey is balanced precariously on his chest. Any second now he'll be asleep. He's taken his suit jacket off and I can clearly see the outline of a vest through his white shirt. Max is the only person I know who actually wears white vests. When I told him how naff it was he looked baffled. 'They keep my chest warm,' he said, and that was that. Anyway I've grown to like Max's vests, they make him look all muscly and I love the way his chest hair curls up around the edges.

Audrey and I are sitting on the floor in front of the fire, feeling the heat of the coals on our faces, sipping our whiskies and not saying much. The room is growing dark around us. Audrey looks so sad and I wonder what she's thinking about. Nan probably. When I'm seventy I want to be like Audrey, sitting on floors and enthusiastic about life. And she's still beautiful. Despite the lines, or maybe even because of them. One day I'll paint her.

Max does a funny splutter and the glass tips over before I can reach it. Whiskey down his shirt and all over the couch, but he doesn't wake. I watch him for a while. Watch the way sleep softens his face and makes his breath even. Sometimes when he's asleep like this I can love him so much it hurts. It's nowhere near as easy when he's awake.

I fill up my glass and take a deep shaky breath. 'I think Nan killed herself,' I say.

Audrey comes back from wherever she's been and looks at me. Her eyes are sad but not shocked. 'Perhaps Irene just let herself die,' she says gently. 'I think there's a difference.'

'You know! Did she tell you?'

'No, no, I would have tried to stop her. But I knew she was ill. She talked about the cancer. She said she couldn't bear the idea of it eating away at her.'

'Why didn't she tell me?'

Audrey shrugs. 'Maybe she thought you'd try to make her have the operation.'

'Of course I would.' I pick angrily at the biscuit crumbs dotted all over the carpet and throw them in the fire. A tiny spark and they're gone.

'Irene was a good kind woman,' says Audrey. 'You have to remember that. Don't see it as a betrayal. At first she was going to have the mastectomy, but then the doctors told her that the cancer was aggressive and quite advanced. She didn't believe an operation would help much. Afterwards there would be chemotherapy and maybe more operations. Irene couldn't bear the thought of being looked after.'

Max is snoring now. I pinch his thumb but he doesn't stop. If anything it gets louder. Big snuffly snores we have to raise our voices over.

'You see,' says Audrey. 'You're young enough to believe in fighting for life. Irene was old enough to see that death wasn't such a bad choice.'

I shake my head, not willing to accept Audrey's excuses. 'But she could have told me! She didn't even leave a note. She could have done that for me, at least.'

That's it. That's the point. I need to know she cared about me because she sure as hell didn't let on. Audrey looks uncomfortable. She might have been Nan's best friend, but she can't answer that one. No one can. Only Nan.

Our glasses are empty. I don't need any more but I don't want the day to end either and I'm past making coffee, so I pour the last of the whiskey into our glasses.

'Maybe this was the note,' I say, handing Audrey the photo of me and Kita. 'Nan left it on her bedside table… My mother didn't die after all. Not then anyway. Not having me.'

Audrey looks at the photograph and smiles wistfully. 'You were a pretty baby'.

'Do you know what happened?'

She shakes her head. 'Irene never did say much about the past and we moved here well after Kita left. You were about four. I still remember you coming over. "To inspect the new neighbours," you told us, but you couldn't say inspect properly and it came out as infect. We laughed about that. A few days later I got a cold and Frank always said it was you that gave it to me.'

'What was I like?'

'You were a serious child. There was a spark in you, but you hardly ever let it show.' Audrey smiles. 'You won our hearts right from the start. Especially Frank, and he wasn't a child person.' She shakes her head. 'Not by then anyway... I can still remember the way you slipped your hand into his and demanded a tour of the garden. He took you around and told you the names of all the flowers, just as if you were grown up, and all the time there was a smile playing around the edges of his mouth... It made me sad to think I'd never given him the chance to be a father ...'

She stops and looks into the fire for a moment and there's nothing I can think of to say in the face of her disappointment. It must be so lonely for her, with Frank dying last year and now Nan.

'Anyway,' she says. 'We heard Irene calling for you. There was a panic in it that sent you hurtling back up the street, carrying a flower Frank had picked for you. A gardenia, I think it was. She never could bear having you out of her sight.'

I think about my solemn four-year-old self, running home clutching a flower, anxious to appease Nan and heavy with the fear of worrying her. It's always been like that with me and Nan. For the first time ever I feel a great sense of compassion for myself, or at least for the child I once was. And for a moment that compassion is big enough to include Nan who was so afraid of losing me, she couldn't let me in and she couldn't let me go.

Finally, the strange detachment I've been feeling evaporates. The hard cynicism that's been tagging along with me all day, disappears with it and I'm back inside myself. When the tears come, Audrey puts her arms around me.

'There, there,' she croons, 'there, there,' rocking me gently back and forth, comforting me in a way Nan never could.

CHAPTER FIVE

Outside, an angry wind has come up. I can hear the howl of it through the thick walls and the scraping of branches against the bathroom window upstairs. Audrey pulls on her boots and coat. When she opens the door, there's a swirl of snow and icy wind that sets me shivering. I kiss Audrey good night and watch her struggle down the path and battle with the gate, before disappearing into the wild darkness.

Back in the warm glow of the green room, the shadows are dancing on the walls and Max is still asleep on the couch. I feel another tug of affection for him. He's so much more approachable when he's like this, with a stain on his shirt and his tie askew. His mouth is open and for a second I can picture him as an old man. Will we still be together? With framed photographs of our children on the mantelpiece and a long history that will take the place of conversation. I don't know. We've been together three and a half years and I still can't believe it's me that Max wants.

I give him a shake, but he just moans and rolls over. Bugger! We're supposed to be sleeping upstairs, in Nan's room. I even made up the bed this morning, with new sheets, still crisp and creased from the packet, because I couldn't bear to use Nan's. But there's no way I'm going to sleep there by myself. I don't want to sleep anyway. I want to talk or make love, though Max doesn't look up to that. But I definitely don't want to sleep.

For the past three nights I've been camped on Nan's couch, having nightmares that make me shout in my sleep and leave me a trembling wreck. As soon as I shut my eyes they come. The same vast dazzling blue that seems to go on forever. I'm very small in it. Small and lost. In fact it's not clear if I'm all there, or if bits of me are missing. Like an arm or a leg or maybe even my head. In the dream I'm looking for something, but I don't know what. And then the wings come and wipe out the blue and that's when it gets worse. I'm mouthing a word, but it won't come, not out loud anyway. Just one word... Mama.

I've started to wonder if Nan's *mula* has come back to haunt me, or maybe Millie's curse is laying its claims on me, now the others have all gone. Max says the dreams don't mean anything, that they're just a part of grieving. But I wonder about that. He says that when you're having nightmares the best thing to do is turn around and face the monsters. You can even tell them to go away and they will. Max is tough like that. I'm a wimp. But he doesn't understand. Some monsters are too hard to face.

I kiss Max on the forehead but he still doesn't wake. I put a blanket over him and top up the fire with the last of the coal from the bucket. It's rare that I get to look after Max like this, usually it's the other way around and it's me that needs him. Even when he's got a cold he won't let me look after him, just wants to be left alone. Maybe that's the Achilles heel in our relationship. I need Max, but he doesn't need me. And now of course, I need him even more.

I pick up the photograph again. My mother stares back at me, a restrained smile, eyes squinted up against the sun, not telling me anything. The light is bright, the sky an overexposed white and the edges sharp, but I can't tell where it was taken. There's still so much I don't know. She's dead. She must be. There's the empty urn, a solid fact I can hold in both hands. But maybe that's a lie too, an elaborate construction of Nan's. I don't know anything anymore. I search the picture, trying to read between the lines. Kita is holding me, but she's looking straight at the camera, not tilting her head towards her baby. I guess more than anything, she looks resigned. Probably she doesn't like the person holding the camera. I'm smiling, but my eyes look uncertain and my face is turned just a little towards Kita. For reassurance maybe. One hand is holding an almost new version of my Peggy doll, which looks so much bigger. The other is reaching up, about to touch Kita's cheek. A moment later she might have reached down and kissed the top of my head, or she might have shaken her face away from my touch. That's something else I'll never know.

I get up awkwardly and my legs almost buckle under me. I've got pins and needles and have to wait a moment, leaning against the mantelpiece until the feeling comes back. I'm so tired and drunk I can hardly walk, but I feel like an enchanted princess drawn against her will toward the stairs. Some force is tugging at my legs, lifting them, one step at a time, up to the landing and then another creaky step up into Nan's room. In here I can feel the weight of all the secrets, hovering about in corners, lurking inside drawers, hiding under cupboards... Waiting for me to find them.

I stumble through the dark, to the window and peer out into the night. It's stopped snowing now but the wet black sludge is covered again - a freshly cleaned white carpet. In the meadow opposite, the wind is blowing clumps of snow out of the trees. There's a fox snuffling about in the corner of the garden where Nan used to leave scraps. I watch it for a while, but when I move just a fraction, the fox senses something. His ears twitch as he looks up at me and we stay like that, frozen, for perhaps a second before he disappears. I don't see him go. He's too quick. And now there's nothing but a few paw prints in the snow to show he was ever there.

The sky is clear now, letting the moon light up the dark outline of the Black Mountains. At this time of year, with the bare trees, it's even possible to see the strange shape of Lord Herefords Knob at the end of the mountain range. If only I could find the room in me to do anything other than bright geometric blocks of colour. I would like to paint what's out there, to catch how impervious it is. How it doesn't care. Somehow I would have to capture the shift between the tiny safeness of in here and the big scary out there that makes me feel small.

Right now though, it doesn't feel so safe in here. Almost reluctantly I turn around to face this room again. I can feel something daring me to take the plunge as I switch on the light and open a drawer at random, ignoring the naughty little girl taboo that tells me it's wrong to look through someone else's belongings. I pull things out, tip up boxes, make piles of mess. Trying not to care. They all owe me some answers.

In the cupboard there's an elaborate hat with bold blue feathers, that couldn't possibly have been Nan's, and loads of umbrellas, at least seven of them. There are dresses too and pointy special occasion shoes, and I don't remember ever seeing Nan wear any of them. I pick up a pair of black stilettos studded with diamontes. They look unworn. I can't believe Nan's puffy feet would have fitted into these princess shoes. My version of Nan doesn't incorporate bright colours, or heels, or plunging necklines. And I'm shocked that this other, more exotic Nan existed, even if it was only in her wardrobe and her dreams.

In the drawers are handkerchiefs and a collection of different sized boxes of jewellery: pearl earrings, a diamonte necklace, a ring with a ruby and a cluster of diamonds. In one of the boxes is the necklace Kita was wearing in the photograph. I take it out and look more closely. A coin strung through leather. Yes, I'm certain it's the same. It might have been Millie's once, then Nan's, or maybe it went straight to Kita. And now it's mine. I pull it over my head, liking the strange new weight around my neck. There's something comforting about it and my hand keeps straying up to finger the coin.

When I find the package, something in me knows it's the thing I'm been looking for. It's right at the back of the middle drawer, underneath Nan's monstrous underwear, underneath even the sweetly scented lavender lining at the base. A bulky white envelope, yellowing around the edges and just a bit crinkled from the damp.

Inside are a few letters and some postcards. They smell musty, but otherwise are in good condition. I pick a postcard out at random. It's a picture of a long white sandy beach, and blue sea. The caption says: Bondi Beach, Sydney, Australia. I turn it over and read:

Having a GREAT time. Miss you.

K. xxx

The post mark is a bit smudged, but I can just make out the date, May 1976. Two months before I was born. This is not surprising. I knew that I was born in Australia. It says so on my birth certificate. *Place of Birth: Sydney, Australia.* Nan couldn't hide that. When I asked, she told me that Kita went over for a holiday, had me and died. I was an accident, which of course meant unwanted. Nan came and got me. Simple. Straightforward. Like making a cup of tea. Except Kita wasn't dead, so it was all a lie.

The next card is a picture of a gigantic orange rock; Ayers Rock, Northern Territory, Australia.

Hey Mum

This is the very heart of Australia. If you

listen really carefully you can hear it beating.

K. xxx

The post mark on this one is September 1978. Two years after I was born and she was still alive. I go through all the postcards trying to work out the dates. On some of them the postmarks are too faint, but it looks as if they span about two and half years. The earliest date I can find is February 1975 and the latest is October 1978. Not once does she mention me.

Why didn't she write about me to Nan? I read them again, searching for some reference, but there's no doubt. I'm missing from these postcards. It's as if I don't exist. Yet I have a photograph of me and my mother. Real, solid evidence. And it's dated 1978. Kita was alive then and still in Australia, so I must have been with her, unless I only saw her that one time when the photograph was taken. Maybe I didn't even know the woman who was holding me in that photograph. My mother.

I pace around the bed, stepping around the junk I've released from Nan's cupboards, my fists clenched around the envelope. More bloody secrets. At least Nan didn't throw these out or burn them like Millie would have done. It's as if she wanted me to know, but she didn't want to be the one to tell. Maybe the lie got too big for her and she couldn't start the process of unravelling it. Secrets are just as bad as lies, and not so different, because like the invisible germs that Millie used to warn me about, they grow and mutate and isolate people from each other. It's hard to climb over the walls secrets make. If Nan had told me things, we might have been closer.

I can still picture her face, those lips drawn up into a thin white line whenever I asked anything important. 'It's bad luck to speak the names of the dead,' she'd say.

But I always persisted. 'You don't have to use her name, just tell me something about her. Anything. Pleeeaase Nan?'

Sometimes my persistence paid off and Nan gave in. Then she'd feed me a tiny story about Kita. Her peace offerings, she called them. She'd tell me how Kita wore trousers, never dresses, how she skipped school and cut her hair short, though it was so curly it stood up in all directions.

'People blamed me you know. They thought I wasn't mothering her properly. They said I was too young.' Nan snorted. 'Too young! I was old well before my time. No, it was Kitty, she was wild. More than any of us could manage.'

'Once,' Nan said, 'Kita climbed to the very top of that big old oak in Grundy's Meadow and jumped off. She broke her leg in two places. It was a dare! Can you believe it?'

'Tell me more,' I'd beg, tugging and twisting at her sleeve as if it was a tap I could open to let all the stories flow out.

'Enough,' she'd say, wiping her eyes and turning away from my insistence. But she was wrong. Her stories were never enough. Each one was just a tiny piece in a huge mosaic. I collected them all and tried to put them together, this way and that. But I had no idea what the big picture was supposed to look like, so I wondered and surmised and elaborated, until my mother, Kita, became a wild, heroic character straight out of an adventure story. But all that time Nan never once spoke about the grown-up Kita and she never talked about Australia.

With the letters and postcards, is a tattered diary. Inside the paisley cover, my mother had written her name in neat round letters: *Kita Cizekova*. And then the year: *1978*. I open the diary to a random page.

October 27,

I've changed my name. Skye. Out here that's all there is. Sky, light and vast and I feel like I'm expanding, up and away, no boundaries. Man, it feels so good. Growing right now I'm filling it.

I flick to another page. I don't know how I expected my mother to sound, but it wasn't like this, not this dated hippie talk.

July 25,

B bought an old station wagon, a Holden. He said nothing else would do, but it looks poxy to me. We packed up the car this morning, just piled stuff on top of the mattress in the back. We've got a cooker and gas because B says there's not much in the way of wood out there. I don't know what to expect and half of me is thinking I'd rather stay in the city and keep working the markets. But once we got going I felt okay. When we left all the houses behind there was this great sense of release. Hello future, here we come.

I pull the cover off Nan's bed, wrap it around me, climb up on the window ledge and keep on flicking through the pages, scanning sentences, trying to work out who B is, looking to see if I feature in my mother's story. I feel frantic now. I need to know if I was there. Maybe she abandoned me. She might have walked out of the hospital, and left Nan to fetch me, while she went travelling with this B person. But if that's what she did, then... This thought screeches me to a halt. Then? I don't know. I don't want to think these things, but I can't help it. Because if that's what she did... maybe it would be better if she was dead.

Then I turn a page and find myself.

August 12

Coober Pedy's a bizarre place. It's a bit like a frontier town from an American cowboy movie. Dusty streets, a couple of shops and a pub. Dirty men and loud women. But there's no guns, at least not around anyone's hips and there aren't any houses either - everyone lives underground in caves, like moles. And the whole town is surrounded by thousands of holes and big piles of dirt because everyone's into mining opals. It sure as hell doesn't look like earth. So we told Storm we were on the moon and her eyes got bigger and bigger. 'Moon', she said. 'Man? Where man?'

The understanding comes in a warm rush. August 12, 1978. The photograph was taken in Australia. Of course it was. I should have realised. The squinting. The hard bright light that never happens in England. And my mother didn't abandon me. I was with her on that road trip in Australia. It feels as if I'm waking from a coma or amnesia. This is a whole part of my life I was unaware of and the tiny seed of hope that I've been nurturing, is growing. She might still be alive. She might still be over there. And I might be able to find her and maybe even my father.

In a hurry now, as if every moment counts, I hunt through the rest of the envelope. There are only two more letters. The first is from someone called Leo Knight. The address on the back of the envelope says Paddington, Sydney. It's a card.

Dear Mrs Cizekova

My deepest sympathy for the tragic loss of your daughter.

Yours sincerely

Leo Knight

In the space of a few seconds my hope has been crushed. Instead I'm filled with a dull certainty. Kita is dead. With this comes a rush of grief. I pull the bed cover tighter around me and lean my head against the window, letting the cold seep into my cheek.

There are no more tears, but this is worse, the sadness is like a lead weight in my chest. My mother has been resurrected and then taken away all over again and the few days of hope have made the loss crueler than ever.

Nan wasn't lying when she told me she'd scattered Kita's ashes on the Malverns. She said that she'd felt it was the right place, like she was almost daring me to protest. As if I would have. As if there were any other possible place. But maybe there was somewhere after all and Kita needed to travel half way around the world to find it. Deep down Nan probably knew that. Anyway, the ashes blew right back in Nan's face, up her nostrils and down into her lungs, sending her into a fit of coughing. They went into her mouth too.

'A last act of defiance from Kitty,' said Nan,

Faced with the decision whether to spit or swallow, she swallowed,

'It wouldn't have been right to spit her out,' Nan said, twisting her mouth into a bitter smile as if she could still taste it.

The second letter is in a larger envelope. It's from Edith Burton and it's from a place called, Mary Kathleen, Queensland, Australia. Inside there's a single sheet of thin blue airmail paper.

September, 1979

Dear Irene,

Thank you for your note. I'm pleased to hear that Storm is settling in well. Some of Kita's belongings have been returned. You said not to bother with her clothes, but there were a few things that seemed right to send on. So I've enclosed the necklace she was wearing and her diary, as well as a photograph. It's of the three of them, so Storm would like to have it. Perhaps you could pass them on to her when you think she's ready.

Please give our love to Storm. Jack and I miss her very much.

Yours sincerely

Edith

It's too much. I don't know these people – Edith and Jack - and yet they missed me. Who are they? What part do they play in my past? How did my mother die? And where is my father in all this? From what Edith says, it must have been him in the photograph. Was Nan the one who took the scissors to him? Why would she do that? The frustration is a painful solid force inside me. For every answer there are more and more questions.

I pick up the diary again. Maybe I'll find some of the answers in here. But my eyes keep shutting and the words on the page are a blur. When Max finds me, I'm half asleep and shivering with cold.

'Hey,' he says, making me jump. He yawns, still groggy from his sleep. He looks a wreck. Me too probably. It's been a long day. 'What's this?' he asks, picking up the diary.

'My mother's diary,' I say, my voice flat.

'You're joking. Really?'

Even though I'm exhausted I find myself telling him about the postcards and not being in them and then discovering myself in the diary. About Kita being dead and alive and dead again. And all the time I'm talking the numbness is creeping back in and taking me over.

When I'm finished Max gives me a look I can't interpret. Wariness maybe, as if I've got something catchy.

'God your life's complicated,' he says.

Complicated? I hadn't thought of it like that before, but I suppose it is, compared to Max's which is excruciatingly simple. He's thirty-six, has a respectable job, with prospects, one sister, two very British parents who still live together, and no skeletons in the cupboard. At least none that he knows of. I'm his only complication.

I'm freezing,' he says, climbing into bed with all his clothes on. 'Come on. Get in.'

I clambor in next to him, but the springs have gone and we both end up in the middle.

Max groans. 'This'll do my back in.'

I slide my hand up under his shirt and try to warm it on his chest, but he squirms away. 'Your hands are freezing.'

I laugh and kiss him. His face is all prickly. His shirt smells of whiskey. I slip my other hand, the really cold one, down into his trousers. He gasps and tries to roll away, but the mattress has him trapped. I keep my hand there, feeling his warmth soak into me. I need to be close to Max, as close as I can get. He's all soft down there. I stroke him for a bit, but it's only half-hearted and nothing happens. In the end Max takes my hand away.

'It doesn't feel right,' he says. 'Not in here.'

CHAPTER SIX

The heating is on, but it's cold in here anyway, because it's such a big room and the windows are bare and wide and tall, reaching from the floor almost to the ceiling. It's these vast windows, not the other people in the room, that are making me feel self-conscious. Through them I can see the sky, a turgid London yellow, reflecting back in on itself and shutting out the stars and the buildings opposite, dark shapes against the night sky. They're dotted with lighted windows, but it's not these bright spots that make me nervous, it's the others, the unlit windows, mysterious black holes from which someone might be peering in at me.

I shut my eyes and let the strong satisfying smells of oil paints, turpentine, linseed oil, rich pastels, and wood shavings waft up my nostrils. The only sounds are the scratching of charcoal, the occasional shuffle of feet, and the muffled traffic noise from the street below. But the intensity of silent concentration in here magnifies each of these sounds until they reach a deafening pitch.

'Hey keep still,' says one of the students. The one who takes himself too seriously and only ever looks at me sideways.

'Sorry.'

I reposition myself, trying to feel my way back to exactly where I was. Usually I'm more professional than this. It's not so hard to stay in one spot for ten minutes at a time. But I'm losing the knack. I think it might be sleep deprivation, which I've heard can be used as a form of torture. After a while your nerves go. You get all paranoid and twitchy. It's been over a month since Nan died and I haven't had a single proper night's sleep. The twitchiness is definitely starting. Too many coffees doesn't help, but it's not just that. It's the dreams too. And something else. It' feels like I've eaten something indigestible that keeps coming back up. Nan's death has imploded my world and I don't know how to recover from it, though I've had to start pretending for Max's sake. He's fed up with me. He thinks I should see a psychiatrist and for the second amazing time in a row, Alison agrees with him. Though she calls it grief counselling.

I can't blame Max for getting impatient. He tried hard at first. Taking time off work. Waiting outside the cottage the morning after Nan died, while I was out on the hills. I found him there, hopping from one foot to the other, rubbing his hands together, trying to keep the cold from getting in. He'd cancelled his important meeting and left London first thing that morning. The roads were icy so he had to leave the car down the hill and walk up. His shoes were soggy and there was a wet line around the bottom of his trousers, but he didn't mind. And then he did something totally out of character. Right on the street, in full view of anyone, he hugged me tight until the relief made my body sag under his strength and I cried some more, making a damp patch on his shoulder, and he didn't mind that either.

When I came back to London, things went downhill. The first couple of weeks were awful. Most of the time I didn't bother to get out of bed, just made little forays into the kitchen and the bathroom. Sometimes I made it to the couch and Max would find me there in the evening watching the movie channel, still in my pyjamas, wrapped in a blanket and surrounded by dirty mugs. He would cook dinner and try to coax me to eat. I was hungry, but not for food. I needed something else to fill the empty space inside me.

Max was being gentle with me, though I could tell he was relieved when he shut the door behind me in the mornings and went back to the life he understood. But I couldn't help it. I was shutting out the world, ignoring the phone, not bothering with the messages. After a while the calls stopped coming. I guess people were relieved I wasn't answering – it's hard to know what to say when words can't make something better. The only one who persevered was Alison, who knows about these things. When I wouldn't answer the phone, she turned up at the door. When I wouldn't open the door, she started shouting.

'Open up Storm, I know you're in there.'

And she kept it up until I was worried the neighbours would call the police. It's always been like this with me and Alison. She just goes on and on until I give in.

When I opened the door, she eyed my greasy hair and crumpled pyjamas.

'God, you're a mess,' she said, sweeping past me and into the bedroom, where she rummaged about in the cupboards, pulling out clothes. Then she dumped them in the bathroom and pushed me in too.

'Hurry up. We're going out for coffee.'

I did as I was told. I always do. It seems I've spent my life surrounding myself with bossy people.

In the cafe Alison ordered coffees and a huge slice of cheesecake with double cream.

'Eat it,' she said, when I protested. 'You can't afford to lose any more weight.'

Alison leaned back in her seat, cradling her coffee in her palms as I struggled with a mouthful of cheesecake. 'So, tell me what's going on?'

'Nan died,' I said not quite able to hide the sarcastic tone. As if she didn't know. As if Nan dying wasn't enough reason to shut out the world.

'And?'

'And what?'

'Max said you found out some things about your mother.'

'You've talked to Max?'

I'm astonished. Max can't bear Alison. He thinks she's too direct, too bossy. Alison's not too keen on Max either, so keeping them both happy has always been a juggling act.

'No, Max talked to me. He's worried about you.'

'More like he's fed up with me.'

Alison sighed.

'I love you dearly, Storm, but sometimes I think you're the most selfish person I know. You're an artist, you're supposed to see things, but you can't see past the end of your nose. Whatever my feelings about Max,' she said, rolling her eyes, there's one thing I'm sure of. He loves you.'

'Well if Max loves me, he might just mention it for once.'

Alison shrugged. 'Maybe that's not his way,' she said, draining her coffee and ordering another. 'Tell me about your mum.'

So I told her everything, right from the beginning, and when I finished my coffee was cold and the cheesecake was still sitting there waiting to be eaten.

'Why don't you find out?'

'Find out what?'

'I don't know... How your mother died. What happened back then. Where your father is... Maybe it's the not knowing that's eating you up.'

'How do I find out anything now? They're all dead.'

'There must be ways. Get on the internet, look up births, deaths and marriages, chase up those people in Australia... ' She picked up my fork and shoveled in the cheesecake. 'I know – you could go to Australia. Have a holiday. God knows, you need one after all this.'

'Australia! No. I couldn't.'

'Suit yourself, but you can't keep hiding in Max's flat. He loves you, but he won't indulge you forever. You can keep grieving, Storm, you should, but some time soon you need to rejoin the world.'

As always, Alison was right. I have to keep functioning. So since then I've eaten and washed and gone to my studio most days, but I still can't pretend everything is fine because it isn't. Over the last few weeks I've abandoned work altogether. I can't paint. Max knows something is wrong, but he has no idea how far behind I've got. There's a bunch of half-finished canvases propped up against the wall, staring reproachfully at me. I've got a hugely important show coming up. My second solo exhibition, my opportunity to really establish myself. So I keep trying, forcing myself to stand in front of a canvas for hours at a time, making little changes, token things that don't move it on. I only give up when the paints I've mixed on the palette dry out.

It isn't just grief I'm feeling. There's also a huge amount of anger. And I don't know what to do with it. I've never been much good at saying how I feel, so Max is just guessing. He knows I'm upset, but he can't help, so he's shut himself off. I heard on the radio the other day that grief puts pressure on your relationships. This woman they were interviewing had written a book about grief and how one of the hardest things about losing someone you love, is that often even the people closest to you can't help. Suddenly all the props disappear and you realise just how alone you are in the world. It's frightening. It feels as if Max and I are spiralling away from each other and there's nothing we can do about it. I can't talk to him. It's the speed of it that's terrifying, as if it was there all the time, waiting, accumulating anger and frustration and hurt and all the petty little irritations: Max cutting his toenails in the bath and leaving them there; or eating cocoa pops for breakfast even though he's thirty-six and should know better; or watching the rugby and shouting 'YES' when they score. All these things which used to rank around five on the partner irritation scale have now reached a whopping great nine and a half. I can't talk to him. There's no connection between us anymore. Max says it's me that's shut off. That I've withdrawn into myself. But there isn't anywhere else to go.

For the last year or so I've been living with Max in his flat more or less full time, but there's still no escaping the fact that it's his flat and I have to fit in around him. He's the only person I know who has a place for everything. Even me. It still amazes me that he has no need to plaster the fridge with bills and notices, not even a photograph. The walls are a clean, intense white, their cold monotony broken up by paintings, all minimalist, with hard, bright lines. Some of these paintings are mine but I don't feel happy living with them. Not like this anyway, as if we're in a gallery. Everything else in Max's flat is black leather or chrome or stainless steel, even the bed. Sometimes when I'm frantic inside, it's a relief to come back to Max's and dredge up some clarity from all this rich austerity. But at other times it's so cold and repellent that I feel like an imposter waiting to be sprung. This is a man's house. It's Max's bachelor pad. My clothes are in his cupboard, my toothbrush hangs in the bathroom, but there's very little else of me here.

Max hates coming to my studio. He's only ever slept there a couple of times and that was in the early days when things were more passionate and he didn't mind slumming it. The studio makes him sneeze. And he hates sharing a shower with strangers, in case he catches some sort of fungal disorder between his toes. But it's not just that. My dirt and clutter make him nervous. He says he wouldn't mind, if only I cleaned it sometimes. He's right, it is a mess. But it's mine, the only place I can really be me. I don't have to pretend to be anything, or fold my clothes or worry about leaving dirty plates sitting in the sink. I don't have a cleaner who comes in once a week and wipes away any evidence I exist, right down to my fingerprints.

A month ago none of this mattered, but Nan's death has changed everything. Max says I should move in properly and use the spare room as a studio. He says he means it, that he's not just being kind because of Nan. But something holds me back. An instinct perhaps. Self-preservation. My studio feels like an escape clause. Or maybe it's simpler than that. It's just good to have my own space. Life modelling, some tutoring, selling a few paintings and getting the occasional grant keeps me independent. Anyway, going by the way Max and I are getting on at the moment, now isn't the time to commit.

'Okay wrap up,' says the tutor, clapping his hands. 'Time for a break.'

I move gratefully. My left leg is cramping and I'm covered with goosebumps like a plucked goose. I slip on my coat, turning my back to the class as I do up my buttons. The worst bit is dressing and undressing, like at the doctors, but at least the doctor slips tactfully out of the room or draws a curtain. I've got to do this in front of twelve students. Nine of them are male and most don't even pretend to look away.

I make myself a strong coffee, even though it will mean another sleepless night, but that's infinitely better than the dreams. Then I wander around the class, letting the coffee warm my fingers and looking at the sketches, amazed all over again that these simple lines connect and make recognisable things. Amazed that these are parts of me transferred onto white sheets of paper. Wondering if in the process I've lost anything.

One of the students has done a vibrant, sensual sketch, almost abstract. He's seen more of me than just edges and lines and when he looks straight at me and smiles, I become painfully aware of my nakedness underneath this coat. I like the hungry way he's eyeing me. I like how upfront he is. It makes me blush and want at the same time and it hasn't happened before. At least not here. I turn away and stand by the window, fixing my eyes on the street below.

I met Max at an opening. It was a group show and I'd just sold my first ever painting so I was feeling pretty good and tossing back the red wine like it was water. It was getting late and the crowd was thinning out. Then I saw him. Well not all of him. Just his eyes. It was one of those across the room scenes in romance novels. He was looking at me with these pale blue eyes, and once I'd seen them I couldn't look away. Something inside my belly took a deep dive. I'd made an effort and got dressed up in a black silk skirt instead of my usual jeans, and I felt strange. Exposed. Usually when someone stares at me I feel all wrong, like my fly is undone, but his look made me feel sexy. Wild and sexy.

I don't remember exactly what we talked about, but my mouth had gone all dry and I was having trouble getting my words out. Anyway at some point I found out he was a financial adviser, which was a big minus. But he was also the one who bought my painting. My first fan. And that counted for something.

'I like it,' he said. 'It's straight forward. Uncluttered, like my life.'

I nodded, gulped back more wine and looked at his crotch. I was flailing about, falling in love or lust or something and trying hard not to, because the last person I wanted to be with was an uncluttered financial adviser. Hell, I didn't know anyone who dressed in a suit.

'Financial advisers aren't called Max,' I said accusingly.

He laughed. 'Actually,' he said, 'it's Maxwell William Taylor.'

For some reason this made me relax. Probably because I knew I could never have any kind of relationship, let alone sex, with someone called Maxwell William Taylor.

I nodded and turned away, but he reached out and held my arm.

'Let's go home,' he said.

You've got to be joking. I heard the words forming inside my head, but they didn't come out and I didn't shake my arm free and walk away, although sometimes I wish I had. His eyes were irresistible, not to mention his body. And that red sticker under my painting was his. He'd bought it. He believed in me. Also, I was drunk. Probably I should have played harder to get that first night, made him work for me. Instead I just nodded like an idiot and let him lead me back to his flat like I was a lost puppy.

I'd never been seduced before, not like this, with all the clichés, so part of me watched in an amused, detached kind of way, as the other part fell for it: the dim lights, soulful background music and expensive champagne in crystal flute glasses. I know they were crystal because I wet my finger and made them sing while I sat on his gleaming leather couch and thought about my dusty old thing with the broken springs and the loose mousy stuffing, and the kitchen bit of my studio, with its collection of empty Marmite jars for washing brushes and drinking red wine, sometimes both. I couldn't imagine taking Max there. I couldn't see him catching his tailored woollen trousers on a wayward spring, or staining the cuffs of his linen shirt on puddles of paint, or drinking coffee out of chipped Bart Simpson mugs. There was no way this could possibly be more than a one-night stand.

Max sat down next to me, took my glass and put it on the floor.

'Aren't you going to slip into something more comfortable?' I asked.

He laughed and pulled me to him. 'Yes,' he said. 'You.'

I couldn't even roll my eyes at how corny he was, because my body took over and all I could think about was how right it felt as he unbuttoned my shirt, and slipped his hands inside, stroking my breasts and nipples and belly, then lifting up my skirt, pushing my legs apart, while my hands pushed him in deeper and deeper ...

'Break's over, let's get back to work then.'

And bang, I'm dumped back into this room with twelve eager students waiting to stare at me all over again. My cup is empty now, but the polystyrene is pocked with absent-minded grooves and scratches, that somehow, maybe, represent what I felt when Max and I made love for the first time. I briefly consider keeping it, maybe even collecting a few and putting together an exhibition, 'Poly Stories' or something. But I can't be bothered and anyway that's not the direction I want to take with my work. I toss it in the bin, go back to my little stage and strip off my coat. That's what it feels like with the way this guy is looking at me. Stripping. And I suppose it is really. I'm self-conscious now and my arms and legs feel superfluous. Pete, the tutor, comes to the rescue. He moves my body around like a rag doll. Puts a leg here, an arm there, until I feel like a contortionist and wonder if I can hold the pose or even unwind it later. He touches my shoulders and I have to stop myself from cringing away from him because I don't like anyone touching them, not even Max.

'What are these?' Max asked that first night as he ran his fingers across the livid, puckered skin.

'Birthmarks,' I said, squirming away from his fingers because he was still a stranger really and this was somehow more intimate than the sex.

'That's odd,' he said. 'To have one on each side, like that.'

I moved Max's hands away that night, but I let Pete touch them as he moves me into position. There's something comforting about being so easily manipulated like this. When there's no resistance, somehow there's no responsibility. And anyway, I'm getting paid for it.

When he's finished he stands back to check and then pats me on the head.

'Good,' he says.

I hold the pose okay, but despite the coffee I keep yawning, feeling heavy with a fatigue that creeps from my feet, all the way up, bit by bit. I struggle through the next half-hour, trying not to look at anyone, especially him, and fighting the urge to shut my eyes, because then I'll start swaying and Pete won't be pleased.

When the class is over I get dressed quickly, fumbling with buttons and zips and laces as the students pack up their work and leave. He's packing his things up too slowly, making it obvious he's lingering. I could linger too. Wait for the others to leave. It would be so easy and probably fun, but there would be complications and guilt and I wouldn't be able to look Max in the eye. I'm not ready for that. Max and I might not be getting on all that well, but I'm not about to blow it with some quick fling. So I pretend he's not there and stumble out of the door, still buttoning up my coat. Damn it, I'm not sure I can go back.

CHAPTER SEVEN

Max is waiting up for me. He's funny about my life modeling work. I know he hates me doing it, but he's afraid to make a fuss. I reach up and kiss him, just a quick peck because I'm on my way to the kitchen looking for something to eat. But Max has other ideas.

'Come on then,' he says. 'Show me.'

'What?'

'Show me. What poses did you do?... No, take off your clothes first.'

Max's breath is a hot pungent blend of beef vindaloo, whiskey and beer. He's drunk, but he seems different, like someone I don't quite know.

'Max I'm hungry. I don't want to do this.'

'You do it for them, don't you?'

The expression on his face matches the coldness in his voice. I'm half frightened and I half want to. We haven't exactly had a great sex life these past few weeks. At first there were cuddles and hardly any sex. Now there's nothing – no cuddles or sex. We're sleeping back to back like book ends, all those unspoken words building a fence between us.

Max pours himself another drink and jiggles the ice in his glass while I undress. As I pull off my shirt, there's an anger rising inside me that's taking over the wanting, but I'm still confused. If this is his way of climbing over the fence, it's a strange one. What's got into him? It's like I'm not here, not really. I'm just an image on the television or in a glossy magazine.

By the time I'm down to my socks, I'm not confused anymore, just filled with a cold hard fury. There's no carpet or under floor heating, so I don't care how silly I look, I'm not going to take off my socks. My stomach is grumbling and I don't feel the slightest bit sexy. The whole thing is absurd. Why is she being so selfish?

'I usually get paid for this.'

I spit the words out at him, but Max doesn't flinch away from them and they don't bring him back to me. He just reaches into his pocket and pulls out his wallet. That's the last straw. I slap him hard on the cheek, leaving a stinging red patch and a face full of surprise. Then I sweep my coat from the couch and leave.

'Storm, wait!'

I slam the door shut on his words and run down the steps onto the street. If I wasn't so angry this might be funny. Me standing in a muddy puddle, on a busy street in Camden, wearing only my coat and socks. To make matters worse it looks like I'll have to walk. My purse is back inside where I left it, sitting on the kitchen bench and I'm not about to stuff up my dramatic exit by going back for it.

I button up my coat. It's red cashmere and reaches almost down to my ankles. It's the most expensive thing I own. A gift from Max of course, and if I wasn't so angry with him, I'd feel grateful all over again. I start walking. The silk lining is icy cold at first and then caressing warm on my skin. My body feels loose and sensual beneath the stroking silk. My feet are cold and wet, but I like walking without shoes. It makes me feel free. The few people I pass only look at my feet. Then they look away again.

I've been doing a lot of walking lately, following the canal through Regents Park, weaving through streets until I find Hyde Park, then past the palace and along the Thames. Or I meander through streets, winding into places I don't know, seeing how long it takes to get lost. It's easy because there aren't too many points of reference in London. Hampstead Heath is good though, I love standing up there with the city spread out before me. It helps give a sense of perspective.

It's surprising how relaxing it is to just walk without going anywhere. It gives you a space to not think. Tonight though, it's freezing cold and pouring with rain. My socks are soggy, there are cold blasts of air making their way up under my coat, my breath is ballooning out in front of me, my teeth are chattering and I have to swing my arms high to generate some warmth.

I know it's dangerous going alongside the canal at night but it's the short-cut and I'm always drawn to this place. After dark it's a no-go zone for most people, because the 'low life' as Max puts it, all congregate here, sleeping under the bridges, drinking on the grassy bits littered with dog shit and broken bottles. It stinks like a public urinal. Hardly anyone goes this way because they're afraid of being mugged or murdered, but anger makes you feel invulnerable, and the danger adds a certain edge.

I walk fast, not looking into the shadows, or at the black, bottomless water. I'm scared of treading on glass or needles, so I keep my eyes on the path and everything is all right for a bit. There are plenty of shadows, but nothing real. No figures lurking about, waiting for lone women in scarlet coats. The rain is getting heavier, dripping down my forehead and stinging my eyes. Then I'm under Camden High Street and it's really dark. I can't even see my feet, but I keep walking, stumbling along blindly and struggling against a growing sense of doom.

That's when it happens. One minute I'm upright and the next I'm flying through the air. I land awkwardly, winding myself, and lie sprawled on the path paralysed with fear. Any second now the person who tripped me will pounce, and that will be it. I imagine the tiny piece in the news-in-brief column: *Early morning jogger finds unidentified body in canal... wearing only a coat and socks.*

How would Max feel when he reads it? Guilty I hope. He'd definitely have some explaining to do. But this is ridiculous. I'm not going to die. There's no way I'm ready for that yet. I refuse to be an ugly bloated corpse, bobbing about on the surface, waiting for someone to fish me out. No. It isn't going to happen like this. I know it.

I slowly become aware of my senses. Of the damp under my knees, the cold burning my fingers and something else. A smell or a compound of smells, stronger than the canal, a crusty smell of piss and alcohol and rotting rubbish.

'Enjoy your trip girl.'

It sounds like an order, but then the rasping voice is followed by a hoarse wheezy laugh, like Millie's before the cancer got her. Peering through the gloom, I get a glimpse of a shapeless bundle of rags. The eyes are two glittering points almost invisible under hooded layers of skin. Just a bag lady, I tell myself. That's all. But I don't wait to see any more. I'm pushing myself up with my hands, onto my shaking legs and running. Hard, so that the cold air tears at my chest, and a stitch needles my belly.

It's only when I'm standing outside the door that I realise I've left the key in my bag back at Max's. I try ringing Warren's buzzer for the upstairs studio. Three long panicky rings.

'Yeah?'

'It's Storm. From downstairs. Sorry. I've lost my keys.'

The door release goes and I push hard. Then I'm tumbling into the foyer and pulling the door shut behind me. My own door is easy. The lock has gone anyway, but it's buckled a bit in the damp and I have to give it a big shove. I turn on all the lights, banishing shadows and darkness.

I'm shivering. Shock, I suppose, and the creeping cold. My feet feel like someone else's. I peel off my filthy socks. There's blood on them where I've cut myself. I didn't feel a thing. This time of night there's no hot water but I have a shower anyway. It's icy cold and takes my breath away, but I wash my feet and the graze on my knee and stay there until I've washed away some of the awfulness of what just happened. I start feeling a bit better. Shaky, but better.

I stand in front of the heater and rub myself dry until my skin turns from blue cold to glowing red. Then I put my coat back on. It's so cold I can see my breath and the bar heater is worse than useless. In a sudden burst of DIY, I hunt about for some alfoil and cover the rusty bits. I might bring some clothes over and move back in for a while. Things are getting too complicated between Max and me.

There's not much in the fridge: some ancient pesto sauce, a bit of rock hard parmesan, a bottle of flat lemonade and some butter. There's a dusty tin of baked beans on the shelf, but I can't be bothered with openers and saucepans. A bottle of wine would be good, but the off-licence would be shut by now, and I don't have any money anyway. So I settle for a hot chocolate, with water because there's no milk.

I push the heater right up near the bed and climb in, still wearing my coat. Tonight I'm even fond of my saggy old mattress and the heavy feather quilt that gave Max acute rhinitis both times he slept here. There's something comforting about single mattresses. They're innocent sex-free places, so when it does happen it feels illicit, like making love in the back seat of a car.

Thinking about sex makes me think about Max again. I can't understand what happened back there. He's never been like this before and I don't know if this is some hidden, warped part of his personality or just the drink talking. Maybe he's afraid. With Nan gone, Max is all I have left and that's a pretty big responsibility for him. I'm scared too, because for the first time I have to work out my feelings for Max. I'm too old to keep running away.

I stare at Kita's postcards on the wall. I've made a square out of them, four rows of four, trying to make sense of my mother's story. Aside from the diary, they're almost the sum total of what I know about Nan and Kita's relationship. The words say nothing really, just reinforce the huge distance between the two of them. But the pictures tell me heaps. Mostly it's the light in them that I recognise. And the mystery.

I remember when Nan told me I was born in Australia.

'Where is it, Nan?' I asked, expecting her to point north or south, because I already knew what lay east and west. But she pointed to the ground.

'Down there,' she said.

At first I thought she meant Australia was underground, like hell or Hades, but then Pop explained that Nan meant right through to the other side. I took Pop's spade and started digging in the front garden but I didn't get far and Pop told me off for mucking up the lawn. After that I made myself forget about Australia. It was the sad place where my mother had died. A hell of sorts. And it was the one story I didn't dare ask about.

But now I can feel the yearning for the past grasping me all over again. The need to know, the need to make it mine. I feel under the pillow for my mother's diary. I keep it here in my studio because I don't want Max to think I'm obsessed with it. And anyway, if Max reads it he'll try to be kind. He'll make Kita out to be some stupid drugged out hippy. And he'll tell me I was better off without her. She *was* a stupid drugged-out hippy. And maybe I was better off without her. But that's not something I'm ready to consider. I need to know who my mother was before I can move on. I need to turn around and face the past, wading through all the lies and inconsistencies until I find something closer to the truth. Something solid I can hang on to.

Nan and Millie and Pop have all left something of themselves with me. When I shut my eyes I can conjure them up, or bits of them. Millie's wild trapped eyes, always darting about between windows and doors. Pop's square hands and the way the air stayed still around him when he moved. Nan humming a tune, while her big red knuckles kneaded the bread dough. One day I would like to paint each of them. Take all the details they've left with me and mix them up. I wonder how to do that. How I could paint their portraits without painting their faces - a montage of features, events, colours and movement. What would they look like in the end?

Kita is still a gaping hole in all this. My mother is an absence. I have two photographs of her, but I couldn't paint her portrait. There are no memories to conjure up. Nothing but her words in the diary. And these are the words of someone I don't know. The more I read, the worse it gets. She's this character in a book, fleshing herself out alright, kind of convincing, but not connected to me. Not at all. I don't recognise her, or me in her, or the Storm she's written about.

Instead of finishing my paintings, I've been trying to reach into the past and put my mother's life in some sort of context. Tea bags were invented in the seventies, and fast-food chains and muesli, as well as boob tubes and see-through crochet bikinis. But underneath the psychedelic orange and purple paisleys and zig zags and swirls, there was serious stuff happening too. Women were standing up for their rights. They were going to university, talking about free love and taking the Pill. My mother wasn't standing up for anything or studying, but she looked like a hippie, she read fortunes for a living and had sex when she felt like it. She also took drugs, too many of them but obviously not the Pill. And she had a baby.

I'm still getting used to the fact that I was with her in Australia. That she didn't abandon me. Not then anyway. Instead she took me through Central Australia with this person called B. I don't know who he is - don't even know his full name. And I hardly know anything about him, except that he took acid, drank too much beer and smoked heaps of joints. He was her lover, that's clear, but was he my father? In the diary he acts like my father. Sometimes. But that's something else I don't understand, because on my birth certificate it says quite clearly that my father's name is Michael. How did it end between them? Is he dead too? Nan said he was, and I believed her then but she lied about Kita so maybe she lied about him. If he's not dead, then why did he leave me? And where is he? There are so many questions jostling about in my head. And not a single answer.

I've been trying to keep myself from feeling anything, because otherwise the pain tears into my heart, churns my stomach and sits like lead inside my limbs. When I go looking inside my mind, the route is evasive, a maze of twists and turns, back and forth, away from the things that hurt. Alison says it's really important to shift the numbness. That I need to feel everything. She keeps telling me to let it out now, otherwise it will fester and ferment deep inside and one day just when I think I've got my act together it will get me. These things always do, she says. You can't run away from yourself for ever.

I don't think Alison realises how hard it is to break a pattern that's gone through four generations. All women. All running. And I don't know why. What from? Pop didn't run though. He was always there. The way Nan told it, Pop was a solid force, facing up to things and keeping them all safe, though she always said that word safe with a twisted edge I couldn't understand.

Nan ran right inside herself. She was like one of those ancient fossils we learned about at school, the ones with the skeletons on the outside. Trilobites. She didn't know she was running though. At least I don't think she did. And I'm only just starting to realise.

With Kita there was no question. She knew she was on the run. It says so in her diary. I look through it for the right entry.

16th September

I wonder what it is I'm running from. There's something big and dark back there. Sometimes it's geometric, like a square and sometimes it's more insubstantial. But it's always there, even on really sunny days when everything seems light and happy. And when it gets me? I don't know. It won't be a blow, not physically sharp like that. More like a kind of soaking, the way dye creeps into a jumper. Maybe it's Millie madness.

I'm surprised at that last sentence. I'd never thought of Millie being mad. She was always just Millie. A little odd maybe, certainly eccentric. But not mad. Millie represented other possibilities for me, outside of convention, outside of Nan's fearful constrictions. I couldn't let Millie be mad. But Kita talks of it as if it were a fact. As if it were a blood line, a genetic thing that gets passed down. Not circumstantial. As if there really is such a thing as 'normal', a baseline from which we can measure. I've never been so certain of that.

Millie ran away too and because of that she survived. But she didn't know that then. She couldn't read her own future. Then she was a wild fifteen-year-old, caught up in a present full of possibilities and the only thing that was clear to her was the impossibility of renouncing a forbidden love. Millie was used to doing as she pleased, and didn't allow for the weight of the past in her scheme of things. But for the Rom it was a matter of survival. For them it was completely necessary to sacrifice one person for the good of the group. And Millie was a Rom.

I have a photograph of Millie and Tomas, taken soon after they arrived in England when Millie was nineteen and Tomas thirty-two. It's a black-and-white photograph, but tinted, and the artist has captured them well. Pop's eyes are like the crests of a wave. And maybe that's what drew her to him, because hers are in opposition to his. Hers are a moonless night. Both sets of eyes are unfathomable, although with the benefit of history, I imagine that in Millie's there's still a hint of wildness, while Pop's show the beginnings of despair. And in between them is three-year-old Nan, staring glumly at the floor.

For those few months in 1936, when Millie secretly went to a Gypsy school which had been set up to help them 'assimilate', she just wanted to learn to read. She didn't expect to fall in love with her gentle, serious gadje teacher. And he didn't expect to fall in love with this dark-eyed barefoot girl in her tatty swirly skirt. That's how they met, student and teacher, Romany and gadje, child and adult, transgressing every rule. And when Millie found she was pregnant she went to her parents and told them she couldn't go through with her arranged marriage to an old man with long dirty fingernails that filled her with an impossible repugnance. I don't know if she was overcome with her love for Tomas or just aware of a need to escape. Nan didn't know either. Even Millie might not have been sure. I asked her once what bit of Pop she'd fallen for.

'His eyes,' she told me. 'I never saw eyes like that... And his hands. Big monster fingers holding my chalk and dancing words on my slate.'

With Pop it was love. Nan was sure of that. Though love changes, she told me once. Sadness strips away at life, so Millie grew up quickly. A baby, a great wide bottom, weariness, despairing eyes and no more children. Even so, Pop never stopped loving Millie. Even when she threw up her skirts at strangers, or smoked her pipe in the front garden or sunk into fits of despair. She was never easy, but he always stood by her.

I asked Nan once, why she thought Pop stayed, even though Millie was such hard work.

She shrugged. 'Who knows?' she said in her 'that's the end of that' tone of voice, but I could see that the thought bothered her, because of the way she splashed the boiling jam over the edges of the saucepan. Usually she was careful.

I waited quietly to see if she would go on and after a while she did.

'I asked him once,' she said. 'He got furious and raised his hand as if he was going to hit me. But he didn't. Pop never hit anyone. "You don't know," he said. "You don't know anything." He was wrong there. I knew a bloody lot,' she said, licking hot jam splats off her hand.

Millie and Tomas married immediately and against the wishes of both families, but their oaths didn't make Millie immune. A few days later her people organised a *kris* and Millie was 'collected'. I imagine Pop putting up his fists, ready to take them all on. And Millie shaking her head, pushing Pop aside and going to face her fate. At the trial the old man she should have married denounced her as a traitor. Everyone had an opinion, people shouted each other down, but in the end the punishment was unanimous. Millie was pronounced unclean and expelled forever from the group. As a final gesture, Millie's mother threw a curse down on her, a curse that would pass through one generation to the next and the next.

I don't know if she cried, or if there was any tenderness. Did anyone wish her well? She had thirteen brothers and sisters and so many aunts, uncles and cousins. It's hard to believe that they could all turn away so completely and viciously. At least one of them must have crept up to her and fleetingly held her hand. Maybe visited her too, in her strange new house. Sat with her, gossiping, plaiting her hair, crooning songs to the baby. She must have been hungry for news and contact with the only world she had known.

When I try to imagine the trial I always see her standing on a chair or table, removed from the rest by her shame. But I can never see tears, only the pride in Millie's face, held up high against the fear inside her. A vicious fear of the unknown, of the dangerous force of tradition, of losing everything that she knew. There's also a new maturity, that comes with the responsibility for the life that is forming inside her. And there's the beginnings of understanding. She has transgressed, moving outside the boundaries of her culture, into a new set of constrictions. For by then she had already spent her first nights in a bed, surrounded by walls and a roof and a tight claustrophobia.

Someone is pressing the buzzer. It's probably Max. No one else would visit after midnight. I stumble out of bed.

'Who is it?'

'It's me.'

'What do you want?'

'Let me in.'

My finger is hovering near the button, but I'm not going to let him off so easily.

'Why should I?'

'Please. We need to talk.'

'What's there to talk about?'

'Come on, Storm, it's bloody freezing out here.'

'And?'

There's a longish pause before Max finally gets his mouth around the words I've been waiting for.

'I'm sorry.'

I hold down the button and wait for the click.

Max is soaking and bedraggled and he's wearing a hangdog look that makes him practically irresistible. That's the problem with Max, everything about him is sexy: the way he stands, kind of a slouch but not lazy; the way his trousers hang off his hips and make just the right number of folds around his ankles; and the way he looks at me. Especially that.

He's brought my clothes.

'I'm sorry,' he says again, handing me the wet bundle. 'I walked.'

It isn't clear if he's apologising for his behaviour or for getting my clothes wet. I don't tell him it's okay, because it still isn't. Nothing is okay between us.

We stand facing each other, not knowing what to do. Max is shivering and looks like he's going to cry.

'What's happening to us Storm? I feel like I'm losing you.'

I shake my head, wishing I could feel something. Wishing away the numbness, but I can't. 'Me too,' I mutter, not sure if I mean him or me. I hate these kinds of talks. They're so unpredictable; you can start in one place and end somewhere else completely. If we're not careful we'll talk ourselves into breaking up.

'Help me, Storm. Can't you talk for a change? Join in. Please ...Tell me what's happening?'

I'm trying to muster up the right words. But I can't find them. I'm so afraid of getting it wrong. So afraid of losing him. If I could cry that would help, but I can't even do that. I'm standing in front of Max, feeling like a schoolgirl called up to the front of the class and not knowing what to do with my hands or what I've done wrong. If writing the same line over and over would fix it between us, I'd write thousands of lines.

Instead I rub his head with a towel, then stand him by the heater and peel his clothes off, one layer at a time. I'm on safer ground now. Trying to make peace. We don't say anything. He's shivering, covered in goose bumps, and his skin is tinged with blue. When I kiss him there's the taste of rain and salt and whiskey. As he picks me up and carries me over to the mattress an immense weariness spreads through my body. He lies me down and unbuttons my coat. Then he gently kisses my breasts and pushes into me, making me gasp. His face is close to mine and

I can see the urgency in his eyes, the set of his jaw, his mouth searching for mine, and my need mirroring his.

Afterwards, he stays inside me and we lie together feeling close again, the barriers between us peeling away. There's a tenderness between us that's rarely there these days. And it's this tenderness that almost makes me change my mind. Almost. 'I'm going to Australia.'

The words are like hot spikes sizzling the atmosphere. They fill Max's eyes with alarm and mine with a reckless glee.

'What?'

'Australia!' I laugh out loud because the decision has surprised me almost as much as Max.

'Why?'

'I need to. I have to find out about M… about Kita. About what happened.'

I can't say mum. I don't know why, though I suppose it's because I never had one. Mother sounds too posh. Even Kita doesn't sound right. And it's wrong that I'm not comfortable saying any of these things out loud.

'But… when? asks Max. The surprise has made him seem vulnerable for a moment. 'What about the exhibition in June?'

'I'll only go for a few weeks, a month at most. There'll still be time to get ready for the show.'

Max shakes his head, appalled.

'You know I've not been painting,' I tell him. 'I can't'

He looks surprised. 'I thought you were,' he says, glancing at the half-finished canvases leaning against the wall. The same one is still sitting there in the easel, as if no time has passed at all.

'I've been trying… It might help to get away for a bit.'

Max sighs. 'Where are you going to get the money from?'

I hadn't thought about money. I've hardly got any. 'Nan's left me a bit.'

'It'll be months before that comes through.'

'Oh.' It feels like someone has let the air out of me. I can't wait months. I want to go now. 'I'll use my credit card. The bank will raise my limit, they're always offering.'

Max shakes his head. 'You're mad.'

I shrug. 'Maybe, but I've got to do it.'

Already I can feel the twitching, tingling sensation, like after a bad bout of pins and needles. It's kind of unbearable and tantalising all at once. I'm coming to life again and it's all I can do to stop myself leaping out of bed there and then. I leap on Max instead.

'Come with me!'

'I can't. I've got a job to do.'

He's sulking and it makes me laugh. 'Quit. Take a holiday. Do something spontaneous.'

'I can't just walk out. These things have to be planned.'

Max likes being a financial adviser. He's sees it as a creative, nurturing role, drawing people and ideas together, creating a seamless world.

'Come on,' I say. 'Admit it, you're just a power freak. You want to feel needed.'

I reach down and kiss Max on the lips. A hard bruising kiss. 'I need you Max. Come with me.'

Max shakes his head. 'My wild c*hiriko*. Don't go.'

I wonder if Max understands the contradiction. They called the gypsies wild birds and then caged them like factory chickens. Nan told me about it one day when I was still only nine or ten and angry with Millie for something. Millie's love was like a seesaw. She took you up and up and then let you down with a giant thud, so I was often recovering from one of her hurts. Nan and I were sitting on an outcrop of rocks, up high on the Malverns, looking out across Herefordshire. It was a beautiful summer's day, peaceful, the warm air sitting calmly in the valleys below. We could hear people calling to each other, dogs barking, the quacking of ducks, smell the cut hay, the sheep dung… A beautiful day. August 2nd. But Nan had something on her mind.

'It's time for you to know,' she said.

'Know what?' I asked, immediately alert for a good story.

'This is the anniversary,' Nan said.

'Of what?' I asked, surprised.

'The *Zigeunernacht*… It means Gypsy Night.'

'I was only seven or eight,' said Nan. 'Playing draughts in the living room with Pop. We were laughing. I remember that because afterwards it seemed so wrong, that we could have been laughing while it all happened. Suddenly Millie appeared in the doorway. I thought she might have been hurt, the way she leaned on the doorframe, as if only that were holding her up. Her face was ashen, even her lips. And when she spoke her words were a monotone, as if she had no energy for it.

'They are dead …'

Nan said she gasped then, at those words, and a chill started at the top of her head and prickled its way all down her spine. She jumped up, meaning to run to her mother, but Pop's hand held her back. Or maybe it wasn't Pop, but something in Millie's face that forbade comforting.

'It is over,' Millie said. 'The devil has won.'

Then she turned and left and the doorway seemed terribly empty after she'd gone. Nan held on tight to Pop, silently afraid, until Pop shook her off and ran after Millie, pleading, comforting. But Millie pushed past him as if he wasn't there. They didn't see her for days. And it was a long time before they understood what had happened. She never explained how she knew, but it didn't surprise Nan, because it had always been Millie's way to know things… The 2nd of August, 1944, was the day four thousand Rom were slaughtered at the Auschwitz- Birkenau concentration camp in Germany. All Millie's family were in that camp. Every one of them. After the war Pop searched and searched, but it was years before he traced them all back to that day in August.

It destroyed Millie. Even though they'd expelled her. Even though she'd made a new life with Pop and little Irene. Even so, her heart was still back there with them. And it broke when she realised it was too late. She'd betrayed them all over again by not being there as they died and denying them the chance to forgive her. And now she could never be pardoned. Nan said it was pointless trying to explain that if she'd been there she'd be dead too. Millie had her own way of reasoning and it didn't always make sense. Pop's heart broke, and Nan's too, because they were all Millie had left and they finally understood they would never be enough.

Nan's words hovered in the air, then slowly settled. I could feel the rare privilege of Nan telling me a story, mingle with the horror and sadness of what she was saying. I wanted to say, 'No thank you, Nan, I don't need to know this.' But these were powerful words and I could never give them back. So I just stared out across the hills and valleys towards the Black Mountains. Everything was different. The shadows in the valleys were dark and unfriendly, the sounds were too unknowing, the whole day had become sinister.

Nan told me it was five days before Millie came back. She was soaking wet, hungry, dirty and empty. That's what struck Nan the most. The emptiness, a kind of hollowness as if someone had scooped out her middle. She'd lost a tooth too and Nan was shocked because the black hole in her mouth made her look old, even though she was only in her twenties. After that Millie got really strange. Although she kept doing most of the things mothers are supposed to do, she did them in an absent-minded way. Only every now and then she'd hug Nan so tightly it hurt. Nan was scared of her.

I had so many questions: How did they kill them? Why the Romany people? Who did it? But I saw that Nan's eyes were red and that frightened me more. Then, instead of hugging her sadness away, I burst into tears and Nan had to comfort me for the murder of our ancestors.

'I thought you should know,' she said. 'I won't speak of it again.'

Over the years I've looked for the answers to these questions. After Millie died, I got hungry for facts, thinking that somehow in them I'd find a reason. I read about the Holocaust, hunting for references, but there was hardly anything, just a sentence here and there. No one denied what happened to the gypsies, they just didn't seem to think it was worth writing about. Finally I found out how it happened. And I knew who did it. But no amount of searching will ever dredge up an answer to explain *why* it happened, because none of the reasons are anywhere near good enough.

Max is staring up at me, looking straight into my eyes. A curious searching look. I wonder if he really loves me. He's never said. Sometimes I think Max collected me, the way he collects paintings. I'm an acquisition and he's watching closely to see if my value goes up or not. If it goes down he'll discard me, like any good businessman would. Other times I know that I'm not being fair. There's more to it than that. I'm what he isn't and he's what I'm not. We need each other.

'Don't go,' he says again. It's almost an order.

I study his face. Max has a look that ages well. He could have been a hero in World War II. The Germans could have modelled their idealised fascist sculptures on him. With his Aryan looks, the square, hard, handsome lines of his face, the perfect triangle of his body, the flashing white blue of his eyes - no one would ever put *Max* in a concentration camp.

'Please stay.' This time he's pleading and I wonder what he's afraid of. 'At least wait for a while. We could go next year when I've got some time off.'

This is the first time I've stood up to Max. The first time I've chosen to go my own way. I'm afraid, but it feels as if there's no choice.

'I'm sorry Max, I can't wait for you.'

CHAPTER EIGHT

'Ladies and gentleman, this is your pilot speaking... We're right on schedule, touching down in Sydney at approximately 4.35pm...'

The pilot's voice is so lazy and relaxed, as if he's about to nod off, and I wonder how he could possibly feel like this when he's flying this monstrosity, defying the laws of gravity, responsible for hundreds of people... but his next words send me into a different sort of panic.

'Looking out of the right-hand windows you'll see we're flying over land. We've reached the far north-western tip of Australia... Welcome to the Lucky Country.'

I bang shut my book, in a flap now because I'm not ready. I need to clean myself up before we land. My teeth are covered with sandpaper scum and my tongue's fat and fluffy from the glass of wine I had with the dinner, which should have been breakfast. I have to wash my face too, and under my arms, and my hair has worked itself into a bird's nest on one side, from when I pretended to sleep, leaned up against the window on the mini complementary pillow, trying to evade the kicks of the grumpy baby next to me.

I check my watch: 12.39 p.m. on the 7 March; four hours until we are due to land and two months and two days since Nan died. I wonder when I'll stop measuring time against Nan's death. Will I gradually forget or will I have to wait until something more momentous takes its place.

I peer out of the window, squinting against the glare of the sun. I expected the desert to be flat, but it's not. Instead its contours are like giant ripples. They remind me of the lines on a beach when the tide has gone out, magnified into huge wavy lines of hills or a mountain range. And crossing this giant, prehistoric landscape is the struggling shadow of our plane, looking tiny and insignificant. A single ash, tossed by the wind, fluttering, insubstantial... like Nan, her ashes sitting perched up there in an urn on the mantelpiece in Victoria Cottage, because when it came to the crunch, I had to leave her there. I simply couldn't do it.

It was the weekend before I left. Max came with me to scatter the ashes. He said I didn't need to rush it, that some people wait a year and some people never do. But I wanted to get it done before leaving for Australia. It was symbolic really, a chance to show him I was moving on from Nan's death. I'd made a bit of a fool of myself, collecting the ashes from the crematorium. When the man handed me a plastic tub filled with ash I didn't know how to react. It seemed ludicrous to walk out of there with Nan tucked under my arm, but even worse to put her in a plastic shopping bag like she was a carton of milk or a pound of onions. So I just stood there, frozen to the spot. The funeral man was exactly how I expected him to be, with his hands behind his back, a reverent bow, the right words - he even called me Madam. It was about then that I felt the laughter rising from deep within me. I tried to stifle it, but it came out anyway. Not a healthy laugh, more the sort that used to get women put away. 'Hysteria,' they'd say. 'Too much stimulation.' That made me laugh again, loudly this time, and they looked at me. Max and this funeral man. Two raised eyebrows, an uncomfortable shuffle, and out came the laugh again. No amount of effort would turn this into a sob, so leaving Nan sitting on the desk, I ran outside and stood in the drizzle. By the time Max emerged, awkwardly holding Nan's ashes at arm's length, I was dripping wet, freezing and ashamed of myself. If I had a tail it would have been curled up between my legs.

Max and I spent the weekend in the cottage, sleeping on the floor in the green room because nowhere else felt right. It was still too much Nan's house and I wasn't up to making it my own yet. The first day we walked the Malverns together, all nine miles or so, from North End Hill up to Worcestershire Beacon, then across Wyche Cutting to British Camp, the terraced Iron Age fortress on Herefordshire Beacon, which is Max's favourite spot, probably because it's defensible. We had lunch in the pub and then went on to Midsummer Hill, Hollybush Hill, and finally to Chase End Hill at the southern end.

At first there was a creeping mist, which meant we couldn't see more than a few feet in front of us. Every now and then it would lift for a moment and we'd get glimpses of how clear it was in the valleys. I'd always hated the depressing mists, the way they sat on the hills for days on end, making everything damp and dark. Later in the day a bitter north wind started up and blew the mist from the hills. Then we could see for miles and miles and I remembered again what I love so much about this place. We drank hot sweet coffee laced with brandy, from Nan's thermos, until my head and my heart were racing and the hills were spinning. We walked all day, our eyes streaming from the cold wind and our faces glowing. The joy of being out on the hills helped us forget the simmering tension between us. That night we lay down by the fire and made love for the first time in weeks, the heat making our fingers and toes and noses sting.

The next morning we traipsed the hills again, still searching for the right place. Midsummer Hill was one of Nan's favourite spots, a magical place of secret pagan ceremonies. Or Worcestershire Beacon because it's the highest point and from there you can see in every direction for miles and miles. Or British Camp because the ancient people carved their own history into it, reshaping the hill their way. But in the end I chose the spot where Nan died, not so far from the cottage, just down from Summer Hill and pointing west across the shadowy mysteries of Herefordshire.

Max and I stood awkwardly, not certain what rituals the act of scattering Nan's ashes called for. Our faces were red and Max hopped from one foot to the other, trying to keep the cold from creeping up through his feet and into his bones. Trying to be patient for my sake, and I was grateful for that. I cast about for the words I needed, something about how much Nan loved the hills and how right it was for her ashes to stay here. But I couldn't get it right. I got muddled with tenses, shocked by how neatly the past tense sweeps a person away. I love you Nan - or should it be I loved you? In the last few weeks even these simple words had become complicated. Nothing was straightforward any more.

It was nearly two months since I had stood in the funeral parlour and kissed Nan goodbye. But standing on the Malverns, holding Nan's ashes, I could still feel my lips tingling from that last kiss. I wondered if they'd removed her slippers before dropping her into the furnace. Somehow it seemed wrong not to, like having a shower with your underpants on. But I was rapidly going numb and Max was rubbing his arms and trying not to hurry me, so I took the lid off the urn and let the wind play with the ash.

I held up the urn. Any moment I would turn it over, allowing the wind to lift Nan into the sky. But the wind dropped suddenly and it started to snow, the flakes falling warm against our numb cheeks. I worried that the snow would make the ashes fall down in a lump on the ground and people would tread on them. And anyway, it was too early to know what I'd lost with Nan's death.

I hadn't worked out what was gone forever and what she had left me. So I put the lid back on.

I look out through the window again, squinting across this dazzling country at a world split in two; blue-white light, deep red earth. And I feel an irrational fear. I recognise this place, those colours… It might be premonition or it might be memory, but whatever it is I can feel the long pointy skeletal fingers of its menace probing into me. Instinctively I want to curl up against it, into a foetal position, a child again, two years old. I want to call out for my mother. I can even feel the word forming inside my mouth… Mama.

We're flying over cultivated land now, vast golden expanses of grain, the cloudless sky, a cobalt blue, richer than I've ever seen. The colours are so unlike England's endless shades of green. Here it's earthier, the tones warm-hot: cadmium orange, burnt sienna, yellow ochre, yellow green… Yet I recognise them. They're almost the same as the dried-up colours caking my palette, the edges of each colour blended into the next. Here though, there's a sharp geometry to the colours and shapes below. Framed by the window, there's a painting down there, already complete. The stamp of human endeavour. Nature made neat. Sometimes I think I can just make out a house, or shed, but we're flying so high it's difficult to be sure. All I can be sure of is that my mother died somewhere down there, but I don't know why or how or where. I wonder about my father too. If he is still alive, then why didn't he ever look for me? Perhaps he doesn't even know I exist.

Suddenly I'm filled with doubts. This whole thing seems impossible. And pointless. I'm spending a fortune I don't have and risking my relationship with Max, just so I can retrace my mother's journey. I should have listened to Max and used the internet or even the Royal Mail, to look for the answers. What if it all goes wrong? What if I get lost in the outback somewhere? Edith Burton might be dead by now and Leo Knight might not want to talk about the past. Even if my father is still alive, my chances of finding him somewhere in this huge continent are pretty slim. I don't know where to begin looking. And Jesus, I don't even know if I really want to. What would I do with a father? There are hardly any men in my life. There never has been. Only Pop, or a vague sort of memory of him. A few boyfriends, one or two brief flings - then Max.

'A bird has to risk falling before it can fly,' Audrey said, when I told her how scared I was of losing Max. And she added something about how she thought I still had rather a lot of growing up to do, which on reflection is quite offensive, though Audrey has always managed to say the worst things in the nicest possible way. So I stayed firm, even though Max and I argued right up to the last minute, me begging him to come and him listing one sensible reason after another why I shouldn't go. I know he's right. There's nothing sensible about this trip, just a strong feeling that I can't ignore. I have to do it, with or without him.

But now Max is not here, I want him so much more, which isn't surprising, because that's the way it's always been with me. My whole world seems to have been formed by neurotic women and absent men and nostalgia for what was or yearning for what might be. Deep down I have a sneaking suspicion that it might be too late for me and Max.

The baby next to me wants to see what I'm looking at. She clambers over my legs as if I'm not there and presses her nose up against the window. The smell of her is sour and sweet all at once and it starts off a yearning somewhere inside me. I've always thought I'd have children one day, but I've never felt this cluckiness before, though I've watched it send my friends to the pet shop for kittens.

'Sorry,' says the mother, reaching out to restrain her child.

'It's okay,' I say and smile as the mother sinks back in her chair, relieved. 'What's her name?'

'Emily. She's just turned one,' she says, 'and won't keep still. It's impossible.'

The mother is weary and frazzled. Her face is drawn into two vertical worry lines starting at the frown above her eyes and sliding right down past her mouth. It reminds me of when I used to make faces at Nan. 'Be careful, she'd say. The wind might change and then you'll stay like that forever.'

I don't want to be like this tired mother who seems to get no pleasure from her child. But I know this can't be true. It's more complicated than that. Nothing is simple between mothers and daughters. That's what Nan used to say. Even so I want to ask this woman if she loves Emily. If she sometimes wishes Emily hadn't happened? But these are stupid questions. Mothers love their children. Of course they do. It's natural.

Emily gets bored with the window and wriggles over her mother into the aisle. She's not quite walking, so she holds onto things and pulls herself along, one wobbly step at a time, stopping to peer solemnly into people's faces until they smile back into hers. When she's too far away, her mother sighs and goes to collect her. Emily screams and kicks and when her mother sits back down, the whole process starts again.

I flick through Kita's diary and reread August 5th for what must be the hundredth time. I could almost recite it from memory, but each time I read it I'm hoping the words might throw up some new meaning, as if the page itself might give me a clue to what she was like and how she really felt about me.

August 5

It's Storm's birthday today. B gave her some little animals to play farms with and I gave her a rag doll, which we've called Peggy because it's easy for her to say. Peggy's already filthy from being dragged about in the dirt. But Storm loves it to bits. I guess it doesn't add up to much, a grubby doll and some toy animals. I know I should tell Mum and Millie about her. Storm has a right to them. They're her blood. But hell, I don't want her tainted with all that.

It's strange how her birthday makes me cry. I've been doing it on and off all day and B is fed up. My tears make him hostile. I guess he feels he's not part of them. And I suppose he isn't. This is about Storm and me. Two whole years since she was born. Two years since I was pacing the floor in Janie's living room, feeling the insides of me tearing open and screaming at how out of control it all was. 'Let go,' Janie kept saying, but I wanted to hold on to something. Not a hand or a pillow, nothing solid like that. Just to what was familiar, to certainty, to what was me, because I was losing that fast. I needed lock eyes with someone else. Demanded it. Got furious when they turned away. 'Look,' I shouted. 'Look at me.' As if I would disappear without them. And I was right. It went beyond that and I was lost. There was just pain and more pain, a guttural pushing, more basic than anything. Me shouting and growling and panting. And then it was finished and I remember how scared I was, counting toes and fingers and turning her over and over looking for the defects I was sure would be there. The awful things I dreamt about. But she was totally perfect. And now two years have gone already. She's turned from the puffy red wrinkly thing that slid out of me, into a tottery little person and she's still perfect. I'm losing her though. Every day she moves a little bit further from me. Part of me wants her to be older and less needy so I don't have to change her nappies or feed her, or wipe her snotty nose, but at the same time I can't bear how quickly she's growing up and away from me.

Emily decides to climb back onto my lap, so I put the diary away again. She's balancing on my leg and peering through the window and the casual intimacy of this makes me wonder at the way it's so easy for a child to trust an adult and also how horribly easy that trust is to betray. Just one betrayal and they've lost their innocence forever, because you can't undo things that hurt and you can't re-create trust. What a responsibility. I can feel a strange tightening in the pit of my belly. It's not the butterfly fluttering I got when the plane took off from Heathrow. It's not the calm lightness that comes in the no-man's land between places. And it's not excitement at arriving somewhere new. No, this feeling is different and deeper and I can't read it. Not yet.

A subtle shift in the atmosphere tells me we're descending. A few minutes later the land disappears below dense dark clouds and soon we're amongst them, bumping around, rain lashing the windows. When I hand Emily back to her mother she howls, the sound adding to the pressure already building in my ears. This is the bit about flying that I hate. If we get to the ground in time then I'll be okay, otherwise, the pain will build and build until it's blinding. One day my eardrums might burst, but not today. Please not today.

I'm still rubbing my ears as we disembark and I feel distant and disorientated, as though I'm peering through the thick glass of a goldfish bowl.

'G'day,' says the customs official and winks at me as he stamps my passport. I'm too shocked to smile back. It's the drawl again, like the pilot's but stronger this time.

'Hi.' My English voice sounds suddenly pompous, but he's already stamping someone else's passport and probably doesn't hear.

When I step outside, the first thing I notice is the light. It's just been raining and the sky is still a heavy purple. There's the rumble of thunder in the distance. The colours are more intense here, like another, a fourth dimension has been added. The reds are the worst, reaching out with an intensity that's seductive and painful and heavy with emotion - a tone I can never capture in my painting. The edges of everything are sharp against the dark sky. The air is a shock: close and warm, steamy, like my local launderette. The smells are strong too: eucalyptus oil, car exhaust, sweat and something else, something exotic, a bruising smell, almost sexual. Jasmine I think. The eucalyptus reminds me of Max, or at least the woolwash he uses for his sweaters. I remember our last kiss, his prickly face and the softness of his lips. I'm trying to hold on to Max, but already he's slipping away.

I queue for a taxi. When my turn comes the driver jumps out and heaves my bag into the back for me.

'Where to love?'

I'm comforted by his familiarity. Perhaps things aren't so very different after all on the underside of the world. But I don't know where I'm going and my guidebook is buried deep inside my bag.

'I'm not sure,' I say. 'I need a hotel or something, cheap but central.'

'No worries,' he says.

It's late afternoon, but the streets are so much emptier than in London. The few pedestrians about are wearing hats and sunglasses and little else. I'm used to seeing people wrapped up against the weather and it's a shock to see so much flesh. When the sun comes out, the city is dazzling. The light is harsher again. Its clarity unforgiving.

We stop outside a backpackers in a street lined with big heavy trees that reach up as high as the two-storey terraces behind them. I pull out some of the strangely colourful plastic notes stuffed in my purse and hand them over.

'Where am I?'

'Kings Cross,' he says, handing me my change. I notice that his hands are covered in sunspots and his face weathered into deep crevices. He gives a little salute before driving back into the traffic. It seems strange that there's a Kings Cross here too. I wonder if it's anything like the one back home.

The backpackers looks run-down from the outside, but inside it's not too bad. Well, at least the hallway is ornate and original. I like the feel of the place and it doesn't smell of disinfectant. I ding the bell at reception and the girl who books me in has a big wide smile. Her hair is cut so close she's almost bald and I wish I had some charcoal or a soft lead, to try and capture the perfect shape of her head, the line of her neck and the curve of her shoulders.

'Come on,' she says. 'I'll show you around.'

She takes me into a huge kitchen which looks new. A few people are cooking in here and it smells good. The lounge has mismatching chairs, but it's comfortable and there's a computer, so I'll be able to email Max.

I follow her into a dormitory with six bunks.

'Take your pick,' she says and disappears back to her desk.

I look around. The walls are painted with flowers and spirals, which makes up for the threadbare carpet and the furniture which is way past its use-by date. Only two of the beds look lived in. I choose a bottom bunk on the other side and push my suitcase under it. The list of rules on the door make me feel like a school girl again: *No visitors. No smoking. No eating or drinking. Lights off after 10pm. Anyone breaking these rules will be asked to leave.*

It's getting dark. I should eat, and maybe explore, but a huge weariness creeps over me and all I want is to lie down, stretched out straight so my stomach can unfold after twenty-six hours of sitting in a very small space. In the seconds before I sink into sleep I realise how good it feels to be here. Nobody knows me. Not a single person. There's a sense of freedom in that. A letting go. In my head is an image of Nan, upstairs in Victoria cottage, sitting up on the window ledge the way she often did, looking out to the Black Mountains. I'm remembering how soft her face would become, how it was only then you saw her turmoil, the yearning in her to be gone. Nan was dismissive of nostalgia, what she saw as stupid sentimentality, the pining to return home. 'To nowhere,' said Nan, fed up with Millie's needs. But Nan was more like Millie than she ever wanted to admit. The yearning was in her too. Maybe somehow this cancer gave her a chance she finally couldn't turn down. A journey from which there was no coming back. Maybe this was her way of moving on. The long road to nowhere.

I wake suddenly from a deep sleep that's blissfully free of dreams.

'Max,' I murmur, reaching out to stroke the smooth skin of his back, but instead my hand hits a wall. My eyes jolt open, and for a moment I have no idea where I am. Outside there are familiar city noises, a busy whir of sirens and shouting. But inside is different. I can hear the sound of regular breathing, and a snore from somewhere across the room. As my eyes get used to the dark I can make out the bunks and it's only then that I remember I'm in Australia.

For the rest of the night I doze and wake, then doze again, my sleep punctuated with dreams. There's an old bag lady rummaging about in a rubbish bin. At first I think it's Millie, but when I reach out to embrace her, she looks right at me and her eyes are small and round. There's a powerful malice in them that makes me stumble backwards. Then it's me there, peering in the bin and frantically looking for something. Whatever it is I have to find it before she does. After a while I look up at myself. 'Enjoy your trip, dearie,' I say, and then she's there again, pulling one of my arms out of the garbage bin and offering it to me.

In the morning I'm groggy. The jet lag is unexpected. I feel like I'm walking on the moon. The air is heavy and thick and it's hard to plough through it. My brain isn't sharp either. Partly the steamy heat, partly the jet lag and partly this new place. I'm just wearing a T-shirt over my knickers and it feels strange being like this in such a public place. Millie would have had a fit at me showing strangers my underwear. Though no one here seems to notice. The other girls get dressed slowly, chatting in German, not worried by me.

The pressure in the shower is good and I let the hot water sting and pummel my back, washing out some of the grogginess. Afterwards it gets awkward. I finish towelling myself dry and then try to get dressed in the tiny cubicle. I drop my knickers on the wet floor and have to put them on damp. Then my jeans get stuck half way because I've got wet feet. I brush my teeth at the basin, looking in the mirror for wrinkles or loose skin. Nothing yet, but when I look close, I can see there are more white hairs amongst the black. It won't be that long before they tip the balance in their favour and then it will look too black when I dye it and everyone will think I'm mutton dressed as lamb.

Back in the dormitory I introduce myself to the German girls.

'Storm,' I say, and they repeat it, puzzled I guess, it's not a common name. They tell me their names are Ulrike and Antje and they're travelling together.

'We go to Byron Bay soon,' says Antje, smiling, 'but it is too much good fun here.'

My stomach is rumbling, so I ask them where there's a good place for breakfast? They go to the window and point. 'Over there,' says Ulrike. 'On the corner.'

'Danke,' I say, which is about the limit of my German.

The cafe is almost full. People are sitting about reading the paper or chatting to each other. They're wearing trendy clothes and sunglasses and they look comfortable and confident, like they've got every reason to be here. It reminds me of London in summer and if it was I'd feel comfortable too. But it's all the way on the other side of the world and I feel conspicuous and uncertain, as if there's a sign above my head saying 'foreign'. Yesterday I felt free and liberated in this new country, but this morning I feel muted and afraid of my difference.

When the waiter comes I mumble something, try to clear my throat, then point, hoping that will be enough.

'What?' he asks.

'A big breakfast,' I say, too loud now. 'With mushrooms and fried tomatoes... and a cafe latte, and a glass of water.'

When the food comes, I wish I had a paper to look at rather than the people at the next table. I pull out my travel guide instead. Now everyone will know I'm from somewhere else and I'll probably get mugged.

After breakfast I go for a walk. It's still early and the main street is only just coming to life again. There's rubbish everywhere and strip clubs too. They look sad in the daylight, without their flashing signs. Some people are still out from the night before, looking pale and out of place with their club clothes and blinking red eyes. There are a few prostitutes standing about, which seems pretty hopeful this early. Kings Cross here is not so different from our Kings Cross, after all. Maybe it's a little more lighthearted. But that could be the weather.

Over the next few days I wander around being a tourist, soaking up the atmosphere and taking lots of photographs, trying to capture details I can work with later on canvas. I go to galleries and museums, catch ferries around Sydney Harbour and look back at the jagged city skyline. I go to Manly and eat chips on an ocean beach that seems to curve forever, watching rows of surfers, waiting for the right swell.

On Saturday I go to the market on Oxford Street. Its busy and bright and I can easily imagine Kita working here. I buy some tortoiseshell sunglasses and a floppy sun hat with a huge brim that's printed with bright yellow sunflowers. I buy skimpy shorts too and a couple of cheap skirts and a pair of flip flops. 'Thongs' they call them here. Little by little I expose my flesh to the atmosphere. In London I would be embarrassed, but here I can be anyone I want to be. Maybe that's what Kita loved about it.

Sydney feels brazen. It's full of shocking contrasts. I walk down a beautiful, tree-lined avenue, then turn a corner and have to pick my way through needles and graffiti and dead ends. Looking up there's the shock of the Harbour shimmering before me, speckled with yachts. I climb a hill and come face to face with the dramatic city skyline, again. Right in the middle is a tower shaped just like a syringe. The map says it's called Centrepoint.

This is a beautiful city. Feminine and independent and bold, like the image I'm forming in my head of my mother. Kita loved it here and it has captured me too. I love that I was born here, emerging into the hot, humid air of this city. I love being free of the heavy winter layers I wore in London to keep the cold at bay. I love the feel of the air on my skin. And best of all, the numbness is ebbing away. I'm starting to feel alive again.

One day I spot an art supplies shop and without thinking walk through the door. I didn't bring anything with me, not even a sketchbook. I didn't think I'd need these things in Australia, but suddenly I want to draw.

It was Audrey who bought me my first sketchbook. She might have seen my drawings and thought I needed encouraging. More likely she saw the need in me. Audrey is good at reading people in that way. It was my ninth birthday and I still remember opening the parcel: a moleskin drawing book, the paper thick and smooth, and a khaki-coloured canvas bag rolled up like a scroll. When I unrolled it there were pencils and charcoals, each with their own place. Every birthday after that she gave me something else: pastels, then watercolours, a complete set of sable brushes, a wooden palette and knives, a beautiful walnut box filled with oils, an easel, canvases, books... Sometimes she took me to London so we could 'view the galleries', as she put it. We went to the Tate, the National Portrait Gallery and the National Gallery, wandering for hours, Audrey patient and smiling over the whispering awe these places inspired in me. Once we went to the Royal College of Art, and I was filled with an impatient yearning I couldn't explain, never guessing that one day I would be a student there. Nan tutted over the expense of all these gifts, but Audrey always insisted that her generosity was rewarded by the pleasure I took in them.

In the art shop I buy pencils and charcoals, a large sketchbook and a small one that fits in my handbag. Something is released then and I can't stop. I do loads of drawings and make exhaustive colour notes in the small sketchbook, referencing them for later. In no time at all I fill a sketchbook and have to go back and buy another. This time I buy pastels and start using colour, trying to capture the intensity of the light, reflections on the water, weathered skin... It's coming back. I can feel it. If I succeed in nothing else, this trip will be worth it for that.

During the day I walk and draw and take photographs until I'm exhausted. At night I cook in the hostel kitchen and chat to whoever else is there, pretending I'm on holiday, that I have no agenda except fun. But most of the people staying here are younger than me – nineteen or twenty, just out of school - and for the first time I feel old. Sometimes Antje and Ulrike persuade me to go out with them. One night we go to a nightclub and I get drunk enough to dance. I sway on the dance floor and a Spanish guy called Marco tries to get up close. He's sexy and I like the way he presses against me. I can feel my body responding, but it's Max I'm thinking of, the way he dances, seductively, like a cobra, his body weaving in time with the music. I turn away from Marco and go back to my dormitory, wishing all over again that Max was here and hoping he isn't dancing up close to someone, his body forgetting me.

I get a wave of guilt when I think about our awful good byes. Max insisted on driving me out to Heathrow when I could easily have caught the train. We were going to have a drink in the bar after I'd booked in, but it was coming up to peak hour and Max was worrying about delays and getting stuck on the M4. And I was all nerves and certain I'd left something behind. He went on and on about the traffic until eventually I lost my temper and shouted at him, right in the middle of the queue. We tried to make up but it didn't feel convincing. When we kissed good bye it was only an absent minded peck and when Max left he didn't look back.

I email Max and tell him about Sydney. *Wish you were here*, I write. *I want you so much*, I add. But I delete that line when I imagine his assistant, Fi, looking at his emails. I want to tell him that my whole body is missing him, that the strange farewell in the airport was just nerves, that I need him here with me. But in the end I don't say any of these things.

The next day I feel lonely. I buy postcards of the Sydney Harbour Bridge, of the Opera House and Bondi Beach and send them to all the friends I've neglected since Nan died. I'm trying to reach back in time and across space. Trying to reconnect. I send Alison a picture of a lifesaver and Audrey one of the city lit up at night. But I can't keep pretending that I'm on holiday. I can't just fritter away my money and my time sight-seeing and sitting about in cafes writing postcards. There's Max, and the exhibition coming up, and my own peace of mind. It's time to do some research.

All I've got is my mother's diary, my father's name, a twenty-six-year-old sympathy card from Leo Knight and the letter from Edith Burton in Queensland. I have to start somewhere, so I go to the post-office and look under 'H' for Harding in the telephone book, but there are hundreds of Hardings and I don't even know if my father ever lived in Sydney. I try another tack, spending the afternoon in the State Library and looking through electoral rolls. But I can't find anything and it seems futile bothering. I don't know where my father was born. He might not even be Australian. I switch to Leo Knight, look up his name in the phone book and find him on the fourth call. He sounds shocked but he makes a time to see me tomorrow.

When I unfold my map of Australia I'm surprised all over again at how few roads there are. In Britain there are roads everywhere, a big huge tangle of them. Nan loved maps. Another contradiction, I suppose. She did all her travel in her head. We'd pore over her giant out-of-date atlas that still called Iran, Persia, looking at all the place names. My favourite names were always the Welsh ones without any vowels and I'd make Nan laugh, trying to pronounce them. It was always good to make Nan laugh because she hardly ever did. I scan the map again; Dubbo, Gunnedah, Wagga Wagga... I don't know what to make of these names.

There's no way I'm going to catch buses, so I'll have to buy a car. My credit card will stretch to that and I'll get the money back when I sell it on. It's scary though. Now I've flown over Australia I know just how big it is. But in a car, that means something else. It means driving day after day, for God knows how long. As Max keeps pointing out to me, I'm not a very good driver and I'm an even worse navigator. Kita went west, to Adelaide, then north again, up the middle, then east to where the diary stops - Mt Isa. She went the long way around. The way I intend to go too. It's tempting to take a few shortcuts, cut across on the Mitchell Highway, but that's a broken line on the map, so it's probably a four-wheel-drive track and everyone says that's suicide, you can't go off track alone. Perhaps I should follow Millie's advice instead. She saw no need of maps. What goes around, comes around she used to say. Follow your nose.

CHAPTER NINE

Walking amongst the suits in the business end of the city, makes me feel horribly insignificant. I'm made little by their easy sense of purpose, and dwarfed too by the cluster of high-rise office blocks that have turned this street into a wind tunnel. Tall mirrored buildings reflect images of other tall mirrored buildings, making the hard-edged towers wobble and dance seductively in the gleaming glass.

I hunch over against the blasting wind. My skirt wraps itself tight around my legs, so I have to shuffle, then blows free and balloons up around me. Grit scours my sunglasses and finds its way into my eyes, making them scratchy and sore. I'm caught in a surreal scene of flapping ties, flyaway hair and billowing shirts, reflected for ever and ever in the mirrors on each side.

The building I'm looking for is just like the others. The lobby is modern - maybe even post-modern or whatever came after that. I check the address again, just to be sure, then tick off the floor number against the list on the wall. Level 23, which is a great deal higher than I'm happy with. The lift is so smooth and silent I can hardly tell it's moving. It also manages to get there very fast, which is a relief, because I don't feel too comfortable about getting stuck between floors or trying to work out at what precise moment I would need to jump as I plummeted twenty-three floors to the basement.

When I step out, the light is dazzling. It's all glass and open spaces and I'm completely gobsmacked by the view out across the Harbour and over the Bridge to the other side of Sydney and beyond. The windows stretch from floor to ceiling and bring the view in so close it feels like I'm falling into it. I have to shift my feet to balance against the dizziness.

I find my way through a glass door, to reception. The girl behind the desk looks up at me with a faint flicker of curiosity. She's perfect and all at once I'm uncomfortably aware that my nails need filing and my calves are all stubbly, there's a giveaway wet ring under each armpit and God only knows what my hair is doing after all that wind.

'I'm here to see Leo Knight,' I say, uncertain whether or not I have an official appointment.

She glances down at his diary.

'Storm Cizekova?'

'Yes.'

She smiles. A big set of healthy teeth, smooth and straight. 'Go right in.'

I follow her directions, through another glass door and into Leo Knight's office. Leo stands up from behind his desk and smiles. He's got a healthy brown tan. All over, I bet. He works out too. Of course he does. But no amount of gym or jogging can hide the excesses; the thickening around the edges, the little paunch, the puffy red nose. Leo's trousers are linen and not even crumpled, and he's wearing jewellery; a heavy gold ring and necklace. He's still got most of his hair, there's just a round bald patch right on top. Probably he looks good for his age. But it's hard to believe Kita was friends with this man. I have to remind myself that nearly twenty-six years have passed since then. A whole quarter of a century. People change. They become more themselves.

Leo stares at me for too long, and I start to wonder if he's in some sort of trance, before he shakes himself free of it. He comes across the room and holds out his hand.

'I'm sorry,' he says. 'I forgot my manners. You're so much like Kita... I must say it was a hell of a shock getting your phone call out of the blue like that. You sounded just like her. And now I see you look like her too. It's disconcerting, like stepping back in time.'

I smile and take his hand. It's soft and smooth, as if it's been powdered. Mine is sticky with sweat and all the scrubbing in the world won't shift the paint under my nails. We are worlds apart.

'I'm sorry if I've put you out,' I say.

'No, no, not all. It's wonderful to meet you. How are you enjoying Sydney?

'It's great.' I only just manage to stop myself from launching into a nervous commentary on the weather. We're being too polite, both of us circling the reason I'm here.

In the end it's Leo who takes the plunge. 'Here,' he says handing me a photo. 'It's the only one I have. Kita didn't like being photographed much.'

It's a picture of him with Kita and another woman. Without the pudge, Leo is handsome. The other woman is beautiful in a cold way, with a self-contained smile. Kita looks gorgeous. She's in the middle, her arms wrapped around the others and she's smiling a huge, open smile for whoever is taking this photograph. I've never seen her like this. Light-hearted. They're standing on the sand, the sea behind them. Kita's bikini top has slipped a little, almost revealing a nipple. She's dripping wet, her hair smoothed back from her face. She's thin, like me. You can see the outlines of her ribs and her hips standing out from her belly.

'That was before you were born,' says Leo.

I nod. In the picture I have of her she was still beautiful, but she'd already lost that light-heartedness. I take one last look and offer it back.

'No, no, keep it,' Leo says, waving it away effusively. 'I've made a copy.'

'Thanks,' I mumble, sliding it into my bag.

There's another silence that goes on for too long. I don't know how to start, even though he's given me an opening. Suddenly I feel silly, like a brassy private investigator, like I should be asking: 'And what were you doing on the night of...' I want to laugh, but for once manage to stifle the urge. He's more comfortable with silences than I am and seems happy to wait me out. But I detect a certain nervousness in him. I suppose it's not always easy having your past raked up.

'Nice office,' I say eventually.

He shrugs and glances around. 'Advertising's a lucrative business.'

'Oh,' I say and there's nowhere else to go from here. But he takes pity on me.

'Come on,' he says, 'it's a beautiful day. Let's get some lunch.'

He walks like he talks, in a purposeful contained way as if he's conserving energy. But in the sudden heat outside I'm pleased to see that his face goes red and he has to pat at the little rivers of sweat with a glowing white handkerchief.

Luckily the wind has died down because the place Leo chooses is outdoors, in Circular Quay. The restaurant is full of business people talking into phones and occasionally to each other. Beyond the tables there are buskers: a juggler; a living statue painted in gold and wearing a top hat; and a street artist, sketching on the pavement. Nearby, someone is playing a didgeridoo, the haunting music accompanying the bustling crowds, as people dart around each other, looking beyond where they are to where they want to be. Behind the crowds are the ferries, coming and going every few minutes; above us somewhere are the trains, and above them is the road, filled with buses and cars – the whole scene framed by the arch of the Harbour Bridge on the left and the curved shells of the Sydney Opera House on the right.

This must be Leo's regular because the waiter leads us to the best spot outside and without a word conjures up a bottle of cold Chardonnay, an ice bucket and frosted glasses.

When the tasting ritual is over Leo holds up his glass.

'To your quest,' he says. 'I hope you find what you're looking for.'

I take a sip, savouring the smooth pleasure of excellent wine. Max would approve. I'll have to be careful or I'll guzzle it and say all the wrong things.

Leo lights a cigarette. 'Excuse me,' he says. 'A bad habit, I know, but I can't kick it.' As he draws back the smoke he relaxes into the chair. A man addicted to the good things. 'So,' he says, 'your mother.'

I take the plunge. 'I want to know what she was like.'

'Ah.' He thinks for a moment, his face softening. 'She was like the sun, radiating energy, heat, passion... She was extraordinary and wild, in a way that no one else was. It made us uncomfortable, you know, threw it back in our faces that we were only pretending. We didn't know it then, but looking back... I mean look at us now. Every one of us, settled and straight.'

Yeah, I think, and she's dead. So who got the raw deal? But I don't interrupt.

'Look at me,' he's saying. 'I was an artist. A painter. I really believed in it. But you know how it is, you get to a certain age and reality rears its ugly head. So I moved into design and eventually a partner and I set up our own agency.' He shrugs his shoulders. 'Money matters. It's good. I've got a nice little beach house and the kids are nearly through school. But there's no time to put brush to canvas... ' He sighs and fills up our glasses. 'I'd give it all up now to be an artist again.'

I nod sympathetically, but inside I'm groaning. Spare me the bleeding heart and the romantic ideals. He's just a coward, giving in and then making excuses. When you really love something you have to do it, no matter what.

'Kita was different though. She had a passion for the now like no one I'd never known before. She was totally engaged with the present. People spend their whole lives aspiring to that.'

He's opening up, leaping from one idea to the next, like a child jumping between puddles.

'You could see it in the way she danced. She was amazing. Like a blazing fire. There was something about her, an aura, as if she was here for a reason... That's why it didn't make sense when ...'

But the waiter is hovering with his notebook and Leo breaks off to order, even though neither of us have looked at the menu yet.

'Oysters, first I think... A dozen should do for starters. Then the barrumundi, grilled?'

He's looking at me for confirmation. I assume barrumundi is fish, so I nod.

'And a green salad,' he adds, handing back the menu.'

When the waiter leaves Leo shifts about in his chair, excited. 'She used to make money fortune telling. It was wonderful to watch. She'd settle herself down with a client, taking her time, like a dog finding its place on a mat. Then she'd clasp the person's hand and stroke it gently, almost absent-mindedly, as if she was daydreaming. Suddenly she'd turn it palm up, holding it more fiercely. And look closely. 'You've got a very unusual hand,' she'd say. Or she'd stare into someone's eyes. 'You've got a lucky face ...'

He laughs. 'You should have heard her, the way she conjured up this solemn, mysterious sort of tone... I asked her about it once. How she knew what to say. And she tossed her head right back and laughed really hard. "It's all a load of crap. But don't tell anyone." God, she was an extraordinary actor.'

In Kita's diary there's a reference to this moment. The only time Leo is mentioned. Something about telling Leo she made it up, but how she didn't really, that things just came into her head and how creepy it was that she was usually right. And then they made love. I can't imagine anyone making love with Leo, and with him right here, looking at me too intensely, that diary entry feels like a weapon. For a second I think I'll mention it and let him squirm, embarrassed. But I can't possibly talk to this paunchy man about his sex life.

Kita must have learned fortune-telling from Millie. Maybe she sat at the table just like I did, with her hands cupping her chin, trying not to be noticed. And maybe she hung about near the door after Millie turfed her out, taking little peeps. It's strange to think that our childhoods were so alike, with Millie, Pop and Nan and Victoria Cottage, the focus of our world.

Women would come and knock softly on the door. Millie was a bit deaf by then and Nan was either at work or simply didn't notice. So I'd let them in and call Millie, but she always took her time. They'd sit awkwardly at the kitchen table, waiting. Titillated and afraid, giggling behind their hands if they came with a friend, or sitting wide-eyed if they were alone. Millie said it helped to make them wait. It made them more nervous, so by the time she got going, they believed everything.

Pop didn't approve. But he'd retired long before and there wasn't much money, only his pension and the tiny salary Nan earned as a library assistant. Nan told me he never said anything. He'd go out in the garden and prune bushes while Millie told fortunes. It was the closest he ever got to violence, snipping away at the rose bushes until there was hardly anything left.

Millie took no notice of Pop. She held the women's hands, staring hard at the lines, then in a strange distant voice she would intone, 'You were born with luck... but only in some things,' or, 'Beware, there is a friend who is not a friend,' or, 'News will come across the water.' I smile, remembering how the women, because it was only ever women, would greedily soak up every word. It seems Millie and Kita were alike. They both had the key to a different way of knowing and the courage to use it.

The waiter brings a plate of oysters. I've only ever had them once before, when Max and I splashed out for our first anniversary. I can't remember if I like them or not. Max told me you're supposed to swish them around in your mouth and swallow them whole, but that sounds pretty disgusting to me, like swallowing slime. So I chew. And they're so good I have to stop myself eating Leo's share too.

'She went weird for a while though,' says Leo. 'When she was pregnant with you she started thinking there was a monster growing inside her. She had nightmares. You know. She got really strange. At the time I thought maybe she'd had some sort of vision, but apparently it's pretty common for women to get like that.'

I finish my glass, not sure how to react. In the diary she's always counting my toes, but still, it isn't very pleasant being told your mother thought you were a monster.

'How was she after I was born?'

Leo looks uncomfortable. 'I don't know. We had a bit of a falling out. I lost touch with her a couple of months before you were born.'

I want to ask about their falling out but when I look up, Leo's watching me intently and there's something hungry in his eyes that makes me retreat.

'You know,' he says, 'sometimes I wonder if I was a little bit in love with her.'

I'm not comfortable with this line, so I help myself to one of his oysters and take the plunge.

'How did my mother die, Leo?'

The colour drains out of his face momentarily and his eyes shift across the room as if he's looking for an escape. His fingers tighten around the glass.

'You don't know?' His voice is almost a whisper.

I shake my head. 'Until a few weeks ago I thought she died having me. That's the official line. I want to know what really happened.'

He fills our glasses again, taking his time, allowing the drama to deepen or simply trying to put off telling me.

'She was murdered.'

Three words. As hard and sudden as a punch in the chest. I look at Leo, searching for more, trying to see if it's some sort of sick joke, but he won't meet my eyes. It isn't possible. People's mothers aren't murdered. We're not in a story. This is real life.

'Murdered? I whisper, struggling to find my voice again. 'How? When?'

'In the Outback. Right up north. She was strangled. You were wandering down the road in the middle of nowhere and someone stopped to pick you up. That's how they found her.'

Leo gestures to the waiter who brings another bottle and fills our glasses. All the time I'm fighting to control myself. I don't trust myself to speak and when I do it's almost a shout.

'Did they get him?' I'm assuming it was a man. The bastard who took my mother away from me.

'They got him all right.' Leo's face is hard.

'So who was it?'

'The guy she was travelling with. Bill somebody. I didn't know him that well.'

I let the horror of that sink in. The man Kita wrote about in her diary. The man who played horsy with me. 'B' is Bill and he's a murderer? It doesn't make sense.

'But... *why?*'

Leo shakes his head. 'He never said. He pleaded not guilty, you know. But there was never any doubt. His fingers left bruises on her neck, for Gods sake.'

The waiter comes with the fish, but I'm not hungry. I've already got too much to digest. My hand is hot and greasy on the glass. I pick up my fork and play around with the fish, but it smells too strong and I feel queasy. I fill my glass up again and watch Leo eat. None of this has taken his appetite away and there's an awkward silence while I drink and he eats. I'm trying to understand what's happening here, but I can't think. My mind's a panicky blank. I have to calm down. I keep drinking, while Leo polishes off his fish and then scoffs the salad.

I wait until the plates are gone and Leo has lit up a cigarette. Then I pounce.

'Do you know my father?'

Leo looks nervous and I can't make out why. Perhaps it's my imagination.

'Bill, I assume... Like I said, I hardly knew him.'

I watch Leo fiddling with the salt shaker. His face is red and shiny now, with the heat and the wine. He's sweating and his shirt doesn't look so fresh any more.

'My father's name was Michael,' I tell him. 'Michael Harding.'

Leo looks genuinely surprised. 'Really? Michael?'

He laughs nervously and I wonder if he'd always suspected I might be his child. If all these years he's been living in fear that I'd come and claim my rights.

'Well it was the seventies' he says, 'free love and all that.'

'How long were my mother and Bill together?'

'Two or three years I'd say. On and off. It was always touch and go with them. I guess Bill got a bit of a raw deal. Kita just wasn't the sort to get tied down. I used to think she was practically begging for a fight sometimes. You know, she pushed and pushed with him. With anyone she got close to. It was almost like a challenge, like she was saying, come on dump me, come on ...'

But I'm not really listening. My mother was murdered. The idea of it is settling inside. Another heavy ugly weight that I'll never shift.

Leo tops up my glass. He's watching me with a concerned look on his face. 'Listen,' he says, 'it's okay'.

'No it's not.' My voice is rising and I'm on the verge of making a complete fool of myself. But I don't care. The people at the next table probably think we're having a lovers' tiff. And I don't care about that either, though Leo's face is getting even redder. 'My mother was murdered! How can it be okay?'

I drain my glass, stand up and push back my chair so it falls over and everyone looks at me while I pick it up.

'Don't go yet,' says Leo, half standing, uncertain what to do.

I shake my head. 'Thanks,' I say. It's all I can manage, but it sounds lame and bitchy at once, like 'Thanks for nothing'.

'Ring me,' he calls as I walk away.

I don't respond. None of this is Leo's fault, but even so I want to get as far away from him as possible. I'm angry with him for telling me all this and then eating his lunch as if it didn't matter. I'm angry he said it was okay. And I'm angry at the way he looked at me. Like I was dessert.

On an impulse I catch a ferry to somewhere called Mosman. I drank most of that second bottle of wine and the bright sunlight on the water makes my head spin. I stand up at the back, staring at the frothing water in our wake and thinking about my dead mother. There are things I didn't ask Leo so maybe I'll have to ring him again after all. Not yet though. I look at the photo he gave me and the force of Kita's life hits me hard, all over again. How could anyone kill my mother?

In the diary I find Kita's entry about Leo. I have to concentrate hard because the words keep jumping about and my stomach is surging.

> *I remember when Leo asked me how I knew things. I laughed at him because he thinks he's in love with me. I said it was all a joke, that I didn't know anything really. Just made it up. But I do know things. Like I know that Leo is straight. That one day he'll put on a tie and be safe again and forget all about me. I realised it that night we made love. At Mrs Macquarie's Point, watching the yachts and drinking champagne straight out of the bottle. I cried because it felt so good and because I knew I was stealing this moment. Leo was besotted with me, but he would never be mine. Nothing I want will ever be mine. He yelped like a puppy when he came, and that made me laugh. We didn't do it again. Leo was too scared of losing his girlfriend or of what B would do to him if he found out.*

I shut the diary and stow it safely in my bag. I think Leo meant more to my mother than she wanted to admit. Kita might still be alive if she'd stayed with him, but then of course, I wouldn't exist. Nevertheless, I'm angry at Leo all over again for being a coward.

I get off at Taronga Zoo Wharf and follow the signs up the hill, but at the gate I can't decide whether to go in. I'm not sure how I feel about these places. The animals always look so sad. Once, on a documentary, I saw a caged Tasmanian devil. It was all ragged, with patches of bald skin, but the thing that really tore at me, was the way it paced, around and around, around and around until my head was spinning. It probably wouldn't even have noticed if someone opened the cage. Millie's groove was like that. I used to watch her pacing about, from the kitchen, through the long room, to the stairs and back again, wearing away at the wood and making a pattern. Nan used to say if Millie wasn't careful she'd go right through the floor, but she never did, the floor was so thick... Milada's groove. Max laughed when I told him. He said it sounded like a new type of dance. But I've always felt the severity of it.

Standing here, staring out over the Harbour, I realise that I desperately need to talk to Max. There's a phone box right across the road. I've only got a few coins though, so the call will have to be short.

He answers in three rings, his voice thick and slow. 'Hello?'

'Max it's me. Are you okay?'

'I'm fine, just sleepy that's all. It's 3 o'clock in the morning here, Storm.'

I'd forgotten about the time difference. 'Oh... sorry. But I've got to talk to you.'

The line's crackly and it's impossible to ignore the distance between us.

'No, no, that's okay. How are you going? Where are you?'

'I'm at the zoo.'

'The zoo? Oh right. You woke me up to tell me you're at the zoo?'

This is hopeless. I just have to blurt it out, there's no other way.

'My mother was murdered.'

There's a short silence. 'What did you say?'

Max suddenly sounds totally awake.

'Kita was murdered, Max. I just found out.'

I feel cold all over and my hand is aching from gripping the phone so tightly.

'Murdered! Jesus, what are you getting yourself into over there, Storm? I think you should come home.'

'I can't. You know that. I'm buying a car. I'll be leaving in a few days. It's not too late to come with me.'

In the silence that follows I can hear his frustration.

'Come home, Storm, please. There's no need to head off on some wild goose chase.'

'I have to, Max. I... Oh shit, I'm running out of coins.'

'Listen, where are you staying? I'll ring you there.'

So I give him the number and then the phone cuts out and I still haven't told him how much I need him. I thought ringing Max would bring him closer to me, but now he seems further away than ever.

I have never owned a car and have no idea what to look for. Someone tells me I should check out the Backpackers Car Market in the Cross. I wander around, looking for something self-contained, like a van. Something I can sleep in and cook in. I want to be secure, like a snail with everything on its back. In the end I choose a Kombi because I like the colour. It's burnt orange, with paisley orange and brown curtains. Very seventies. The New Zealander I buy it from is long and thin and tanned.

He pats the van. 'It's a good one,' he says. And I believe him.

I buy supplies: tea bags and a kettle, and long-life milk, food that won't go off, a saucepan and frying pan, a mug, a plate, cutlery, a pillow, some tapes, matches, a new gas bottle for the cooker. I'm surprised at how efficient I am because all the time the word is going round and round in my head. Murdered. Murdered. Murdered. And I can't seem to shift the heavy queasy feeling that's been sitting in the pit of my stomach ever since I met Leo.

I go back to the State Library and look through the 1978 newspapers. It doesn't take long to find an article, in a paper called *The Australian*. There's not much to it, but it clears up the sneaky suspicion I had that Leo was lying.

WOMAN FOUND MURDERED

A British woman, identified as Kita Cizekova, was found dead yesterday alongside the Barkly Highway in Northern Queensland. Miss Cizekova's two-year old daughter was found near the body. She was dehydrated and severely sunburnt, but otherwise unharmed. Police want to question Bill Harding, who was believed to be travelling with the murdered woman.

It makes it indisputably real. I'm there, dehydrated and severely burnt. That was me. It's a fact, but I still can't really believe it. And there's something else. The strands are coming together. Bill Harding and Michael William Harding are probably the same man. Bill is my father. My father is a murderer.

When I get back, Max has rung the backpackers and left a message for me to ring him. He's been looking at maps again and asking questions. Now he's really worried.

'It's huge out there,' he tells me. 'You can hardly drive.'

'The roads are straight.'

'What if you break down?'

'Come with me.'

' It's a desert,' he says. 'Take plenty of water… Be careful, Storm, don't do anything stupid.'

It's good to know he still cares. But I'm numb with shock and the M word and the other thing that's left me feeling dirty inside and out. How can I tell Max that my father is a murderer? He'll worry that it runs in the family. How do you clean out that kind of a taint?

'Don't worry Max, I'll be careful.' Then I hang up before I can tell him anything else.

I collect my bags and kiss Antje and Ulrike goodbye. We exchange addresses and promise to visit each other one day. There are cracks appearing in their friendship. Antje has met someone and wants to travel south with him. Ulrike still wants to go to Byron Bay, but not alone. Neither of them are going my way.

As I pack everything into the van, the numbness is joined by butterflies. And a bad feeling. Like the one my mother had when she set out all those years ago. I climb in the van and reread Kita's first diary entry.

26 July

When I left England, it was in such a rush. I didn't want to go back there. Not ever. I thought I was leaving the darkness behind. I thought it was possible to start fresh. That was stupid. Of course I brought it with me, people always do. Millie knew though. She gave me a blessing when I left. Held tight onto my shoulders and stared into my eyes. 'May your road be open,' she said with such force that I suspect she was trying to conjure up the luck, clearing the road ahead for me. It made me stop and look at everything again for one last time. Millie was troubled about something. I wonder what she saw. But Mum looking away like that. What is it with that woman? Why doesn't she see? All I wanted was a hug. When I thought about that today I gave Storm a huge hug. I'm not going to be like mum.

Now I'm setting off again. This time there's no one to bless me and that sends a chill all the way down my spine.

I kiss Kita's amulet which has hung around my neck since I found it in Nan's drawer. And in the absence of anyone else to do it, I bless myself.

'Lucky road,' I whisper and start the engine.

CHAPTER TEN

28 July

We're still in New South Wales. It's not what I expected out here, more golden than red. Yellow wheat fields and big blue skies. This makes me think of American prairies, not arid deserts. The air smells sweet and sort of cloying. But still it's wild and it's worlds away from the gentle fields back home, with their buttercups and clover and overripe apples. Sometimes I wish I could just pop back for a few days. I'd like to walk the hills and the fields with Storm and show her the things I loved.

29 July

We're sitting in the car puffing on joints with the music up loud and it feels as if we're watching a great big TV screen. There's 'in here' and then there's 'out there'. Today everything's changed out there. We're on the Hay Plains and nothing's cultivated anymore. There are hardly any trees either, so I guess it's a desert now, but it's not sandy, just barren foreverness with little bushes. Some of them don't seem to have roots. They're round and roll along the ground with the wind behind them. At first we go through dead towns with crumbled houses, then bigger towns with wide open streets and I wonder about the people with closed faces who live in them.

1 August

B wanted to see the ocean. He said we won't see any other water for months. So we decided to drive into Adelaide. It's strange seeing a city again. So many people in one place. The streets are narrower than the towns we've just been through, and it's flat, with wide low houses, as if someone has taken to the suburbs with a rolling pin. We stopped and asked a woman about the beach. Another closed face, but she pointed. 'That way,' she said. 'Glenelg.' 'Hey,' I said winding up the window against her sniffy hostility, 'it spells backwards.' So we went there and I took Storm on the merry-go-round and it reminded me of Christmas time in Hereford, and the creaky old rides. Then we made a sand castle and played chasey with the waves. But Storm fell over and got wet and the sand stuck to her and the wind was biting cold and she wouldn't stop crying. So B put her on his shoulders and we walked out onto the jetty, me trying not to look down because I could see the surging water through the planks under my feet. And B leaning over the edge with Storm, and them both laughing, but I wanted to scream at them to stop. It's Storm that's done this to me. If it wasn't for her I'd be dancing on that bloody jetty. Being a mum is like serving a bloody prison sentence. Everything is different. It's as if I've lost me.

3 August

Storm has a fever. She's listless and floppy and her hair is matted wet against her head. I'm furious with B for taking her on the jetty in the cold wind and her wet clothes, and furious with myself for letting him. All night she tossed and turned and sometimes sat up calling for me, looking right through me. 'Mummy,' she screamed, 'Mama.' 'I'm here,' I said. 'It's all right sweetheart, I'm here.' But she kept calling anyway and all I could do was try to hug her rigid little body against me and wonder about finding a doctor in this place. I keep wiping her face with a damp cloth, I try to make her take little sips of water, but she fights me off and I'm so afraid of losing her.

4 August

Storm's fever is better this morning but now she's sneezing and coughing and sending out gobs of stretchy yellow snot and B keeps shouting at her to cover her face. I told him she's too young for that, but he just said, she'd better bloody learn before he whacks her one. It's because he hasn't had any sleep.

9 August

We're stocking up in Port Augusta. B's got a few days' work helping out in the caravan park, so we're sticking around. It's feels like a frontier town. Right on the edge of something. 'Nowhere,' the park manager said. 'On the edge of bloody nowhere.' B shuffled about nervously when the guy told us that, because you can go north or west or east or even south from here and mostly it's thousands of miles till you get anywhere. He's worried about the car and the heat and bitey things and other people, but I like the idea of how little we'll be when we get out there.

It's strange seeing Aboriginal people. I never saw any in Sydney. The black is so black, sort of matt, not shiny, except that sometimes the little ones are different. Big brown eyes and blonde hair. Gorgeous.

11 August

It went down past zero during the night and we had to put all our spare clothes on just to keep warm. We lay there wrapped up like mummies and Storm thought that was a huge adventure, until she wanted to suck her fingers and couldn't reach her mouth. I didn't expect this sort of cold out here. Sometimes there's even ice, not much because it's still pretty dry. But it reminds me of home. B's never seen snow or ice, so I told him and Storm about our little cottage on the hills. How Jack Frost came each night and froze everything and how in the morning we'd have to scrape ice off the windows and pour water on the pipes and hope they didn't burst. I told them how sometimes in the morning the hills were crusty with snow and I'd go out in it, sinking up to my knees, and make snowmen and snowballs and angels, until my fingers turned blue and then I'd come back inside and warm up by the fire, savouring the delicious pain of thawing out - and I never got chillblains, even though Mum always said I would. And other times outside was like icy jewels, everything dipped in crystals, shimmering and smooth and priceless. On those days the hills were slippery and treacherous and desperately beautiful and I'd come home bashed and bruised from slipping and sliding all over the place.

While I talked Storm watched me with big wide eyes, and B was quiet. I can tell he wants me to take us there. Maybe I should. Maybe we can make it together. The three of us. He's not such a bad father for Storm. I should be grateful. But hell no, what am I thinking? I can't go back there. Not ever.

12 August

There's a rhythm to the road, not like music really, rather an inevitability, if there's a rhythm in that. It's like giving up purpose and letting something else draw you along. I feel as if I was born to this. And Storm's so good. She sleeps a bit and then looks out the window and we sing Bob Dylan songs and nursery rhymes and take turns telling stories and when we stop the car she totters around and around, burning off all that energy, and when I watch her I'm bursting with something. Maybe that's what being a mother is all about.

13 August

For the first time in ages I feel right.

A drop of sweat lands on the page and sits holding itself in a little self-contained ball for a moment, trembling with tension until it can't hold on anymore and breaks free. I watch it spreading, letting it dissolve the ink and blur the date on this page. There's another on its way, trickling all the way down my right cheek and hovering for a moment on my jaw before falling onto the diary. It's impossibly hot in this van.

For the first time in ages I feel right. I read this line again, trying to feel what Kita meant. But I can't. I can't reach back in time like that and understand someone I don't know. Why couldn't she go back home? I don't understand this and she never explains, not once. It's still strange to think that the woman who wrote these words is my mother. That she was a human being, not just an absence in my life. That I was once hers. That she loved me and she blamed me, and that the snotty little helpless Storm I'm reading about was really me. I slam shut the diary. What's the point of all this? Why am I sitting in this van on the other side of the world looking for someone who has been dead for twenty-six years? I'm filled with a useless fury at how big a waste it is, not knowing her.

For three days I've been driving away from myself and from the M word, as if speed could keep things at bay, already clocking over two thousand kilometres. I've been following my mother's footsteps, but faster, driving long days, sometimes eight or ten hours at a time, trying to see through her eyes, trying to equate her physical journey with the emotional spaces she occupied in her diary. Maybe even trying to catch up with her, as if I can reach back into history and change what happened. The whole time I thought I was facing things, but I'm not. I'm running, even faster now, like one of those cartoon characters, revving up and up, then whooshing off and disappearing in a cloud of dust, trying to outrun the dirty, horrible knowledge that I can't swallow or spit out. Mothers aren't supposed to be murdered. Fathers aren't supposed to be murderers. Where does that leave me?

I'm stiff all over, my right arm is lobster red, there are black spots dancing about in front of my eyes and shooting pains in my legs. I should slow down. I've driven through wheat fields and arid plains, through broken-down towns and prosperous towns with wide streets. I've stopped in Adelaide, looked at the ocean and walked on Glenelg jetty, in thirty-eight degree heat, trying to imagine the wind and the cold and my mother's fear. And I've been to Port Augusta and slept in the caravan park Kita slept in, on *the edge of bloody nowhere*.

I haven't taken any photographs or made a single sketch. All the time I've been seeing the landscape through my mother's words on the page, not through my own eyes. I feel detached from this country, as if I'm not inhabiting myself. Maybe I'm afraid of what I'll find if I look inside.

This morning I turned right onto the Stuart Highway and came face to face with the full force of my fear. Every bit of me wanted to run away from this world out here that's too simple and hard, and way too big. The bright white light, the big sky, the heat, and the sharp line of the horizon, slicing the world in two. I feel like I've walked up to one of my paintings and stepped in. But that only happens in Mary Poppins and then it's supposed to be fun. This morning I entered the world of my nightmares.

I sat for a long time by the side of the road, gathering my courage. This was a major highway. Maybe the equivalent of the M1, but there were no cars at all for ten minutes. Then one passed, heading the other way, back to Port Augusta. I watched in the rear-vision mirror as the car slowed, turned and pulled up alongside me. A man with a weathered craggy face peered out.

'You okay love? Need any help?'

'I'm fine... Just having a rest,' I said trying to raise a smile for him... 'I'll be heading on soon. Thanks.'

He nodded. 'Yeah,' he said. 'You wouldn't want to break down out here. You'd fry.'

After he left I sat for a few minutes more, remembering something I once saw on television, an Aussie man, frying eggs on a car bonnet. When I turned the key in the ignition there was a moment of tension while I waited for the engine to start.

'You can do this.'

I had to say it out loud, letting the words break through the quiet sound of the engine turning over, the pounding of my chest and my tight breaths. I planted my foot on the accelerator, spinning the wheels on the dirt, then steered back onto the road, pointing north, fear tunnelling my vision so that all I could see was the road ahead, not the sky, or the earth, not the horizon, Just a long stretch of road, shimmering in the heat as though I was driving into an illusion.

That was only a few hours ago, but it seems like days. I pull the map out of the glove box again. Already the creases are tearing because I've looked at it so often, folding it back the wrong way every time. Map folding is a puzzle I haven't managed to solve yet. I've already drawn my mother's journey in red ink. Alongside it I'm drawing my own, in black ink. But so far, my line from Sydney to this tiny speck called Woomera, covers just one corner.

There are lots of fences in Woomera and not many trees. Even the caravan park has a big fence all the way around it. Inside is a toilet block, a few old caravans and a load of empty sites. On the other side of the fence is the vast empty expanse of desert. Neither side appeals to me.

Twenty-six years ago there wasn't a detention centre for refugees in Woomera, or even the strangely surreal public display of life-size weapons and aircraft in the centre of town. My guide book says that back then Woomera was all top-secret military stuff and rocket launching. It's still top-secret though and the camp has a tall barbed wire fence. Detention centres, they called them, not prisons. I'm shocked at the way politicians take the meaning out of things, stripping people of their value. Reducing them to an unwanted delivery. *A boat load of human cargo*, they say, *arrived for processing*. This is appalling. I remember Nan telling me about the boat loads of Jews in World War Two, turned away from one country after another, until finally they had to return - for processing.

All dead.

And the Rom. Dead too.

I wonder what Millie felt when she arrived in Great Britain in 1940. Relief, probably, because she was finally safe. And fear too, of this strange new country. But what else? Regret for all the things she'd left behind, no doubt. Did she really love her daughter in that unconditional way mothers are supposed to? Or was there a whole lot of resentment there too? Irene was the anchor pinning Millie to the future but she was also the knife that severed her from her past.

For Millie, arriving in Great Britain meant the end of four centuries of oppression. It was just over four hundred years since the first anti-gypsy laws were passed in Bohemia; two hundred and something years since Joseph the First in Prague ordered that all Roma men should be hung without trial, and women and boys mutilated; eleven years since a law in Bohemia had been passed, allowing Romany children under fourteen to be forcibly taken from their families; six years since Hitler ordered the sterilisation of all gypsies; and only three years since gypsies had their voting rights taken away. The gypsy school had been closed down and Pop was left without a job.

Millie and Pop and Irene left just in time. Soon the German army would march into Czechoslovakia. Already they were starting to round up the gypsies. In four more years, four thousand Roma and Sinti would be gassed in one night, and well over a million would be dead by the end of the war. Even so, Millie still wanted to stay in Bohemia. She told me that only days before she died. 'I never wanted to come here,' she said in her raspy voice. 'I never wanted to leave my people. Always I was hoping for a pardon.'

'This is our home,' she'd argued at the time, and for the first and the last time in their marriage, Pop lost his temper with her.

'If we stay, you will die,' he shouted. 'And Irene too.' It was this that made him angry. Millie could choose her own fate, but

Irene was only three and it was their responsibility to do what was best for her.

Knowing that Millie and Irene would not survive the war in Czechoslovakia, Pop contacted an old acquaintance in England who agreed to support their application for a visa. Then he sold nearly everything they owned, packed up what was valuable or sentimental into trunks and borrowed money from his parents to buy false papers for Millie. And all the while Millie sat and watched, feeling a sick helplessness deep inside of her. When Pop finished the preparations they turned their backs on everything they knew and began the slow perilous journey to England and a new life.

I remember seeing a report about the Woomera detention centre on the BBC. It closed last year, after protests inside and out. After escapes and suicide attempts and hunger strikes and sewn-up eyes and lips. After all this they moved the refugees on, sending them back to their countries to die, or into other prisons that strip them of what's left of their hope and self-respect. Then they shut this place down and I suppose that's a triumph of sorts for the protesters. It's quiet here now. There are no prisoners standing at the fences staring out into the desert. There are no television cameras either, or protestors. But still the fences are here and the dust. I'm not staying in Woomera.

It's too hot to leave the van shut up any longer, so I open the window, but it's no better out there. Within seconds the van fills with flies. I know you're supposed to ignore them, but I can't. I can't stand them buzzing about me, crawling all over my skin, into the corners of my eyes, my mouth, my nose, trying to suck out the last bits of moisture. I reach for my keys. I'll have to keep driving with the windows open and the hot air sucking the flies back out where they belong.

My fourth day on the road and already the sounds of the engine turning over and the click of my seat belt, are two of my favourite things. It's part of why I can't slow down. Moving helps balance out the fear, forcing it somewhere into the back of me, where it nags and niggles but doesn't overwhelm. Finally I'm beginning to feel the rhythm of the journey. Maybe that's what Kita was talking about when she said she felt right.

I drive on into late afternoon. The sun is big and low to my left and the shadow of the van is huge, rippling across the dusty scrub. The road is heavily fenced on both sides and the fences are punctuated with signs: KEEP OUT: PROHIBITED AREA. My guidebook says that in the sixties the British did nuclear testing just west of here. And it still feels like a poisoned place. When the wind starts up it feels worse. Mini tornadoes stir up dark eddies of dust and push them on a twisting journey across the landscape. My foot's flat to the floor but even so, the van is going slower, struggling against this hostile head wind, and guzzling fuel. I can practically hear the poor thing panting.

The shadows are stretching right across the road, so I'm driving through a dappled world of light and dark. Soon the sun will dip and there'll be kangaroos bouncing about, so it's a relief when I see a rest stop ahead. It's a pretty desolate place to stop - gravel and dust and no trees. But it's just me and one other car at the far end; a battered old station wagon, blue and white and spattered all over with red dust. It looks abandoned. I hope it's abandoned. Up to now I've stayed in the relative safety of caravan parks. This is the first time I've risked a rest stop and I don't fancy spending the night out here with anyone else.

I stare at the car for a while, but there's no movement, so I settle in: popping the top, clipping it up and unzipping the canvas windows to let in some air. Then I switch on the gas and put the water on to boil for a cup of tea even though it's about fifty degrees out here.

I'm getting better at setting up. The first day or two were fumbly-feely days when I didn't know how anything worked and despaired of it all, but now I have a routine and it's easy, easier than at home, wherever that might be. I seem to be collecting homes. Victoria Cottage is mine now. Then there's my tiny, cluttered studio in London, and my side of the bed at Max's. And now this little orange van that I'm getting attached to despite the thin foam mattress that leaves my bones aching. Each place has a little bit of me, so it's like someone has got a knife and spread me about. If I had to choose between them I don't know what I'd do. Maybe being in just one place all your life has something going for it. Being absolutely and entirely there. Nan never moved again after her terrible journey through Europe, her three-year-old eyes seeing everything through the sharp lens of her parents' fear. She was afraid to move after that, I guess, her spirit locked deep inside her. Or perhaps the locking came later, after she had Kita and threw away her life. Millie stayed put too, but her spirit was never there, she'd left it back in Bohemia.

The kettle whistles, a homely urgent sound in the middle of a desert. I dig out some biscuits and drink my tea sitting on the van's step, sheltered from the worst of the wind and watching the dust swirling about me. I don't know if they have cyclones this far south, but the wind is definitely getting stronger, each big gust, lifting and shaking the van. I wonder what it would take to tip it right over. Bang! And then where would I be? Stuck in the middle of nowhere.

A man crawls out from the back of the station wagon and immediately my shoulders tense. This is just the sort of thing Max warned me about. I check the mobile, which Max made me buy, 'In case you break down,' he said, but the bloody thing's useless anyway. It's out of range. It's been out of range practically the whole time since I left Sydney. And it doesn't do international calls either, which makes it pointless as well as useless. Who else would I ring besides Max?

He glances over at me briefly and waves. Then he opens the bonnet, peers in and fiddles with something, but even from here I can tell he's half-hearted about it. I keep watching, trying to read him from a distance. He's young. I can tell from the way he moves. He's tall and thin, a bit gawky looking, but strong too. Nan would have said lean, not thin. And he doesn't seem the least bit interested in me. All at once I know he's safe. He's also stuck. I wonder how long he's been here. There's no way I can help, but I decide to trust my instincts. Ignoring all Max's dire predictions, I struggle over, the wind whipping my hair into knots and sending stinging grit into the corners of my eyes. He's wearing long baggy shorts and a very old T-shirt, with something about uranium mining written on the back. Up close he's all sinewy and even younger than I expected, probably not more than early twenties. But he's sun beaten too, the way Australians get, with messy bleached hair and dark tanned skin.

'Hi.'

He straightens up too quickly, bumping his head on the bonnet. 'Hi there.' He rubs his head, and when he smiles his eyes crinkle up. Two big crow's feet.

'Sorry, I didn't mean to startle you.'

'No worries.'

'Where are you heading?'

'Nowhere fast, I reckon.' He laughs again and gestures at the car. 'I bought myself a dud. Know anything about cars?'

'Not much. I guess I've been lucky so far... touch wood,' I add.

'Yeah well, I've fiddled with just about everything that moves under this bonnet, but I can't get a spark of life out of it. I'm gonna have to give up on it. The bloody thing's probably not worth fixing.'

I like the look of him. The way he's smiling, even though everything has gone wrong and he's stuck in the middle of nowhere.

'I'm Storm.'

'David,' he says and the smile gets even deeper, making his eyes crinkle up even more.

I've got the beginnings of an idea, but I can't tell whether or not it's a good one. I stare at him for too long, weighing up the pros and cons, wishing I was more decisive about things, like Max.

'I'll give you a lift,' I say eventually. But as soon as the words come out I wish they hadn't. He could be a serial rapist for all I know. I know he's not but he might be. And what would Max think about me travelling with another man? This thought is immediately followed by another. Who cares? Max isn't here and he should be, so stuff him.

'Yeah?' He's looking at me searchingly. Without the smile I can see that his eyes are a hot afternoon blue.

'I could drop you off in the next town if you want to get this fixed,' I say, pointing to his car.

He laughs. 'Nah, I'll have to leave it. I reckon it's beyond help, and anyway I haven't got the money.'

I nod. 'Where are you heading?'

'Darwin.'

I think it through. I'm turning off before Darwin, up past Tennant Creek. I could take him most of the way, but I'm not willing to commit yet.

'I can take you some of the way,' I tell him.

'Great,' he says, his face opening into a smile again. 'I'll help with the petrol.'

He wipes his greasy black fingers all over his T-shirt, before reaching out and shaking my hand.

CHAPTER ELEVEN

For one long confusing moment I don't know where I am. And I'm caught in the foggy remnants of a nightmare; my face up close to the cracked hard earth and giant bull ants crawling up my legs. I can't move. I'm calling out, but my throat is too dry and no sound comes. Then finally I come back to myself, recognising the familiar texture of my sleeping bag and the swirling paisley of the curtains. I pull one aside and look out. The wind has stopped and the sky is clear. David is up already. I watch him packing his stuff. The way he concentrates on what he's doing as if that's all there is.

I sit up too quickly and am overwhelmed by nausea. Lying down again only makes it worse. Seconds later I'm leaping out of bed, into the front and sticking my head out of the window, just in time. There's not much there. Even less now. Just the bitter burning taste of bile and a growing ball of anxiety, because it happened last night too. That was the first time. I didn't even get to eat anything, just a whiff of the instant risotto was enough to set me off.

I've been feeling sick ever since I met Leo for lunch. At first I thought it was fear, something to do with the awful things Leo told me, but then I decided it was more likely some sort of bug, maybe giardia. I've been blaming the oysters and trying to ignore the glaring fact that my period is late, not that they've ever been regular anyway, so two weeks, give or take a bit, is normally fine. But this time I'm not so sure. I wipe my face and put the kettle on, pushing the worry aside, willing it to be a false alarm. It's impossible. I can't be pregnant. It's too complicated.

Hot black tea helps. But when David comes over I'm still in a crumpled T-shirt, with messed up hair and a bad taste in my mouth. God, I hope he doesn't tread in my puddle of bile. I quickly slip on some shorts and watch him approach, liking the way he moves, sort of gliding across the ground, conserving energy. He's wearing a fresh T-shirt with *Stop Old Growth Logging* printed in bold letters on the front.

'Morning.' He smiles, but around the edges he's uncertain. So am I.

He's not carrying much, just a rucksack with a sleeping bag strapped on top.

'Have you got a tent?' I ask.

'Nah,' he says. 'Didn't need one in the wagon.'

'What about a mat or something?'

He shakes his head.

'Well you're not sleeping in the van. Okay.'

His face screws up again into those crow's feet, but he manages not to blush. I'm blushing like an idiot. Damn it.

'Guess I'll kip on the ground then.'

'What about your mattress. Why don't you bring that?'

I know it'll take up a heap of room, but he can't just sleep in the dirt.

'Yeah,' he says. 'Good idea.'

It's only a foam thing, so isn't too heavy. We lay it on top of my mattress and somehow that seems symbolic. Like I'm giving up something. I don't know what. Anyway I feel irritated, probably because I haven't eaten anything since lunch time yesterday.

He climbs in, puts his feet up on the dashboard and leans back like he's right at home. It gets to me and I have to try really hard to bury my bad temper.

'Haven't been in a whiz-banger for a while,' he says.

'A what?' I snap. I can't help it.

'That's what they call these things. You know, the sliding door... whiiizzzz, bang!... We used to have one when I was a kid.'

'Oh,' I say switching on the radio.

David gets the hint and shuts up. He goes straight to sleep which is a relief because I don't know what to say to him. At least he trusts my driving. Unlike Max. I try to imagine what it would be like if Max was with me. David wouldn't be here for starters, because Max would never pick up a stranger. He wouldn't have his feet up on the dashboard either. And there's no way he'd wear shorts, not even long baggy ones. He'd be wearing trousers and long sleeves to keep the sun off. His skin would be dazzling white in the bright sun, not like David's. I smile. If I was driving, Max's eyes would be glued open. But if he was here, I wouldn't be the one doing the driving.

The road is unnaturally straight and on either side is flat monotony, broken only by termite mounds and a few low bushes. My stomach is still churning and I can't swallow away the watery metallic taste in my mouth. What if I really am pregnant? The very thought sends me into a panic. I wonder how Millie felt when she realised she was. She must have known there would be no forgiveness. At best she would swap her huge family for a half-half baby and a gadje husband. At worst she would lose everything. No one would want polluted goods. She wouldn't have expected Pop to stand by her. Why would he? The gadje hated the Roma. I wonder if she was afraid of being alone with a baby to bring up. Or if she thought about ways of getting rid of it. Maybe she even tried. Boiling up some bitter concoction that was supposed to kill the thing in her. Maybe that's where Nan got all her bitterness from.

I've never been to Bohemia. But I imagine there are forests and tall mountains peaked in white all year. The forests would be thick and in summer they would be a deep leafy green, letting only thin twists of sunlight filter through. Not like here, where the sparse gum trees make a light mottled shade that scarcely works.

When I think about Millie in Bohemia it doesn't seem idyllic anymore. There's still Millie running barefoot behind their wagon, Millie suckling the warm milk from their mare, Millie sitting by a camp fire surrounded by her huge extended family… the wonderful sense of freedom she felt. But now I've grown up and the world doesn't seem such a kind place, now I can't forget that mostly it must have been difficult. With the cold and the hunger and all the laws; some telling gypsies not to move, others telling them not to stop. And there was worse. Much worse. Hitler's holocaust, the *porajmos*, the devouring. More than a million Romany murdered. After Hitler, when the world should have learned some lessons, Romany children were taken from their families in Czechoslovakia. Then in the 1950s nomadism was banned; police killed the Roma's horses and took the wheels from their wagons and put the Romany people in prison. And in the seventies when Kita was travelling through Australia with me, a sterilisation programme for Roma was beginning in Czechoslovakia.

Millie knew none of these things. But they wouldn't have surprised her. She was Romany, her blood steeped in centuries of oppression.

'Huh,' she would have said, tossing her head proudly. 'We laugh in the face of bad things.' But I bet she didn't laugh when she got pregnant to a Gadje and was faced with the prospect of losing her people forever. I wonder how Nan felt, too, pregnant so young and having to give up school and all the dreams that went with it. How did Kita feel, on the other side of the world, with me in her belly? And how will I feel, if this isn't a false alarm?

I glance over at David, who's fast asleep. There's a fly crawling over his face and I reach out and brush it off. He seems so relaxed, so accepting of where he is, as if there's nothing in life to worry him. Unlike me.

Having no family feels like being in freefall. I have no connections, nothing to ground me, no anchors, no sails, nothing. I'm dizzy with the freedom of it and the fear. My foot is right down to the floor, pushing the van as fast as it will go. I can feel it shuddering with the strain. We're ploughing through space in a little metal box. Moving through this country, but not touching it. Not really. I can feel the heat and the stickiness and the burning hot wind on my skin. I can smell the dust and see the harsh light. I'm here, but not part of this hostile alien world.

When David wakes he stares ahead, mesmerised by the road, lost in his own thoughts.

'Do you feel part of all this?' I ask, waving my hand about to show I mean 'out there'. 'Australia. Does it feel like you know it? That it's yours?' I give up. Not sure what it is I want to know.

David doesn't answer for a minute. 'Yeah,' he says finally. 'Sort of... It's complicated... I'm not Indigenous and that makes it harder because this land is theirs. But I kind of feel like I belong. Our family's been here five generations now so the place has got in my blood and that kind of makes it mine too, I reckon.'

I think about my family. Four generations of us living in our little cottage on top of the Malverns. And before that Bohemia. How long can you keep looking back? How long before it's okay to be where you are?

'It's a speed thing,' David says, reaching into his bag and pulling out a water bottle. 'Australia's a bloody old country and slow. Us whites are too impatient. We spend all our time trying to squeeze more life out of the land, instead of learning from it. That way we'll never belong.'

He takes big swigs from his water bottle. 'We're killing this place faster than you'd believe,' he says offering me the bottle.

I shake my head.

A speed thing. It's not really what I meant. But maybe David's right and I just need to slow down. I ease my foot off the accelerator, suddenly tired.

'Maybe I need to walk on this land,' I say.

David laughs and his laugh is wide and open just like this country. 'You'd last a micro second,' he says.

'I bet you wouldn't do much better.'

'Point taken,' says David.

Up ahead in the distance is the telltale cloud that signals a road train. My fingers automatically tighten on the steering wheel. It's the first vehicle we've seen for an hour or so and I was getting used to having the road to myself.

'Bloody road trains,' says David. 'They drive through the night and plough into everything that gets in their way. Then the wedge-tails come for the carcasses and they get ploughed through too. So they're dying out and the ones that are left are forgetting how to hunt.'

I don't like the road trains either. They're big and brash, with awful names like *Big Shifter* and *Pussy Foot* and, more often than not, naked dolls strapped to the front. The road isn't wide enough for us both so I slow down and pull over to let it by. But even going slow I can feel the tug into its slipstream and its hypnotic roar.

My arms are getting stiff and my left knee's locked. I'm too hot and getting really hungry.

'I need to stop soon,' I say, pulling back onto the strip of bitumen that passes for a highway.

I hand David my map. He must notice the lines I've drawn but he doesn't ask.

'We're nearly in Coober Pedy,' he says. 'Probably only another thirty k's or so.'

The landscape is changing. It's a bit like I imagine the moon would be, silvery grey and pitted with lumps and holes. In this middle of the day heat, there's a strange low-down rippling effect across the horizon. At first I think there's a river running across the road, but it never gets any closer and I soon realise it's a mirage. I wonder if it would be possible to capture this in a painting. Watery illusions and shimmery heat. This kind of fluidity in such a harsh dry landscape. The contradictions intrigue me.

After a while I notice signs along the sides of the road, telling people not to step backwards or run.

'It's the opal mines,' explains David, 'People stop and take pictures of each other. They step back to get everything in frame and disappear down one of the holes. Happens all the time.'

I make a mental note to avoid all roadside toilet stops until we're well clear of Coober Pedy.

Suddenly David starts laughing. 'Hey, get this ... You know what Coober Pedy means? I shake my head. 'White man in hole... Now that's good, that's really good.'

The town is full of broken cars and piles of dirt. The only things on the road are trucks and utes and they've nearly all got EXPLOSIVES written in big letters on them. We drive past the golf course. Aside from little pieces of astro turf for teeing off there's not a scrap of grass to be seen.

'It's a bit of a frontier town.'

'Yeah,' says David, 'it looks like a post-nuclear hell hole.'

We park in the main street and order steak sandwiches in a greasy cafe with plastic tables and pinball machines. There's a purple light hanging in the corner which buzzes every time it zaps a fly. The steak sandwiches are the best I've ever had: beetroot and pineapple and egg, bacon, steak, sauce, onions, lettuce, tomatoes, cheese, soggy white bread… The whole thing is bigger than my mouth and drips all over my hands and down my front. I don't have any tissues so I have to lick my fingers. The dust mingles with the juice and my face smells of meat and onions.

'How about we meet in an hour?' I suggest.

'Sure,' he says. 'I'll see you in the pub.'

I go to the chemist and scan the shelves for pregnancy tests, hoping no one will ask if I need any help. At the counter I can't look the man in the eye.

'Is that all?' he asks and I feel like shouting at him. 'Is that all! This is monumental.' Instead I blush and nod then hide the kit right at the bottom of my bag. I'll keep it for later. If it comes to that.

The bookshop is underground, the walls roughly carved from stone. It's cool and quiet and feels a long way from the messy chaos above ground. I buy more postcards for Max and Alison: one of a pockmarked lunar landscape and another of the night sky with wide circles of light showing the path of the stars. I also buy a new sketchbook. Inside is thick, handmade paper and the cover is a pastiche of leaves and twigs and rough paper in earthy colours. The book itself is a work of art and I'm afraid I won't be able to do it justice.

Lastly I go into one of the shiny tourist shops and buy a plastic goanna and a chunk of rough stone with a tiny seam of raw opal through it. I'll put them on the dashboard with my growing collection of leaves and sticks. I try on hats too, because I'm having a crisis of confidence with the flowery yellow one I bought at the markets which takes off at every gust of wind and looks too conspicuous out here. In the end I buy a leather one called an Akubra even though it's expensive, because the sales assistant says it looks good.

'Thanks hon,' she says when I pay.

The pub is full of huge guts, leering eyes and noisy machines that make me wince. Someone wolf-whistles. Someone else shouts. 'Hey babe, you can wrap those legs around me any time.'

I pretend I haven't heard, but feel horribly self conscious as I wind my way between tables and chairs, wishing my shorts were longer or my legs shorter or I was somewhere else entirely. Why couldn't we have met in the bookshop?

I order a lemonade with lots of ice and sit down opposite David who is calmly reading a book and sipping on a beer. He looks up and laughs at my Akubra.

'Now you really look like an English tourist,' he says and goes back to his book.

Embarrassed, I take the hat off and hang it round my neck. I can't believe David can read like that, so casually, with me sitting opposite, twiddling my thumbs. We hardly know each other. Where are his manners? Why doesn't he need to fill up the silences like everyone else? I'm not quite comfortable with it, but in a way it's refreshing too. Not having to bother.

With nothing better to do, I pull out the diary and reread part of the Coober Pedy entry. It feels strange to be sitting in the same pub so many years on. It doesn't look like much has changed.

23 August

In the afternoon we went to the pub. It was full of men with loud voices and the noise got noisier as night fell. We bought dinner too, although we shouldn't have because we're running out of cash. Greasy fish and chips and floppy lettuce, and thick sliced tomatoes. It got so smoky it was hard to breathe. Storm started whimpering and that drove B mad because he never has room for her when he's drunk. He shouted at her to shut up, but that only made it worse. So I took her outside and smoked a joint while she flicked stones around. When we went back in, someone spat on me, a great big glob. 'Bloody hippy,' he said. I told him to fuck off and he put on a show of being scared, scrunching up behind his bloodshot eyes. 'Ooh,' he said, 'the lady's got spirit.' B wanted to kill him, 'Come on,' he shouted, hopping about with his fists clenched, 'I'll show you. Picking on a woman.' But I stopped him because suddenly he looked so stupid. They both did. All puffed up and ready to kill each other. For what? I mean aren't hippies supposed to be about peace and love and happiness? Or have we lost the plot somewhere along the way?

I can imagine it. Right down to the floppy lettuce. And me, eating soggy chips dipped in tomato sauce, whimpering and whining, while B gets into fights and Kita smokes joints outside. That's easy. But it's still impossible to equate my hippie mother with murder.

I have the basic facts. Bill murdered Kita. My father murdered my mother. He drew his hands around her neck and squeezed, gently at first probably, just to see, and then harder as she struggled, because she must have struggled. She must have fought for the most valuable thing she had. And for me. Or maybe he was in a fury and squeezed hard right from the start, blindly and so as not to think about it. I don't know what else he did to her. I don't want to. Knowing that kind of stuff is hard to live with. It fucks you up. Images sneak in when you let down your defences. And I have no idea how much of this I saw. What can a two-year-old remember? A shudder goes all the way down my back. I've got goose bumps and my toes are curled. This is the closest I've let myself come to it yet.

David has put down his book. He's looking at me. Maybe he's said something. I pick up my lemonade and take a sip, but the ice clinks against my teeth and makes them hurt. David is still looking at me. I try really hard to pull myself together, to steer my mind away from the details. It's important to keep it abstract, to keep away from anything more than the basic facts. But it comes anyway, straight out of my nightmares. First there's bright light and a whirring noise. I can feel the air shifting about and brushing against my face. Then the light goes and everything is black. In it is a curved, sharp shape, and skin - soft, soft skin.

'Hey, are you okay?' David's voice brings me back to myself. He's holding my arm, which is shaking like mad. All of me is shaking, even my teeth.

'Fine... I'm fine.'

'You don't look crash hot.'

His hand's still on my arm. I brush it off. 'Look, it's nothing,' I say, but my voice is too high. 'Really. Can we just leave it? Please?'

'Okay,' he says, backing off. 'Okay.'

He picks up his book again, but I can tell he's not concentrating because he keeps sneaking looks at me. Maybe he thinks he's travelling with a madwoman. Then the awful thought comes - maybe he is. When I pick up my lemonade it slops all over my hand and leaves me sticky.

It's getting late and David suggests staying here. I think he's nervous I might freak out again. We look around but all the caravan parks have fences and that puts me off. I don't want to be constricted like that. Not out here.

'This place is too big for fences,' I tell David.

'That's why we've got them, to make it feel safer.'

But I don't want to be here. I don't want to stop yet and the idea of it is too big to explain to David.

'I need to keep moving,' I tell him, hoping he'll understand.

He stares at me curiously for a moment and I think he'll probably decide to catch a bus or something. But he doesn't.

'Fair enough,' he says, studying the map again. 'How about the Breakaways? They're a bit north of here. Not far.'

'Okay.' I like their name, and besides, I feel absurdly grateful to David for not asking, so I'd probably agree to anything. Well almost anything.

It's a rough sandy dirt track and the van slips a bit, but we make it through all right. The Breakaways still look like a moonscape, but there are different colours, soft ones, more like moonstone or pale opal. Not what I expected from the richly coloured opals in the souvenir shops back there.

David lights a fire. I collect rocks to put around it, remembering what Millie taught me about camp fires. He discards some of them.

'You've got to be careful about which rocks you use. Some types get too hot and they explode, you see.'

'Really?' This is the first I've heard of exploding rocks. I wonder if he's having me on.

David looks at me quizzically. 'Don't they have Brownies over in England.'

'Brownies?'

'You know, miniature Girl Guides?'

I laugh, trying to imagine myself a part of all that. 'Me, no way!'

He's looking at me, amused and I'm irritated that he knows things I don't. I'm not going to let David take over. I'm not going to tell him that I've never camped before.

'Look,' I say. 'I don't know much about camping and I'm not keen on snakes, but I'm not some squealy city girl with perfect nails.'

'Hey,' he says, waving his hands in the air. 'There's no need to get so defensive. I'm just trying to help. Okay?'

I take a deep breath. 'Okay. Sorry,' I add. 'I grew up in the country, but it's so different here. Like another planet.'

'Yeah,' says David. 'It is.' He stands up and stares out at the landscape. 'I grew up in the city, but I love it out here.'

He sighs and for the first time I notice that underneath the laugh lines and the open face, David is sad. I wonder if he's running from something too.

'Dinner's on me tonight,' he says. 'Baked spuds.'

I watch him wrap potatoes up in foil and tuck them into the coals. His arms are lean and strong and the veins stand out, patterning them in blue. I'd like to draw them, but I'm too tired to look for my sketchbook. David pulls out a six-pack and hands me a bottle of beer. It's warm lager, but after the first couple of sips I don't mind. We don't speak, just sit watching the sky change colour as the sun sets. The few wisps of cloud glow golden orange for awhile, then the colour drains from them and it's as if someone has switched off the light. The wind dies down and now there's a silence that's only broken by the occasional thump of a kangaroo and the sounds of insects I can't identify. We could be the only people on earth. I'm amazed at how easy I feel with David and pleased that I offered him a lift. I would never have had the courage to come this far off the road alone. Being with David is slowing me down, and easing out the tensions. Maybe I can stop running now and start noticing where I am.

When the potatoes are done, David tips baked beans on them and sprinkles a bit of parmesan on top - the disgusting powdered sort you get in shakers.

'There,' he says, 'practically a gourmet meal.'

It tastes great. Anything would out here. And this is the second meal of the day I've got down without any trouble. Maybe I didn't need to buy that pregnancy test after all.

I find some gooey chocolate that's melted twice already and give half to David. He hands me another warm beer. There's something special about warm beer and gooey chocolate and we sit quietly, savouring it and the silence.

'Why are you going to Darwin?' I ask after a while. The silence has gone on too long and I need to fill it.

Straight away David tenses up. He's trying to look casual, but it doesn't work.

'I don't know.' He laughs bitterly. 'I guess it's about as far as you can get from Adelaide without leaving the country.'

'Are you running away from something?' I ask.

'None of your business,' he says.

'Actually it is,' I tell him. 'I don't fancy harbouring a criminal.'

David laughs again. But this time it's convincing. 'Nah,' he says. 'I'm on the run from my girlfriend. She dumped me.'

'Oh,' I say. I'm sorry,' which sounds lame, but I can't think of anything else to say.

David turns his face away and starts drawing patterns with a stick in the dust. He looks pretty glum and I'm scared he's going to cry — then I wouldn't know what to do. I can't hug an almost stranger in the middle of nowhere, even though suddenly I want to. I change the subject instead.

'So what do you do?'

'I'm at uni, doing environmental studies.'

'Are you an eco-activist then?' I ask.

'A what?'

'An eco-activist. We have them in England. You know, they tie themselves to trees and dig bunkers underground.'

David laughs. 'Not really,' he says. 'What made you think that?'

'I don't know. The way you talk sometimes and your T-shirts. You're a walking billboard.'

'Yeah well, some things are worth saying.'

He's blushing, which is kind of sweet. I can't imagine Max blushing, he's too certain of himself. And I can't imagine him wearing a T-shirt with a message either – not a brand name or an issue. He always says there's enough advertising in the world without him paying to join in too. David's right though, there are some things worth saying, and some things worth saving.

We're quiet for a while. The beer has gone straight to my head and it's been ages since I've felt this relaxed. I lean right back, looking up at the night sky. The Milky Way is thick and so close it feels as if any second I'll fall into it. The sky is almost clear, just a few light clouds.

'It's going to rain,' I announce.

David laughs again. I seem to have that effect on him. 'Come on,' he says.

'It's a wet moon. See the way that cloud is cutting across it.'

'Oh yeah,'

'Tomorrow some time, you just wait.'

But I'm laughing too and it seems like a long time since that last happened.

'Okay,' he says. 'I'll bet you a six pack.'

'Make it a bottle of red... A good one.'

'Right, you're on.'

We shake on it and I like the feel of his hand in mine. When he looks at me, his eyes draw me in. I don't have any defences against eyes like that.

'Do you have a stigmatism?' I ask and he cracks up, bending over double, like he's got a pain in his gut.

'You know what,' he gasps, 'you're really weird.'

And that makes me laugh too. 'Well, do you?'

'No I don't have a stigmatism.' he says. 'Why?'

But I don't want to get into that. That's one of the things I fell for in Max. His eyes have a piercing intensity, a kind of concentrated squint that always makes people feel special. It's why he gets away with things and why women follow him around I suppose. Anyway it worked on me. After I'd moved in he explained about his eye problem and I remember thinking, Oh my God, I've fallen in love with a stigmatism. But it wasn't just that. Nothing is so simple.

David's still looking at me expectantly, but I'm not about to tell him.

'Good,' I say. 'I'm going to bed.'

CHAPTER TWELVE

In the morning I feel sick again and filled with the worry of it. I try to ignore my stomach, but my mouth is watery and I have to keep doing little swallows while David builds up the fire and makes coffee. I watch him take out the beans, grind them in a little machine with a handle and then pull out a percolator.

'Now who's weird?' I say.

'Coffee has to be done just right,' he says.

As the coffee bubbles on top of the fire, the smell takes me back to Victoria Cottage. Nan sitting at the kitchen table taking that first sip of coffee for the day. Strong and black with three teaspoons of sugar and all the pleasure of it in her face.

'You would have liked my nan,' I say.

'Yeah?'

'She had a thing about coffee.' I can feel the tears welling up, and turn away, trying to brush them off. David's going to think I'm crazy all over again. 'She died a few months ago.'

David squeezes my shoulder and doesn't seem to mind that I'm crying. At least he's not embarrassed.

'She had cancer, and didn't want to get treated.'

I pull away from David and wipe my eyes. He hands me a coffee.

'Sorry,' I say. 'It's just that she didn't… ' I'm on a roll now and about to tell him everything, but we're interrupted by the roar of engines. There's a convoy of trucks approaching. David jumps up, splashing his coffee all over my knees and not noticing.

'Hey, it's a television crew.'

'Yeah sure.'

They park just up from us and make it pretty obvious that we're in the way. David thinks it's hilarious. Maybe he's trying to cheer me up.

'Here we are in one of the hottest, most remote parts of Australia,' he says, 'and we're taking someone's spot... That's fantastic.'

He goes over to ask what's going on and comes back beaming.

'A car ad. Can you believe it? They're filming a commercial out here.'

But I'm resentful. Our wonderful quiet has been broken by busy city voices issuing orders. They're working to a deadline and not seeing and because of them this place doesn't seem beautiful anymore. I want to be somewhere else.

'Let's go.' I throw the rest of my coffee into the dust. It doesn't even have time to sink in, just darkens the ground momentarily before evaporating.

It's too hot. Even with the windows down the air is so hot it burns. Deep cracks have formed on the soles of my feet, and it hurts when I push my foot down on the accelerator. If I smile my lips crack. I keep licking them but that only seems to make it worse. We pass dead kangaroos on the road. Sometimes there's a dead wedge-tailed eagle next to them. Other times there's one perched on a kangaroo carcass, tearing at its flesh. They rise up into the air as we pass and I have to look away. There's something about them that makes me shudder.

We've been driving north about twenty minutes when I remember.

'Oh shit.' I slam on the brakes and turn the van around.

'What?'

'I've forgotten something.'

We drive all the way back to the Breakaways. David looks out for last night's spot, while I negotiate the soft track and all the film trucks.

'There it is,' he shouts, pointing to a ring of rocks in between two trucks.

I get out and dig up my wallet from under one of the rocks around our camp fire, while the film crew look on suspiciously.

That's bizarre,' David says when I get back in. 'You really are weird.'

I smile. 'Just cautious... It's a Romany trick.'

David looks puzzled. 'Romany?'

'You know, gypsies.'

Then I tell him a bit about Millie and how she taught me some of the Romany ways.

'Yeah, well,' says David. 'She forgot to tell you not to forget you put it there.' He's laughing, but I can tell he's impressed.

'So what else did she teach you?'

'All sorts of things. 'Like what to do with plants and how to find them – chickweed, nettles, dandelions, comfrey, coltsfoot, that sort of thing.'

'They're all considered weeds here,' says David dismissively.

'Really?' I'm surprised, but I guess it's all about the way you look at it. I remember how Pop hated weeds. They were the bane of his life and he was always down on his knees pulling them out. When his bones ached too much I'd do it for him, though I could never tell the difference between good plants and weeds.

'See that one *chiri*?' he'd say pointing, and I'd pull it out. More often than not I'd pull the good one, not the weed. Then he'd sigh and I'd feel stupid. But I never did understand what made one thing a weed and another not. I asked Pop about it one day.

'I don't know *chiri*,' he said. Who decides these things? Some people say God is repsonsible.

'But what makes something a weed?'

'The weeds are too many,' Pop said. They threaten to swallow everything else.'

But weeds were important for Millie. She didn't care for a flower simply to look at it. For her, weeds were nutritious and healing. Comfrey for broken bones, coltsfoot for asthma and bronchitis, dandelion roots for the liver and the leaves for water retention, aniseed for indigestion, elderberry for colds... She taught me loads more but I've forgotten most of it. We would walk the hills and meadows and study the sides of the roads, picking flowers, leaves and berries, and digging roots. For Millie everything had a purpose.

'They're useful,' I tell David.

He shakes his head. 'Maybe, but they're taking over the native plants.'

'You can use that argument on refugees,' I say. 'People do... And Hitler thought Millie was a weed.'

David looks surprised. 'Yeah,' he says after a minute. 'It's difficult... in global terms I guess you could call the human race a weed... Anyway, most of those plants wouldn't grow out here in the desert. And most people wouldn't survive. You'd have to know about bush tucker. We do a bit of that at uni.'

Australian plants, I think. A whole other alphabet of food I know nothing about. David's right, I wouldn't last a 'micro second' without all the props.

'So what more did your wise old great-grannie teach you?'

I laugh at the idea of Millie being wise. 'Wacky? Yes,' I say. 'Wise? No.'

I wrack my brain for more interesting titbits. There's not much there. Nan always did her best to stop me going off with Millie. She hated that I wanted to learn her ways.

'Millie showed me how to roast a hedgehog once. On hot coals.' David pulls a face. 'No. It tasted good, a bit like pork. And I know how to kill a chicken. Millie used to break the necks of our chickens because Pop couldn't stomach it. She never minded doing it. She said it was okay so long as you ate it. "Otherwise," she told me, "you must never hurt an animal." She'd get both hands around its neck and twist until I'd hear it snap. I used to watch it flapping about, still squawking sometimes, even though it was dead ...'

'Spare me the detail,' David groans.

'It wasn't that bad,' I laugh. 'I used to be fascinated. The way she dipped it in hot water so she could pluck it more easily. Then chopped off its head and feet and wings, slit it open and took out the insides. She always threw out the heart.' I wag my finger sternly at David and imitate Millie's raspy voice. "Never eat the heart of a chicken, because it will be full of fear and when you die your heart will be fearful too."'

David laughs and I'm happy that I can make him laugh like this. Max isn't interested in my past. It's as if he's ashamed of it. Then it strikes me that perhaps it's me that's ashamed. I don't talk about it much with Max because I'm not what I think he wants. Over here I feel free of all those constraints and suddenly my story is interesting not embarrassing. Well at least that part of it anyway.

'So what else?' David asks, eager for more.

'Ah,' I say, drawing it out. 'We have a curse... handed down from generation to generation.'

'Creepy,' says David. 'What sort of curse.'

'I don't really know. No one would ever say, but I think it runs really deep. When I was little I thought it had something to do with men. We never had them, you see... only Pop, but he died when I was ten.'

Then I tell David about Millie meeting Pop, and getting ostracised and Millie's mother throwing down the curse on her.

'And her offspring… which I guess is me. I don't know how it's supposed to work. Maybe it's a bit like a virus, adapting to each new environment and finding ways to get in and do its worst.'

David's staring at me, with his mouth open. Now he thinks I'm really, really weird.

'Know how to break a curse?' I ask him.

He laughs. 'Nah, can't help you there, sorry. It's not my area.'

'Nor mine.'

'I don't know. Maybe you have to stop believing in it? Maybe that's the only way you can break its power.'

I nod. He's right, but I think there's more to it than that. There's some sort of genetic inheritance, a miasmic link from one generation to another, patterns that repeat, pain that's inherited. It's hard to recognise those patterns though, and when you do it's even harder to unravel them. Maybe we all have curses to contend with, scar tissue that stops us being ourselves. For a moment I wonder about my painting. Maybe that's what I've been trying to express in these abstracts I've got stuck on. The pattern of a curse. Or my own scar tissue. The thought makes me shudder.

'Tell me more,' David says. But I can't think of anything else. Only Millie lying on the couch downstairs. Dying. And angry about it. Scared too. She wouldn't be left alone to wait for it. She told me all the *mula* were crowding around, waiting. She practically begged me to stay with her, but the idea of sharing the room with a bunch of vengeful spirits scared me so much I only sat with her during the day. Nan slept on the floor next to her at night, while I lay upstairs in bed, terrified by the shadows that played dreadful patterns on the wall next to me.

I knew exactly what vengeful spirits looked like. They had pointy teeth and long fingernails, but no lips or legs, just tattered strips of clothes. Mothers are supposed to love their children, but I knew I killed mine and that must have turned her into a vengeful *mula*. The trick was to keep my eyes open. I used to lie on my back, staring at the ceiling, with the lamp on if I could get away with it. Every time my eyelids slipped shut I forced them back open again. When I got desperate I held them open with my fingers until they went all dry and sore. In the end sleep would always win though, then in the morning I would open my eyes really slowly just in case the spirits had got me. But they never had.

'When Millie died,' I tell David, 'a whole part of my life shut down.'

'Yeah,' says David. 'That's how I felt when Dad died.'

We're quiet for a bit. Lost inside our own heads. I'm wondering whether to ask about his father, or if that's too forward. I don't know the rules in this country. Then I notice something right on the edge of the horizon.

'Clouds,' I say, pointing

'Yeah. Doesn't mean it'll rain.'

It starts just before we get to Kulgera. Big splats on the windscreen. Slowly at first and then faster and faster until it's hard to see through the water.

David's shaking his head in amazement. 'You win,' he says. 'Bloody hell.'

I can tell I'm going up in his estimation.

'Population, nominal,' reads David as we drive past the 'Welcome to Kulgera' sign.

'What does that mean?'

'God knows.'

It isn't exactly a thriving metropolis. There's not much here, just a hotel and filling station, and outside the hotel, a camping ground where I park. It's too late to drive on and too early for dinner, but it's pouring with rain and we don't know what to do with ourselves. David's feet are up on the dashboard again. His skin is dark tanned and I'm fascinated by the hairs on his legs. They're white. David sees me looking and I turn away, blushing again.

'I'm going to the pub,' I say abruptly and open the door.

'Good idea,' says David, unfolding his legs from the dash.

We run through the rain, dodging puddles, but we're soaked by the time we get there.

Inside there are only two or three other customers, but the whole place reeks of smoke. We sit at the bar on tall stools and my feet don't reach the ground. The bar runners smell of old beer. The barman nods and pours us icy cold lagers.

'So, where are you guys heading?'

'North,' says David, 'To Darwin.'

I let it stand. It's easier than explaining. He can think we're together.

'Darwin! You should have left it a couple more weeks. The wet season started late this year. It usually eases off by the end of March, but it's still bloody hellish up there.'

'It can't be worse than here,' I say.

'Wanna bet.'

I shrug. No I don't want to bet. I haven't got a clue.

David launches into a conversation about the weather. He's passionate about his subject and the barman seems genuinely interested. I'm content to listen, fading in and out while I sip my beer. The barman's talking about the drought, even though the rain's coming down in sheets outside. He says something about the wildflowers coming out at the wrong time. And David says there's nothing for the native birds to eat …

'And the frogs! How long have they got?' he asks in a broken voice.

'It's a bloody shame,' says the barman, shaking his head and pouring us more beers.

'Shit yeah,' says David.

I like it that David feels so strongly about everything. It's an antidote for the numbness inside me. And it puts my problems back in perspective.

'What are you planning to do in Darwin?' I ask him when the barman goes off to serve another customer.

'Nothing really, just hang around for awhile. I'm staying with an old friend. He went up there a few years back to protest about uranium mining in Kakadu, and ended up staying on.'

There's a silence. I have to ask. 'So why did your girlfriend leave you?'

Suddenly David looks really miserable and I wish I hadn't asked quite so bluntly. I watch him tearing up the drink coaster. He's really hurting.

'She met someone else... You know how it is.'

I nod, but I don't know. It hasn't happened to me yet and I send out a silent prayer that it won't.

'I'm sorry,' I say.

'How about letting on where you're heading,' says David, changing the subject. He's smiling again and I'm surprised at how quickly he can recover.

This sends me into a spin. I haven't really thought about it like that for a while. I've been absorbed in following my mother's journey, not heading anywhere in particular.

'Mary Kathleen,' I say eventually.

'Who's that?'

'It's a place. Near Mt Isa.'

'Never heard of it.'

'It's on the map – it says something about it being a uranium town.'

David looks horrified. 'Uranium! What do you want to go there for?'

'I have to see a couple of people up there. I think they know some things I need to know.'

I'm sounding like a private eye but David doesn't laugh. 'Uh-huh,' he says, and drains his beer.

I order more beers and tell him the story. Though it's hard to decide where to begin because every starting point needs an explanation, so I find myself going further and further back until we're in Europe in 1921, even though I've already told him bits of that, and then I have to make my way into the present again. It takes ages. Halfway through we order counter meals to help soak up the beer. And all the time I keep talking and David keeps buying more beers. After a while mine are lined up next to each other and I have to tell him to stop. I'm used to sipping on thick warm English ales, not guzzling this cold light stuff.

'So,' I finish, 'the last diary entry is around Mt Isa. I guess she was murdered somewhere nearby… I'm pretty sure Edith and Jack Burton were the people who found me.'

David is gobsmacked. 'Wow,' he says. 'That's pretty full on.'

His mouth is gaping open like a hungry goldfish and it makes me want to laugh. I guess the whole thing does sound pretty crazy.

'You want any more drinks?' asks the barman. 'We're closing up early.'

I shake my head. I've had plenty.

Outside the rain is still coming down in sheets and the ground has turned into one big puddle.

'It's still pissing down,' says David, stating the obvious. There's no way he can sleep outside tonight.

It's too hot for sleeping bags and neither of us plan to get undressed anyway, not in front of each other. So we both lie down on top of the mattress in our damp, steamy clothes, permeated with pub smells: beer slops and second-hand smoke.

'Night.' David rolls over and faces the door, his back to me.

'Goodnight,' I say and lie on my back, willing sleep to hurry up. But I'm woozy with the beer and it feels strange lying next to someone I've only just met. I don't even know his second name. And what if sometime in the night I roll over and cuddle him, or call him Max. Jesus! What would Max think if he saw me now? The worst I imagine.

'What's your other name?' I ask.

'Huh?'

'Your surname?'

David rolls over and smiles. 'Ah,' he says. 'Time for formal introductions. Mine's Field... and yours?'

'Cizekova,' I say. 'Goodnight.'

David stays near one side and I stay near the other but I can still feel the edges of him, and the space between us. It's buzzing hard like electricity. After a bit I start to feel a tight, full roundness inside. My bladder. I need a wee.

'Excuse me,' I straddle David, pulling at the door, blushing, trying not to touch him, but I can't open the door from this angle so eventually he pulls it open for me, but then I've forgotten the torch and have to climb back and look for it and my flip-flops are somewhere and I'm not about to walk around out there in bare feet, with mud and spiders and snakes. By the time I find my flip-flops all the mosquitoes have got in and David has switched on the light and started swatting like mad.

I go round the back of the van where he can't see me, turn on the torch and scan the ground for snakes. My eyes and ears are on full alert for slithery noises, any movements. I can feel the tension, tight across my shoulders and somewhere inside my chest, like the slightest thing and I'm going to start screaming. Kita was murdered out here somewhere. Murdered! And it's insane that I'm out here too, on the other side of the world, in the middle of nowhere, picking up strange men and squatting in the rain and mud in the middle of the night.

About an hour later I have to wee again and the whole embarrassing ritual is repeated. When I straddle David for the third time, he sighs and opens his eyes.

'Hey,' he says wearily, 'why don't we swap places.'

'Sorry,' I say. 'It's all that beer, I'm not used to it.'

Then it's ages before I get to sleep and when I finally do, David wakes me up, calling out, 'No, Jade, no.'

In the morning I've got a fat revolting tongue and eyes that don't want to open. The sun has been up long enough to turn the van into an oven and my stomach is churning. I leap out barefoot into a puddle and make a run for it, throwing up on the way and hoping David can't hear.

When I get back he's awake and grinding coffee beans. His hair is a mess, but he doesn't look a bit hung over and when he sees me his whole face creases into a smile.

'What, another piss?'

I'm not in the mood for teasing. 'It's all right for you,' I mutter. 'You can just stick your willy out the window.'

After the rain, the sun turns everything into a steamy sauna, until there's hardly any air left for breathing. I take quick little breaths and concentrate on the road. My whole morning is fuzzy and nauseous and bad tempered. The pregnancy test is burning a hole in the bottom of my bag. It's all I can think about and I promise myself I'll use it today.

We stop at the turn off to Ayers Rock, but it's not called that anymore, it's called Uluru, its Aboriginal name. It's a long detour, nearly six hundred kilometres all up and I'm not sure David will want to do it.

He boils up coffee again. The same long ritual. My stomach is way too empty, so I rummage around the cupboards and find half a pack of stale biscuits to dunk in our coffee.

'I have to go there,' I explain. 'You can go on if you like. It shouldn't be too hard getting a lift from here.'

He's quiet for a bit. Weighing things up. I leave my biscuit in too long and lose half of it, then have to look for a spoon.

'I'm in no hurry,' he says eventually.

I nod, all business like, fishing soggy biscuit out of my cup and smothering a smile. There's no way I want him to see how pleased I am.

CHAPTER THIRTEEN

I have to read the instructions three times before I work out how to do it. When I lift up the toilet lid the stench immediately hits me immediately, twisting my stomach into knots of nausea. The flies buzz even more frantically, excited by the stink. When they land on me I brush them away, revolted. I stick the little container under me and start weeing, but most of it misses and I have to wave it around to get enough. Then I wait for something to happen on the litmus paper, willing it to hurry up before a queue forms outside. It doesn't take five minutes, not even two. Almost straight away the line goes bright blue. I read the instructions all over again, just to make sure, but there's no question. I'm pregnant.

I am standing inside a pit toilet in the heart of Australia. There's at least one person shuffling about outside, waiting their turn. But I can't go out there yet. I can't possibly walk out of here as if nothing has happened. Because no matter what decision I make about this, my life will never be the same again. I'm deeply shocked that this could happen to me, but I'm also not in the least surprised.

I stare up at the thin strip above the door that's filled with a clear blue sky. In the corners are perfectly formed spider webs. Fine and strong and dotted with trapped flies. I wonder what they feel, paralysed like that, waiting to have their insides sucked out and knowing it's only a matter of time.

The shuffling outside is getting more urgent so I lift up the lid again and tip the wee down the hole. Then I put the litmus strip in the container, the whole lot back into my bag and open the door. I smile apologetically at a lady with a perm the colour of the line on my litmus paper. She frowns and bustles past me, with no idea of the monumental thing that has just happened inside that cubicle. As I walk back to the van I'm filled with a sense of urgency. There must be something I have to do, other than wait for my belly to stretch. But I have no idea what. I don't even know if I want a baby. Or if I want Max's baby. And what about him? Would he want a baby? I don't expect so.

His parents would be appalled. They hate me. He says they don't, but I know they do. That first time, staying in their sterile country house with its well-mown lawns. The grounds, Max calls them. And there's even a fountain. They were terribly polite but I couldn't help noticing they talked to me very slowly and a bit too loud, the way people talk to foreigners. Then at dinner I used my dessert spoon for the soup. Nobody mentioned it and that somehow made it worse.

Let's hope Max hasn't mentioned the latest developments in my chequered past. I don't imagine he would dare. They know nothing about gypsy blood, illegitimate children or murders. To them I'm just a girl with a strange name who grew up in the Malvern Hills with her grandmother. And who has unfortunately 'latched on' to their son. They'll think I planned this.

Oh God! One slip up and look what's happened. It was that night. I know it. When Max was drunk and I ran along the canal back to my studio and he came with my clothes and we made love. And it was special. But Max didn't pull out and neither of us said anything, though we both knew it was dangerous.

I get lost amongst rows and rows of caravans and tents and end up having to retrace my steps to the toilet and start all over again. When I finally get back to the van, I climb in knowing something huge and David doesn't even look up from his book. I want to check in the mirror to see if I look different. There must be something new in my face. But David would wonder what I was doing, so I sit in the back, waiting for him to ask me what's wrong, so I can snap 'NOTHING' at him. But he keeps on reading. How dare he! I have to work really hard to stop myself from leaning over, grabbing his book and throwing it out of the window. In the end I can't bear it anymore.

'Come on,' I say, 'let's go and look at this rock.'

David shuts his book. 'Sure.'

I've seen loads of pictures of Uluru so I knew it was big, but I never expected it to be this huge. Sitting here, so powerful, so certain of itself. Way, way beyond us and our petty little emotions. It makes me feel tiny but also somehow safe. We stand at the bottom for a while, looking up at the track to the top, watching puffing red-faced people hauling themselves up by a chain. I have absolutely no desire to join them, even though Kita climbed it back then when it was still Ayers Rock.

'Lots of people don't make it,' says David. 'And at least one person dies every year trying. A heart attack or they wander off the path and slip. The Anangu people believe it's the spirits taking revenge. They don't want people walking on the rock.'

We start walking around the rock and end up doing the whole thing, all ten kilometres of it. Close up there's so much more detail: subtle shifts in colour; folds of rock that look almost liquid or like soft flesh; dark still caves; shallow crannies; cool shady bits with plants and small trees tucked in them; and fenced-off sacred places. I bend down and pick up a small stone.

'Look,' I say. 'A tiny piece of Uluru.'

'You'd better put it back,' David warns. 'Lots of people steal pieces of the rock, but apparently they bring bad luck, so each year thousands of pieces are sent back.'

I imagine all those bits of Uluru tucked safely in padded envelopes, travelling thousands of miles, hitching rides in planes and ships and buses and trains and postal vans, their paths criss-crossing with other pieces, all drawn like magnets back to their home. I put the stone down. I don't need any bad luck.

Soon I'm too tired to think about anything except sitting down. When we get back in the van, I'm puffing and absolutely exhausted. I thought I was fitter than this, but the heat is somehow hotter and there's less air, so I have to puff hard to get enough. David doesn't even look tired. He tells me we're lucky that it's only thirty-something this time of year.

'In January,' he says, 'it can climb up into the fifties... Imagine that.'

I'd rather not.

I park early at the viewing point and we settle down to wait for the sun to set. I take some photographs, but they don't capture it at all. I knock David's feet off the dashboard, pull out my sketchbook from the glovebox and start sketching shapes and shadows, trying to remember the rock's flesh-like fluidity. Then I pull out the pastels, looking for colours but none of them will do it justice.

'Hey that's good,' says David, peering over from his book.

But I know it isn't. My pencil's too hard and that makes the edges too sharp. There's no subtlety, just a silly cartoon shape, and then the lead breaks so I give up. I'll have to buy a postcard.

Soon we're surrounded by buses and cars and people sitting on bonnets, leaning on the fence, waiting with cameras poised to capture whatever it is that's supposed to happen. David's not too keen about staying with all these people about, but I'm driving so he has no choice.

'It spoils it,' he says, sounding sulky.

Normally I'd feel pretty cynical about this tourist mecca thing too, but there's something about this rock that makes it worthwhile. Kita thought it was special too. When David goes back to his book, I skim through Kita's diary until I find the entry.

5 September

We weren't going to come here because it's about a hundred miles off the highway, we've hardly got any money left for fuel and as B said, it's only a bloody big rock. But at the turn-off I suddenly really wanted to go there. I'm glad we did. People talk about the dead centre, but it's not like that at all. This rock's more like a vital organ, a living throbbing heart. B stayed down the bottom with Storm, but I wanted to climb it. So I joined the others hauling themselves up the side of this obscenely smooth rock. God it was a hard slog. Then I was standing there looking out every way forever. I held my hands out and felt the beginnings of a breeze, and the sun beating down on me. There were no clouds in the sky, but I felt a shadow cross over me anyway and I remembered what Mum told me when I left. 'You can't leave yourself behind', she said and I thought she was talking codswallop, but now I think I know what she meant.

I shouldn't have gone up the rock. It didn't feel right. Like walking on sacred land. There were people everywhere clicking away. 'Wow, Look at this. Wow.' Snap, snap snap. Tourists with big cameras and matching bellies. I forgot to take water or my hat, so by the time I got down again I was dizzy and shivering and feeling pretty weird. B said it was probably sunstroke. "You looked like an ant up there," he said. "Ant, ant,' laughed Storm and I was pleased because she's starting to talk more now. She's really trying to get her mouth around words, though still not stringing them together. I won't have to worry so much if she starts talking properly.

That night we watched the sun set and the rock change colours, from orange, red, to a deep dark purple. And I thought, this is the most 'here' thing I've ever seen.

The sun will be gone any minute now and already the rock is flushed blood red. Kita felt Uluru was alive – *a living throbbing heart*, but for a moment I get the odd sense that instead it is the earth's pregnant belly, swollen tight and ready to give birth to her spirit children. I feel my flat belly, trying to imagine it round, holding a life that isn't mine and yet is intimately connected to me. But it's too early, the knowledge of my pregnancy is still only in my head and written on a thin strip of litmus paper.

I get out and climb up on the bull bar, so I can see above the heads of all the other tourists. Everyone is going 'Oooh, aaaah' and I'm thinking how great it would be to see this alone. But even in a crowd it's something special. I know exactly what Kita meant about it being the most 'here thing' she'd ever seen.

David told me that all sorts of dreaming lines intersect here and I wonder if they're linked in some way with the ley lines that crisscross the Malverns because sitting here on this bull bar, watching the rock changing colour, is the only other time I've felt such a strong sense of connection to a place. It's as if standing on the other side of the world in the very heart of Australia, I'm still somehow linked to Victoria Cottage. That these places are on my journey. And that it makes no difference if you stay still forever or never stop, so long as you stay on your path.

And then for a split second I get the sense of being on the right track, of everything slipping into place. For a moment I understand what Millie meant about following your nose. Letting one thing lead to another and living in the now. But it doesn't last. It never does with me. A second later and I'm anxious again, in a hurry and thinking about something else. Then the sun goes down and the buses leave and all that's left is a memory of something that felt incredibly light and free.

CHAPTER FOURTEEN

12 September - Alice Springs

B's got some more labouring work, so we're going to stop here in Alice Springs for a while. He goes off every day first thing and then after work he goes to the pub. Storm and I hang about in the caravan park, splashing in their dingy pool and waiting. We've rented a caravan. It's pretty old and the fly mesh is lifted away from the edges of the window so at night everything just flies right in. I can't make the cooker work properly either. The bloody thing practically explodes every time I try and light it and I have to send Storm outside just in case. But she loves it. I suppose for her it's like a cubby house, everything her size.

14 September

I've met a couple of other women about my age, maybe younger, but they're not my type. They're big and fat and already old. All they do is heave themselves in and out of chairs, shout at their snotty-nosed kids and talk about babies. There's only so much you can say, isn't there? It doesn't take long for them to work out that Storm is the only thing we've got in common. At night their men come home late and there's always angry voices and heaving caravans. When B got back tonight I told him I wanted to move on. I said I don't want to get stuck living in a park like this. The very thought of it makes me want to throw up. He put his arms around me and I could smell his yeasty beery breath, 'Soon honey,' he said, running his hands all over me. 'Soon.' And then his voice got urgent and his hands more insistent. 'Come on,' he said, but I didn't want to. Storm was awake and I hate B drunk like that. So I pushed him away. He stumbled and fell over the table. 'Bitch,' he shouted. 'Ya snobby bitch.' Storm cried and that shut him up, but not before everyone else heard. Maybe he's right. Maybe I am snobby. But I imagine all those women smirking in their beds and I hate it that we're getting to be just like them. There's a lump inside my throat, but it's not tears coming, it's a ball of anger that's growing and growing. What's happening to us? B isn't who I thought he was. He's changing, or he was only ever pretending.

19 September

I couldn't bear hanging about here any longer. So I walked into town with Storm. It was further than I expected and I didn't bring the pram, so she walked a bit and then I carried her on my shoulders for a bit and then she walked again. We went along the river bed. It's dry and sandy, with big beautiful shady gum trees. Hard to imagine what it would be like with water rushing through it. We played a game, dashing across the hot sand from one piece of shade to another, and when Storm tired we sat down, leaned against a tree and watched a line of ants marching somewhere. They were full of the sort of purpose, which I always envy. I feel more like a startled butterfly, fluttering from one danger to the next.

There were some Aborigines sitting in the shade along the river bed. They smiled at me and Storm. Some waved. One old woman with no teeth gave Storm a sweet. I don't know anything about these people but they seem okay. I wonder why people despise them. Why they want to destroy them. People are like that with the gypsies too. Maybe underneath the scorn, it started as envy. In the way that people who are trapped envy the freedom of open space and movement. There would have been greed in there somewhere. There always is. And the destructive fear of what we don't understand. Guilt too, because people always take their guilt out on someone else. Why is it that ownership is linked to staying put? If you have a fence or a piece of paper, then that's supposed to make you superior to everybody else. At least back home there are rights of way. Here they're so paranoid, you can get shot for walking on someone's land.

I tried to talk to B about it, but he wasn't interested. He said not to worry, they're just boongs, which made me take another long hard look at him. When I talked to Millie about being a Rom, she told me you can't run from it. 'It's in your blood,' she said. 'What about Mum?' I asked. 'She's got it too,' said Millie, 'but she won't see.' Mum was good with birds and squirrels. Even foxes trusted her. The birds would come right up and sit on her shoulder and she'd stroke them, her face soft and open. 'I want to be a bird. Turn me into a bird,' I once pleaded with Millie, because all the kids thought she was a witch and could do that kind of stuff. 'A bird?'

she asked. 'Why?' 'So Mum will love me too,' I said. The words hit Millie like a stone. 'Irene is hurt in here,' she said, pointing towards her heart. 'You must be careful with her. She is lacho jilo. *Do you understand? Her heart is good. But the curse is pulling her one way and then the other. Like this,' she said, wrapping her fingers in a monkey grip and tugging.*

I shut the diary and put it back in the glove box. I don't really understand what the curse is. I just know that it's made us all unhappy. Nan used to laugh at talk of a curse. 'Don't be ridiculous,' she'd say, but her voice had the brave worried tone that children always see through. Millie tried to explain it once. She said the mingling of our blood made tugs of war inside us, so we could never be at peace. I wonder if curses dilute in the way blood does, generation by generation? If so, how much is left for me? Not much I hope.

David is taking forever in the toilets. I'm waiting for him in the van, watching the traffic lights changing over and over. They're the first ones I've seen since Port Augusta. It's also the first time I've had to concentrate on other cars for a while. And it's left me tired and bad tempered. I'm feeling sick all the time now, and being accosted by smells, and the heat is too hot even though it's only thirty-three according to Alice Springs Radio, which I had to switch off because everyone's shouting and urgent as if we're all about to miss out on something. There are too many decisions I'm not making and too much that's been left unsaid. A couple of months ago there was certainty in my life, but now my past is a lie and my future seems more and more terrifying. Oh God, I just want to find somewhere cool and sleep forever.

David comes sprinting back to the car and jumps in, excitement lighting up his face.

'It's running,' he says. 'The Todd River. Can you believe it?'

And I'm thinking: Does he really chat to people in the toilet. All lined up in a row with their willies hanging out? How embarrassing.

David leans over and waves his hand in front of my eyes.

'Storm, come back... The Todd River is flowing. This is amazing. It hardly ever does. Can we go and see it?'

He's sounding patient, the way Max does when I'm not getting something. Spelling out his words and talking in short sentences. I hate that.

'Please.'

I sigh. 'Okay,' I say, starting up the van.

The river is beautiful. The wide sandy bed, the gentle flow of water meandering through the centre, the banks dotted with giant trees; some I recognise as red gums, others have trunks and branches that are dazzling white.

'Ghost gums,' says David. 'Aren't they beautiful?'

I nod, thinking how apt the name is. There's something melancholy about them, as if they've been around forever and seen too much.

In the distance are hills, or ranges as David calls them. They're long and low, with gentle rounded contours, and they look ancient like the Malverns. I feel a tug of yearning for home, but it has no face and I wonder if, like Millie and my mother, the yearning I feel is *o lungo drom*. A nostalgia for something that doesn't exist.

I don't want to stay in Alice Springs. I'd rather keep going, further north and then east. I'm impatient again. I want to get it all over and done with: find out what happened to Kita; tell Max what needs telling; make a decision about this baby; and start painting again. But David points out that we need to do washing and stock up on food. He's right. And I'm tired. So we book into a caravan park with glossy new amenities and a swimming pool, squeeze all our washing into one machine and go for a swim. David wears boardshorts and jumps in, whooping. But I feel self-conscious in my bathers, as if it's obvious there's a baby growing in my belly. I haven't shaved around my bikini line, so there's a mass of curly black hair, and my breasts feel huge and tight as if they might burst. David stares at me for just a bit too long and I think he's noticed. But then he wolf-whistles, so I jump in and splash him. That starts a splashing fight and pretty soon I feel much better.

The centre has a glossy shopping mall and lots of souvenir shops. I buy a plastic thorny devil lizard to keep the goanna company on my dashboard. Then we wander around, revelling in this oasis of people and noise and movement, almost forgetting that just a few kilometres away the desert is waiting. There are surf shops here, which doesn't make sense considering we're about as far as you can get from the sea.

David wants to go his own way around the shops, so we agree to meet later outside the supermarket. I visit all the galleries and buy some postcards of Indigenous paintings as well as a book on Indigenous art. I'm fascinated by the dotty, pointillist style done in ochres that match the landscape. I love the way the paintings tell stories and how bold and brave they are in form and colour. They're distinctive, and most importantly they have a purpose that's bigger than them. This gets me worrying about my own work all over again. I don't want my painting to be just shapes and colour, without meaning or purpose. There needs to be something more, some exploration that will help me make sense of the world. If there's not, then I should stop. This is a worrying thought, considering there's not much else I'm good at. There's the exhibition coming up too. And Max would never forgive me. Once again I wonder if it's me he loves or just the idea of me.

I find an art shop. It's small, but well stocked and I can't resist browsing. I buy some soft leads and look at the oil paint catalogues. One of them is Australian and when I open up the brochure I'm met with a feast of colour. They're here, and ready mixed, all the colours I've been getting so tantalising close to blending: Pilbara Red, Flinders Red Violet and Blue Violet, Australian Red Gold and four completely new types of green that capture the colour of the Australian bush. I buy them all. I can't resist, even though I won't be doing any painting until I get back to London and I'll probably have to pay excess baggage.

'Aren't they gorgeous?' says the woman at the counter who has dreadlocks tied back from her face and hands that paint too.

Afterwards I go into the library and check my emails. The real world descends with a thud and I wish I hadn't looked. There are two from Max, sounding worried. Why haven't I rung? Where am I? Am I okay? I'm relieved to see only one from Trevor, the gallery owner, asking me about the exhibition. Petra's emailed that she only sold three paintings in her last exhibition and her dad wants her to train as a teacher. I shudder. Will that be my fate too?

In the end I don't answer any of the messages. I don't want Max to worry, but I don't know how to say the things I have to. There's too much between Max and I and it's not just miles. Email is too casual anyway and not private enough, not with Fi organising Max's life for him.

Instead I pull out the postcards and scribble a short message to Max, saying I miss him and everything is fine. I write one to Audrey too, telling her about the river and the new paints I've found. Then I have to find the post office so I'm ages late for David, but he's there, leaning against the wall, reading a book about global warming. He's bought a couple of fly nets from an army disposal store.

'Here,' he says, handing me one.

He shows me how to wear it under my hat. It looks ridiculous, but hell, at least it keeps the flies off. I take mine off. There's no way I'm walking around a crowded shopping mall in one of these.

We sit in a huge food hall and drink two cappuccinos each and I don't feel sick.

'We could be anywhere,' grumbles David, not happy about 'invading monocultures'. But I like the air-conditioning. I can feel myself beginning to relax in here. All the tensions releasing as my body temperature goes down. If it wasn't for the caffeine, I could sleep here, deeply, for the first time in ages.

At the next table there's a mother feeding her baby. Just looking makes me want to cry. I'm awash with hormones. Every time I see a mother pushing her baby, the same thing happens. Suddenly they're everywhere.

In the supermarket I linger in the nappy aisle, looking at bibs and bottles and tins of baby food. Fascinated. And frightened. It's a whole new world.

David comes looking for me, and stares. I wonder again if he's guessed.

'Come on,' he says. 'Let's get out of here.'

His basket is already full. But I've hardly started. The coffee has left a foul taste and now all this food is making me feel sicker. I keep picking up things, feeling the watery mouth sensation and putting them down again. There's only one thing I want. Chicken.

But David screws his face up. 'They're factory farmed,' he says. 'You don't know what's in them.'

I struggle with myself. I've heard stories about pregnant women eating really strange things. If I don't get chicken maybe I'll start craving rocks or something.

'How about fish? suggests David.

But the fish counter makes me want to puke.

'Steak?' asks David. 'That'll be fresh. We're in beef country.'

'Okay', I say, not looking. I give him some money. 'Get what you like. I'll be outside.'

It's better out here. There's still noise and colour, but not so many smells. I'm standing right next to a phone box and I know I should ring Max. Really I should. But I still don't know what to say. We've never talked about babies. I could write instead. That would be better. A long letter, telling him how I feel about it all. Except I don't know how I feel. And I have no idea how Max will react. I think he'll tell me to get rid of it. But maybe he won't. Maybe he'll say, 'Great, I've always wanted a baby.' And that will be that. But somehow I don't think so.

The day before I was supposed to leave for Australia, I almost changed my mind. Max went ballistic. He accused me of never being satisfied, of always swinging from one thing to another. 'Like a bloody pendulum,' he shouted. 'Maybe one day you'll learn to stop whingeing and just get on with things.' Then he looked away and muttered something about how if I didn't watch out it would be too late for us. It left me speechless. I mean, I thought he didn't want me to go to Australia. And there he was practically pushing me out the door.

Not for the first time I consider the possibility he's trying to dump me. Maybe not coming with me is Max's roundabout way of getting the message across. Maybe I've been really, really thick about this. The thought leaves me shivering cold, even though it's too hot out here. Could I bring up a baby by myself?

David comes out carrying bags of stuff.

'Let's have a barbecue,' he says.

While David cooks dinner, I try doing his portrait. I've always found portraits difficult. People aren't static, they're fluid. One expression captures only one thing about them. The trick is to find their essence and get that down on paper but it's really hard to do. Even trying is fun though and I feel happy all of a sudden. I love the feel of the pencil in my hand. I love it how I can vary the pressure, ever so slightly and change everything. It makes me feel like a magician.

David looks over my shoulder. 'That's not bad,' he says. 'You could do that for a living.'

'I do.'

'Really! You're an artist?'

I nod, wondering why I always have difficulty saying that word – artist. Perhaps it's because most of the time I feel like a fraud. Though something is changing. Despite Nan's death and Kita's murder and me risking this trip without Max – despite all this, or maybe because of it, I'm freeing up. It's tentative and I couldn't begin to explain it, but if I can just look the other way and trust it, not fiddle or force anything, then maybe a new style will emerge.

'You're lucky,' says David, turning back to the barbecue. 'I wish I could draw.'

He serves up barbecued onions and crispy potatoes and steak that's black on the outside and too bloody inside.

'Just right,' he says.

But I make him cook mine until all the blood is gone.

He produces a bottle of red and a corkscrew.

'Here', he says. 'I owe you.'

I hesitate. Even *I* know that you're not supposed to drink when you're pregnant. But one glass won't hurt and I don't even know if I want to keep it yet.

I don't know much about Australian wine, but it's a good one, a pinot noir, smooth and woody. The nights are still warm at this time of year, so there's no need for a fire. We sit on the ground and drink it out of metal mugs. Max would have a fit, but it tastes just as good. We sit close together. Not touching, but close enough to feel each other. I feel a tug of regret that in a few days' time we'll go our separate ways.

My washing is still hanging out on the line David rigged up between two trees. I forgot to bring it in. Millie would be appalled. It makes me smile to think of it. My lacy knickers on public display. Suddenly embarrassed, I stand up and grab them off the line. Remembering how Nan took a grim satisfaction in hanging our clothes out to dry in the front garden for all to see. She said it was because it was sunny out front but really it was to make Millie suffer. We all knew that. When Nan wasn't watching I'd sneak out and rearrange things, using the tea towels to screen off the underwear from passersby. There was so much tension between them. I felt it and so did Kita. She wrote about it in her diary.

Mum's been on my mind a lot lately. This family has already got way too many secrets. I should tell mum about Storm. She needs a grandmother. If only I could go back. But what would I do with B? I don't know if I love him enough. Or if he loves me enough to cope with the things I should tell him. Keeping secrets does bad stuff to relationships. And this is a big one that's making us all wrong together. Sometimes I see B looking at me with questions in his eyes and all I can do is look away.

But I can't go back. It's too hard. Mum and Millie fighting it out. Tugging me back and forth between them. I'm not sure I want to put Storm through it all.

They were chalk and cheese.

Millie: Never be afraid. Always pay what you owe. Never steal from friends. Mum: Never do anything scary. Never owe anything. Never steal

The only thing they agreed on: 'Asking is no way to get an answer. So when they do tell, it's like being blasted in the face with a grenade.

It's as if Kita's and my lives are running parallel. Our childhoods shared. Sometimes I feel as if she's my twin, or she's me, but we just made different choices. She seems so young, not like a mother at all. I'm starting to feel older than her and that's the weirdest feeling. Then it strikes me for the first time that I am. Kita was only twenty-one when she wrote this stuff. She was young and lost and didn't know how to be a mother.

I should have got it. Walking into the room that day, hearing that stuff pouring out of Mum. It was like someone had unlocked a door into my mother and it was too late to stop it. We all had to stand there and listen to these words she couldn't take back. Then Millie's hand swinging through the air, a resounding slap and Mum storming out of the room, a stinging red patch on her cheek.

Millie told me once never to be afraid of facing up to what I am. But back then neither of us really knew what that meant.

I can't imagine what Kita heard, or understand what she was running away from, but it's apparent she wanted to hurt everyone around her, as well as herself. It's strange to think that Nan, Millie and Pop didn't even know I existed. What an awful shock it must have been for them when they found out. There would have been a phone call or a telegram, or a letter, or even a knock at the door. And then their world plunging down around them. Kita murdered. And an unexpected grandchild, brought back to the cottage to take her place. All over again. History repeating itself. Another tug of war.

I throw the clothes in the back of the van then fill up David's glass again. He's worlds away. Back with Jade I guess, wishing he had the power to rewrite history and start again. This makes me think about Max. I wonder what he's doing now. Just waking up maybe. Reaching out for me in bed. Or is there already someone else taking up my space? One of those high-heeled women he works with? Or worse, one of my artist friends. Another acquisition. That doesn't bear thinking about.

David leans back and stares up at the sky. 'Dad always used to say that the best thing in the world is a glass of wine under the stars'

When he looks at me I can see the sadness in his face, but even so I feel a twinge of envy. He really loved his father.

'When did he die?' I ask.

'Ten years ago… when I was fifteen. He was only forty-three. A truck swerved onto his side of the road and hit him …'

I can hardly imagine how awful it must have been for David to lose his dad like that. Pop was the closest thing I had to a father. I remember being fascinated with the hair in his ears. It was a gingery colour and fluffy. I would tug at it and that was his signal to tickle me. Then I'd giggle so much I couldn't breathe, except in long silent gasps, until Nan would put a stop to it as she always did. He wore brown corduroy trousers and I would rub my hand along his thigh, watching the colour change, then back again, making velvety patterns. Sometimes for a joke I would slip my feet into his massive shoes and stagger about pretending to be Pop and wondering how it must feel to have so much to balance on. Pop was kind and gentle and I loved him, but he wasn't like a father and when he died I was sad, but it didn't feel wrong, probably because he was so old. And he didn't leave a big empty space in my life.

'Are you like him?' I ask.

'Everyone says we are. Not just in looks either. Mum reckons I take after him. What with the stupid jokes and the way I love nature …'

David stops. I can see he's thinking about his dad and I don't want to interrupt. I've never studied genetics. I don't know what things are handed on to children. Hair colour, height, build … they're all obvious. Then there are gestures and personality. But what about tendencies and trauma and pain? What about fear? What about violence? Do these things leave a genetic imprint? My father is a murderer. What have I inherited? The thought scares me into filling my glass again.

'I learned a lot from Dad,' says David. 'Plus we had a good time together… We used to go fishing sometimes. I was always too impatient, but he loved it… And Dad was the one who taught me to respect the land. It's because of him I'm studying at uni.'

He laughs and gulps down the rest of the wine. His teeth and his tongue are stained red.

'And he taught me how to pick up girls. Not very effectively I might add… He sure as hell didn't teach me how to keep them.' There are cracks in his voice and I can tell he's close to tears.

'Everyone else knew except me. That was the worst bit. She didn't care… She made me into a fool.'

I reach out and take David's hand. It feels right.

What is it about hurt men that turns women into putty?

CHAPTER FIFTEEN

October 15

It's good to be back on the road again. This is a country where movement is natural. It's staying put that's wrong. The land doesn't want people to stay put, it's not generous in that way. Perching on the edge of things, filling yourself up with fear and building fences against unknown enemies. That's what the white people do. The Aborigines have got it right. I watch them walking through the bush, barefoot, treading lightly, taking only what they need, reading their world in a whole other language of signs. It's as if they're tuned in to some dimension we can't even see.

David is driving. It's the first time I've let him and it's strange being chauffeured through the Outback like this. Surrendered into someone else's hands. I've got used to being in control. It's good to be moving again too, back on the road and a passenger, just looking out the window, dreaming and not worrying. I can feel my shoulders relaxing and I like watching him drive. The way he changes gear, the muscles flexing on his arm. The other arm sitting on the window, air rushing in. All of it helps me forget the things I'm supposed to remember and the decisions I'm supposed to be making.

We stop at a roadhouse to get petrol. I can't stand the smell, so David does it, but even so I can feel the nausea building inside. We're somewhere between Alice Springs and Tennant Creek. The telephone box is sitting all by itself in the middle of nowhere. The wind blows dust in swirling eddies. The sky reaches out forever. There are no trees. Just the termite mounds and the long straight road cutting through them.

I don't let myself think about it, just dig out some coins from the bottom of my purse and dial Max's number. The ringing tone goes on and on. The answering machine hasn't switched on, so I know Max is there in his cool clean flat. So many worlds away from here. Right now I'd die for just a little piece of his world. I want to suck on it, like an ice lolly, feel it wash clean the cracks in my lips, smooth out the dryness in my throat and calm the churning in my belly.

The phone cuts out. I retrieve my money and ring again. We need to talk.

He answers quickly this time.

'Yes?' His voice is impatient, probably because it's the middle of the night over there.

'It's me,' I say.

'Storm! Where are you? What's happening?' His breath is heavy and quick as if he's been running. He wasn't asleep. I know that because the phone is next to the bed. What if there's someone else in bed with him? I can almost hear the swish of sheets. Max and someone else. I tell myself to stop thinking like this. I'm going mad, having delusions. Perhaps it's being pregnant. Kita had delusions about me being a monster. I'm pinning my delusions on Max.

'Why are you out of breath?'

'What?'

'You're panting Max.'

'I was in the shower and I ran for the phone. It's 6.30 in the morning... Storm? What's going on?'

His voice sounds strange, so English but I love the deep round notes. And I trust him again – for now. But I can't tell him I'm pregnant. Not like this when he's rushing to work.

'I'm in the middle of Australia, just above Alice Springs. I'll only be another week or two.'

'Trevor rang,' says Max. 'He's getting worried about the exhibition. I told him you had it under control.'

'Thanks,' I say, pushing more coins into the slot. Then I blurt it out. 'My father killed my mother. He's a murderer. He strangled her somewhere out here... It's awful,' I finish lamely.

'What! Your father ...'

Max is speechless for a moment and I hope he's not considering the genetic implications.

'Hell, this is getting worse and worse. Please don't go looking for him, it's too dangerous! Come home Storm, there's nothing for you over there.'

The nausea has reached my throat now and my mouth has got that awful watery feeling again.

'Soon,' I promise and hang up before I can make any other promises. Of course I'm going to look for him. And if Max was so worried he'd be here.

I get the door open just in time and throw up outside. David's walking toward me, holding out a sandwich, and some of my vomit splashes over his feet. He jumps back.

'So that's how you feel about me,' he says.

'Sorry.'

'Guess you're not hungry then.'

I shake my head and we both head to the toilets to clean up.

I'm driving this time. Faster than David. Trying not to think of Max or the sour ugly taste in my mouth. Trying to outrun all the things that are bugging me. We pass a herd of camels and I have to look twice to be sure. I thought camels only lived in the Sahara Desert.

'They're feral,' David says. 'They came over with the first Afghan workers and liked it. They do masses of damage out here. But hey, they're a multi-million-dollar industry now. People round them up and sell them to the Arabs.'

We pass a cyclist. He's wobbling dangerously all over the road, swatting ineffectually at the flies.

'Stop!' shouts David.

I pull over and David gets out. The cyclist is young and Japanese. He can't speak any English, so David mimes, shows him the fly mask, helps him put it on, then waves and jumps back in the van. The cyclist bows and smiles and bows, and cycles off in a straight line. When we pass him again he waves.

'This time of year,' says David. 'Can you believe it? Hopefully he'll live to see the day out.'

In the late afternoon sun, everything looks suddenly bloody. Not benign anymore, but murderous. Waiting. I feel a shiver of apprehension. I'm getting close to whatever it is I'm looking for but now I'm not so sure I want to find it.

We stop for the night at Devil's Marbles. The giant boulders are glowing orange and precariously balanced, as if a child has built a marble house and at the slightest touch they might tumble and roll back down again.

'Fantastic,' says David. 'They're supposed to be the Rainbow Serpent's eggs, you know. She laid them as she was passing through during the Dreamtime.'

In my guidebook it says they're *granite rocks of volcanic origin, eroded over time...* but out here it's easy to imagine a monstrous rainbow striped snake slithering through the desert and laying her eggs.

'Just think,' says David. 'In about fifty million years they'll be little pebbles.'

He climbs to the top of an egg and stands there beating his chest and yodelling. A pretty poor attempt at a Tarzan act. I can't help laughing, but I don't do a Jane and follow him up. Instead I look in Kita's diary for her entry about this place.

19 October

B and I dropped tabs and it made everything funny. Towering behind me are the Devils Marbles. They're crazy, Huge. Incongruous. It's crazy being here and not in Malvern or Sydney or even Alice Springs. B put a tape into the cassette player. We didn't worry about running the batteries down. We danced, spinning Storm between us. She was half afraid, but happy too. Our excitement rubbing off on her. I felt close to B again, the way it used to be. I lifted up my skirt and twirled, around and around, sending up clouds of dust, startling birds and lizards, confusing lines of ants. Kept twirling. Spinning right back into the kitchen at the cottage. The day Pop brought home a record player. A record too, something from Czechoslovakia - gypsy music. When he put the record on, Millie got taller. Regal. She shone. Then she started dancing. Slowly at first, letting go, bit by bit, until she was spinning. Twirling. Lifting her skirts. Mum standing back as always, tight and closed off. And Pop, with red-rimmed eyes, tapping his feet and clapping Millie on. Then Millie took my hands and spun me with her, around and around until I felt something rising within me, a wild swirling freedom and joy and power. The music changed then. It became a long slow lament, tearing at my heart. I didn't understand the words, but I felt the deep yearning in them for something, the tug. Millie stopped twirling and subsided into a heap of skirts and tears, sobbing, and wailing and tearing at her hair until Pop knelt down and took her in his arms. Then she wiped her eyes on his shoulder and laughed her anguish away. I wiped my eyes and laughed too, a hard knot bursting out of me. Then Millie looked at me. 'Kita,' she said. 'You are like me.'

Millie used to say it's in your blood. Go on the road and you'll be one again. She was right. I'm a fucking gypsy. Here I am back on the road. I dress like a gypsy. I feel like a gypsy. I do fortunes like a gypsy. What am I trying to prove? That I'm more like Millie than Mum? That one way is better than the other? That I've taken sides, and for me it has to be like this? Jesus, they're asking too much. It's not my fault. Millie or Mum, Romany or gadje. I shouldn't have to take sides. I don't want anything from any of them.

20 October

I'm still flashing with the acid, so when I saw the snake, B thought I was hallucinating. I felt my breath draw in - a silent scream. It was there all right, only a foot away from where Storm was playing. I froze. Horribly afraid of what was about to happen. Storm looked at the snake and laughed, a friendly giggle. 'Don't move,' said B. 'Hello,' Storm said to the snake as it slithered past her big toe. But she didn't reach out and it didn't strike and seconds later it disappeared into the scrub and I ran to Storm and plucked her off the ground and then she must have felt my fear because she started to cry.

We're driving along listening to Joni Mitchell. Storm sitting between us, picking her nose, snot and red dust, unaware of how close she came to dying. I watch her serious little face. She's so precious it makes me hurt inside.

I shut the diary and wipe my eyes. This bit always makes me cry. She did love me and because of this I can almost forgive her for being such a crappy mum.

It's strange to think that I've been here before. I look around, but don't remember anything. The boulders look familiar, but that's probably from a tourist brochure I've seen somewhere.

I climb up the boulders and join David.

'My mother took acid here,' I tell him. 'Twenty-six years ago.'

'Wow!' he says. 'That's weird.'

We stand together looking out to a horizon that seems forever away across the flat desert plains. I turn in a full circle and see that it's the same everywhere and for the first time I *really* feel how tiny I am in comparison to this. How awful to be left alone out here in the desert. I try to push away the thought, but it comes anyway. *I was.* The cruelty of it hits me hard. He left me out here, a two-year-old, with a dead mother and nothing else. With that thought comes a dread which makes me reach out and clasp David's hand. We watch the sun sinking, the heat and the harsh light draining from it as it turns from blinding white to glowing orange and then dull blood red.

We share a big tin of baked beans for dinner, but I'm not really hungry. David looks at me curiously, but he doesn't say anything. I wonder if he feels sad that tomorrow we'll be going our separate ways. Part of me wants to draw it out a bit longer, but that would be crazy. We've both got messed-up lives to sort out.

I climb into bed early, but can't sleep. Tonight is a full moon and maybe that's the problem. I'm just wearing a T-shirt and knickers, but I still feel too hot and really claustrophobic in the van. I envy David his cool space outside, looking up at the stars and the moon. I toss and turn for ages, and in the end can't bear it any longer. When I'm sure David's asleep I take my mattress out and put it on the ground. Then I lie on my back, looking up at the stars and the silhouette of the huge round boulders. The whole world is illuminated in a soft milky glow. The shadows are glistening silver. The stars are pale, washed out by the moonlight. There's a grainy element to it, like blowing a photograph up too big for itself. I do some sketches by the moonlight, letting the pencils sweep across the page, trying to capture the grain and the silver shadows. Then I lie down again, waiting for sleep, but I'm too energised by the night. Out here I'm acutely aware of my body opening up to the gentle caress of warm night air. I wish I dared to be naked.

'Don't move.' David's voice is quiet and urgent.

I tense. Knowing he's looking at me and wondering how long he's been there. I should be angry, but the urgency in his voice fills me with fear and I freeze. In a moment I feel it, not slimy wet like I'd always imagined, but dry and soft. A sort of scaly slow slithering as the snake slides right across my foot. It must feel my heart pounding and the panicky rise and fall of my belly. I'm holding my breath now, but in a minute my lungs will explode and startle it and then… It must sense my fear because it pauses for a second, right there. I'm afraid to look at it, afraid to take my eyes off the sky. Then it moves on and away, fast now, fleeing, but I'm still frozen, staring up at the sky. Lost in fear.

'It's gone.' David's voice is close now, but I want it closer. I hold up my arms, like a child and he takes them, lifting me up to him. He holds me tight while I cry. I nuzzle in under his arms, breathing in his sweat. The smell is beautiful. In this moonlight I want him.

I seek out his mouth. We kiss. A long slow exploratory kiss. He lifts my T-shirt over my head and then holds my heavy breasts, weighing them in his hands. Then he moves down and gently takes a nipple in his mouth. When we make love, our skin sticks together. He feels strange. I'm used to Max's round hairy chest, not sticky-out ribs and smooth skin. All the shapes are different, and the textures. I think about Max. Not in my head. It's my body that thinks of him. Reconstructs him from a physical memory. And I wonder if David is feeling the same. If some part of him is pretending that I'm Jade.

Afterwards we lie next to each other, our fingers linked loosely together, not saying anything for ages. There will be consequences, I know it, but right now I feel too good to care.

'Tell me about the place you grew up,' says David.

I roll over and draw a picture in the dirt with my finger. 'It's the sort of house little children draw in kindy,' I say. 'Two windows up, two windows down, a door in the middle. A path out the front, smoke twisting out of the chimney, a tree at the side… There. Just like that.'

And all the while David's fingers are running lightly across the skin of my back, playing it, like I imagine you would play a harp.

'There's even honeysuckle growing up the wall,' I say, missing it as I speak. The smell, and the feel of the old stone walls. 'Sometimes I'd sit in the field opposite. Grundy's Meadow it was called. And I'd try to look at the house as if I was a stranger. You know, like for the first time.'

I roll over and David's fingers trace patterns on my front, around my belly button and then my nipples which by now are hard. Wanting all over again.

'I've stopped believing in my childhood. It used to be an anchor, something certain that let me function out in the world. It made me real. But when Nan died it felt as if everything changed. Nothing was how I thought it was. So now who's to say any of it really happened? Maybe I dreamed it, then drew in all the little details that make things seem real. Drawing was my best subject at school... Maybe that's why I took up painting. To kind of hold things together, because underneath everything, I knew there were fault lines and one day I might fall down one.'

I watch David for a moment. He's watching his finger tracing patterns on me. His head moving too, ever so slightly. Head and finger together. They look so graceful. Playing out a slow sensual dance.

'Do you think I'm crazy?'

His finger stops. He looks at me for a while. Squinting hard, as if he's trying to make me out. Pretending to concentrate. Then his face breaks into the broad grin with the crinkled-up crow's feet. 'Nah. No more than anyone else.'

I laugh. 'Well that's good news.'

Our eyes meet and we can't pull them apart even though it's getting embarrassing. David's eyes are the same colour as Max's, but they're completely different. I push the thought away, I can't think about Max now.

'You have singing eyes,' I say. 'I always fall for eyes.'

David smiles briefly and then it's gone. 'What are you going to do?' he asks. 'About this.'

His hand is on my belly and I'm shocked that he knows. Though I shouldn't be. I've dropped enough clues. I look up again at the stars, searching for the Southern Cross. Trying to find my way again. I could open up to David now and tell him everything. He wants me to. I could tell him how exciting it is to have a life growing inside you. And I could say how afraid I am – of the responsibility, of being a bad mother, of what's in my blood, and of telling Max.

David is looking at me searchingly. He wants to know. He cares. I can read these things in his eyes. And the thought of that makes me want to cry. But David doesn't know anything about Max. It's strange how I've told him so much about my life, but I've never once mentioned Max. Did I know this would happen between us? Did I plan it? Would David have made love with me if he knew about Max?

I want to tell David everything, but I have to push him away.

I tear my eyes away from his and look up at the sky again, more lost than ever.

'I don't know,' I say finally. 'None of the options look attractive right now.'

This sounds hard, like mind your own business, and it's not what I mean, but I can't find the words to explain all the conflicts inside me.

David sighs and takes his hand away from my belly. He's distancing himself and I don't blame him.

'Well,' he says, 'it's official. Your life's more fucked up than mine.'

CHAPTER SIXTEEN

Driving into Tennant Creek the next morning, everything is different between us. David doesn't try to talk or make me laugh. He just sits there looking miserable, with his feet up and his eyes shut. Blocking me out. I stare ahead at the road, plagued with fear and embarrassment. What if he wishes it never happened? That would be too awful.

There are things I want to say, but I can't bring myself to speak. It's always been easy talking to David, not like Max who I'm careful with. Yet now there's something important to say and I can't. It's so bloody frustrating. I keep asking myself the same question: How is it possible for something to be right and wrong like that, at the same time?

All morning it hangs in the air between us. In Tennant Creek we stop for a drink and check the map. It's only then I realise how close we are to Threeways. In less than an hour we'll be parting. That gives me a jolt. It's too sudden. But when I turn the keys in the ignition, nothing happens. The whole thing is dead. I try again. Then David has a go.

'Maybe we've over heated,' he suggests.

'This is a VW. There's no water.'

'Yeah, but it can still overheat. The air's supposed to cool it, so if it's too hot, it seizes. Then the engine blows.'

There's a mechanic right near where we've stopped, but we have to wait most of the day before he can look at it. So we eat ice-creams in the shade, then walk around, looking in the shops, having coffee and sharing a newspaper... killing time and talking about things that mean nothing. There are lots of pubs in this town and they've all got metal grates on their windows and doors, like prisons. It's not clear if it's to keep people in or out.

Finally the mechanic has a look.

'Ah.' He grabs a hammer and bashes it somewhere underneath. 'It'll start now,' he says, waving away my money.

And it does.

'Well,' says David, 'I reckon that's the fastest fix I've ever seen.'

Even so, it's too late to drop him off at Threeways so we book into the caravan park and try to celebrate our last night together with a bottle of wine. David does another barbecue and I make a sad-looking salad with tinned beetroot that makes everything look bloody.

The wine is a warm Riesling with a sharp edge.

'Like battery acid,' David says, drinking it anyway.

He drags his mattress out and I climb in the van. And that's that. Except he sits up late finishing off the bottle and I lie still for hours, pretending I'm asleep.

In the morning David makes coffee, both of us aware that this is probably the last time we'll ever share that ritual. We sit together, drinking it slowly, putting off the moment. But we're miles away from each other. Further apart than we've ever been. Already being pulled in different directions. There's nothing more we can do to draw this out and I know we shouldn't try, but the sadness I feel is a solid force around my heart.

Even when we say goodbye we hold each other tentatively. David is looking at the ground, making lines in the dirt with his toe and it hurts that he can't even bring himself to look at me. But then he does and I realise he's braver than me.

'I'm really glad it happened,' he says, and suddenly everything's okay again.

'Me too,' I tell him. 'Thank you – for everything.'

I open my sketchbook and carefully tear out the portrait I drew of David. Then I write on the bottom corner – *with love from Storm* – and give it to him.

He wraps his arms around me and we kiss long and hard on the lips, savouring the taste and feel of each other. And storing it. A farewell kiss that doesn't want to end. When I get back into the van, David stands near the window and points at the dashboard. Next to the plastic thorny devil is a plastic snake.

'A king brown to remember me by.' He puts his hand out and touches my arm. 'Hey, he says. 'Good luck.'

'Thanks. You too.'

I leave him standing there at Threeways, next to a sign that says no hitchhiking. Then I turn right onto the Barkly Highway and straight into the blinding glare of the morning sun.

I drive fast, squinting into the sun and trying not to think about David or the feeling of dread that's building inside me. At first I think it's just morning sickness and the sun in my eyes, but then I realise there's something else too. A kind of vertigo has set in. Maybe these endless flat expanses are giving me the same dizzying vertigo I sometimes feel at the top of the Malverns. The desire to jump. Just to see. To step over a line, with no way back. My hands are slippery on the steering wheel. I can feel my fingers twitching with temptation. They're telling me to give the wheel a little twist. Plunge off the road or into the path of a road train. Just to see if it's real out there. Because I can't tell anymore.

After a while the feeling gets so strong I have to stop and walk away from the van, just to make sure I don't give in to these bizarre temptations. The earth is over-baked, spread with a thin line of cracks like the bread Nan sometimes left in the oven for hours on end, until it shrivelled and hardened and cracked, while she got lost in something else. On her knees in the garden pulling weeds, miles away and then, 'Oh lord, the bread!' I haven't thought about Nan properly for days. Perhaps that's what happens; the dead just slip your mind bit by bit, fading away like a summer tan. But suddenly she's so real I could almost reach out and help her up off her creaking knees.

Then I'm plunged back here, into this landscape of death, littered with dazzling white bones. The world moving under my feet. Nothing solid. Nothing certain. Except the hideous stench of the bloated corpse twenty feet away. More road train kill. I've seen dozens of them today. Swollen cows and kangaroos. Legs sticking straight up in the air, caricatures of themselves. Out here death doesn't seem to mean very much. The world moves on.

This urge to step over a line has shaken me. I don't trust myself anymore. I have to be careful and concentrate harder, so I don't give in to a sudden whim. But there's something else that's been playing on my mind. When Bill wrapped his hands round my mother's neck and squeezed, he was stepping over a line too. He wasn't insane. It must have been a whim, or a surge of fury or an idea that he'd got fixed in his head. It's made me think. Maybe I am my father's daughter after all. And that's not a nice thought.

Things get worse when I climb back in the van and sit on my sunglasses. They snap, right in the middle. I try to perch each half on my nose, but they keep slipping off. Bugger. I can't drive into the sun without them so I'll need to wait until it gets a bit higher. There's no shade here and the temperature inside the van is suffocating. But when I look at the map there's nothing for miles and miles and I can't remember the last tree I saw. So I open all the windows, put on my fly mask and have dry biscuits and warm water for brunch.

I've been reading the diary so much it's starting to look tattered. Yesterday's pages are stuck together where I spilt coffee on them. I carefully unpeel them and turn to where we are now. Kita's trip was getting pretty weird. They were off their faces most of the time and it's hard to accept that Kita could have been so irresponsible. How could I have been so precious and yet so neglected? It doesn't make sense.

29 October

We're taking heaps of acid and I can't tell much what's real and what isn't. It's getting hotter. Too hot to eat much. B's drinking a lot. He drives along with a beer jammed between his legs, passing joints back and forth over Storm's head. So out of it. We're here and not here. Just a pressing heat, a big sky and music. The world out there is huge, but our world seems to be shrinking down and down. It's closing in on us.

4 November

Threeways is nothing except a turn-off. We can keep going or we can turn right. I wanted to go on, up to Darwin. But B said it's too hot there, that the rainy season is coming and we'd be better off in Cairns. He's probably right, and I know he wants to see his sister, but I'm not comfortable with this road. Or with Kate and her sneaky ways.

We're driving into the morning sun. Blinding. And hot with the sun beating down on our laps. Even the wind is hot. So we start out later each day, waiting until the sun is above us. I don't like this road. It's like an evil path.

There's something bad about it. Rotten. Since we turned onto the Barkly Highway things have changed. There's an atmosphere. An edge. Something menacing, either in my head or out there. Can places be bad? Can roads be bad?

This morning I tried to read the cards but they were cloudy. I don't know what this means. But it left me feeling strange about things. All day I've wanted to hold Storm close. Of course she doesn't understand and it's so hot she wriggles and whinges until I let her go. But I don't want to let her out of my sight. Is it me or her or B? I don't know, but something is going to give. When we stopped at a roadhouse to fill up, I went into the toilets and stared at my face in the mirror, looking for something... there must be some sign. It has to manifest itself in some way. But I can't see it. Not in me, or in Storm. Not yet.

6 November

This heat is grinding me down, into rocks... pebbles... blood stained dust, until I am so fine that the wind picks me up, spreading me thinly into the atmosphere, particles tossing and turning until it tires of its game and lets me settle, slowly rocking toward the ground. In my head I can't shake the image of death and erosion. Ashes to ashes, dust to... desert, out here where there are no clouds, just the sun washing out the sky and me spreading myself wide like the horizon and wanting B to fuck me, hard and slowly, pushing right through me until my bones break apart, so that I can feel the tearing, like when Storm was born. I want to lie down with him in the dirt, and feel it scorching my skin, feel the sun burning through, sizzling my flesh, feel the bull ants crawling across, nibbling, until there is nothing left, just dry bleached white bones.

B says I'm sick in the head. But I just want to feel - everything. I'm greedy for everything. I want to open my arms and take it all in.

7 November

It doesn't feel right anymore.

I'm trying to pinpoint the exact moment when everything changed for Kita. The thing that made her lose herself in acid. Though maybe it was the acid itself that did it. But I imagine there was a moment when a shadow crossed into her world. Everything would have been the same, but different too, like she was seeing life from an odd angle. To make it better all she had to do was shift back a few degrees, but she couldn't. I wonder if she woke up one morning and felt it creeping in, or if it was more definitive than that, something Bill said or did. A threat. Or it could have been something about me, a sense of despair about the permanency of being a mother. Nan told me once that even when your children go away or die, you're still their mother, you can't take it back. Or maybe it was a genetic thing. An inheritance of some disorder. Millie Madness. Or the curse Millie always warned about. A steady seeping dissatisfaction tugging at her. It might have been a gradual thing, a surreptitious, slow darkening, creeping up from behind. Kita blamed it on this road.

She called it a menacing evil place. I don't know if a road can really be bad, but I feel it too.

I drive on. The sun is above me now, so it isn't as bad without sunglasses. Still the sky and the road are glary and I can feel a headache starting. Without David to talk to, without his jokes and his routines, everything is getting strange. All I'm doing is sitting here, holding a steering wheel, putting my foot on a pedal, and this machine is hurtling me through space towards the next twist in my mother's story. I'm not even sure I want to turn any more corners and find out what horrible thing is at the end.

As I approach the Queensland border the desert is turning into dry yellow grasslands. There are more cattle and a sense of order. It's a relief to drive into a new state. Though I'm not sure why - a punctuation point and the pleasure of starting something afresh, though there's no actual difference, just a half-hearted welcome sign riddled with bullet holes. I stop in the next town, another tiny place built around a road and a fuel stop. I wonder about the psychology of that. How would it feel to grow up in a place where the focus is a throughway. I guess it would feel like you were missing out on something.

The road is lined with gleaming road trains, some so big that I'm only as tall as their wheels. I drive into a fuel station. The attendant is wearing greasy overalls.

'G,day, he says. 'You want me to fill 'er up?'

'Yes, please.'

'Good weather, we're having, hey.'

'Yes,' I say, feeling the sweat dripping down my back. He wants to talk. I don't. The smell of the petrol is making me gag.

He looks at me curiously. 'You travelling by yourself?'

Straightaway I can feel the tension in my shoulders. Why is he asking this? I want to tell him to mind his own business, but instead I just nod.

'You make sure you've got plenty of water then. You don't wanna get caught short out here.'

'Thanks,' I say and go into the roadhouse for something to eat. The restaurant is air-conditioned which is a relief, but the television is on full blast and the air is thick with smoke and big men's talk. I get one or two wolf-whistles, but there's rugby showing and they're more interested in that, so I manage to sit in a corner and eat my greasy chips in peace.

Kita came to this town. I wonder if it's the same roadhouse, or a later version of the same thing. Either way I imagine it wouldn't have changed much. I open up her diary and read about where I am, or at least Kita's version of it.

8 November

B's acting really weird. He tried to sell me tonight. In this truckie town on the border. We were sitting in a cafe, having chips for tea. He was out of his head and winding himself up about something. Maybe he thought the guys at the next table were eyeing me up because he got all agitated and called over, egging them on, 'Have her... go on... she's a good fuck.' I didn't wait to find out if it was a joke or not. Storm and I got back in the car and locked the doors. When B staggered back much later he couldn't get in and stood there ranting and raving, threatening to break the windows. Then he started sobbing. 'Sorry, I'm so sorry...' When I still didn't open the door he lay down on the ground and passed out. Arsehole.

There's something wrong with the car. It wouldn't start this morning and B was swearing and kicking the tyres and getting nowhere with it. He's stiff and sore from spending the night outside and he's got a filthy hangover.

Serve him right. He wasn't any use, so I fiddled with the alternator and got it going again. B was furious. 'For Christ's sake leave something for me,' he shouted. He hates it that I'm good at fixing things.

10 November

The car's still not right and we had to go slow all the way to Mt Isa. It's a shitty mining town, full of smoky smelters and hotted-up cars, but it's big enough to get our car looked at. The mechanic's name is Mick. He was wearing these tiny tight shorts (B says they're called stubbies) and a vest and nothing else, except tattoos up and down his arms. I'm still angry with B so I played up to Mick a bit. Stood near him and leaned over into the bonnet, letting him see right down my top and then let my hand brush up against the front of his shorts. He didn't move away, just kept on peering with a big smile on his face. Then B stepped in and started talking engines with Mick.

We've booked into a caravan park for a few days while we wait for the car. The sky is getting heavy with clouds. They're pretty dramatic looking, all dark and brooding. Storm and I play games looking for shapes in them, dragons and birds and funny faces. They look like rain clouds to me and I wish they were, just to relieve things a bit, but the locals say they won't break. Not yet. Though someone told B that further north the crocodiles are laying high up the river banks. That means a bad wet season and probably an early one. I can't wait to get up to Karumba, right on the gulf, and then Cairns. I can't wait to see crocodiles.

11 November

Storm's covered in mosquito bites. It looks like chicken pox or something. Poor thing's scratching away all night, whimpering. She's got prickly heat too, and she won't sleep. B's fed up with her. Says, Christ, it's enough just coping with the heat, let alone a bloody whingeing child. And sometimes I'm scared he'll hit her. But then all of a sudden he's kind again, and crawls around on all fours with her sitting on his back screaming with delight. I can't predict it anymore. Every reaction is over the top. Maybe it's just the heat because we're all bad tempered.

I jump, startled as a huge roar fills the roadhouse. Someone must have scored. For a moment I think of Max, in his flat in London, sitting on his leather couch with a designer beer, watching rugby and shouting 'YES!' Worlds apart, yet not so different after all.

I finish my chips and leave. It's probably best to get out before the rugby finishes and they all look for something else to watch. The van won't start. It's the second time in two days. I hope this isn't the beginning of the end. Max always says that once they start being unreliable they never stop. Like people, he says, though I'd rather not think about that.

I try again, but nothing happens. It looks like there are a lot of 'fix-it' men about, but I don't want to go back inside and ask for help. I don't want to be a useless female and give all these men a chance to strut their stuff. So I grab the hard piece out of the tyre-changing kit and try to remember which bit the mechanic bashed. Feeling like a complete idiot, I hammer a few times in different places, just to make sure. The petrol station attendant is watching and so are a couple of other men, feet planted firmly on the ground, legs apart, arms crossed over their bellies and wearing amused faces. Perhaps they mean well, but the overall effect is sinister.

One of them strolls over. 'Need a hand love?'

'I'm fine, thanks,' I say, getting back in and praying that it will work. I'm holding my breath while the engine turns over. It grabs. Yes! I give them all a triumphant wave. There, that wipes the knowing smiles off their faces. Even so, as I drive back onto the road, they can't resist calling out:

'Can I come too?'

'Take me with you… pleeeaaase.'

CHAPTER SEVENTEEN

I've made all the classic mistakes. Being too ambitious about getting to Mt Isa in a day. Then when I knew I couldn't, letting the way I feel about this road take precedence over practical good sense. So I've kept wasting time, humming and haaing over where to stop and thinking there'd be something better further on. Now I'm exhausted and have to keep pinching myself so I don't nod off. I've got to the dangerous point where I feel like I'm playing one of those racing car games in amusement parlours. It doesn't matter if you crash, you just put some more coins in and start again. I'm looking for a rest stop. The alternative is to keep driving to Mount Isa. But I'm too tired.

Twenty minutes later I find one. It's pretty unattractive. There's rubbish dumped everywhere and the door of the pit toilet has been ripped off its hinges. Inside there's dirty toilet paper on the floor and too many flies. I'd be better off going behind a bush. There's no one else around, which is good. And bad. I'd feel a bit safer if there was a nice old couple camped just across the way. It I lock all the doors I should be okay, but I still wish David was with me. I don't know if it's because I've got used to having him around, or if it's this road, but I'm spooked. Maybe I'll just have a rest and then risk driving at night for once.

I can't make up my mind what to do, so I don't pop the top, just connect the gas and make tea, even though it's awkward doing stuff in the van, all bent over. Then I wander over to the nearest picnic table with my mug and Kita's diary. The table is splattered with bird shit and graffiti - Nazi swastikas, and right in the middle in big letters someone has gouged the words 'White Power' into the wood. I suppose this is what David means by rednecks. It's like there's a whole load of ugly hate and violence hovering about just under the surface, waiting to explode.

There are only a few more entries left in my mother's diary. Tomorrow will be the last day of her journey. After that I'm on my own. Maybe this is one of the things that's spooking me. I already feel too alone out here.

12 November

I'm thinking about death a lot. Thinking about all the Aborigines that died. And the Rom and the Jews too. Thinking how all those Romany deaths are in me, how my genes are loaded with Romany history. My blood feels heavy with them, and the other thing that's sent me hurtling across the world, trying to keep ahead of it. Though you can't keep ahead of something that's in you. I can't even say it, can't even get my mouth around the words, so maybe it isn't Nan or Millie's fault that they couldn't say it either and I had to find out for myself. I wonder if Storm will be heavy with all these things too. Maybe she'll be let off the hook somehow. That's what I'd wish for if I could. Peace for Storm. Contentment. None of this restless wildness that takes me over and sends me into self-destruct. There's my blessing little one, that you can find a way through all this. Not like Mum who's shut herself off, or Millie, trapped between two worlds. It's my turn to carry the weight of secrets, for Storm's sake.

I study Storm's face while she's asleep. It's so peaceful and certain and trusting. I stroke her cheek with my finger and she stirs ever so slightly and smiles a little half-smile. I try to imagine her grown up, what she'll look like, She's like me, people say, but I'm not so sure, there are bits that remind me of her father. Some of her gestures, little ways she has, and the eyes - at least the shape of them. Storm gives me hope. Maybe we can find a way through this together. Maybe we can stay friends.

The whoosh and squeal of air brakes makes me jump. A road train is pulling up on the far side of the rest stop. I tense up and watch it for a minute, but there's no movement, so I relax. The driver's probably having a kip.

I look at the diary again, wishing I knew what Kita was running from. I can't imagine anything so bad that she would turn away from Millie and Nan and Pop like that. Her life was falling apart. She was afraid. And trapped too, with nowhere to go. Yet even then she found the space to bless me. Despite every stupid decision she made, I love her for this blessing. I can judge Kita's actions, but I won't condemn them. There is a difference, I'm sure of it.

13 November

We've run out of acid and B's drinking beer like water. He disappeared for hours last night and came back with a black eye and a swollen lip. There was perfume on him too, but I didn't care. Things really are falling apart between us. He wouldn't tell me what happened, he just looked edgy and said he wants to move on. But we can't.

Today he wouldn't get out of bed, so I took Storm in the pram and walked over to see about the car, which is taking forever because Mick's had to order a part in from Brisbane. When I got there Storm was asleep so I parked her in the shade and went looking for Mick. He had his head stuck up under a car, whistling along to a crackly radio. When I called out he emerged from under the car and reached for a cloth to wipe some of the muck from his hands. I really was just going to ask about the car, but his hands caught me, I couldn't take my eyes off them, they were so big and messy and certain. Above all, certain. I wanted to know the feel of them. So when he showed me under the bonnet I let him reach in under my shirt. I liked how coarse his skin felt against mine. Then we were fucking. We didn't kiss or anything. It wasn't tender like that, the way it used to be with B. We just both had the need. Afterwards my shirt was filthy and I had a greasy mark right down one cheek and dirty hand marks on my hips where he held me. Neither of us said a word. He wiped at my face with the filthy cloth and went back to work. I started pushing Storm back up the hill. 'It should be ready tomorrow,' he shouted after me. When I got back B was still in bed. 'Tomorrow,' I said, throwing my shirt in the wash bag. 'You can pick it up.'

Maybe Leo was right about Kita. She was desperate to be close to people, but then when it happened, she hit out. Every sexual transgression, every argument, every time she took acid or smoked too many joints - all of it a sort of insurance to make sure she'd push someone away. Maybe eventually she would have pushed me away too. I suppose she did in a way. Being murdered like that. I know it wasn't her choice, but even so, it was a betrayal of sorts. She abandoned me and on one level I'm angry with her. She should have looked after herself better. For my sake if not her own.

I take a sip of tea, then spit it out, fly and all. For a few minutes I have to fight the nausea that's rising up again. So far I've only been sick once today. I'm distracted by a high-pitched buzzing in my ear and slap myself hard on the cheek. It's dusk and the mosquitoes are out. I can feel the itching already around my ankles.

Then I'm startled by the sound of a door slamming. I'd forgotten about the truck. A man has got out. I assume he'll go over to the toilets, but he turns towards me instead. Jesus, he's coming over here. It would be stupid to get up and run now. The chances are he'll be friendly, but even so my heart is thumping in my ears as I watch him approach. He's wearing shorts that sit low under his belly, a filthy T-shirt and flip-flops on his feet. He's also wearing a big grin and holding a can of beer. When he gets closer I can see his eyes. I don't like them. They're shifty, and a bit glazed, like he's on something. And they're running about all over me.

'G'day,' he says.

'Hi.' I'm not about to launch into conversation, but I don't want to offend him either.

'So what's a good-looking girl like you doing all alone in a place like this?'

It's the sort of line that ought to be funny, but it sends me into a panic. I can feel the sweat breaking out in my palms. My whole body tightens into a tense ball.

I force myself to look him right in the eye.

'I'm not alone. David's in the toilet,' I say, wincing at how English I sound.

He raises one eyebrow. 'Saw you back there at the roadhouse.'

I look at him cautiously, knowing that he knows and not knowing what to do about it.

'Where you heading then? he asks.

'Cairns,' I tell him.

'Oh well, I'll be seeing you.'

'Bye.'

He saunters away and I wait for a minute, trying to look casual, listening to the lazy *slap, slap* of his flip-flops. The dark has crept in on me. I really need a wee, but I'm too scared. I shut the diary and pour out the rest of my tea, all the time trying to remember where the keys are. Hoping they're still in the ignition. The van's not far away but I only get about halfway there when the truckie reappears. I haven't heard him coming and it's so sudden I can't help jumping.

'Thought you might wanna beer, hey.'

'No thanks.'

I keep walking, trying to look calm. As if keeping up the pretence will make it not happen. But when he reaches out and grabs my arm he's not being friendly.

He puts his face right up close to mine. 'So where's your boyfriend now, hey? Fallen in the dunny?'

When he laughs his gut wobbles up and down. He smells of insect repellant. He pulls me even closer, so I'm squeezed right into his gut.

'Fuck off,' I shout, kneeing him in the balls. Then I twist free and run.

'You bitch! I'll have you… '

He's chasing me but I get to the van first, throw myself in the side door and pull it shut, just as he gets one hand in. There's a tug of war. He's stronger, but I'm scared and I push with everything I've got and trap his fingers until he's yowling. I let go briefly, just long enough for him to get his fingers out, then slam the door shut again and lock it. Thank God the back door's locked already. I hurl myself into the front and lock both doors.

The keys are in the ignition. I turn them, pumping the accelerator, revving the engine, praying it will start.

'You fucking cunt,' he's shouting.

'Oh God, Oh God, get it together,' I'm muttering frantically. Then the engine catches and I remember to take the hand brake off, but my foot's right down and that's making the wheels spin.

'Fuck off, Fuck off, Fuck off!' I'm shouting at him like a bloody mantra. Then I lift my foot a bit and screech off too fast. The fucking bastard. I wish I'd run him down. I wish I'd killed him.

I drive on and on. The road gets windy, which makes it harder but I don't care. I'm going too fast and the van leans dangerously around every curve. But I'm not about to slow down. I've got visions of him coming after me. A bloody great road train chasing me down. The adrenalin is pumping through me. I'm scared. But I'm angry too. At what he tried to do to me. And I'm angry that even though I got away, his ugly mean face will always be there, and his hands and the awful smell of him. Just because I'm a woman. Just because some bloody man wasn't there to protect me. I don't want to be scared. I don't want to be afraid of empty spaces and dark alleys and strange men. And I don't intend to tiptoe through life, just because of some stupid bastard with a big belly and a twitchy cock. This is exactly what Max warned me about. I can practically hear his 'I told you so'. Okay, I tell myself, that's it for roadside stops, from now on its caravan parks or motels. From now on I'll watch my back.

The clouds have built up, covering the moon, so it's too dark. Sometimes I see eyes caught in the headlights, flashing green or red, but I never see what's behind them. When a car comes the other way I forget to switch off high beam and they flash their lights. Stupidly I do it too late, after they've passed.

In Mt Isa there are street lights and traffic lights and neon signs around the shops. I'm confused by it all and not sure where to go. The main street into town is lined with motels. In the end I choose one of the newer ones, not caring how expensive it is, so long as it isn't seedy. I fish around in the glove box for my credit card, then climb awkwardly out of the van, my limbs stiff with shock and a long day of driving.

It's past 10 p.m. so I ring the after-hours bell and wait. Eventually a man comes and lets me in. He takes my details and I give him my credit card, but my hands are still shaking and I have to sign twice.

'Are you okay?' he asks.

'Fine,' I say and my voice sounds shaky too. 'Just tired. I've been driving all day.'

He hands over the key, but he looks concerned.

I lock the motel door behind me and go straight to the bathroom. In the mirror my eyes are red and wild. I take off my clothes and stand under the shower until the whole room steams up. Afterwards I wrap the towel around me and climb into bed. But when I shut my eyes, he's there. So I keep them open for as long as I can, staring up at the ceiling. Trying not to think.

CHAPTER EIGHTEEN

I'm dragged out of a heavy black sleep by a persistent knocking, and have to struggle to work out where I am. The radio clock says it's already 11 a.m.

'Who is it?' I call.

'The cleaner. It's past check out time. I gotta clean your room.'

'Oh, sorry. I won't be long.'

I pull on some clothes, splash some water on my face and leave the key in the door on my way out. Driving into the centre of town, I'm still bleary eyed and slow and it's hard to negotiate traffic lights and lots of cars. The fuel gauge is down past empty and I realise with a cold shiver that I could have run out anytime on that stretch of road last night.

I stop at a roadhouse and fill up with fuel. It drips over my hands, making me want to puke. Then I sit in the tacky cafe and order a sandwich to stave off the morning sickness, and a coffee to wake me up. The cafe smells of fatty, greasy things and burnt cooking oil, and the sandwich is squishy white bread with too much margarine and revolting pressed ham inside. But the coffee isn't too bad and I sip slowly on it, trying to quell my insides and get my head working again. I'm in Mt Isa, Kita's last stop, only an hour or so away from her death. I open her diary.

14 November

B came back with the car late this afternoon. Said it was cheaper than he expected, but that doesn't help us much. We're almost out of money anyway. There's no way B can get a job in his state and there's not much I can do either. I can't imagine anyone wanting their fortune's told out here. I'm also starting to feel trapped. I don't want to stay in this town and I don't want to stay with B. The only thing left between us is the memory of what we once had. But B doesn't realise that yet. He's clinging on to his idea of us and that makes me feel guilty because he still hasn't got a clue. It's a big lie and we need to sort things out.

It must be the bright fluoro lights in this cafe, but when I turn the page I notice for the first time, a ragged edge of ripped paper, right up close to the binding. Someone has torn out a page. I wonder who. And I wonder why. Maybe Kita tore it out to keep Bill from seeing something too awful. But why that page and not the one about the mechanic, or Leo, or about leaving Bill? What could be worse than those things? I wonder if Bill read Kita's diary. Did she hide it or carry it about with her all the time, so he couldn't? Or did some part of her want him to find it? Did she leave it lying around? An open invitation for a snoop. If she did, he might have read something awful and tore out that page in a fit of fury. Then again, it might have been Nan. She ripped their photo in two, so why not a page in her daughter's diary? Or maybe it was more innocent than that. Just two-year-old me, being mischievous. My scribbles are all over the place. First artworks, an out-of-control pen wobbling across pages, right through Kita's words and her elaborate doodles. I wonder about that. If I could translate those doodles, I'd probably find out all her secrets.

> *I'll leave him soon. We'll see this through, but when we get to Cairns I'll take Storm and go. Maybe he knows that already, because he keeps looking over at me. Nervous. As if he wants to see inside my head. Sometimes I'm scared he will, because there are things in there I don't ...*

There's a bit missing here where the page has been torn. Then:

> *... this morning B slapped Storm for nothing. Of course she burst into tears. I grabbed her away and shouted at B not to ever hit my daughter again. 'Yours?' he shouted and poked me hard in the chest. 'Your daughter? She's mine too and don't you fucking forget it.' Then he pounded at the car with his fists and made a dent in the bonnet and that got Storm really howling. B looked at her and burst into tears. He's getting scary.*

> *The road has changed. It's windy and hilly now and there are some trees too for a change. It's a relief after months of straight roads and empty horizons. But it still feels all wrong and I can't do anything about it because I don't know what it is. I feel like a rabbit caught in headlights.*

That's it. The last entry. Now I'm left me with nothing but blanks and the ragged edge of a missing page. I close the diary and finish the dregs of my coffee. Mary Kathleen is less than an hour's drive away. It's time to get some answers.

I forget to buy new sunglasses in Mt Isa and have to drive squinting into the sun. Kita was strangled somewhere along this stretch of road, between Mt Isa and Cloncurry, but I don't know where. I expect it was close to Mary Kathleen, where Edith and Jack Burton live. I scan the sides of the road, half expecting to see a cross or a monument, something to pinpoint the spot. But there's only the usual crushed cans, broken glass and rotting carcasses. When I try to imagine a two-year-old child wandering along this road it sends shivers up and down my spine.

I miss the turn-off to Mary Kathleen and have to drive back. I go over in my head all the things I've planned to say to the Burtons, the questions I need answered, but I'm so nervous I can't even decide what to say when they answer the door. *Hi, I'm Storm*, I guess, but what about the tone? Should it be light and friendly, or serious? I practice different ways of saying the same three words but the more I do it, the more fake they sound.

There's always the possibility they won't live there anymore. Twenty-six years is a long time. They might be dead too, or moved on. In a way that would be a relief. I wouldn't have to face things, just keep on driving. Though there's still Bill's sister, Kate, just outside of Cairns. That's if she still lives there. Leo wasn't sure. And Bill himself. If I can find him. If I want to. I keep changing my mind about that.

There's no sign, just a crumbling bitumen road, full of potholes. I drive slowly, trying to avoid the holes and worrying about punctures because I don't have a clue how to change a tyre. I drive back and forth, thinking maybe I've missed it. But the town simply isn't there. Mary Kathleen has disappeared.

I follow the road to where it stops being bitumen and drive up a bumpy dirt track. At one point I'm so worried about getting stuck, that I stop the van and walk the rest of the way. Eventually the track ends above a lake filled with shockingly blue water. The lake is in a huge, stepped amphitheatre that has been carved out of the hill. The walls are wet striped, with leaking metallic oranges and blacks and blues in a gorgeous abstract pattern. I stand on the edge, watching the wind blow soft patterns across the surface of the water and trying to shake off the sinister feeling that the whole town is hiding somewhere. Watching.

Finally understanding dawns on me. This is an old uranium mine, closed down years ago by the looks of it. When the map said 'a former uranium mining town', it meant a former town. God, that's crazy. I knew Edith might have moved on, but I never imagined the town would be missing too. Towns don't do that. They might shut down and turn into ghostly wind tunnels, with weeds growing through the floorboards of houses. But they don't disappear.

Then I start worrying about radiation. I walk back to the van, trying to hold my breath, as if that will make a difference. There aren't any signs warning people off, but that doesn't mean much. I drive back down the pitted bitumen road, looking for evidence of a town, trying to imagine this as a bustling lived-in place. But there are no houses, no crumbling chimneys, no abandoned washing lines. There's something terribly poignant about it. Human endeavour reduced to nothing so easily, leaving just a network of broken streets and a few brightly coloured bougainvillea's gone wild. Except for the wind and the sound of the motor, it's completely quiet. And creepy. I remember David telling me how Indigenous Australians keep away from places like this, with bad energies in the earth. I turn the van around and head back on to the highway, towards Cloncurry, not certain what to do next.

CHAPTER NINETEEN

The sign into Cloncurry says that it has 4828 people and a string of tidy-town awards. The streets are wide and empty, no litter, no dogs, no people… It's eerie, like a ghost town, but too orderly for that. More like it's been suddenly evacuated. And this gives it a sense of imminent disaster. I dismiss the prickles crawling up and down my spine, and try to ignore the urgent need to spin around and catch whatever is there just outside the corners of my eyes, because good sense tells me that it's mid-afternoon and thirty-six degrees Celsius and all the very normal people of this town are probably inside biding their time until the relative cool of the evening. Then they'll come out.

I pull up in the main street, outside a supermarket and sit in the van for a while, wondering where to begin. I need to make enquiries about Edith Burton but I'm putting it off. Afraid that, after all this effort, she won't be here. And maybe afraid that she will be. I feel lost, as if I've crossed a boundary into a world that isn't mine, and in a sense I have. This is new territory. Kita didn't make it this far. But I did. That's what's so weird. I'm going on without her.

Inside the supermarket it's deliciously cool. I wander up and down the aisles feeling like Gulliver in the land of the giants. Everything is big. Two-litre bottles of tomato sauce, giant tubs of margarine, monstrous tins of baked beans, ten-litre tubs of oil… I find a reasonable sized ice-cream and take it back to the counter.

'I'm looking for someone called Edith Burton,' I say, handing over the money.

The woman's bored face is suddenly curious and suspicious all at once. I can almost read her thoughts. She's studying me, thinking maybe I'm a relative, looking for likenesses.

'She used to live in Mary Kathleen,' I explain, 'but it isn't there anymore, so I thought maybe ...' I stop, feeling suddenly stupid. What are the chances she moved from there to here?

'Edith. Yeah, she's just up the road. Number 32, I reckon it is.'

I can't believe my luck or just how easy it was. I bet people in this town know everything about everybody. Not like London, or even Malvern, although it was a bit like that when I was a kid. Everybody reporting back. I can still remember the wonderful sense of freedom I felt when I first moved to London. How fantastic it was to be anonymous.

'Great,' I say smiling. 'Thanks.'

But there's no smile on her face. She's looking at me. Waiting. A battle going on inside her. She wants to ask. Really wants to. But it's up to me to offer and when I don't, she scowls.

'I reckon she'll be in. She usually is on a Wednesday,' she says dropping my change on the counter and turning away.

My ice-cream is already melting. I stand outside, under the broad verandah, eating it as quickly as I can before the whole thing drips off its stick, and watching a woman in her Sunday best, supervising the trolley boy loading her shopping into the back of her four-wheel-drive. One cool box after another. And then carton after carton, until it's squeezed full.

I lick my fingers and get back into the van. I'm not going to think about this. Just do it.

Less than a minute later I pull up in front of the house. It's neat, like the town. White, no smears of dirt, no flaky paint, nothing out of place, not even a blade of grass. In a way it's a fairy tale house, like Victoria Cottage. Not quite real.

I push at the gate it swings open easily and I'm absurdly relieved that it doesn't squeak. The path running up to the front door is neatly raked gravel. Not a piece out of place. It shifts and crunches under my feet, making me feel like an anarchist, planting seeds of chaos into this order. The path is lined with carefully pruned rose bushes, which look completely out of place in outback Queensland. Even the glorious creeping purple bougainvillea is not allowed its freedom but has been carefully trained around the entrance in a neat inverted U. The effect is pretty, but I'm not going to like these people. That much is certain. David told me it's a control thing. They're scared of what's out there. Neat houses, tight fences, lawns and trimmed rose bushes help keep the wilderness at bay.

'It's like they've brought England with them,' he said. 'It doesn't matter how many generations they've been here, they're still in denial.'

When I asked him what was so awful about England, he smiled,

'England's great… over there. We don't want it here'.

On the door there's a ceramic sign saying 'Welcome'. Around the words someone has painted a pattern of roses. I take a deep breath and reach for the knocker, then wait nervously because I've no idea what sort of reception I'll get. When the door opens, I'm surprised. There is no resemblance between this woman and her garden. She's wearing a grubby apron and her hair looks as if she's stuck her finger in a power point. It's gone haywire.

'Mrs Burton?'

'Yes?'

'You've moved.'

She looks puzzled. 'Not recently.'

'I'm Storm Cizekova, you wrote to my - '

'Storm!' she cries, stepping back and taking me in, all the way from my feet to the top of my head. 'Oh, my dear how you've grown.'

It seems weird all over again, the way she knows me like this. Strange too that she's so pleased I'm here, because there's no doubt about that. I've sent her into a flap and now she's doing everything at once, tugging off her apron, puffing the flour off her chest, wiping the perspiration off her face, patting down her hair.

'You caught me doing the baking,' she explains. I start to apologise, but she interrupts. 'Don't say another word! It's just me in a mess, that's all. It won't take a minute to fix,' she says, grabbing my arm and pulling me through the doorway.

'Come in, come on in girl. Jack! Jack! Storm's come.' Then to me. 'He's going a bit deaf, love, I'll have to give him a shout. JACK! '

Then she turns and takes a good long look at me. There are tears in her eyes. 'Oh Storm, I knew you'd come one day.'

In the living room I sit down on a vinyl couch that squeaks when I move, while Jack shuffles about looking uncomfortable and Edith goes to the kitchen to rustle up some afternoon tea. Despite the couch squeaks and Jack's shuffling, I'm getting the strangest sensation. It's like I've come home. I yawn and feel rude for it.

'It's been a long day,' I say to Jack. He smiles and nods, but I'm not sure if he can hear me.

'I went to Mary Kathleen.' I raise my voice for Jack, but it's Edith who responds, reappearing in the doorway, hand over her mouth.

'Oh my. You didn't?' She bursts out laughing. 'That must have been quite a shock'

'It was.'

'Did you take a dip in the lake?' Edith asks.

I shake my head, horrified at the idea.

'Sensible girl. There's plenty around here that do, though. Some people swear by it. They reckon it's got special healing qualities. I reckon the uranium's gone to their head,' she adds, then disappears back into the kitchen.

I ask Jack what happened to the town, but again, I'm not sure he's heard. He takes his time, flicks a switch on the side of his chair and a footstool pops out. That's when I notice how thin his legs are, poking out of his baggy shorts. They're brown and bowed and knotted with veins.

'Well,' he says, clearing his throat. 'Twenty years ago, it was. Some idiot fella banned uranium exports and they had to shut down the mine. There wasn't much point staying on after that, so they pulled some of it down and shifted the rest back here to the museum.'

Oh.' I'm wondering if Jack's one of those rednecks David talked about, and decide to steer clear of politics just in case.

There's a painting on the wall above Jack's head, and I can't resist going over to have a look. It's a print, but the detail is still there. Soft delicate tones, but the right colours and the edges are almost cartoon-like in their sharpness. Despite the tones, the colours and the subject matter are quintessentially Australian, but the artist has captured something else. The fragility of the landscape, its delicate balance.

'Albert Namatjira,' says Jack. 'One of our best.'

'Here we are.'

Edith plonks down a plate of pink and white coconut slices and golden biscuits that she says are called Anzacs. It's a sticky hot summer day and the perspiration is making little tracks down her forehead, but she still puts a cosy on the tea pot. It's a knitted one with crocheted yellow flowers, daisies probably. She sees me looking.

'Made that myself,' she says proudly.

The cups and saucers are so fine they're almost transparent.

'Hand-painted,' says Edith, when I comment on their delicate floral pattern. 'I did china painting classes a few years back. Painted everything I could get my mitts on,' she adds, waving her hands about the room. I hadn't noticed before but there are plates hung on the walls and lining the mantlepiece.

'They're great,' I say smiling appreciatively.

Edith beams. 'Jack thinks I'm mad, all that dusting. And what'll we do if there's an earthquake, he says. All that china falling on our heads. Well, I say, there hasn't been an earthquake around here for as long as I can remember so I won't let it worry me.'

The best crockery makes me nervous. I can't get my fingers through the handle properly and in the end pick it up all crooked and spill some tea into the saucer. It's so different from sitting around with David burning my lips on metal mugs. In the space of that difference is a tiny hurt. I wonder if he's in Darwin yet. If he's rung up Jade and if they're patching things together again.

Jack finishes his tea in a big gulp, and bangs the cup down so hard all our teaspoons rattle. 'A good cuppa, that,' he says in a voice that's too hearty. When he eases himself out of the chair I can hear his knees crackling. 'I'll just go and ...'

'You will not.' Edith is outraged. 'You'll stay right here and talk to the girl. There are things she'll want to know.'

'It's okay,' I say. 'I can come back if it's not convenient.'

'Convenient? Of course it's convenient. You can't come all this way and it not be convenient.' Edith's voice is shrill. 'You'll stay with us of course.'

I shake my head, unsure about being drawn too far into their world.

'No, no, that's very kind, but I've got a campervan, I can just book into the caravan park.'

'The caravan park! Nobody's going to say that Storm Cizekova came all the way from England and Edith and Jack Burton didn't put her up. Hey Jack?'

Jack nods along with Edith. Two bobbing heads. Suddenly I like them both.

'Well, if it really is alright, I could stay the night.'

Edith's face lights up. 'You stay as long as you like, love. The bed's already made up, I'll just give it an airing.' And she's off again, leaving me alone with poor Jack. He fiddles about with a magazine while I eat another Anzac biscuit. When I look over again, he's nodded off. At first I think it's not for real, but nobody would pretend like that, with their mouth wide open and long chugging snores.

After a while I hear Edith in the kitchen, so I tiptoe out past Jack.

'I'll just go and get my things,' I tell her.

'Good girl,' she says. 'Your room's second on the left.'

I put my bag on the bed and look around. The wallpaper is a soft floral pattern of pinks and whites. The flowers are raised slightly. Three dimensional. I reach out and touch one. It feels velvety soft. There's a white cupboard and a white dressing table, with a brush, comb and mirror set on top. This is exactly the sort of room I dreamed of having when I was a kid.

Back in the kitchen it's sweltering hot and Edith is making dinner.

'Sorry,' she says, 'the oven's been on all day.'

'Can I help?' I ask, struggling for breath.

'No love, I'm right. You just sit down here and have a chat,' she says, clearing a space on the table.

I watch her cutting up apples. They're bruised and she has to dig out all the off bits.

'For a pie,' she says, seeing me looking. 'It's not easy getting fresh fruit and vegetables out here and the apples are always floury at the shop. Jack grows some things.' She sighs. 'We're a long way from anywhere, some would say. But where's anywhere? Know what I mean love. What makes somewhere else better than this? We've got everything we need and all the company we want.'

Edith pulls a cask of moselle out of the fridge and a couple of glasses. I can't believe she keeps glasses in the fridge.

'Here,' she says, filling up my glass. 'It'll do you good.'

Edith takes a big gulp of hers and starts rolling out the pastry. I take a sip and try not to wince at how sweet it is. But the glass is frosty and it's fantastically cold. I hold it against my forehead for a minute, savouring the spreading coolness.

Edith finishes the pie and pops it in the oven.

'There. I had to make you a pie. You loved them so much. Warm apple pie and ice-cream, that's what you always wanted.' She's back there, remembering. Smiling happily, and it leaves me disconcerted. I still don't understand how she knows these things about me.

'How did you and Jack get to look after me? Wouldn't the police have taken me away after… you know …?' I can't say the words out loud.

Edith nods. 'Jack was the police love. The only one around for miles.'

'Oh.' I let that sink in. 'How long was I here then?'

She looks hard at me. 'No, I don't suppose you would remember. Didn't Irene tell you?'

When I shake my head a hurt starts up in Edith's eyes, but she blinks it away and gets on with peeling the potatoes.

'Never mind,' she says.

Nan didn't tell me anything,' I say. 'It was only when she died …'

'She's dead? Oh, I'm sorry, and so young too.'

Edith pours oil over the potatoes and puts them in the oven. In hardly any time they're sizzling and I'm wondering how much longer I can bear the heat in here.

'How long did I stay with you?' I ask.

'Well, let's see now. You were here for nearly eight months. And my, didn't we get fond of you. It was a real wrench to see you go. Though we all knew it was for the best.'

At first I think it's perspiration, but when she sniffs I realise Edith is crying. I'm puzzled.

'We couldn't have any of our own you see. It broke Jack's heart, that. It isn't right, a house with no children. When you came along you filled up our lives. We got a glimpse of how it could be. And after that nothing was the same for us. We started fostering kids and that helped a lot. Helped us all. It was a two-way thing… The poor mites needed someone to get them through …'

There's a hard something forming inside my gut. A kind of foreboding. Already I'm building a wall against whatever it is. I'm not really listening to Edith. Just forming the question I don't want to ask.

'Nan took eight months to get here?' There's a sharp edge to my voice.

Edith looks uncomfortable. 'It took that long to sort all the details out. Everything was slower back then. We had to find your next of kin …'

Edith fills up our glasses again. She's reluctant, but she can tell it isn't enough, that I need to know more.

'Then she had to find her way out here. Wade through all the police stuff … You know. As far as we were concerned there wasn't any hurry. We loved having you. Didn't we, Jack?' she says raising her voice for him as he shuffles past, wearing a glowing white terry toweling hat.

He nods and bangs the screen door shut behind him.

Edith looks after him fondly. 'He's a man of few words, my Jack. But he feels things deeply. He loved having you here. Used to carry you everywhere on his shoulders. And sit up with you at night when you cried out... Oh dear,' she dabs at her eyes with the back of her hand. 'You poor little mite. Losing your mum like that.'

I'm fighting back tears too because I don't want to cry in front of Edith. I can't tell if it's self-pity or a kind of empathy with the child I was, abandoned out here and no one bothering to come and get me, or maybe it's just a response to the kindness of these people, taking me in like that as if I were their own. Probably all three.

It starts raining, the drops beating down on the galvanised iron roof. Edith runs around opening windows to let some cool in, while I wonder how stable the house is. The roof and the walls are so thin, there's hardly anything between inside and outside. A big wind and it would blow away. Suddenly I miss solid old Victoria Cottage with its three-foot-thick walls.

Edith serves up a hot roast dinner - beef and roasted vegetables, boiled frozen peas and bread and butter. For afters there's hot apple pie with ice-cream and I still love it.

Jack devours two huge servings and then uses Edith's bread to clean the gravy off his plate. Despite her size, Edith eats very little. I scoff my food down, almost keeping up with Jack. It's a combination of things: the relief of finding Jack and Edith, and the simple luxury of being in a house again, sitting on a chair, eating at a table with a knife and fork and not worrying about what's crawling up my shorts or lurking behind the bushes. Not just snakes, I think, remembering that truckie's fat fingers and greedy cold eyes. There's also the amazing fact that I don't feel sick. I make the most of it and help myself to a second serve of apple pie. Maybe I'm already past that stage.

Afterwards I help Edith with the dishes while Jack nods off in front of the television. I've had two glasses of wine and feel pretty good. I'm telling Edith about Nan dying and how I found the photo and Kita's diary, but then I get to the bit about how I'd always thought Kita died when I was born.

'That's what Millie and Nan told me,' I say, the outrage sliding into my voice. 'So I always believed it was me that was to blame for my mother's death.'

I clunk a dish down on the table, then pick up another and wipe out the moisture, knowing that I'm being too rough and I'll most probably break something soon. But I can't stop thinking about how the guilt has shaped my life. Pulling and pushing at me. Making me better than I should be and worse too, sometimes. Jesus, I've spent my whole life trying to make up for my mother's death.

Edith gently takes my tea-towel and dries her hands on it. Then she wraps me up in her arms.

'I thought I'd killed her.' There's a huge lump pushing up into my throat and next thing I'm crying into the bold sunflower pattern of Edith's apron, breathing in the heady chemical fragrance of her washing powder and wishing I could go back and start everything all over again.

'There, there,' she's crooning. 'Never mind. You poor dear, you must miss her so.'

I wipe my eyes, trying to halt the tears but her sympathy is making it worse.

'You get it all out dear. That's right.' And I'm off again, sobbing and shaking.

After a while the sobbing stops and Edith leads me down the hallway to my room. She helps me undress and practically tucks me into bed. She pats down the sheets and brings a hot chocolate to help me sleep, although the weather's all wrong for that.

'Goodnight, love, I'm so glad you came. It's the right thing.'

And then she's gone, shutting the door behind her. I lean back in the bed. The mattress is so soft it feels like I'm lying on a cloud. The sheet over me is crisp and smells of the sun, but underlying that is the neglected mustiness of an unused room. Edith and Jack have no children. Audrey had no children. And Millie only had one, despite the fact that she came from a world in which family was everything and believed that having many children was both a necessity and a blessing. For Millie it was both a failure and a punishment. She must have thought it a miracle that Pop didn't leave her.

'*Nane chave, nane bacht,*' she would say, sadly. 'If there are no children, it is bad luck… Have many children my *chiri*.'

For Millie every child was wanted. To be infertile was a tragedy. To kill a baby in the womb was beyond comprehension. Despite the consequences, I don't believe Millie would have tried to abort her baby. And neither did Nan, or Kita. Though we were all accidents, unwanted but loved in a complicated way. I rest my hands on my belly. What should I do? I can't keep putting off this decision. Time doesn't stay still and the baby is growing.

The crying has taken its toll. I feel all emptied out, like the cicada shell I found outside the hostel in Sydney. If I held up my hand to the light I could probably see right through it. I switch off the lamp and stretch out in the bed, savouring the fresh sheets and soft mattress and the sense that I'm being looked after. Despite the thin walls I feel a long way from the elements. And safe, though after all this time in the van, it's strange to be sleeping in a house again.

Millie's first night in a house must have been so weird. How did she cope with running water, a bath, electricity? Did they even have any of that in Bohemia in 1937? I don't know. But there was certainly a roof over her head, and walls around her and a bed with a mattress. Did she miss the stars? Was the mattress too soft? Did it frighten her, the way she sank deep into it?

And how did the silence feel? She would never have been alone before, always sharing a space with her parents and brothers, sisters, cousins, aunts and uncles. There was no such thing as privacy in her world and now all of a sudden there she was - just Millie and Pop and a great big silence that Pop could never possibly fill, even if he tried, and Pop was never much of a talking man.

I wonder if Millie understood how to work the wood oven. Or if she made everything burn. Did she cook too much? Did Pop lean back and laugh at the mountains of food on the table? Or did he frown at the waste and make her feel silly for not knowing? I don't think so. Not Pop. Maybe they laughed together and made light of these things. Or maybe the empty space around them was already filled with the fearful anticipation of a future of differences and a single child working overtime to hold everything together and at bay.

Poor Nan, it must have been impossible for her. She indulged Millie, even I could see that through my child's eyes. Sometimes it seemed to me as if there was a debt Nan felt she owed her mother. A bottomless one that could never be paid. Or perhaps it was simply that Nan recognised the hurt in Millie. Though they had wild fights, she was patient right up to the end. But with Pop she was tough. He was a mild man, always caught up with his garden and the birds and the tiny delicate figures he would spend hours at a time carving from pieces of wood, leaving trails of sweetly scented wood shavings while Nan with a dustpan and broom muttered to herself as she swept up after him. I hated the way Nan went for Pop, pushing and pushing, but he never fought back. It was only ever Nan, bashing her head against her father.

I'm finding more and more contradictions in my feelings about Nan. The old frustration and anger are still there, along with a deep hurt, but there's compassion for her creeping in as well. For the first time I'm seeing Nan as a person, with all the complications that entails. I wish more than anything that I'd been able to cross these lines when she was still alive. Sensing she's nearby, I lie very still, drawing her gently in, closer and closer, until I can feel her breath on my forehead.

'It's alright Nan,' I whisper. 'I think I understand.'

The rain starts up again, but this time the steady drumming on the roof lulls me into a deep and dreamless sleep.

CHAPTER TWENTY

In the morning I'm surprised all over again that I'm here. And pleased. I lie in bed, savouring the worry-free space I've found myself in, but at the same time knowing it can't last. As soon as I get up, all the worries will come tumbling back, jostling for space. They're sneaking in already, taking the pleasure out of things. I still haven't told Max and the thought of that sends a cold wave of terror rushing through me. Then there are the things I'm learning, like Nan not coming for me, and the things I'm about to learn. God knows what. Today is going to be hard. I do a big sigh, roll over and curl into a ball, trying to shut it all out.

I'm starving, and it's only that, and my urgent need for a pee, that eventually drags me out of bed. I pull on a fresh sleeveless top and crinkly shorts and let my grumbling belly lead me to the kitchen. The stench of burnt milk stops me at the door. Edith's got her back to me, standing over the sink scrubbing at something and muttering to herself. Her great big bottom is encased in a vast pair of shorts and her thick, dimpled legs wobble when she moves. All of a sudden one of my first memories of Millie emerges. She's down on her knees in the kitchen, skirt spread around her, bottom up in the air and scrubbing at the floor stones until they gleamed. The whole house was like some sort of battleground, with Millie fighting valiantly to keep the germs at bay. Her face flushed pink, scouring red hands, and all the time a huge bottom waving defiance in my face. Over the years she wore deep ruts into the spaces between the stones and everyone kept tripping over, until finally Pop broke his nose and Nan had to get someone to put in tiles. It was much smoother after that, but even then she scrubbed so hard at the grout, we had to keep redoing it.

Edith must sense me standing there because she turns round and smiles. Her face is flushed and sweating.

'Morning love.'

'Good morning.'

When I open my mouth the burnt milk smell goes right in and I have to concentrate hard to stop from gagging.

'Sorry about the smell. Jack likes his milk warmed for his Weetbix and I went and left it on while I had my shower… Here this should help.'

Edith opens the door and waves a tea towel about, trying to clear the smoke out. But there's no breeze and it stays put. Then she switches on the oven fan. It's noisy but soon the smoke starts to clear so I venture in.

'Hungry?'

I nod half-heartedly, not certain anymore.

'Get yourself a bowl. There's Weetbix, Cornflakes, you name it, the cupboard's full of cereals. Jack has his fads and then I'm left with any number of half-empty packets… That one love, second from the left.'

I settle for Rice Bubbles, though the use-by date is well past, and cold milk. Edith opens a tin of pineapple and plops some on top.

'To make it sweet,' she says.

'I'm sorry about last night,' I say. 'I really shouldn't have …'

But Edith breaks in. 'No need for apologies, love. You have to get these things off your chest. And heavens, if you can't cry when you've got something to cry about, when else are you going to do it? Now, would you like tea or coffee?'

'Coffee, please.'

Edith gets out the jar of instant, spoons in some granules and within seconds it's made. 'Here you go - ' she says then stops abruptly, mid-sentence. I can feel myself tensing up. She's staring at my shoulders. When she gently runs her fingers over the marks, I have to steel myself not to pull away.

'I thought they'd scar,' she says.

'What?' I look up, surprised.

'These.'

'They're birthmarks,' I tell her.

She looks shocked. I can see she's uncertain what to do next. But she's committed now. 'No they're not, sweetie, they're scars. That... day, you were out there in the hot sun for God knows how long, with just a singlet and a grubby nappy, half falling off. You poor little mite, you were burnt to a cinder. Third-degree burns they were. We had to race you to the hospital. It's a wonder you survived. You were in shock and dehydrated and so weak, you didn't make a sound even though it must have been agony... They kept you in a week, attached to a drip. So forlorn, with those big frightened eyes and not saying a word to anyone.'

Edith smiles fondly. 'Found your voice later though when we took you home – screaming blue murder every time we put the cream on.'

I run my fingers along the familiar rough texture of my shoulders, trying to absorb another new version of my history. Why did Nan lie about everything? Was the truth so appalling? I guess one lie makes another and another until you can't go back again. That's what she taught me as a kid. Not to lie. 'It isn't right,' she said. Yet she fed me one great big lie after another.

Edith is smiling at me. Her face is gentle, but I can tell she's angry. She doesn't understand. She's thinking, why did that woman keep things from me? Edith is being polite about Nan, but it's obvious she didn't like her. They wouldn't have got on. They were poles apart.

'I wrote, you know,' Edith says. 'I was hoping she'd send a photograph or just let me know how you were going… But she never answered.'

I take Edith's hand. I feel sad for her, but inside me there's a shift happening. For the first time in ages I feel willing to defend Nan. Her lies and secrets weren't really malicious. They were more like a habit she couldn't break. She was protecting herself, and me too.

'Nan was okay really,' I say. 'She was just brittle with people and kept things to herself.'

I sip my coffee, feeling the hot sweet liquid burning all the way down. It makes me think about David again, with his grinder and the black charred percolator he carries about with him. And Max with his shiny stainless-steel plunger. And me, here, with Edith's instant International Roast. Each of us with our own private grief, trying to protect ourselves in whatever way we can.

Edith clears the table and brings out some photograph albums. I have to steel myself against whatever it is that's coming next. I feel like a boxer in the ring. What is this? Round five or six? I can't remember. One of the albums is covered in a 3D image of a great wave with surfers on boards. Depending which way you move it, the wave and the surfers go backwards or forwards. I concentrate on this while Edith flicks through the other album. She's looking for something, but on the way she can't help stopping here and there, cooing over old memories.

'Look,' she says, 'these are my kids… That's Alice, that's Micky and there's little Roddy.'

I look at the children, with their arms wrapped around each other and wide wicked smiles spread right across their faces. I shouldn't be shocked. But I am.

Edith notices my surprise. Yes,' she says, 'Indigenous kids. It wasn't unusual up here.'

She tells me that Alice has three children of her own.

'They're up at Normanton now,' she says sadly. 'So we don't get to see as much of them.' She turns the page. 'And there's Roddy, he's a mechanic now, working in Mount Isa. A good strong boy he's turned out to be. '

'And Micky?' I ask. 'What about him?'

Her eyes cloud over. 'Dead,' she says, shaking her head sadly. 'It broke my heart.'

'I'm sorry.' I don't know what else to say and Edith is lost in her own thoughts so I just sit here making the surfer dance back and forth.

Then Edith turns the page. 'Ah,' she says. 'Here you are.'

It's a picture of me on Jack's shoulders. Jack looks younger of course, but he's already got those dark stringy legs. He's smiling, but my little face is quite serious. There's not a hint of a smile around my mouth and my eyes are solemn. My shoulders are bandaged and my face is red and peeling. Edith has tried to tame my hair. There's a ribbon in the top bit and she's combed the rest down, but it hasn't worked. Already there are bits sticking up and it's obvious that some sections are longer than others.

'Lucky you had such a great mop of hair,' says Edith. 'It shaded your face a bit. You had so many tangles, bird's nests everywhere. Your scalp was so badly burnt that I couldn't even try to tease them out so I had to get the scissors to them... You were a real sight.'

I look at this damaged, unkempt child, with her solemn eyes. How long does it take to get tangles like that? Obviously Kita must have given up on me. I wonder if she'd ever bothered much, or if it was the darkness she talked about in her diary that made her forgetful.

Edith turns the page and suddenly I'm looking at a picture of a much younger Nan. I can't begin to imagine Nan here, in Edith's house in this isolated part of Australia. It's bizarre to think of her sitting in the living room sipping tea from fine porcelain cups, nibbling on Anzac biscuits and talking about the weather. Because I don't believe she would have talked about me, not if she could help it. Not with a stranger.

I look closer at the picture. It's taken outside what must have been their place in Mary Kathleen. Nan is in a summer dress, surrounded by dazzling light and bright bougainvillea. She's standing stiff and straight, one hand at her side, the other holding onto my hand. I'm wearing a dress too. It looks brand-new. Pressed smooth, with a full skirt and puffy sleeves that cover my scarred shoulders. My hair is neat too and tied with a shiny ribbon. I'm wearing white sandals without scuff marks. My face is scrubbed clean. I'm smiling, but the smile hasn't reached my eyes. It looks more like someone's told me to say cheese and then I've had to hold it like that too long. There's nothing light-hearted about this photograph. We're both posing for the camera as if it's a formal photograph. We're strangers. We don't know what to do with each other.

'Irene stayed a week,' says Edith. 'She had to. There wasn't a bus. It did her good in the end. You see it gave her a chance to get to know you.'

I look at the photograph again. Nan's dress has a bold floral print that looks so out of character. In all the time I knew her, Nan never wore dresses, only trousers and shirts, practical, comfortable clothes. And yet here she is on the other side of the world in a polyester bold print. I can tell it's polyester from the way it clings close to her legs, and sticks to her arms and chest. She was still quite young, only thirty-eight or so, and for the first time I can see that if Nan had just let go a little, she would have been beautiful.

It's time to face the thing that's been nagging at me. 'Nan didn't want to come, did she.'

Edith sighs. 'Sweetie, you have to understand. She'd just lost her only child. She didn't even know you existed. When they contacted her, she insisted she had no grandchildren. We had to send papers and a photograph, to convince her. It must have hurt her terribly that your mother never told her about you. And don't forget that she did come in the end. That's the important thing.'

Edith's right. Nan did come. If she hadn't, probably Edith and Jack would have adopted me. I try to imagine it. Growing up out here! Would I still be me? Or a different me? How arbitrary that it was one thing and not another. How fine the line must have been between me and Nan. The only line I had left back then, the only thing connecting me to family. It would have been so easy for her to snap that line forever. She could have just turned away. Oh God, how horribly fragile everything is. I shudder, suddenly afraid. I'm also uncomfortably aware that there's a baby growing inside my womb and I'm its only line. My decision is everything for it, one way or another. With this realisation comes a new sense of responsibility. It feels like a burden but maybe just maybe, it's a gift.

I sit in the kitchen all morning talking to Edith, then in the afternoon Jack drives me out to the place where Kita died. Edith's not happy about it. She thinks I should take things slowly. But I've already agreed to stay another night and I don't want to stretch it out any further. The past is pressing in on me but so is the future. I need to make some decisions and sort things out with Max, and I need to finish this journey.

The car isn't new, over ten years old, but it's still Jack's baby. It's silver and shiny, with not a single scratch or dent. The seats and steering wheel are covered with sheepskin. From the rear-vision mirror hangs a green thing shaped like a pine tree. It stinks. I can taste the smell, in my mouth, my throat and up my nose. My head starts to ache. There's no winder on the window, but eventually I find a button and slide the window down. Straight away Jack presses a button on his side and it glides back up again.

'No need,' he says. 'There's air-conditioning.'

So I sit there in the cool stinking air, trying not to breathe and feeling my mood turn sour as the stench enters my nervous system.

We drive past the Mary Kathleen turn-off and I ask about the memorial I saw yesterday, an inscription, riddled with gun shots and racist graffiti.

'Bunch of Aborigines massacred,' is all he says.

I wonder what's underneath that gruffness; try to imagine him lumbering about with me on his shoulders. 'A heart of gold,' Edith says. She should know. Maybe with Jack you just have to read between the lines.

When we pull up, Jack points across the road. I don't know what I'm expecting, something special I suppose, some marker that says - this is it. This is where it happened. There are loads of crushed empty beer cans that have been tossed from passing cars. There's a road sign too, peppered with gun shots. But nothing else. It's completely arbitrary. Why did it happen here? Why not there, or there, or somewhere else completely? My heart is banging away in my chest as I get out of the car. The hot damp air claws at my throat as I cross the road, feeling conspicuous, with Jack sitting in the car, not looking. I'm also filled with an intense fear and keep glancing back to check Jack doesn't leave me alone out here. There's a crackle in a bush and I jump. The ground is still damp from the rain last night. And there are bones. None of them are my mother's. She was scooped up and shipped back to England for processing by Nan.

I look closely at the ground, at all the ants, not marching in neat lines, but swarming about chaotically. According to David this means it will rain soon. I look up at the sky, pushing thoughts of David away. I want to concentrate on Kita. Force myself to look at her, lying dead in the dirt. Face down maybe, or the other way, eyes peering sightlessly into the sun. I don't know which is worse. But Nan keeps intruding. In her shiny coffin surrounded by sprays of flowers, quiet blank faces and empty sentiment. The stupid little speech I gave. How pedestrian it was, in the end. And how angry I was.

'What does it matter?' I said, when the funeral man asked about coffins. 'You're going to burn it anyway.'

His indrawn breath as he turned to Max. I'd been dismissed. A childish idiot. It didn't help, me butting in about Nan not being a Christian, when he asked about the service. Then the final straw when Max told me off later.

'It wasn't just some stupid protocol you transgressed,' he said. 'You actually offended him. Don't you get it? You demeaned his job.' He banged his fist down on the steering wheel and accidentally beeped the horn. We both jumped, but it didn't lighten the atmosphere. 'God Storm, you need to learn a bit of respect for people.'

But all I could do was sit there and fume until I couldn't hold it in anymore. Then I shouted something about him not being my bloody father, so he should stop telling me off. We didn't talk for the rest of the day. Standing here at the place where my mother was murdered makes all that seem so... petty. Looking back on it, I can see that Max was right. I acted like an idiot and standing here on the spot where Kita died, I feel ashamed at how selfish I was and wish I could turn back time and do it all differently.

Of course I have no memory of Kita's funeral, the one they had back in England before Nan came and got me. No one ever gave me the chance to say goodbye. And no one gave me anything of Kita's. Nothing to remember her by, except one poxy photograph. And now I'm angry again. Angry that I was abandoned like this. Out here. With snakes and bones and litter. Left out in the sun. And no one ever asked what I wanted. Or helped me grieve. Or even bothered to tell me what really happened.

I kick at the ground. The mud squeezes up through my toes and hardens almost immediately. It's always been the same. Murdered Kita frizzling out here in front of me. Then Pop dying. Me having to help Millie get him in his best suit because Nan wouldn't do it. His body was there and we changed him like you change a rag doll's clothes. But there was no spirit, even ten-year-old me could tell that. Then Millie gasping for breath on the couch in the green room and afterwards Nan tossing out all the sheets because 'that's what Millie would have wanted'. Then Nan killing herself out there in the cold. Not once did anyone ask me what I wanted. Or even give me a chance to shout NO! They were all just as selfish as me.

The roar of an approaching road train jolts me out of my thoughts. I don't know how long I've been standing here, but I can feel the sun burning through my hair, and Jack's eyes burning into my back. The roar is getting louder. I look up. The shiny metal is blinding in the sun. The road train pulls the air into its path and then pushes it out again, battering me with its ferocity. I stagger back from its huge power and turn my face away as it passes. How easily it would crush me under its wheels.

When the road is clear I walk back to the car. There's more I need to do here, but this is not the time. When I get in next to Jack, a blast of hot air comes with me. He's left the engine running and the air-conditioning on. I shut the door on the heat and let my breath settle. I try to smile, but find I can't.

Jack switches off the radio and hands me a big envelope. 'News cuttings,' he says, staring ahead. 'From back then… We don't know what you saw. You never talked about it. I found you standing on the edge of the road. So small.' His voice breaks and when I look over I catch him rubbing his eyes. 'It made everything else seem very big,' he says and looks at me. 'Do you see?'

I nod and he looks away again.

'You struggled a bit when we put you in the car. Not much, because you were dehydrated. After that you were quiet. Didn't say a word for ten days. Not in the hospital, or when you came back home with us. Except at night. You'd wake up screaming and stare straight through us as if we weren't there.'

Jack's all talked out now. He starts the car and turns back toward Cloncurry. I'm holding the envelope, afraid of what's inside but after a while I can't resist it anymore. I open the envelope and slide the cuttings out. In the first one there's a photo of us all together. It's the one I already have, where Kita is holding me. But this is before Nan sliced it in two and threw Bill's half in the rubbish bin, or more likely burnt it. This is the first time I've seen a picture of Bill. I search for a resemblance, something to pinpoint this man as my father. I try to check the shape of his eyes, but he's squinting, and it's a black-and-white print, so I can't see their colour. I don't recognise him. He's just a stranger standing right up close like he's part of the family. I look to see if there was already something there, a shadow of the future. But no matter how hard I try, he doesn't look like a murderer.

I pull out another cutting and the headlines hit me in the face.

INJURED TODDLER FOUND AT MURDER SCENE.

There's a photo too. A face filled with hurt, mouth tight shut. I remember reading somewhere that when a baby wants something it cries and shouts, but when it feels really threatened it shuts up. Silence is the only defence it has.

That's enough. I slide the cuttings back in to the envelope and press it shut. We drive back in an awkward silence that's filled with the stench of synthetic pine. Edith opens the door, a face full of questions I'm not prepared to answer. I look away.

CHAPTER TWENTY-ONE

I get down on my hands and knees and check under the bed. There's an old slipper, a cracked porcelain potty and lots of dust, but none of my socks or dirty undies. I haven't folded anything, just stuffed it all in my bag, so it's bulging and I have to sit on it to force the zip closed.

'Shit.' The zip pinches my finger. I suck at the blood and wait for the pain to go away, then take a long last look at this room. There's a part of me that's sorry to say good bye. Despite the wallpaper, I like it. I like Edith too and am even fond of stiff old silent Jack. I'm grateful too, for everything they did for me back then - and what they've done for me now, the way they recognized the need in me for the truth. They didn't have to do any of it. Yet they did. Unlike Nan.

Edith is sweeping the back 'patio'. That's what she calls it anyway - a big slab of concrete with a barbecue, an outdoor table and a see-through roof. After more rain overnight it's steamy early morning but the concrete is already dry. I don't understand how anyone can function in this heat. It makes me languid and slow and lazy but Edith does everything so vigorously. I watch her making clouds of dust, humming away to herself, totally absorbed, in the way Millie was when she was taken by one of her 'enthusiasms', as Nan called them. Millie with her skirt so long it swept the ground. And Nan always saying, 'Who needs a broom when you've got Millie?' But I don't have Millie or Nan, and pretty soon I won't have Edith either.

'I'm leaving today.'

The swishing stops and Edith looks at me, surprised. I can sense her disappointment. 'There's no need to rush, love. You can stay as long as you like.'

I study the fine cracks in the concrete and shake my head against the temptation. 'No, I have to get on... I'm sorry, it's been great to stay with you and I'm so grateful for everything.'

'No need for that,' says Edith putting aside the broom and wrapping her arms around me. 'You're a very brave girl.'

But I don't feel brave at all. More like a snivelling soggy coward. I want to stay. I really do. And that's the problem. It's even more terrifying than the prospect of leaving. There's a massive lump growing inside my throat. Was it Nan who taught me that it's safer not to love?

'Got time for a cup of tea before you go?' asks Edith.

I nod and let her lead me inside. Then sit at the table and watch her fussing about the kitchen.

'What are your plans now, love?' she asks, spooning sugar into both our mugs. She's never once asked me if I take sugar and I've not had the courage to tell her I don't.

'First I'm going back to the place... you know... where Jack found me.'

Edith nods and sips her tea.

'Then I'll finish my mother's journey for her,' I say, watching the tea steam up her glasses. 'As far as Cairns, anyway. And then home I guess.

I don't tell her that I'm going to Kuranda to visit Bill's sister, Kate, and then I'm going look for Bill. Probably because I'm afraid she'll talk me out of it. Jack told me they let my father out a few years ago. It wasn't mentioned in the papers, but Jack got word of it because he used to be a policeman. He was surprised the police hadn't warned me. Probably they spoke to Nan and that's as far as it went. Bill is living somewhere in northern Queensland, but Jack doesn't know where.

'I don't know why I've had to do this trip,' I tell Edith. 'It feels almost like a pilgrimage.'

'It's important, love, that's why. We all have to make peace with the past so we can move into the future.'

We sit quietly for a few minutes, sipping our sweet syrupy tea.

'And what about that?' Edith asks, pointing at my almost flat belly.

I'm surprised enough not to deny it. 'How can you tell?'

She laughs. 'I might not have been blessed with any of my own, but I know. I was brought up on a station. I can pick a cow in calf before most people... no offence, love. It's in the eyes and the way they move.' Edith leans back in her chair and looks me over with a professional eye. 'There's a bit of a glow about you, and even though it's early days, you've already got that careful way of walking, like you're carrying a piece of fine porcelain.'

I blush. 'I don't know what to do,' I say. 'I can't decide... It wasn't planned.'

Edith nods. 'Sometimes you have to make decisions in your heart, not your head. How do you feel about having a child?'

'Scared,' I say, then correct myself. No, terrified! I think maybe I'm too selfish to let a baby take over my life.'

Edith looks at me sadly and I feel guilty. 'Babies don't take over,' she says. 'They join you. They make your life even richer.'

'Well that depends, doesn't it?' I say, bitterness creeping into my voice. 'Our family doesn't exactly have a great track record for mothering: Kita was crap; Nan was like living with a marble statue; and Millie was all over the place.'

I sigh, remembering that passage from Kita's diary.

I don't feel like a real mum. It's more like I'm pretending. Other mums make raffia dolls and pretty little cakes... I'm scared that one day someone's going to see right through me and I hope it's not Storm. Mum wasn't too good at it either, nor Millie. They weren't devoted in the way people expect mothers to be. I always thought they were protecting themselves, not me but maybe it was a bit of both.

Edith reaches out and takes my hand. 'You know, love. What you've got going for you?'

I shake my head, thinking, not a lot.

'You've recognised how bad they all were. You can change it. You can be a wonderful mother.'

Edith has more faith in me than I have in myself but even so her words ignite a tiny spark of hope. Maybe she's right.

'What about bringing a baby up alone, with no money and no family to help? I ask.

'Oh,' says Edith. 'What about the father, love?'

The sad gentleness of her voice calms me. I think about Max, trying yet again to imagine a child breaking into his orderly certain world. Toys strewn all over the polished floors, crumbs and mushy food stuck to the walls, dirty nappies spilling out of his gleaming, stainless-steel pedal bin... I smile at the absurdity of it. Edith is waiting for an answer. The father? What about him?

'He doesn't know yet. I'm afraid to ...'

I break off as Jack comes in, wearing his terry-toweling hat and looking more embarrassed than usual. There's no room for intimacy anymore, just small talk and hugs and a kiss from Edith, along with a tin of Anzac biscuits to keep me going.

'I'll keep in touch,' I say as I climb into the van.

Edith and Jack nod and smile and we all try not to cry as I leave them all over again.

I have to drive back and forth, before I recognise the spot. There's a freshly killed kangaroo, probably ploughed down by a road train during the night. The ground is still muddy from last night's rain.

I've brought some things. Two sticks, some string and a few hydrangeas Edith gave me from her garden, nothing lavish. I'm going to make a little cross. I've seen lots of these tiny tributes dotted along the highways and I want to mark this place out too. I want to create a ritual, to make this sacred in some way. For Kita. But also for me, so I can move on.

I collect some stones and build them up into a pile, then I kneel in the mud and pat globs of it in between the rocks to cement them together. It looks good. A little English cairn in the great Australian outback. I weave the string around and around the sticks to make a cross, then push it into the top of the cairn and step back to see how it looks. The flowers are pretty around the bottom of the cairn. They'll wilt in no time, but it's enough. I'm satisfied.

I think about grief and all the ways it manifests itself. For me? I don't know. A kind of restlessness, I suppose. Anger too, and a numbness that descends when things go really wrong. I wonder how Nan grieved. What happened in those eight months after Kita's death? I imagine she went very quiet, with an outward composure that would have infuriated Millie and made everyone else think she didn't care. Millie would have wandered the house and the hills, tearing at her hair and wailing. All of it out there for everyone to see. That didn't leave Nan anywhere to go, except inside. And Pop? He probably spent more time in the garden pouring life into his plants.

I think about Kita lying dead by the side of the road. What happened to her spirit? When did it leave her? At what point was she just another dead animal, already starting to rot in the sun?

Ants, flies, crows, eagles, all feasting on my mother. Stripping her bones down to a gleaming white. Nothing wasted. But it wasn't like that after all, because Kita got scooped up and put in a box and shipped across to the other side of the world, where they burnt her and scattered her ashes across the Malverns. And then they burnt her things. All gone, as if she never existed.

But she did exist and in a way she still does. She's not gone, not while I'm alive to remember her. Perhaps as Millie said, it's only other people's memories that make a person live on? Perhaps that's all life after death means. Or is there something more? As I pat more mud between the rocks it suddenly strikes me. I'm kneeling here, surrounded by death, and yet there's a brand-new life growing inside me. That wouldn't have been possible without Kita. This baby isn't just about me and Max; this baby is Kita's too, and Nan's and Pop's and Millie's *and* Millie's mother, the one who threw down a curse on her daughter and didn't live to watch it pass on through us all. Then I realise that I've already made my decision. I will have this baby. Whatever Max says. I will create a new life out of all this death. I'll make raffia dolls and pretty little cakes and go to parent/teacher nights and sit through school concerts. Suddenly I feel an expansion around me, a certainty that is visceral and deep, a sense of being no longer alone.

Almost immediately this new found certainty is replaced by the same old fear but in its wake it leaves something solid behind for me to hold on to. The morning is getting steamier, the sun already white-hot and beating down on my bare shoulders, opening up old wounds, reigniting the terror I felt so many years ago. I glance back at the van, checking it's still there, and resist the urge to jump in and drive away from this place as fast as I can, not looking back. I can't go yet. There's more to do.

All this time I've been retracing my mother's steps, I've also been retracing my own, moving closer to the dreadful thing that happened here twenty-six years ago. And maybe that's what this journey is all about - following the thread of my fear back to its source. Whatever it is, I have to look at it.

There are only a few facts and hardly any details, so I have to imagine... We're in the car. A beaten-up old Holden station-wagon which I am certain is red, though I don't think anyone has ever told me that. I'm sitting between Bill and Kita. Bill is driving. It's only mid-morning, but he's drunk and when he talks his words slur around in his mouth. Kita's in a bad mood. She needs the toilet. There are no rest stops, so Bill just pulls up by the side of the road. Maybe they're arguing. Maybe not. He stays in the car. Or he gets out. He lights a cigarette. It's already hot, the sun is beating down hard. I climb out too. Or maybe he pulls me out after he's done it. Anyway, he comes up behind my mother and strangles her. And then he drives off. Later he panics and throws her things out of the car. He isn't thinking straight. He's drunk and adrenaline is surging inside him. But there are no excuses. And maybe he already knows that.

Then there's me. And this is where it gets really hard. I'm standing on the edge of the road, clutching my filthy Peggy doll. I'm filthy too. My nappy is dirty. I've been tugging at Kita, trying to make her answer me. Pulling her hair, tickling to make her laugh. I've been calling: "Mummy, Mummy, Mama... ' Shouting. But after a while I have to stop because my mouth is getting too dry. Maybe I even lie down next to her. Maybe not. But what's bigger than all this is the terror. It's the kind of fear that wipes out vision and leaves everything a blank.

Twenty-six years later I feel the same terror I felt back then, because just a few feet away, a wedge-tailed eagle has landed on the dead kangaroo. I watch its powerful beak tearing through the skin, at the meat inside. I can't breathe. I've forgotten how. Then finally the air comes out in a gasp. Startled, the eagle spreads its giant wings and soars up, its silhouette framed by the bright blue sky. As it takes off there's the whoosh of its wings and the round cold eyes and I'm face down in the mud, curled up in a little ball, head tucked under as if this will keep me safe. Suddenly I see a flash of the sleeping toddler cuddled in beside her mother, one little arm wrapped around her neck. I see her dirt-smeared face and searing skin and the mother who doesn't move. Something disturbs the child and she opens her eyes. Just inches away are the talons, clutching into her mama's back. She watches the way they poke through her mother's T-shirt. Watches the hard curved beak, the nervous shifty head. She stays very still and quiet, but something, maybe even a flick of her eyelids, startles the eagle. Alarmed, it spreads out its wings, lifting up into the sky and away. When it's gone, she sobs on and on, clinging onto her mother and tugging at her hair. Then finally she gives up. She turns away from her mother and walks back to the road. A grubby white figure, alone. out here with a fear that has silenced her.

CHAPTER TWENTY-TWO

I drive fast, not stopping for drinks or food, or even the toilet. Not noticing anything, just driving - away from that spot, that time, that memory, which has been inside me for twenty-six years, a slow invisible poison seeping through my life. By the time I reach Normanton I'm exhausted, but calm. The fear has gone and I feel lighter.

There's a life-size replica of a crocodile in the main street. It's 8.6 metres long, some sort of record, and caught by a woman. I stop the van and walk all the way around it, running my fingers along the croc's side. Then I put my head in between its jaws. Imagining. One little snap would be enough. I touch the teeth, but they're not sharp, probably worn down by thousands of curious fingers.

When I check into a caravan park, I wonder why the woman at reception looks at me strangely. In the toilets, I see why. There's mud all over my face, my arms, my legs. Dried-out caked-on mud, peeling off in places. For a moment I have the sense that this dirt is mine, that it's the fear that was inside me. Now it's risen to the surface where I can wash it away. I stand under the shower for ages, letting cool water flow over me and watching the dirt form rivulets as it runs down my skin, to the floor and into the drain. All gone.

It's time to write to Max.

Dear Max, I'm pregnant. To you ...

I cross out the *to you* bit. It would only make him wonder.

Dear Max, It seems I'm pregnant ...

No that's not right. Either I am or I'm not. I cross out *it seems*, but then opening with *I'm pregnant* feels too direct. I tear off the page and screw it up. That makes at least ten balls of paper littering the back of my van. But I can't get the message right. Or the tone.

All the time I'm thinking, what if Max is seeing someone else? Maybe he's already forgotten me. When she asks, he'll refer off-handedly to his neurotic ex in Australia. Whatever the case, this letter is sure to come as a pretty rude shock. I feel so far away from him out here. And time is doing funny things. It seems like I've been away forever, but it's less than a month. Apart from a few postcards and a couple of emails, I've not shared any of this journey with him.

I start a fresh piece of paper.

Dear Max, You're going to be a father...

No, that sounds really stupid. I screw this page up too.

Dear Max, I've just found out that I'm pregnant. I worked out the dates and it's probably around ten weeks. Do you remember that night in my studio, when I told you I was going to Australia? It must have been then. That's nice isn't it? I'm glad it was then.

I stop writing for a minute. Not certain if 'nice' is the right word, or 'glad'. Not certain what I want to say to Max or what I expect him to think. The chances are he won't think it's nice at all. A drop of sweat lands on the page making a crinkly round splodge on the paper and smudging the last couple of words. He'll think I've been crying.

I've almost forgotten what Max looks like. If I concentrate really hard, I can remember his eyes, the line of his jaw, the coarse feel of the hair on his chest and shoulders, even the shape of his ears. I can see David quite clearly but no matter how much I concentrate, I can't put all the pieces of Max together and make a picture.

> *... I want to keep this baby, Max. I don't know why, and there are probably loads of reasons why I shouldn't, but it feels like the right thing to do. I don't know if having a baby will make things worse or better between us and maybe that's not the point. It's not why I want to keep it. It's not a carrot I'm dangling to keep you hanging on, or a threat to stop you from moving on. I don't want a shotgun wedding or anything... I have the feeling you've got fed up with me. Maybe you've even been seeing someone else while I've been away. It makes me afraid to think about how little it would take to wipe me from your life, without a trace. You could get the cleaner to do it Wednesday morning while you're at work. A quick sweep of the bathroom cupboard, empty the shelf in the fridge that's got the things I like on it, toss out the photo of my mother on my bedside table (please don't, it's my only copy) and that's about it. I don't seem to have made much of an impact on your life, do I? But being pregnant changes all that. This is our baby that's growing inside me and despite all our problems, I like the idea of that.*
>
> *I'm nearly finished here. Another week or two and I'll come home, although I'm scared at the prospect. I'm also scared about what I have to do here next. There's one more monster I have to face.*

Max is easily alarmed, so I decide to cross that last bit out. As I sit chewing the pen and wondering what to say next, I have the uncomfortable sense that something is watching me. But when I look around, there's nothing. The curtains are pulled shut and there aren't any cracks between them to let in prying eyes. I turn back to the letter, but the feeling persists. Then I notice a stick attached to the back curtain. When I look closer I see it has big round eyes. When I move they move, back and forth. I am being spied on by a stick insect. I leave it there, tensed up, waiting for its prey and perfectly camouflaged against the brown leaf-like pattern of the curtain.

> *... I'm sorry I couldn't make you understand how important this trip has been for me. We're all a mishmash of everything that's happened to us, or at least that's how it seems to me. I went along thinking everything was okay and then Nan died and I found out that the past and everyone in it had tricked me. That's a pretty big shock to the system. I had to find out what happened so I can make sense of me and Nan and Kita all over again. Sometimes you have to go backwards to move forwards. Maybe after this is over, I'll be able to let them all go.*
>
> *I'm going to wait to hear from you, Max. I'll be in Cairns in a few days. You can send a letter poste restante there, or an email.*
>
> *Love Storm xxxx*
>
> *PS: I've enclosed the litmus strip. The blue line means it's positive. Weird isn't it.*

Finished. I put the letter and the litmus strip in one of those thin airmail envelopes and address it, then I roll over and sink into a light sweaty sleep, watched over by my stick insect.

In the morning I walk into town, looking for the post office. Within minutes I'm wilting. Yesterday the temperature reached thirty-nine degrees Celsius. Today it feels hotter. It's still sunny, but clouds are already gathering on the horizon. Thunderheads, David called them, and they do start off that way, a sharp point like the head of an arrow, then spreading out, filling up the sky. All day they'll build up and up, until it's unbearable, and then it might rain. The rain will bring some relief, but make it steamier tomorrow. If it doesn't rain, the pressure will build until it's too much and then something will have to give. I don't know what, but I can't bear another day of this. David warned me about 'the Wet' up here, the heat and the stickiness.

'At least we missed troppo season,' he said. 'That's when all the murders happen.'

I walk past the Normanton public pool. There's a bunch of kids in the water, playing ball. They're shouting and laughing and splashing, filling the air with glittering white diamonds. The water looks greeny-blue and deliciously cool. I want to get in with them. I want to feel my skin contract with the cold tightening shock as I slide into the water. But they've laid claim to it and anyway there's stuff I have to do.

Between us is a thin wire fence, and a lot more I suppose, that's not so easy to see. I wonder if these kids feel a sense of belonging, and an ease with where they are. That's something I've never had. Because in English terms I've always been not quite. Not quite one thing or another. Not British, not Romany, not this school, not that.

'You don't fit,' Nan used to tell me. 'They'll never let you, not in this country.'

Not very comforting, but she was right. Max fits in and I don't, and that's why it's so hard for us to work together.

Back home we have all these layers between us and the world. A kind of thick armour, so we spend our time all trussed up and pretending. But out here there doesn't seem to be any of that crap. Just the freedom to be what you are. I know I'm being romantic. It's easy to do when you're travelling and looking in from outside, but things are never that simple.

In the pool they're passing around a baby, casually, each person taking it in turns. Then one of them lifts herself up onto the edge of the pool. She takes the baby, slides a breast out of her bikini top and stuffs a nipple into its mouth. She can't be more than fifteen or sixteen, but she's breast feeding her baby so easily, as if she's done it forever. I can't take my eyes off her, can't imagine me in her place. The others are playing around her, taking no notice, as if it's the most natural things in the world. And it is, I guess. But I don't know if you can do that in public in England or if you've get arrested.

I walk on, past a petrol station with its galvanised iron roof and a couple of old pumps outside. The stench of oil and petrol and rubber rises up with the heat of the morning and forces me across the road. There's a shop on the corner, in an old wooden building, with rickety verandahs and cold blue posters advertising ice creams. As I walk past the door there's a welcome blast of cool air. Then a passing car backfires and makes me jump. The shock hits me in my chest and somewhere new. Deep inside my belly.

Millie was only sixteen when she had Nan. Fifteen when she got pregnant. With no one to ask. But with all those brothers and sisters and cousins, she must have been used to babies. Except when it was her turn everything was different. Expelled from her family and not welcomed by Pop's, she would have felt so alone. Just Pop's awkward wonder at her changing body, with him treating her like something breakable and keeping away. When Nan was born, there were no cries of wonder, no words of wisdom, no one to hold the baby except Pop, and he was away six days each week, working long hours. I can see how she might have been torn between an immense protective love and a seeping, growing resentment. Millie's hugs were followed by slaps and never made sense but finally they made Nan into what she was.

And Nan, when she had Kita, moving away from her friends and her hopes. A fatherless baby. At least she had Millie to help, and Pop. But she also had the shame. In 1957 it wasn't the 'done thing,' and single mothers didn't get welfare support or any other support for that matter. Then Kita. A baby at nineteen, the drugs, the clothes, the road trip… In the seventies she was the height of fashion. But didn't live to see her baby grow up.

And now me, twenty-eight and pregnant. Nearly twice Millie's age when she had Nan, but I still feel too young. I don't have any family either, maybe not even Max. A few friends, but they'll think my life is over and stop inviting me out. Trevor will probably roll his eyes and cross me off his list. No more exhibitions for Storm. And it's hard to imagine Max's parents doting over my baby, knitting booties, blue ones because they'll want a boy, and buying little packets of those all-in-one things babies wear. Max is their only child. They'll want better for him.

A woman walks past me pushing a pram. She's wearing a loose dress and a straw hat and a dreamy half smile. I peer in at the tiny baby, fast asleep. It can't be more than a few weeks old. When I look at the mother's tired face, there's a kind of clarity and radiance in it, which makes her look beautiful, despite her body which is still too big for itself.

I don't feel any of that radiance, just nausea, and a difference inside that is hard to pinpoint. It feels like my body's been taken over by an alien. There's a metal taste in my mouth and no spare energy, my heart's going too fast and I'm way too hot, although that might actually be the weather. There's also a new weight sitting low in my groin. It's tiny but I'm aware of it all the time. It's not just the foetus, but also the terrifying weight of responsibility. All the certainty I felt yesterday has gone. What will I make this baby into?

I've forgotten my hat and the sun is beating into the top of my head, my skin has broken into beads of sweat which are quickly turning into rivulets. Already Max's letter is damp and limp between my fingers. A tired-looking letter and I haven't even sent it yet.

In the post office I buy a stamp, lick it and stick it on the envelope. The ink is smudging a bit and I worry that the address will be blurred and Max will never get my letter. I can still taste the sweet glue on my tongue as I stand in front of the mail-box, putting off the moment when I drop the letter in. That's the point when I won't be able to change my mind and take it back. I wait a few seconds more, take a deep breath, then let go.

CHAPTER TWENTY-THREE

Instead of turning east, I make a short detour and drive north up to Karumba on the Gulf of Carpentaria. I'm doing this for my mother. She wanted to stand at every edge of Australia and look out over all the different gulfs and seas and oceans, but she only managed two; the icy cold waters of the Southern Ocean at the very bottom of Australia, and the Pacific Ocean to the east. For Kita's sake I'm going to stand on the north coast of Australia.

Kita also wanted to see a crocodile. So do I, a real one, but not up close. Karumba is riddled with red and yellow signs warning about giant saltwater crocodiles and deadly jellyfish, so I like my chances. I walk along the shore keeping well away from the water, my head full of horror stories about monster crocodiles dragging people in, shaking them about and then spiralling them under in a frenzied death roll. What makes the idea of it so much worse is knowing the crocodiles only eat a little bit and then store the rest for later.

I was hoping for a sea breeze to help ease the tension of this heat. There is one, but it's hot and wet and salty, not refreshing, and the water is tantalising, but out of bounds. I stand still, savouring the feel of the warm coarse sand between my toes and scanning the surface of the sea, looking for glittering eyes or a long snout, a swishing tail, anything. Aside from a few dogs and kids playing in the sand, there are no other signs of life.

I wish I could pat myself on the back and say, good girl, Storm, you've done it. You've turned around and faced your monsters. But it isn't over yet. I walk shakily back to the van, open up all the windows and doors and lie down, dozing in a pool of perspiration. I'm so tired even the heat can't hold sleep at bay. This afternoon I will rest. Tomorrow I'll gather up my courage and start looking for Bill. There are still things I need to know and there's no other way of getting the answers. I want Bill to tell me why he murdered my mother. I want him to explain why he left me out there to die. I want to know what was on that torn-out page of Kita's diary. And I need to find out if I'm like him.

When I wake, it's late afternoon, heavy with sleep and hungry. I have a shower to wash away the sleep and the sweat, then decide to go out for a meal, even though my credit is running out and I should be practising austerity. Everything in my bag is crushed and smells of mildew. In the end I choose a clean denim skirt and a dressy cotton top and get dressed, trusting gravity to sort out the crinkles. I let my hair out of its scrunchie and tug at the tangles. The mascara makes my eyes look too big for my face. I put on some lipstick too, but my skin has gone so dark its almost lost on me.

I find a restaurant on the foreshore. It's busy and I wish Max were here ushering me through the crowd. Even David would do, in his slogan T-shirts. Alone, I'm suddenly too aware of myself for comfort. I want to glide in gracefully, but with each step I feel more robotic. I'd turn and leave right now if it wouldn't attract more attention. I find a table and order fresh king prawns and a glass of champagne. To celebrate, I tell myself: the end of Kita's journey; the letter on its way to Max; and the growing sense of clarity that's descended on me with all these decisions. In short little bursts, life has stopped seeming impossible. When the champagne comes I hold the long elegant glass up to my face and let the bubbles tickle my nose.

'For you, Mum,' I whisper.

The sun slips quietly down under the sea, leaving a livid burning sky and the water a rippling ecstasy of silver and orange. A quiet grows around me and I wonder if everyone feels the same tugging sadness, the poignancy of the day's ending, a regret that what's done is done. I imagine my letter hurtling towards Max, being shuffled and sorted and packed on trains, planes, trucks, vans, and finally into our postman's bag. One morning sometime this week, it will pop through the slot in the door and lie there all day on the slippery polished wooden floor, waiting for Max. What I can't begin to imagine, is Max's face when he reads it.

Gradually the sky turns a rich blue and the sea darkens to a deep dangerous black. The quiet is replaced by a surge of voices as people turn back to where they left off. All the time the pungent smell of seaweed hovers in the salty air.

I finish the prawns and order a lemonade with lots of ice, then rummage around in my bag for Kita's diary. It's stained and ragged now, with a few torn pages. Now her entries have finished, I'm left with the other half, the blank pages Kita left behind. Their clear potential stares out at me, a glare of white, slightly yellowed around the edges. I think about writing in them myself. Adding my voice to hers and in a way, finishing her story. But the empty pages already have their own story. It's futile wondering what more she might have written or what might have happened in our lives, or how we might have been together now.

For weeks I've been scouring the pages of this diary, reading lines over and over, memorising passages, trying to read between the words and decode the doodles - hers and mine. I've been running my finger over the paper, feeling the indents that the pen made and straining to see the woman writing them. Was she left-handed or right-handed? Was she sitting up when she wrote, or lying down on her belly? What sort of pen did she use? Did she chew the end like I do? Was I crawling all over her? Or trying to get away? Did she keep half an eye on me, or didn't she bother? Were we driving along while she wrote, the letters bumping and zigzagging with the rough road? Mostly her writing is messy and haphazard. I wonder what a handwriting expert would make of it. What verdict would Kita get? Unstable? Flamboyant? Psychotic?... How does her writing mirror the awful tragedy that was building up through the pages? And how is it that the blank pages at the end say more than any of the words?

For weeks I've been looking for my mother in words on a page, looking for her in the places she's been. Trying to understand what happened and why. I'm only just starting to realize that instead of finding my mother, I've been finding myself. That's what my journey's all about. I'm gathering up the pieces of me that I lost so long ago.

I put Kita's diary away and pull out my small sketchbook. My mother's diary is finished, but mine has only just begun. Unlike hers, mine is a visual diary. I flick through the pages. There are colour notes, studies of the light, and details: a leaf, a termite mound, a pair of weathered eyes, the rocky cairn I built for Kita, Jack asleep in his chair, Edith's smiling face, Uluru, a stick insect... but not David. There are also a few tentative studies for paintings. It's in these that I can see a new style emerging, in the colours and the composition, but also in the emotion. It feels as if a door is opening. The armour is coming off, but I'm not quite ready to look at my vulnerable new self.

I wander down to the beach and sit on the sand well away from the water's edge, just in case. The moon is up now and its light plays patterns on the rippling water. Behind me I can hear the murmur of voices from the restaurant, but it's peaceful here. I put Kita's diary on the sand in front of me and dig around in my bag for some matches. I've done with it now. This is not how I want to remember my mother. It's only a fraction of who she was. If Kita had been given the chance to live, then who knows, perhaps she would have faced her own monsters, perhaps she would have grown into someone special... perhaps we would have been friends. I tear out the pages, one by one, and screw them up into balls, then pile the balls together in front of me and set them alight. After a moment the flames burst out and up, sending their light into the darkness, and it feels as if her spirit is released with them. Then they subside, flickering orange and black in the sand.

'Goodbye Kita,' I say, the tears welling up. A drop lands in the dying embers. I remember something Millie used to say, an old Romany proverb: *Sar shaj jivas, te ne janas jekh avreske te od mukel?* How could we live at all if we didn't learn to forgive each other?

Next morning I pack up and drive back to Normanton and then east, into the sun, heading for a town in the mountains outside of Cairns and another meeting I'm not looking forward to. Bill's sister, Kate Harding. My aunt. Probably my only living relative, aside from Bill. Surely she'll know where he is.

I drive through angry purple skies and shooting diagonal sheets of rain. In between, sharp slivers of sun spotlight a termite mound, a bush, a tree, a blue-black crow, luminescent against the horizon. There are more colours in this landscape than I ever imagined. A painter's paradise. I store the colours and shapes in my head. The sharp line of the horizon slicing through the land and sky. Massive cloud formations, shaping and reshaping, weighing down the sky. A burnt-orange van, hurtling through space, and me inside feeling very small. Maybe one day I'll paint all this.

There are more cows now. They're like the Indian holy ones, all angular bones and too much skin. Sometimes there are trees, big broad shady gums that the cows shelter under. A couple of times I stop under their shade and do some sketches. I try to capture the colours, the tone, the textures of the scenes before me. Other times I just sit, staring at the clouds, watching and waiting. Just looking. Not thinking.

After two days not hurrying, I drive up to the Atherton Tablelands and everything suddenly changes. The long straight road begins to curve and there's more traffic. I have to negotiate other cars for the first time in ages. It feels like I'm screeching too fast around corners and almost slipping off the road. Although in reality the speedometer says I'm going stupidly slow and in the rear-vision mirror there are cars banked up behind me. I can't day-dream anymore. I have to stay with the road and concentrate.

First there's a twisted ancient vine scrubland, a tiny remnant from Gondwanaland, when there were dinosaurs. Max would love that, he knows all their unpronouncable names. When I laugh at him he gets huffy and tells me I wouldn't understand. 'It's a boy thing,' he says.

After the scrubland it becomes tropical and bright, with thick lush forests and round soft hills. I drive through Ravenshoe and Atherton and Tolga, pretty towns with painted wooden houses on stilts, and real lawns. The shops have food in them again. And most importantly, fresh fruit. I scoff ripe mangoes and pawpaw. My senses are in overdrive. Everywhere there's grass and flowers in rich vibrant poster colours, and powerful sensual smells that knock me about inside. The trees are getting closer and closer together, blocking out the horizon, refocusing everything, zooming in, such a huge contrast from the vast spaces I've got used to. I drive up towards Kuranda, and into a rainforest that's so thick it shuts out almost all the light and the air, so I have to struggle with each breath.

At the turn-off there's just a rusty old can for a mailbox and on top of that the name of the property, 'Clear Light'. The drive is steep and rough and muddy. My wheels keep spinning, making deep ruts in the ground, and I'm terrified I'll either get bogged or slide right off into the rain forest. I stop the van in a clearing and put on my boots. I'd rather walk than get stuck here, and the idea of reversing back down is a chilling one.

Behind me there's the low sound of a whistle, followed by a high sharp crack like a whip. The sound is beautiful and hard, slicing through the atmosphere.

CHAPTER TWENTY-FOUR

The house blends in so well with the rainforest that I don't see it until I'm almost there. It's on stilts, with wide-open verandahs and hardly any walls. There's not really a door to knock on, so I bang on a pole. No one comes.

'Hello,' I call

I don't hear her approaching. She's just suddenly here in front of me. Her long straight hair is streaked with white. Bare feet, an amethyst around her neck, and matching earrings. A hippie, but well groomed and her clothes look expensive. A designer hippie. I recognise her. She's an older version of the woman in the photo Leo gave me. It's like she's been caught in a time warp. She's hardly changed. Just got money. And got harder.

She looks puzzled, as if she's trying to place me. Then she takes a step back, unsettled for a moment. 'God!' she says and there's a quick flickering uncertainty in her eyes, fear maybe, before the lines sharpen around her face again. 'I'm sorry... I didn't expect anyone... I didn't hear a car.'

'It was so muddy I walked up. Are you Kate Harding?'

'Not for the past twenty years or so. My name's Almira.'

I assume this means she was Kate, once.

'I'm Storm Cizekova. I think you knew my mother.'

There's a slight pause before she smiles. And when she does it's only with her mouth. I can't read anything welcoming in her eyes.

'Yes, I knew Kita ...' She pauses and I can see she's reluctant, but curious too. 'You might as well come in.'

I take off my muddy boots and follow her into the house. Notice the quiet delicate way she walks, not making any noise, her feet hardly touching the ground. The way her loose silk trousers swish. Her straight back. She makes me feel like a clumsy elephant.

'How did you find me?'

'I met Leo Knight in Sydney. He gave me your address.'

'Leo! I haven't seen him for years... How on earth? Oh, that's right, he came up once. Years ago, when we were still building. It wasn't his scene.' She laughs. 'Too many leeches.'

I smile. It's hard to imagine Leo dealing with a leech. Me neither, for that matter.

'You've got an amazing house,' I say, peering out across a verandah that's probably bigger than the whole of Victoria Cottage. And unlike the cottage with its thick walls and clearly defined spaces, here there don't seem to be any edges. I can't make out where the house ends and the verandah begins.

'Isn't it. It took us ages to build. We had to live in a caravan for a couple of years because we didn't have any money to finish it. And it would've taken longer, only Mum and Dad died... '

She trails off and I look back at her in time to see a shadow crossing her face.

'Sit down out there if you like. I'll make some tea. It's not every day my "niece" comes to visit,' she adds, putting little apostrophes around niece and making it sound stupid.

'I suppose not,' I say, wondering if I'm imagining the spite in her voice. She's never bothered to track me down, so I didn't expect open arms, but I didn't expect this either. In a way it's a relief. I've never had an aunt before and I'm not sure I want to start now. Aunt Almira? Aunty Allie? No, it just doesn't sound right.

Almira opens a cupboard and I get a glimpse of all her clearly labelled tea tins sitting in a neat row. Nan used to say you can tell a person by the state of their cupboards.

'Let's see. There's chamomile, peppermint, lemon verbena, a fruity thing or the real stuff.'

'Real, please,' I say, needing something with an edge. Something to hold onto, so I don't spread out to nothing in this strange house.

I go outside and sit on a lopsided wooden chair. It's handcrafted in a fashionable rustic look. Uncomfortable, but the cushions help. There's a rainbow-striped hammock strung between two poles on the edge of the verandah. I'd like to lie in it, but that would be making myself at home. And I don't feel safe enough for that. I can't imagine how Almira manages to relax here. The rainforest is brushing the edge of the house. It feels dangerous, as if it's poised there waiting to take over. If I dozed off, I'd wake to find myself part of it, rooted to the ground, surrounded by twisting, choking vines.

I close my eyes for a minute, playing with the idea, listening to the sounds of the forest, a buzzing, whirring, busy noise that gets too loud if you let it. Then I focus on my neck, my shoulders, back, calves, releasing tensed-up muscles, lowering myself deeper into the cushion.

I wonder if Almira's had kids of her own. Somehow I doubt it. There are no family photographs on show, no trophies, stray shoes, or abandoned toys, no evidence of children at all, past or present. Her parents are dead, she's got a murderer for a brother and an unwanted niece. I can feel her aloneness. It's a force field around her, something repellent that makes me step back, rather than reach out.

When I open my eyes, I see something that sends my muscles into tight knots all over again. Right above me there's a monstrous snake coiled around one of the verandah poles. I shut my eyes then open them. Hoping. But it's still there, so close I can see the intricate pattern of its skin, can even see the scales. With my eyes fixed firmly on the snake, I edge very slowly out of the chair and then back around the coffee table, into the kitchen.

Almira sees my face and laughs. 'So you've met George. He adopted us a year ago. We kept taking him back to the forest and he kept coming right back. We've given up bothering now. He eats rats and mice, so he's worth having around.'

'What sort of snake is it?'

'A carpet snake. Don't worry, he's not poisonous. He just strangles - '

She stops and a flush rises up into her cheeks. Neither of us know where to go from here.

'That's alright then,' I say finally, 'so long as he's harmless... Here I'll take these.'

I grab the two mugs and a jug of milk and carry them back out to the verandah. I choose a different chair, as far away as possible from George.

She brings out a pot. It's fine china, with a slender long spout. When she pours the tea, I notice her fingers are long and slender too. Terribly fine, but the bones are too sharp and there's something about them that makes me shudder. She reminds me of a cat. Not a cute fluffy one that lazes about on people's laps. No. Almira's more like a Siamese. Sinuous and slender, perhaps even treacherous.

The tea is perfumed. Jasmine maybe. And there are thin almond biscuits, the sort you get in Italian coffee shops.

'We run a cafe in town. That's where Julian is. My partner. You're lucky to find me here. I'm usually working. But it's off season, so I don't go in as often.'

We sip our tea. The pause goes on for too long. She's staring at me which is disconcerting and makes the almond biscuit I'm chewing sound way too loud.

'It's uncanny how much you look like your mother,' she says. 'Nothing at all like Bill. How unsurprising.'

When I ask what she means, Almira puts down her cup and looks at me, eyes narrowed, savouring her moment.

'Billy thought he was your father. Kita put his name on your birth certificate, so I suppose legally he was. But I'm not so sure.'

Why am I not surprised by this? Almira has already made it perfectly clear she doesn't want a niece. I suppose I should be relieved at the possibility Bill might not be my father, but instead I'm angry. How dare she think I'm not good enough to be part of her family. I want to shout at her; tell her I never wanted Bill for a father; tell her it's crap blood and she's got it too. More than anything, I want to wipe that superior smile off her face. But if I do I'll have to leave and there are things I need to know first.

'Why not?' I ask, trying hard not to spit the words at her.

She hesitates, not certain where to start. Or just making sure she gets it right. Either way, I get the distinct impression of a cat getting ready to pounce.

'Kita was a beautiful woman. She was wild, in the sort of way that draws men, you know?'

I nod. So that's why she hated Kita. Because Almira is so contained. She's still attractive, maybe even beautiful, in the way a marble sculpture is beautiful, cold and carefully chiselled. But the only way anyone would penetrate her would be with a hammer. I wonder if there are any soft spots left, deep inside her somewhere, because people aren't born like this. It takes lots of hurt to get so brittle.

'She thought it was all a secret, but you'd have to be blind to miss what she was up to. In front of Bill too, half the time, though he was usually too stoned to notice.'

'So you don't think he was my father?'

'Who knows?' she says. 'The chances are he was. But really it could have been anyone's.'

It feels like she's hit me in the face 'That's me you're calling *it*,' I say, but she doesn't seem to notice.

'You know he turned up here after the... after your mother was killed.'

'Murdered,' I hiss and she looks at me, bristling.

'Yes,' she says. 'Murdered. It was two days later. They were on their way here anyway, so he just carried on ...'

She stops and refills her cup. She's taking her time, pouring in the milk, adding half a sugar and stirring for too long. When she stirs, the spoon makes a gentle rhythmic clink inside the cup.

'We'd just bought the land and hadn't started building yet. It was pretty basic. We were still in the old caravan.' She takes a sip and stares out into the forest, remembering. Anger is creeping into her voice. 'The police said I was harbouring a criminal. They wanted to get at me anyway. You know, hippies living in the forest in the seventies. It was too much for their petty little brains to handle. But it took the police a week to find me and by that time Billy had left.'

I take a deep breath. 'Why did he do it?'

Almira shrugs. 'I don't know. The papers talked about drugs and too much alcohol. But that wasn't all of it... '

She nibbles slowly on an almond biscuit while I shift about impatiently on my seat, holding myself back, determined to wait her out.

'Kita ate away at Billy,' she says, then looks at me nervously as if afraid she's gone too far. 'Of course that doesn't excuse what he did. Nothing does. But he wasn't strong enough for her. He couldn't bear not having her.'

Her cat eyes are almost shut now, just two thin slits across her face. 'She taunted him. She brought him right down until he wasn't a man anymore. Not even man enough to leave.'

Evidently one of us has got it wrong. Kita's diary made it clear she was the one who wanted to leave Bill, not the other way around. But Almira seems determined to cast her brother in the role of victim.

'He loved you.' Almira sighs. 'That's partly why he stayed... Wait,' she says, getting up. 'I'll show you something.'

She leaves me contemplating the nature of love. Can you kill for love? Can you abandon what you love? How complicated can it get?

Almira comes up behind me, close enough so I can feel her breath on the top of my head and smell her perfume, a rich woody smell like sandalwood. She thrusts a picture in front of me. I recognise him straight away. He's young here. Even younger than when he killed Kita. But he looks healthy and there's something in his eyes that's missing from the newspaper clippings Jack gave me. It's hard to pinpoint. Maybe it's a future.

'Look at him,' says Almira. 'Look at those eyes. How sweet they are. He was so innocent.'

But I'm not looking for innocence. I'm scanning his eyes and nose, the curve of his mouth, the length of his ear lobes. Looking for a resemblance. In her diary Kita said my eyes were like my father's, but I can't tell. Of course he's my father even though I wish he wasn't. His name is on my birth certificate. Why else would it be there?

'Why would he do anything like that?' asks Almira, snatching the photo back from me. 'Billy's never said. I don't think he even knows. But I've thought about it. For years I've wondered. And I keep coming up with the same answer. Someone like him had to be pushed and pushed... and then pushed some more.'

I think about the newspaper cuttings Leo and Jack gave me. How I've forced myself to look at the man who killed Kita. My father, with his puffy self-pitying face. He pleaded not guilty, even when there was no doubt he did it. The baby brother. How weak he was. And contemptible. I wish Almira was telling the truth. I wish I could wipe his name off my birth certificate and extract his blood from mine.

'Everyone said Kita could see the future,' says Almira. 'In the future. Oh, she laughed it off, but you know, she really thought she had a short cut into universal consciousness, that one.'

Almira's practically hissing now and I'm completely repelled. There's not really anything more to say. This woman hated Kita and she's still stuck on it.

We sit looking out into the forest wondering where we can go from here.

'The rainforest is an amazing thing,' says Almira so suddenly I jump. 'Every plant, every animal, fighting for its own survival. We're all parasites here, feeding off each other. It's an incredibly hostile place.'

I briefly wonder what she's getting at, but am distracted by the feel of something wet under my sock. A fat slimy leech is attached to my ankle. I squeal and flick it away and blood spurts out.

Almira laughs. 'The rainforest is crawling with them. Don't worry, they won't hurt you.'

I lean back, trying to look relaxed. My tea has gone tepid but I take a sip anyway. There's only one more thing I need to know but if I ask it straight out, she won't tell me.

'Is he still in jail?' I ask. Jack has already told me he's out, but I need to keep her talking.

'No, they let him out six years ago. He's not a pretty sight.'

I wait, holding my breath like I used to with Millie and Nan when I wanted a story. If the silence stretches out long enough people usually break.

'He's just down the road, living in a caravan in a tourist park in Cairns. I visit him once a month. Take some food and clean up a bit for him. He's a diabetic and doesn't look after himself. It's sent him blind.' She stops, realises she's said too much and loses her temper again.

'It's pathetic. Such a dreadful waste. She brought him to this, you know. It killed our parents. Dad had a massive heart attack not long after. Then Mum got cancer.'

I put down my cup in a hurry and the tea sloshes over the table. Who knows how people become murderers? Maybe it runs in this family. It's time to go. I've found out what I needed.

'It killed my mother too,' I say, standing up. 'Thanks for the tea.'

I see the alarm registering in her eyes.

'You're not going to see him are you?'

'Of course I am.'

'Please don't. It will kill him.' she says, practically begging now.

I smile, surprised that she's failed to see the irony.

CHAPTER TWENTY-FIVE

After two weeks of Outback towns and roadstops, it feels good being in a city again and on the coast. Cairns is small but cosmopolitan; the foreshore's lined with perfect palms, white sand, and lots of thin people wearing wrap-around sunglasses. The outdoor cafes serve pastrami and bocconcini foccacias, oven baked spicy wedges and soya smoothies, instead of the standard steak sandwiches, greasy chips and chocolate milkshakes I've been bringing back up all over the Outback.

I choose a place near the water and order a cafe latte. The tables and chairs are elegant fine metal and the coffee comes how I like it, burning hot, with a paper napkin wrapped neatly around the glass. I watch people walking past. The men wear board-shorts and dark tans and sandals and the women all seem to have bare middles and perfectly flat bellies. Looking at them, I feel a surge of panic. For the rest of my life I'll probably have to wear loose T-shirts and stretchy pants to hide the flabby post-baby bits.

I take a sip of my coffee, but it turns my stomach and I have to leave most of it. Then I wander around for a while, absorbing the feel of the place and peering wistfully at the slinky fitted dresses and designer bikinis in the shops. It doesn't take long to come down from my city high. Cairns looks exotic and romantic, just like in the tourist brochures but I can taste the exhaust fumes in the back of my throat and the hard concrete pavements are making my feet and lower back ache. It's sticky and wet and you can't swim in the sea because it's full of stingers and I've got itchy fungus growing between my toes and a rattly problem with my exhaust pipe that means I'll have to venture into the industrial area, looking for a mechanic.

I stop at the first place, not sure if it looks promising or not. There are cars everywhere, in various states of decomposition. The mechanic comes out of his workshop, wiping his hands on a smelly rag. His face is old and wizened, like a dried-up apple and he's got a white scratchy chin.

'Cor,' he says, 'it's hanging on by a thread. Reckon you'll lose it any sec.'

'How long?' I ask. There's no need to point out that I sleep in it.

'Leave it with me,' he says. 'If I can get hold of the parts you'll have it back tomorrow arvo.'

I don't have a lot of choice, so I stuff a few things into my bag, graciously accept his offer of a lift back into town and resign myself to a night in a motel.

It takes ages to find somewhere central that's cheap enough. The room smells of insect spray and mould. The bed is wearing a dirty beige cover with listless ragged tassles. It sags in the middle and the pillows look sad. But the sheets are clean, there's a fan and fly screens on the windows. There's also a full length mirror, which makes a change. I've got used to looking at little bits of myself in the rear-vision mirror.

I wash away my sticky sweat under the shower, switch on the fan and then stand wet and naked in front of the mirror. I cup my breasts in my hands. They're huge and heavy and sore, but I knew that already. What surprises me is how much darker my nipples are and the way my veins are more pronounced. A mess of blue lines crisscrossing my breasts. I turn sideways on and run my hands over my belly. A little curve, but no one would know.

Even so, I can't wear most of my clothes, can't bear anything tight against my womb. There are distinct tan lines on my arms and legs, and around my neck, marking the various edges of my shorts and different shapes of my T-shirts. I stare at my face. It's dark, but the rings under my eyes are even darker, almost black it seems in this light, and so like Millie. I'm searching for something, but there's nothing in my expression that says, this girl is pregnant, this girl is going to be a mother.

When I ring the next morning the mechanic has bed news.

'Sorry love, he says. 'I had to order the part in from down south. It's going to take three days.'

There's nothing I can do about it. I tell myself there's no rush, that Bill isn't going anywhere, that I'm waiting to hear from Max, that it's probably a good thing. But the impatience still tugs at me, sapping the pleasure out of now.

In the market I buy a couple of colourful sarongs to wrap around my growing belly. I go into the library and check my emails, hoping for something from Max, though it's only been six days. There are heaps of messages, all trying to tug me back into my old life, which seems impossibly remote. Pete, the life drawing tutor, wants to know if I'm planning to do anymore modelling. Trevor wants a guest list for the exhibition. And Max wants to know where I am, so he obviously hasn't got my letter yet. I answer what I need to, putting people off, promising lists and commitments later. And I ignore all the other messages, including Max's.

Then I go into a bookshop, looking for a novel to pass the time, but instead I'm drawn to the pregnancy books. The one I choose has a series of drawings of the baby in the womb; at six weeks, nine weeks, twelve weeks and all the way to forty weeks. I stand, blushing, at the counter, fixing my eyes on the stress toy sitting next to the till; a soft Mr Potato Head, with *Squeeze Me* written across the bottom. The woman puts the book in a paper bag, but I still feel embarrassed, like someone with the runs buying toilet paper.

I spend the afternoon sprawled out on the bed in just my knickers, with the fan on, reading my pregnancy book. Words like episiotomy and epidural make my toes curl. I avoid the pictures that come later in the book, women spread wide open, their faces sucked inwards with pain, wet babies heads… They make me cry. But I'm greedy to find out what's going on now. Week eight throws me into a panic. *You should be thinking about arranging childbirth classes,* it says. And I haven't even seen a doctor yet.

It tells me the baby's organs, brain, hands and feet have already formed and the foetus is one and a bit inches long, with fingerprints. There's more blood circulating through my body, which is why I get puffed out so easily, and I need to buy a bra with good support. Week nine is only a few days away and by then the foetus will be making breathing-like movements and be able to bend its fingers around an object. I push down the panic that's rising inside me and work out the due date. October 25th. God, it's getting real.

On the second day I force myself to visit the lingerie section of a department store and tell the sales assistant I'm pregnant.

'You'll be needing a maternity bra then,' she says.

She's all matter-of-fact as she prods and pushes me into a horrible white thing with wide straps and absolutely no sex appeal. But it feels comfortable, so I resign myself to its sexless functionality and buy two.

I can't help it, my feet take me straight from there to the baby section. There's so much equipment: baths, push chairs, prams and cots, car seats and bouncers and so many other strange expensive things that don't seem to have any function at all.

I wonder if it's all necessary. But it's the little clothes that get to me, with their fiddly buttons, and the fluffy red booties with teddy bears and elastic round the ankles. I pick up a booty. It's so tiny in my hand. As I stand here holding it, there's a flooding sensation deep inside my chest and seconds later my nipples start leaking. I can't believe it. My book says this doesn't happen until later on. It's not much, just two little dots on my T-shirt. But it's enough to bring reality crashing down on me all over again.

On the last day I rise out of my baby stupor and go on a tour to a crocodile farm. The tour comes with a crocodile burger. I offer mine to a guy with long sandy hair and stoned far-away eyes.

'You sure?' he asks.

'Yeah,' I say. 'I couldn't.

We walk around for an hour or so, looking at massive crocodiles sunning themselves. They're like sharks, with those cold eyes and no sentiment. Real hunters. You can't tame them or talk them out of it.

'You have to admire them,' says the crocodile keeper who's got a gaping scar on his right thigh. 'Yeah,' he says, when he sees me looking. 'It got me. Take your eyes away for a second and you're a goner.'

'In here,' he calls and the group gathers around for the grand finale. The crocodile keeper walks into an enclosure which is empty, except for a shallow murky brown pool.

'The water's only knee deep, he explains, marching up to the edge holding a stick with a bit of bloody chicken on the end. It's still got its feathers.

'See that,' he says, pointing at a slight ripple on the surface of the water. 'He's felt the vibration from my feet.'

Seconds later there's a mass of displaced muddy water and jagged teeth as a giant crocodile leaps out of the pool at the man.

'Lordy,' shouts the woman next to me. 'He's a big bugger.'

I let out a yelp as it grabs the stick and goes into a death roll with it, over and over and over. Only knee deep! But it's the ripple that's got to me most. It's hard to imagine a ripple like that being so menacing. And the fact they can shut down and stay for ages under the water. Waiting.

I'm still shivering when the sandy-haired guy asks me out.

'For a drink,' he says, looking the other way.

I'm taken by surprise and catch myself opening my mouth to say okay. That's when I realise how lonely I am. I imagine reaching under his shirt to touch his skin, and have to shake myself free of this crazy desire to have sex with a stranger. Maybe I'm more like my mother than I ever imagined.

'Sorry,' I say. 'I'm pregnant.'

CHAPTER TWENTY-SIX

As soon as the van is ready I start working my way through the caravan parks in the outskirts of Cairns.

I find him in the third park.

The woman at reception looks blank when I ask for Bill Harding. 'No,' she says, shaking her head. 'I don't think so.'

'He's blind,' I say.

'Oh yes,' she says and her tone is surprisingly affectionate, as if she really likes him. 'William. That's nice, he doesn't get many visitors.'

Maybe she doesn't know.

I tell her my name is Sandy Smith and book in for one night, thinking that's all I'll need. Then I drive towards his caravan and set up camp nearby under a giant fig tree. It's not a very big caravan: off white and rounded at the edges, with scratches and dents here and there. There's a big stripy green and white annexe on the side. Through the narrow flap it's murky dark, but I can just make out a couple of plastic outdoor lounge chairs and the white outline of what's probably a fridge. I can't see the television but I know it's there because it's flickering flashes of colour.

I knew it would be hard, but I didn't expect this kind of paralysis. An aunty is one thing, but a father, that's in a completely different league. I've run out of courage. I can't do it. Can't bring myself to walk up to the door and knock. Can't make one foot follow the other to cover that short distance. I need to see him first, so I know what to expect, so that when he opens the door I don't fall apart.

I end up waiting for two days, watching his van in a haze of sweat and indecision. It rains the whole time, in a steady torrent, so thick its almost solid. The wind knocks figs and small branches onto my campervan in scraping thuds. I only go into town once, for supplies, and to check for an email or a letter from Max. I only leave the van to go to the toilet block or do the dishes in the camp kitchen where there's hot water and company. Even so, I don't see him.

At night the fruit bats come out and feast on the bursting overripe figs. They crap on the van in big purple splodges and all night there's the plop of figs splatting on the roof. There are possums up there too. They make blood-curdling shrieks that wake me up in a trembling sweat of worry. All day and night the tree is a mass of feasting and squabbling. Too many things are not what they seem: sticks that move, a giant praying mantis and luminescent green leaves that flutter on my towel and fly off when I reach out to touch them. At dawn the birds start calling in a building cacophony of sound that blends together into a screaming mess like a Jackson Pollock painting. At dusk the dengue fever-carrying mosquitoes emerge and the air is one giant buzz. There's no peace here. And it's driving me nuts.

I lie in the van, peering through the rain, waiting and watching, while time winds down to almost a stand still. I fill up my sketchbook, focusing on details, drawing the fig tree, insects, a leaf, anything to hold my fear at bay. There's hardly any sign of life in his caravan. The only way I know he's in there, is the flickering light from the television, the occasional bang or creak as he moves about inside and the muttering that starts late in the evenings. He's probably drunk and talking to himself, because I haven't seen any pets. What I can't get used to is the way the lights don't come on in the evenings.

I make myself look at the newspaper cuttings again. In one there's a mug shot of Bill. He's looking at the camera, sullen and straight-faced. Another photo looks like it was taken just after they handed down the life sentence. He's looking at the floor, or his eyes are shut. The sag of his shoulders, the angle of his head, it all spells despair. In one he's flanked by police and surrounded by a crowd. He's covered his head with a shirt in an attempt at anonymity. This is the only photo that shows the rest of him, and I can see he's not the lean idealistic man Kita fell for. He's getting puffy, and his belly is already hanging just a little over his trousers. He's weak. I try to see what Kita saw. Why she was still with him. In the diary she made it clear she wanted to leave. So what made her stay? Me? Or was it fear? Or money? Because she didn't have any. But then neither did he. I know she didn't love him. At least not by then. He wouldn't have killed her if she did.

I don't know if Bill loved Kita or me. In the diary she writes about the good times too. How sometimes he was funny, and kind. There's him crawling about on all fours with me on his back or pretending to be a monster and making me laugh and squeal at the same time. And him leaning over the jetty at Glenelg, with me on his shoulders and the wind in our faces. But those moments weren't enough in the end. If he loved me, like Almira says he did, then why did he leave me in the desert like that?

On the third day when the rain finally stops and I'm sitting outside soaking up the early-morning sun, I hear Bill's door open and seconds later he comes out through the annexe carrying a garbage bag. Time springs back into life as he emerges into the light. I'm shocked. He can't be much more than fifty, but he's an old man, shuffling about in worn-down flip-flops, his shorts sitting under a great fat belly. I wonder if he's proud of it, the way David said Australian men sometimes are; going on about how much they've invested in their guts. They look stupid though, all these tough blokes, waddling about like pregnant women, with fat tight stomachs and poppy-out belly buttons.

When he looks my way, I panic and have to force myself to stay put. He's blind, I tell myself. He's blind. But he doesn't stumble or wear dark glasses, or carry a little tapping stick. The only clue is the cautious way he walks and way his eyes stare straight ahead, not shifting about from one thing to the next.

I study him greedily, searching his face for clues, trying to see past the sagging jowls, the livid layers of his neck and the balding scalp, pockmarked with sun-spots. I look for his expressions, his gestures, anything that might be familiar. My father. Just the idea of a father, any father, leaves me helpless. I'm not used to them. I've no experience.

He turns and disappears inside again, leaving me staring at the empty space he's left. I've hardly started looking at him and he's gone again. I almost get up and follow him in. Almost. But then he comes out again and makes his way to reception. This time he has a stick to feel his way along the path. His back is a curve and his face is permanently pointed at the ground, as if he's looking for something he's lost. His trousers are baggy and too long, the cuffs scraping along the path behind him. He's the image of a broken man.

Half an hour later he's back. I don't move, just sit quietly and watch him approach, waiting for him to disappear back inside the caravan, but instead he turns around and looks right at me.

'I know you're there.'

My heart is banging away so loud he must be able to hear it. I don't know what to do. Don't know if I want a confrontation. Don't know anything yet. I grab fistfuls of grass to stop myself from running.

'Maggie at reception, she asked about my visitor. You're it I suppose?'

I still don't say anything. I'm taunting him with silence, but it's not intentional, I just don't know where to start or how to get past the thumping in my chest.

'What do you want? If you're the press, I've got nothing to say.'

There's an edge in his voice. He's scared and for some reason that makes me feel better.

'My name is Storm,' I say eventually, and watch him wince.

One emotion after another flashes across his face. At first there's a kind of backward longing, then he half smiles, then it's fear, then something like greed and somewhere underneath there might be anger too.

'I thought you might come one day.'

He comes closer, feeling his way over to me. When he reaches his arms out I duck away, not willing to grant him that intimacy.

There are tears in his eyes. This close I can see they're brown and I'm surprised at how intact they look.

'It's been a long time,' he says and the self-pity in his voice hardens me against him.

'And whose fault is that?' I ask, turning away. Disgust is welling up inside me, so strong I feel like throwing up. Every instinct I have is telling me to run, but I force myself to climb slowly into the van.

'Please don't go,' he begs. 'Please.'

There's a rock in my heart as I drive off. I want to keep driving, away from this, all the way back to England. But it's not over yet. And I'm angry with myself, almost as much as him. I won't let him ambush me again. I'll come back in my own time.

CHAPTER TWENTY-SEVEN

The post office is always busy and today the post restante section is the busiest of all, with a queue that snakes back and forth all the way to the door. Each day I've stood in this queue, squeezed between backpacks and watched other people walk out with letters and parcels and expectant eyes. Why doesn't Max write, or at least send an email? It's been ten days since I sent that letter and still nothing. Maybe I forgot to put an airmail sticker on it. Or Max is away. There are bleaker possibilities, of course, ones I don't want to dwell on. But I can't be sure about anything until I hear from him.

It's a good ten minutes before I get to show the man my passport. He shuffles through the C box, pulls out a letter and hands it over. Just like that. I nervously scan the thin envelope, aware that one possible future is contained inside. *Storm Cizekova, c/o Poste Restante, Cairns, Australia.* There's no doubt. It's Max's writing.

I force myself to wait until I'm back in the van and by then my fingers are trembling so much I can hardly open the envelope. Inside there's a small slip of paper: *I'm in Room 19 at the Seaview Motel on the Esplanade. M x*

I check the envelope more closely. The handwriting is definitely Max's, but the stamp is Australian and post marked Cairns. He's here.

I stumble over myself to get to him. Put the wrong key in the ignition, then can't do up my seatbelt. I stall twice before I get going and then pull out straight into the path of another car. The driver blares his horn and yells at me and my nerves are shot, but it's enough to get me concentrating again. The traffic lights are against me all the way but even so it's only a few minutes before I pull up in front of the Seaview Motel.

It's a fancy one, with a view across the water and a glistening polished foyer. Normally I'd feel the need to be dressed up for a foyer like this, but today I stumble through without noticing. There's a mirror in the lift and I stare at myself distractedly, not really seeing. Until I'm suddenly aware of my messy hair and furry teeth, the sexless bra and the tatty knickers I'm wearing. And the sarong! God, he won't recognise me. I tug at my hair and scrape at my teeth with a fingernail.

When Max opens the door I can hardly believe this is really happening. I stand there taking him in. Hungry for more, but too afraid to step forward and wrap my arms around him, as if that might break the spell and he'll disappear. He's wearing boxer shorts. And that's all. He's paler than I remember and unshaved. There are dark rings under his eyes and a strain in his face that I haven't seen before. He looks exhausted. He's beautiful. He's here.

'Hi,' I say and it doesn't seem enough.

I smile because otherwise I'll cry. His face breaks into an answering smile and he reaches out for me. I bury my face in his neck, my cheek rubbing against the soft down of his ear, remembering him all over again. His own particular smell of warm Max sweat and the lemony starch he does his shirts with. And there's another smell, a rich new spice I can't quite identify. Maybe cardamom. When my fingers find the coarse curled hair on his chest, something inside me lets go. There's no doubt anymore. I'm in the right place.

He searches out my mouth and when we kiss it's fierce and hungry. But through the need, I'm getting whiffs of his half-eaten breakfast. It's on his breath and wafting about the room. I haven't eaten yet today, so that makes it worse. The nauseating stench of bacon and eggs and the oily fungal smell of fried mushrooms, is making my stomach heave so much I have to push past Max and run into the bathroom. I get there just in time and throw up loudly in the toilet.

Oh God, talk about destroying the moment. In the mirror my face looks washed out, exhausted like Max's and my chin and lips and the space just above are rubbed red from his bristles. I clean up slowly, flush the toilet and wipe around the edges.

'Are you alright?'

Max's concern comes floating through the door, but he doesn't come with it. Thank God.

'Fine,' I say, filling up the sink with hot water. But the plug doesn't fit properly and all the water runs out again. Unlike the foyer downstairs, the bathroom isn't exactly perfect. The toilet seat is wobbly, the laminex around the bowl is peeling at the edges and the mirror is speckled with toothpaste spit. A first-class foyer and second-class rooms. I hold a washer under the tap and scrub my face with lots of. Then I wash my mouth out, before using Max's toothbrush. When I venture back, I'm prickly and vulnerable all over again.

But he's grinning. 'Nice to see you too,' he says and it's so very Max that I have to laugh.

'Sorry,' I say, grimacing. I walk away from him, over to the window. 'You got my letter then.'

'I did.' He takes a deep breath. 'It was a bit of a shock.'

Max's is the first proper English voice I've heard for weeks and I'm surprised how foreign it sounds.

'It gave me a shock too,' I tell him, circling round the point. 'When did you get here?'

'Yesterday afternooon. It's a hell of a long haul. I'm shattered.' He pours himself a coffee. 'You want one?'

We're being polite with each other.

'No thanks. I can't drink it anymore …'

Max raises an eyebrow but doesn't say anything. He's surprised. I've always been a coffee junkie, like Nan. Coming off it has been an agony of headaches, but that's better than the watery throwy-up feeling I get every time I take a sip, or even a sniff these days. I've got so sensitive.

'I'll have your orange juice though, if that's okay.

'Sure.'

I pick at the left-over bacon on his plate, soaking up the runny yellow bit of the egg with some cold toast. Now the nausea is gone, I'm starving hungry.

Max sits down with his coffee. 'So, he says. We've got a lot to talk about.'

I nod and gulp down the rest of the orange juice nervously. I don't know why I'm always so afraid of talking things through. Max and I haven't done much of it before. Not about us anyway. Mostly we've both preferred to look the other way.

'First up,' he says, waving my letter about like he's fanning a stink out of the air. 'We'd better clear up this bollocks about me seeing someone else.' He reads out loud. *'I have the feeling you've got fed up with me. Maybe you've even been seeing someone else while I've been away… '*

I wince at how incredibly stupid it sounds now.

'So where did you dredge this up from?'

I shrug. 'I don't know… Everything was so bad between us before I left.'

Max is shaking his head and swearing under his breath. 'Storm, you're so paranoid. Can't you just relax and accept what you have. Stop expecting everything to be taken away. That's what I'm fed up with, not you. I am not fed up with you. Do you believe me?'

I nod. He's doing the spelling-out thing again and making me feel stupid. I hope we can move on from this as quickly as possible. I'm ashamed and maybe that will be enough for Max. I'm also relieved. At least my head will be free of the image of some other woman's long, smooth, spot-free legs, languishing on our sheets.

But Max won't let it go. 'We've been together for nearly four years. Isn't it about time you started trusting me?'

He's looking at me expectantly, but I don't know what to say. This isn't fair. Max has always been the one with the uncluttered life and no commitments and now he's making it my fault.

When I don't answer he gets even more frustrated. 'Can't you step outside yourself for a minute and try seeing the world from someone else's shoes. Stop making excuses. Stop blocking me out. I don't have a little black book with a list of girls' phone numbers... I love you, Storm. Don't you get it?'

That's the first time he's told me he loves me and it must have been hard for him because he's not an L-word sort of a person. For me it's like a blast in the chest. I feel a surge of joy and terror. No one has ever told me they loved me before. Not straight out like that anyway. I want to. I really do, but I can't seem to say it back. Can't shape my mouth around those words.

'I'm scared of losing you,' I blurt out instead.

'You're not going to lose me.'

'But our lives are different. We want different things. You're a financial advisor, for God's sake.'

I bite my lip. I shouldn't have said that. It's not what I mean, but I can't find the right words.

'What do you want me to do? Grow my hair and chain myself to trees?'

I shake my head, wondering all over again why it was so much easier talking to David. But even as I think this, I know the answer - with David there was never anything to lose but with Max there's so much at stake.

'Jesus Storm, there's a place for everyone… Every time I advise a client to put their money in a green fund, I make a difference. I might wear a suit, but I'm trying. What are you doing?'

He stands up and kicks the table. The cups, plates, everything jumps and clatters down again higgledy-piggledy and the violence of it makes me close up inside.

'Can you see it?' I ask. 'The two of us. You sitting about on Sundays, reading the paper while I scurry around changing the water in the vases and making cups of tea… just like your mum and dad.'

I don't know why I'm pushing like this. Winding him up. It's like there's a little demon inside me gleefully putting a spanner in the works, as Nan used to say.

'It doesn't have to be like that,' he says. 'And even if it was, there are far worse things. Don't try to make me ashamed of my family, Storm. My parents are still together. They love each other, for God's sake. That must mean something.'

Max walks over to the window and stares out, at the mass of angry clouds forming over the sea, at the people on the street, at whatever. 'Don't you think it's about time you stopped being ashamed of me, Storm? And take a good look at yourself. You're way more respectable than you like to admit.'

Max doesn't understand. It's me I'm ashamed of. Not him. It's me that doesn't live up to the picture. I stare miserably at his back. My need to make him understand is so strong he must feel it.

When he turns around again he's calmer, but he hasn't finished yet. 'You've done your best to destroy our relationship.'

I brace myself for more accusations. I can feel myself buckling under the torrent. I know he's right in a way, but he's wrong too. If only I could explain. But I'm in shock and I've never been any good at quick come-backs anyway. I usually lie awake for nights afterwards, churning over all the things I should have said at the time.

But Max's voice is suddenly gentler. 'I know you've had an incredibly tough time since your nan died, but things were bad for me too, you know. My job was on the line.'

'What?' I'm shocked. 'Why didn't you tell me?'

'Because you didn't want to know! Every time I mention work you shut off.'

I shake my head. This hurts. Of course I care. He should know that. 'You could have tried me.'

'There was no point,' he says in a tired voice.

He starts pacing, back and forth from one end of the room to another.

'They were laying people off. Rumours were flying around but no one knew anything. I was tearing my hair out but all you wanted to talk about was your nan. You were having a bad time and I didn't want to upset things even more, so I held all my stuff in. But in the end I got so resentful. I had to tell you enough was enough. So what did you do? Stopped talking. No dialogue. Not even the bloody monologue I'd got used to.'

He looks at me and tries to smile but there's so much pain in his face I want to cry. 'You need to sort yourself out, Storm. Stop blaming me for being me. Stop blaming me for this relationship. You're here. You wanted it too.'

I've never seen Max cry before. It leaves me helpless, seeing him standing there so open and vulnerable, his arms by his sides and tears on his cheeks. I have to wade through my fear to get to him and when I put my arms around him his tears turn into great heaving sobs that tear me apart.

'I'm sorry,' I say, the word echoing around and around in my head. Sorry. Sorry. Wondering if that will be enough.

We stand like this for a long time. I'm watching the clouds come closer, flashes of lightning dividing the sky, and thunder rumbling and rolling across the horizon. Max's head is on my shoulders, his tears mingling with my sweat, my tears soaking into his hair. My fingers are stroking his back, soothing him. It's never been like this before. He's never let me look after him.

Eventually he pulls away from me and goes to the bathroom. I can hear him in there splashing water on his face and rearranging himself. I wipe my eyes and start making tea, just for something to do. Max comes out and sits down on the couch, looking at the approaching storm, his face turned away from me. We're closer now, yet somehow further apart too, and that makes a kind of awkwardness between us.

I bring over two cups of tea and sit down next to him. 'What did you tell them at work?'

'I told them it was an emergency. My girlfriend was barefoot and pregnant and lost somewhere in the Australian Outback, hunting a murderer.'

'Really?'

'No.' Max turns and looks straight into my eyes. 'I quit.'

'You *quit*?'

'I did.'

'I don't believe you.'

He smiles. 'When I got your letter, I told them I needed time off. They said no. That was the last straw for me. It's going to be okay, though. I've got enough clients to set up on my own and at least now I won't have to answer to anyone.'

We stare out the windows, not remembering to sip our tea. I'm in shock. I can't quite believe that Max has quit his job, for me. Outside the sea has turned slate-grey and the palms are a vivid green against the dark sky. They don't look real.

I turn to face him. 'I don't know why it's so hard for me to believe in us. And I'm sorry that's hurt you. I'll try Max. Really, I will. But I'm scared that the minute I start believing in us, you'll find someone else. Someone more... suitable.'

'Suitable! What does that mean?'

His voice is going up again and it makes me panicky.

'I don't know,' I say, grabbing at anything. 'Someone your parents would approve of, I suppose. With a plummy voice and a mummy and daddy.'

'God, Storm, you've got such a chip on your shoulder. You go on about how terrible English class structures are, but you're the one keeping all the boundaries intact. I can't help it if I went to a public school. It's not my fault.'

A huge roar of thunder makes us jump and that breaks the tension somehow.

'So what *do* you see in me?' I ask.

Max laughs and looks me up and down.

'Well,' he says. 'You've got great legs... and gorgeous breasts... and you're pregnant with my baby. What more could a man want?'

There, that's the first time he's mentioned it. I feel myself tensing up again, getting ready to break it to him that it's too late. I've made up my mind. I'm going to have this baby anyway. But what Max has just said is slowly sinking in. The idea that there might be nothing to defend after all.

'You don't want me to get rid of it?'

He shakes his head. 'God, no. I want you to have this baby' His voice is urgent. 'I want *us* to have this baby.'

I never expected this. Had never thought of Max and me in this way. Mum and Dad. God it's scary.

'I don't exactly have a history of happy families. I mean, my family's probably enough to put anyone off: murdered women, abandoned women, crazy women, mothers who betray their daughters. And no men, except a murderer for a father, and Pop. At least *he* was normal… Are you sure you want to go through with this?'

It's meant as a joke, but Max doesn't laugh. 'Look,' he says. 'History doesn't have to repeat itself. We can make our own pattern. A good one this time. But you've got to let me in. You've got to trust me.'

When we kiss there's a new certainty that dissolves the boundaries between us. It makes kissing a bit like drowning, but in the nicest possible way.

Then Max pulls off my T-shirt and comes face-to-face with my bra.

'What's this?' he asks, staring at it in horror.

'A maternity bra. Attractive, isn't it?'

'It looks like body armour. Here, how do I get it off?'

'It undoes at the front. For breastfeeding.'

'Oh my God,' groans Max, hit by a burst of reality. 'I don't think I want to know.'

He puts his hand on my belly. 'Does it show?'

I undo my sarong and let him see the gentle curve.

'It's only about three inches long,' I tell him, 'but it's already got eyelids and fingernails, even testicles or ovaries. Isn't that amazing?'

'Amazing,' says Max, pulling off his boxer shorts.

Just the touch of him is as powerful as the storm that's building outside. My skin is tingling all over and electric shocks are shooting through my middle. I'm realising how much I've wanted him. Not just the past few weeks, but ever since we met. Since we started building all the walls between us. Even my womb is shouting at me. It's as if the baby's saying, 'Yay, here comes dad.'

'Is it safe?' he whispers.

'What do you mean?' My voice is husky with the need for him.

'You know... I don't want to... poke it or anything.'

I laugh so much we lose the moment and have to start again.

'It's fine,' I tell him, but even so he's careful inside me, lying still until neither of us can bear it anymore. And then he forgets to be gentle and pushes hard into me in a frenzied rush. When he comes, he stays inside and I run my hands along the round muscles of his thighs and the taut curve of his bottom, all the way up his spine, feeling for the familiar oval-shaped mole just under his right rib and then up to the nape of his neck. Remembering him all over again.

We lie half next to each other, squeezed up tight on the couch, listening to the thunder. There's a calm between us, but the atmosphere is prickly with expectation.

'Tell me about your trip.' Max says. 'You've hardly told me anything.'

'It's a long story.'

'That's okay. I'm not going anywhere.'

So I tell him about Sydney and Leo and how I found out Kita was murdered, which he already knows. I tell him about doing a pregnancy test in a pit toilet and that makes him laugh. But I don't mention David. Then I tell him about the truckie attacking me. I love the worry on his face and the way he's tensing up as I talk.

'Jesus!' he says. 'I knew it was dangerous out there.'

'I saw him off,' I say, snuggling up even closer to Max. Then I tell him about Edith and Jack in Cloncurry, and visiting Bill's sister, Almira.

'What a bitch,' he says.

I go back a bit and tell him about me wandering along the side of the highway with third-degree burns and not speaking for ten days. But I still don't mention David though he keeps getting in the way.

Max pulls me even closer and kisses me.

'Poor you,' he mutters.

Lastly I tell him about Bill and how I haven't had the courage yet to talk to him.

'Do you need to?'

'Yes.'

I wish I didn't. I wish I could just walk away from here into a future with Max and our baby. But there are some questions only he can answer.

Right now, though, David's on my mind. He's the big gap in my story. It would be easiest to avoid him completely, only that won't make him go away. He'll still be there between us and if I don't tell Max, he'll hang around forever, I know he will, until eventually one way or another Max will feel that something is missing. Not telling is just as bad as lying and there has already been too much of both in my life. I can't live like that with Max. But if I do tell him? Oh shit. Not now. Not when we've only just finished sorting things out.

So I tell him.

I say I met this guy whose car had broken down and I gave him a lift up through the middle bit. Just a few days, I tell Max, and it only happened once. But as the words tumble out I can feel Max slipping away from me.

'You're telling me you had sex with a hitchhiker?'

I nod. What can I say? Although it wasn't like that. 'There was a snake -'

'A snake!'

'I was scared.'

How can I tell him? I was drunk on moonlight and fear and uncertainty and I thought Max had already abandoned me.

'It didn't mean anything,' I say. 'Honestly.' But even I can tell it sounds half-hearted.

Max is closing up on me, his body tensing up. 'You're pregnant!' The horror in his voice makes me cringe with shame. 'Did you know?'

I nod again. 'I'm sorry. I'm so, so sorry. But I had to tell you or it would always be there between us.'

'Well, at least you're honest.' He sits up abruptly. 'Can't you see it Storm? The way you push people away? Every time anyone gets near you. I'm your partner, for God's sake, your lover, the father of your child… and still you're pushing me away. When's it going to stop?'

Every time anyone gets near… It's going over and over in my head, taking its time to sink in. Where have I heard that before? Something in the diary? No, something Leo said. How Kita pushed and pushed. Like she was saying, come on, dump me, come on. When I finally make the connection I can't believe how blind I've been. How I've spent weeks, months, maybe even a whole lifetime looking for my mother. How it isn't only about hair colour or how long your fingers are. So much of Kita is right here inside me, still pushing people away.

'I'm so sorry, Max. I wish none of this had happened. I need you. I love you. I want us to be together.'

My voice is cracked with tears and Max won't look at me.

'Maybe it's too late,' he says. 'Maybe you've pushed too far.' He gets up. 'I'm having a shower.'

He's washing me off. He's never done that before. My first instinct is to leave, to run out of here and away from his disappointment, which is even worse than his anger. But Max is worth more than that. *I'm* worth more than that. I get dressed and force myself to wait it out.

I'm even more like my mother than I imagined. That's a shock. Like Nan and Millie too. All lost and struggling in our own ways. There's a thread through us, a pattern none of us could see. It's taken Max to show it to me. That's the curse I guess. A virus, creeping through generations, changing and adapting for each new environment. David was wrong - not believing in curses isn't enough. Max was right all along. You have to turn around and face your monsters, get to know and understand them. Let go of your fear and then watch the monsters dissolve as they lose their power over you. Though when it came to it, he didn't want me to.

I can feel a new sense of resolve forming. Maybe I can break the curse. If it's not too late. I'll make amends forever if Max will let me.

Max is in the shower for ages and when he comes out he's wearing a fluffy white towel and a smooth face. Just under his chin there's a drop of blood where he's cut himself. When he looks at me, his eyes are cold and there's an awful 'Are you still here?' expression on his face, that reduces me to pleading.

'What do you want me to do?' I ask him. 'I'll do anything to make it up to you. Please, Max… Please give me another chance.'

'I don't know,' he says. 'I don't know anything …' His voice breaks. 'This wasn't how I imagined it would be.' He shakes his head. 'Maybe you should go.'

'I don't want to leave, Max. I don't want to lose you. I've only just found you again.

There's a flash of anger on his face. 'It's always you, isn't it? I want this. I don't want that. Well right now I couldn't give a toss what you want.'

It's like he's hit me in the face. The shock of it makes me step back. But I'm not going yet. 'Okay. What do *you* want then?'

'I just told you. I don't know.'

He's freezing me out the door but I won't go. Not until he's heard me out. I'm not too comfortable about being the villain in all this. Sure, I'm most at fault. But it isn't just me. Things are never that simple. Max has to step out of his safety zone too and face his own monsters. Right from the start we've been hiding from each other. Yet that night at the gallery when we met, we each saw something we recognised. Under all the walls and barriers and patterns we've established to get through every day, we're not so different.

'Look,' I say. 'I made a big mistake and I know I've hurt you. I'm sorry. Really, really sorry. But this is getting way too one sided. For the past hour and half you've made me feel guilty about everything.'

I can't believe things have changed so quickly. Now it's me pacing back and forth across the room, trying to sort out what I want to say. Letting the frustration build up inside me, so I'll have the courage to keep going, even if it means the end of us.

'It's not only me that's been stuffing things up.' I tell him. 'You say I'm not interested in your work. Well, why don't you try me? You never take me to your work functions. It's like you're ashamed of me. And now you say you love me and then act surprised that I don't already know. But you've never told me that before. I've had to work things out for myself. I might not be easy to live with, but hell, Max, you want everything your way. There's no room for me. Everything's always been on your terms… you can't have it both ways.'

I'm standing right in front of him now, but he won't look me in the eye.

'I was scared out there, Max. I needed you. More than I ever have, and you wouldn't come.'

'I couldn't.'

'I know that now. But you didn't tell me. You just said no. I'm not a mind reader! And then you tried to stop me from going at all.'

Just for a moment Max looks at me. 'I was scared of losing you, Storm. You were so distant. And you seemed so self-contained, flying off to the other side of the world. I thought you'd never come back.'

He turns away and I stare at his back, amazed. I'd never even considered that Max might be afraid of losing me.

'You need me now,' says Max. 'I'm here.'

I hate how flat his voice is. All the life gone out of it. 'No, you're not,' I tell him. 'You've just asked me to leave.'

There, that's it. My knees are shaking, but I've done it. While I look around for my keys I tell Max I'm going back to the caravan park to visit Bill.

'Then I'll come back here,' I say. 'And see if you think it's worth starting again.'

'Wait,' Max says. I'm coming with you.'

I breathe a sigh of relief, but when he gets dressed he turns his back to me, like I'm a stranger.

CHAPTER TWENTY-EIGHT

We make our way along the corridor, down the lift, across the foyer and over the road to the van. Walking alongside each other and not saying anything. I'm still in shock. I've never stood up to Max before, not seriously anyway. I'm not sure why I always hold back. It's probably because I've been too scared of losing him. That's usually why people keep quiet. But it's pretty bad that I had to get beyond that and all the way to a point where I didn't care, just so I could be honest. Then, after all that, the sky didn't fall down on my head. And Max is still here. At least for now.

Everything is back to front from what I'm used to. Max is wearing shorts. Longish khaki ones, with side pockets and a neat line down the front where he's pressed them. But still they're shorts and I never thought he'd do that. He's wearing sandals too, woven leather ones that make the curves of his ankles look so sexy I have to keep sneaking looks at them. Once I would have said something, made a joke and we'd have ended up back in bed. But now it's all too awkward.

Max doesn't say a word about the van, doesn't raise an eyebrow, even though it's a bright orange Kombi and that must warrant a mention. It's also splattered with mud, filthy from front to back. It takes Max three tugs to open the passenger door and then it creaks horribly like it's about to come off in his hand. But he just hoists himself in and fiddles about untangling the seat belt.

And he doesn't say a word about me driving either. No jokes. No token resistance. Not even any real resistance. I don't know if this is the new Max working on our relationship, or if this is the it's-too-late-to-bother-now Max. Either way, it's making me extremely nervous. I forget to take the hand brake off and then I get the clutch confused so we lurch off in a series of bunny hops. Max only winces when the lights go red and I don't stop.

'It's a good van,' I say, to break the silence between us. I try to keep the tone light, but a defensive note creeps in anyway. Why am I always defending myself against Max?

He inspects the dashboard which is covered with all the things I've gathered on the way: sticks and stones, leaves, a long piece of stringy bark, and lots of plastic creatures, the green tree frog I bought in Normanton, sitting dangerously close to the king brown David gave me. Then he looks in the back. There's my open bag, clothes spewing out all over the place, the lurid seventies curtains I used to like, and David's wrinkled foam mattress with one chewed corner. Through Max's eyes it must all look squalid.

'So is this where you fucked your hitchhiker?' he asks. There's a kind of cold curiosity in his voice and nothing I can read in his eyes.

'No,' I say in a small voice, knowing I deserved that and anything else Max might choose to throw at me. But even so I wish he wouldn't keep making it seem sordid. Because it wasn't. It felt so right at the time but in the end it wasn't anything special after all. Just two people reaching out to someone else through each other. Scratching our itches, as Max would say. Which should make it seem pathetic, except that it's done all this damage. God I wish it had never happened. I wish I could take it all back. And I hate it that I wish that. I change the gears roughly and there's a screaming crunch as my foot comes off the clutch too early. Will we ever find our way through this?

In the caravan park I put the little card they gave me into the slot and wait for the barrier to come up. We drive past tents and caravans, and empty grass sites with square dead bits where the tents have been. The atmosphere is so close it's shutting out the air. Max isn't used to this heat; he's come straight from the end of winter. There's sweat dripping down his face and his shirt is wet through already.

I pull up under the fig tree and point at Bill's caravan. 'That's where he lives,' I say

Max studies it. I don't know what he's thinking. Maybe that it's strange to come halfway around the world and find out that the grandfather of his child-to-be, is a murderer living in a rusty old tin can in a corner of a caravan park. Because it is. Even without anything else, it's reason enough for Max to tell me he's finished with me and walk away forever. But he doesn't say that. He doesn't say anything at all.

I look at his handsome profile. I can see the pain in him and how strong he is. Noble even. It must be so hard for him, sitting here like this, waiting for me to finish sorting myself out. Max's biggest childhood trauma was getting lost for a few minutes in a department store, aged five. It felt like forever, he told me. They announced him over a loud speaker and his mum found him straight away. Max's world has always been so much more straightforward than mine and it's a big leap for him to understand the need in me to delve into all my complications. But he's trying. I rest my hand on his arm and reach over to kiss him on the cheek.

'I'll go in then. Wish me luck.'

I'm still not ready for this. But chances are I never will be and it has to be finished with. I have to move on. For me and for Max and for our baby.

'Do you want me to come in with you?' asks Max as I climb out.

I pause in the doorway. Surprised. And touched. It hadn't crossed my mind. I try to imagine us both knocking on that door, shaking hands, introductions… 'Bill, I'd like you to meet my partner, Max'.

'No,' I'd better go myself.'

Max nods and looks away. I know he's thinking I haven't changed. That I still don't let him in and I probably never will.

'He's nervous,' I explain. 'I don't think he'll talk to me if there's someone else there.'

I watch Max absorbing this information. 'Is it safe?'

He looks worried and this makes me feel a whole lot better.

'I think so. He's old and he's gone blind, but I'll shout if there's a problem. Okay?'

'I'm not happy about this,' says Max, frowning over at the caravan.

'Well, it's good to know you still care,' I say, kissing him on the lips. He responds for a just a second, before pulling away.

For the past few days I've been imagining this moment over and over again. Walking across to the van, through the annexe, knocking on the door. So straight forward, yet I haven't been able to take the first step. Now, without even thinking about it I've crossed the space between my van and his in a few seconds. I take a deep breath, lift the flap into the annexe and with one simple step, enter its shadow world.

I expected dirt or grass in here, but there's a rough canvas floor with a big muddy rip near the caravan door. The television is where I expected, in the far corner, and there are two mouldy-smelling lounge chairs. They're cloth covered and might have been blue once, though most of it has gone grey black with sweat and dirt and beer stains. One has got a spring sticking right through it, but it's the other one he sits in. There's a stool for his feet and a glass side table, streaked with ash and spilt beer. He's emptied the ashtray but hasn't cleaned it, so it's thick black in the bottom, with a sharp, stale nicotine smell.

My heart is pounding in my chest as I tap on the door. When it opens I could swear he's looking straight at me. This close I can see a dark mole just under his left nostril. His shirt is dirty and missing a button right in the middle, revealing a patch of round belly and off-white vest. His fly isn't quite done up and there's a stain near his crotch. But it's his bare feet that are the worst of all. I can see the filthy bits between his toes and the revolting curled-over nails, pointy sharp at the edges.

'Why are you here?' he asks. As if there is any question. As if it isn't normal for an abandoned child to look for a parent, or natural to try and find out why. But standing here in front of him feels so far outside the bounds of normal, I'm left with nothing to measure things up against.

The silence stretches between us, taut and fragile. He's staring so intently I have to remind myself he's blind. I have no idea how he knows it's me. Wondering it makes me uneasy. Perhaps being blind has given him some sort of second sight or sixth sense. But more likely it's because he doesn't get many visitors.

'What do you want?' he asks nervously.

He's waiting for something from me. I've rehearsed this moment so many times these past weeks, but now I'm here, all my prepared lines disappear. I stumble over the words and I'm angry with myself for falling apart like this. It's me that should be asking questions. Not him.

As I talk his face crumples. 'You sound just like Kita,' he says in a broken voice and reaches out with both hands trying to feel my hair and face. It takes a second before I understand he's trying to create an image of me through his fingers. I step back. It's involuntary. But I don't want him that close and he doesn't deserve to know anything about me.

He looks hurt but I don't let myself feel bad. Eventually he sighs and moves out of the doorway to let me through. 'You'd better come in then.'

For a wild moment I want to run. But Max is out there, waiting. He's hurt, and trusting me to see this through. That gives me the courage to take another two steps into Bill's nasty world. The smell of body odour and old man's piss sends me reeling. God, he must go in the sink.

The curtains are drawn. I suppose it doesn't make any difference to him, but the gloom makes me uneasy. The cupboards are filthy with finger marks and dribbles from the kitchen bench. The ceiling is discoloured, riddled with rusty patches, from leaks probably. The whole place is dirty, but neat and uncluttered. If anything it's austere. Almost minimalist. Except for the squalor and the tacky furnishings.

'Sit down, sit down,' he says, waving me to the table. I slide along a bench seat and sit tucked up close to the table. It's more dirt-beige now than white and there's nothing on it, except an open can of beer. But the surface is covered with black melted burns where's he's rested his cigarettes, and an abstract pattern of stains. Perfect beer circles from endless cans. My head is spinning from the yeasty smell of beer and smoke and the pre-storm ions. Briefly it crosses my mind that this would be a good idea for an exhibition. Life marks - a stained table top, a broken mattress, worn paths in a floor... Patterns of repetitions. But I push the thoughts away. It's time to stop evading the point of all this.

Bill pulls out a chair opposite me and feels his way into it. I watch his hand explore the table, looking for his beer. He's uncannily accurate.

'I thought you'd come one day.'

'Yes,' I say, surprised at how measured I'm being as I try to avoid dwelling on the fact that this man spawned me.

'Tea or coffee? Or beer. That's all I can offer.'

I shake my head, then realise he's still waiting for an answer. 'No. I don't want anything.'

'Come on. Have a cup of tea. It's the least I can do.'

I don't know what he means by that. As if any number of cups of tea will transform history and make everything all right. But I've been brought up well enough to be polite. Even to a murderer.

'Okay, tea then.'

I watch him feeling about for the things he needs. There's a tentative gentleness in his movements that contradicts what I know about him. Sometimes it's hard to tell he's blind. The way he knows where things are. And when he's finished he puts everything back exactly where he found them. Max would approve.

He must sense me noticing because he launches into an explanation. 'I've had to learn to tidy up after myself,' he says, putting the tea down in front of me. 'When you're blind, you need to know where things are.'

Outside the clouds cover the sun sending the room from dim to almost dark so I switch on the light. 'It's gone dark,' I tell him when he starts at the click.

He nods. 'Reckon there's a monster of a storm brewing.'

A clap of thunder makes me jump. The distant angry rumbling has changed to a sharp cracking fury. I wonder what Max is thinking out there. He'll be all taken up with the thunder and lightning and won't be able to hear anything from where he's sitting inside my van.

Bill lights a cigarette and opens another beer. 'Cheers,' he says and takes a big gulp.

I push my tea away. It's time to stop pretending. 'Why did you kill my mother?'

He freezes, the beer half way to his mouth. It's like he's playing statues, right down to holding his breath. Then the air comes out in a burst as he puts his head in his hands and starts rocking back and forth, groaning. From this angle I can see the sunspots on his shiny scalp. Apart from the electric light bulb it's the only bright thing in this place.

'She was going to leave me... I read her diary. Hell, what did she expect? She left it lying around all the time like she wanted me to see. There were things in there - Oh God - it tore me apart.'

He breaks into sobs and right then the storm breaks too. A sharp crack of thunder splits the air in two, dividing now from then. A burst of wind rocks the caravan so hard I have to reach out and steady myself on the table. Something has been let out that we can't put back.

Suddenly he's angry. 'Fucking the mechanic, for Christ's sake. And that poncy city bloke, Leo something or other. And who else? She was worse than a bitch in heat. I just had to look away for a second and she'd be off with some other arsehole.'

The force of his rage pins me to the back of the seat. It hurts. I don't have to listen to this. Not from him, or Almira. They've got their own reasons for hating Kita. Okay she did sleep with Leo and the mechanic. Bill was jealous and maybe he had good reason. But Kita wrote about feeling trapped; she said jealousy was worse than anything. A disease that ate away at people. I wonder how much of it was in Bill's head and how much was real. Probably a bit of both. These things usually are. Letting him read her diary like that though. Taunting him with it. That's really cruel. I'm all too aware of the symmetry here. Of what I've done to Max. Of the awful realisation that I'm like my mother in more than looks. Still, at least I've seen it. You have to see it, to break it. And I didn't taunt Max.

When Bill stops crying, I ask him if he's my father.

He looks at me with red puffy eyes. 'Hard to tell isn't it? Back then you were so much like Kita. Almira reckons your Leo's kid. She reckons I was a cover. Leo wasn't having it, so stupid gullible me would have to do.'

He takes another gulp of beer while I ponder again on the possibility that Leo could be my father. I wish he was, but I didn't see any resemblance. He could draw though and that's some sort of connection. Storm Knight? An interesting name, but it isn't me. No more than Storm Harding would have been. I don't know whether to be relieved or horrified all over again.

'Kate… Almira always had it in for Kita. I never could work out why. She used to drive me mad with her catty comments.'

He slams the can down on the table. 'Damn it, I should have listened to my big sister. Still, there's a bloody better than good chance you're mine. I'm there on your birth certificate anyway. They can't take that away from me, though they bloody well took everything else.' He sweeps his arm around the caravan in a regal gesture. 'It's all yours when I'm gone. There. Isn't that something to look forward to?'

He starts crying again, lost in some sort of deranged sentiment. 'I loved you though. I really did. And it broke my heart losing you like that. My little Storm.'

He smiles up at me through watery eyes, but I'm not falling for this.

'You didn't *lose* me. You left me out there in the middle of nowhere. I nearly died.'

'I didn't think… I panicked… I wanted to come back. Really.'

I shake my head. I'm disgusted. There's only one thing that matters. 'You left me.'

His eyes are pleading with me but I look away. When I look back again, his face is set in a nasty scowl. 'Jesus, I loved that woman,' he says, banging his fists down hard on the table and making his beer jump.

I'm starting to wonder if Bill is mad. He's between me and the door and that makes me uneasy. I stand up as quietly as possible, but he notices straight away.

'Please don't go.'

I'm surprised at how easily he can follow my movements and realise with a jolt that I shouldn't assume his blindness gives me an advantage.

'No, no,' he says, waving his hands in the air, like he's surrendering. 'I'm sorry. Don't be afraid. I'm not a violent man... Don't go, please... I want to tell you what happened out there. You deserve that.'

When I sit down again he breaks into a childish grin then lights up a new cigarette from the last, even though there's already more smoke than air in here. Then he gets himself amother beer. When he opens it, there's a whoosh of gas that's been trapped in there waiting to come out. With it comes the rain. First in big slow drops, *splat*, *splat* on the roof. Then in a rush, battering the roof and drowning out his words, so I have to lean closer to hear.

'It was bloody hot out there. Hotter than I'd ever known it. We were arguing.' He gestures dismissively with his hand. 'I don't know what about. Probably nothing much, we were always fighting. Then she wanted a piss, so I pulled over and she took you with her so you could stretch your legs. We'd been driving for a couple of hours.'

Somewhere behind me, there's a steady thud of drips. I look around and see it, almost a stream, right in the middle of his bed. Another, sharper drip has started up next to my chair, pinging on the lino floor.

'Bloody rain,' he says breaking off to find some bowls to catch the drips. I watch him feeling about for the right spot. I don't offer to help.

'So... I saw her there, squatting in the dirt, and suddenly I knew I was about to lose her. Do you know what that feels like?'

'How would I?' I ask. 'What have I ever lost?' But my sarcasm is lost on him.

'Well it feels bloody awful, I can tell you. I couldn't bear to lose Kita. You know? I couldn't bear that. I had to stop her going. I didn't even think about what I was doing. Just came up behind, put my hands around her neck and squeezed. She struggled a bit, but not for long. I remember being surprised at how easy it was... Now you're here, now you're not. So easy.'

He laughs in a kind of nervous burst then controls himself again. 'I've never told anyone this before,' he says, looking at me like he expects a trophy, or at least a pat on the back.

I look away and wait.

'Oh shit,' he says. 'I'm getting shaky.' He gets up again and feels about in a drawer, then lifts out a packet of something.

'My medication. I'm a diabetic. That's what sent me blind. The circulation's going in my legs too. The doctor reckons I'll lose them if I don't watch out. I'm supposed to give up the cigarettes and the drink.' Bill laughs in a wheezy burst. "Be a good boy," the doctor said. "Well doc," I said. "I reckon it's a bit late for that."'

Am I supposed to laugh at this?

The packet is full of syringes. He doesn't have to measure out his dose, it's already there, pre-packed in the syringe. When he pulls up his shirt and sticks the needle in, I have to turn away.

'You didn't even see. You were looking at a bull ant. Watching a bull ant while your mother died ...'

He leans over to me, so close I can smell his rotten-liver breath. I lean back as far as I can, pressing myself against the seat.

'I hated you too. You and your mum. She wouldn't let me have either of you.'

Then he's crying again. I look down at my hands, see how they're gripping the edge of the table, the knuckles white. There are chills racing up and down my spine.

'She wanted me to, you know. She practically begged for it. *I want to fuck the desert... I want B to fuck me, hard and slowly, pushing right through me until my bones break apart, so that I can feel the tearing ...*'

His voice is mean and mocking and high like he's mimicking a woman. He's quoting from Kita's diary. After twenty-six years he still remembers what she wrote.

'So I did what I was told like the good little boy I was. I left her there with the bull ants and the sun just like she wanted.'

'Why?' My voice is a whisper. The chills are spreading from my spine into the rest of me. 'How could you do it?'

'I drank a lot of beer,' he says, as if that's a reason for anything. 'She was going to leave me. She made me beg and then she laughed in my face. And all the time there was the dirt in her. She was filth. Even she knew it. She knew she deserved it.'

There's a huge burst of laughter rising up from deep in my belly. It gets all the way to the top of my throat and I have to keep swallowing to hold it in. I wonder if Kita was like me, laughing at all the wrong times. I wonder if being scared made her laugh. And if that was what got her killed in the end.

'It seemed so bloody straight forward back then,' he says, taking a big puff out of his cigarette and leaning towards me again. 'If I couldn't have her, no one could. Makes sense doesn't it?'

There's a long pause while he waits for me to tell him it's fine. I don't. I just sit here listening to the drips. Watching the lightning illuminate the walls, then leave them in grey shadows. The wind is still rocking the caravan back and forth, but the anger has gone out of it. Back and forth. I can feel my body slipping into line with its rhythm. Comforting itself.

'Then I heard you saying. "Look Mummy, look, ba'nt." That's what you used to call a bull ant. Ba'nt. That's when I realised what I'd done.'

Suddenly he starts sobbing and knocks his beer all over my lap. I jump up gasping at the shock of the cold liquid.

'I'm sorry, so sorry.' But it isn't clear what he's apologising for - spilling the beer or murdering my mother.

I don't hate him. I can't. I can't forget my own vertigo out there. Can't hate him for losing it. But he's revolting and pathetic and that's even worse. With his puffy ragged face and livid nose and the greasy thin strips of hair he's flicked over his scalp. I can't stand his self-pity. He's not my father. Even if he is, he's not. I don't know what Bill would have become if he hadn't murdered my mother. And frankly I don't care. Some actions in life are so big they define you forever.

He reaches out and grabs my arm just above the elbow before I even realise what he's up to. He holds it so hard I can feel bruises forming in the shape of his fingers.

'You know what?' he asks.

I don't want to hear any more. It isn't funny. It isn't a *game*. He's a murderer for Christ's sake and he's gripping my arm too tightly.

'What?' I whisper, playing along, but my heart is thumping hard. I hold myself very still. If I can get him to relax and think it's okay, then maybe he'll let me go. But I'm filled with the kind of terror that makes me want to run, squealing like a small child with all the monsters in the world behind her. I have to use every bit of my willpower to stop myself.

'I loved you,' he says, reaching over with his other hand and stroking my hair. 'Oh Kita, don't go. Why don't you stay with me?'

Jesus! He's got it all wrong. He's all the way back there.

'Please stay. Please. We've got something special. Things are good.'

'I'm Storm,' I tell him, trying to keep my voice under control. 'Kita's dead. Remember? You killed her.'

He shakes his head and nods impatiently, like I'm an idiot for saying it. 'Yep,' he says sitting up in his chair like he's proud of himself. 'And I've had to relive the whole thing, all over again, every bloody day of my life. You know, I nearly ripped that diary up into shreds, like Kita would have wanted, but I left it just as it was. That way everyone would know what she was really like. They'd see she wasn't worth anything. Tainted like that. And you too...' He shakes his head sadly. 'I really thought the bastards would let me off when they saw what I was up against.'

He pulls me closer and grabs a big handful of my hair, yanking my head back, so I have to look into his face. Tainted? I'm trying to concentrate, trying to understand what's going on, but the fear is getting in the way. He's had too much beer. He's too close. I can't think. Tainted? I don't know what he means. Maybe it's the gypsy stuff. Some people have got a thing against them. But surely he would have known all along. Kita was never secretive about it.

'And you thought I was bad, didn't you? Hey?' he shouts, tugging some more. 'Didn't you?'

I try to nod, but he's holding on too tight and he wouldn't see anyway, so I squeeze out a yes, desperately wishing Max would walk in and make everything safe again.

'That's right. You've been looking at me, praying this bloody old wreck isn't your dad. I thought you'd know all about it. But you don't, do you? Do you?'

He starts giggling and lets go of my air. My head snaps forward and I feel a muscle pull in my neck. It must have been Nan who tore that page out of the diary. But what could have possible been worse than the things she left in?

'Ever wonder who Kita's father was? Hey?'

'Yes,' I say, wincing with the pain in my neck. Of course I have. Nan would never say - her lips got thin and tight every time someone mentioned it. I watch Bill's face twisting into a smiling ugly blend of pity and malice.

'Your pop.'

He's not making sense.

'What?'

'Pop. Your bloody pop. He liked them young, the old bastard. Couldn't keep his hands off his own daughter. And then she went and got pregnant on him. Filthy bastard,' he shouts, poking me in the chest with his finger. 'So don't you mind having me for a father. Your mum was a filthy inbred bitch - and so are you!'

He takes a big swig of his beer, looking triumphant now, like his team has just won the grand final. I can't believe it. Not Pop. Gentle old Pop.

'You're lying.'

But even as I yell the words I know Bill is right. This is the secret Nan shouted out in that room so many years ago. This is what sent Kita running to the other side of the world, knowing she could never go home again. Pop was Kita's father.

Now he's crying again. I need to get away, need some space to think, but I'm numb, inside and out. We stay like this for minutes, him gripping my arm and stroking my hair and me in a kind of horrified stupor I can't seem to break free of.

Then Max comes to the rescue. 'Storm? Are you okay?'

His voice breaks something in Bill. It takes his attention away from wherever he is and brings him back to the present. He looks towards the door. Then back at me. He lets me go and I walk away, too numb even to feel relief.

Bill reaches his hands out towards me. 'I love you, Kita. Please stay with me. I'll look after you. I won't hurt you. I promise.'

I shut the door on his words. There's no space left in me for feeling.

Max is waiting for me outside the annexe, wet through and uncertain. I rest my head on his chest for a moment, then lift my face into the rain, wanting it to wash everything away. I'm still holding myself together, afraid of what might happen if I let go.

'Will you drive?'

Max nods. He doesn't ask questions and I'm grateful. In the van he leans over and rests his hand on my belly.

'Are you okay?'

I nod automatically. He kisses me on the nose, then starts the van. I look over at him, wanting to tell him that I've worked it out. That it's over. I know what I want to say, but my mouth is moving like a goldfish and I have to give up.

We bunny hop out of the caravan park because Max doesn't know how to work the Kombi. He finds the wipers, but they go too fast at first, frantically racing back and forth across the windscreen and he has to fiddle with them to get the right speed. Then we're turning left into the traffic. Everything is shiny wet. It must only be early afternoon, but all the cars have their lights on. Max fiddles about some more, swearing and looking for the lights. In the end I have to lean over and show him.

We're moving through the rain, not talking. The traffic lights reflect sad red streaks onto the road. There are other cars too. People are going shopping or visiting friends. Living normal, ordinary lives. I'm wondering how anything can ever be normal again, after what Bill said. I want it to be a lie but know it isn't. Everything has fallen into place: Nan tearing out the page in the diary; the friction between Millie and Nan, always there bubbling away beneath the surface, a festering blend of pity and resentment and guilt; and the endless secrets wound tightly around an even more repulsive secret. The ugly core they all wanted to forget. Pop a paedophile. How could that be?

Suddenly I remember how I used to sit on Pop's knee and he'd jiggle me up and down pretending he was a horse. First he'd trot, then canter and finally a rough kind of gallop that usually sent me flying off his knee and onto the floor. Nan never liked it, but I used to beg Pop for a ride anyway. Then one day Nan came in with her face set like a block of ice. 'Get off him,' she shouted. 'You're too old for that.'

I caught the look that passed between them. Nan's anger, verging on panic and Pop's sadness as he pushed me off his knee for the last time. Then Nan leaned over to Pop.

'*Vyusher*,' she hissed.

When I asked Millie later, she told me it meant wolf.

I used to think Pop should have given Nan more protection from Millie, but it was the other way around. Poor Nan needed protection from her own father and she spent her life protecting us all from that knowledge. When did it start? And how often did it happen? Did Millie know all along? It's hard to believe she did. Though she might have known and not known at the same time, the way we do with things we can't face.

Incest was the very worst crime for the Romany people. Poor Millie. Ostracised by her own people, then abandoned by her husband as soon as she lost her youth. A double betrayal. Then her husband turning to their own daughter. And Millie forced to live with, and love, the consequences. No wonder she believed in the curse. Nan said Pop always protected Millie, that he wouldn't hear a word against her, that he bought her things… But nothing could have made up for what he did or the way he must have looked past her. Millie needed love and passion, not kindness and filthy betrayals. And Nan? She needed to be free of them all.

How did Kita find out? Pop might have tried it on her, but I doubt it. Nan would have been a formidable and ever-watchful enemy. In her diary Kita mentions walking into a room as Nan and Millie were arguing. She describes Millie slapping Nan. Probably Kita heard something too. Enough to want to know more. Enough to send her running to Australia, swearing she would never come back.

I rub my neck where it hurts. Max has turned the wrong way and we're driving away from the motel, but I don't have the strength to tell him.

'Are you alright?'

I nod, but it doesn't reassure Max. 'It's okay, he says. 'It's okay.'

I can tell he's starting to panic. He doesn't know what to do, so he keeps saying it as if just the words are enough. But I know they're not. The reality of what's just happened finally rushes in on me and pushes away the numbness. I burst into tears.

'It's okay,' Max tells me again, patting my knee in between gear changes. He's concentrating on driving so it makes him sound absent-minded, and that makes me want to scream because nothing is okay. I thought this was the final thing, that after today I would be free. But Bill has given me another secret I don't know how to tell.

'He's mad. He told me how he did it. All the details. Can you imagine how awful that is?'

'It's finished. He can't get you.'

Max is right and the relief of that is starting to sink in. I wipe my eyes and try to pull myself together. The rain is slowing. The atmosphere is getting lighter. It's almost cool and much easier to breath.

'I'm so tired.'

'Nearly there.' Max reaches over and takes my hand. 'You can rest in the motel.'

I'm almost nodding off now. I'm safe. Max is here. And I've done what I needed to do.

'What's that?' asks Max.

I'm clutching a box in my left hand so tightly that my fingers are white with the tension. I didn't even know it was there. I stare at it blankly for a moment, before I recognise Bill packet of syringes. I don't remember picking it up.

'It's his medication.' I say. 'He's a diabetic.'

'Jesus! We'd better take it back.'

'I'm not going back there.'

'I could drop it off at reception.'

I look at the box and wonder at the power of it, sitting here in my hands. Life or death. I can't forgive Bill for murdering my mother, or for being so pathetic. And when I think about him driving off and leaving me in the desert to die. When I think about me out there all alone, I can't forgive him that either.

'Storm, he might die without it.'

'I know.'

'We have to do something,' he says.

I wonder if Max realises how tempting it is. It would be so easy. I could just throw the box out into some bushes. Soon the rain would dissolve the cardboard and no one would ever know whose it was. So tempting… I reach for the winder, pause for a moment, then reluctantly pull my hand back.

'You're right,' I tell Max. 'We'd better take it back.'

My motives are purely selfish. I don't care whether he lives or dies, but I don't want to be like him.

EPILOGUE

I pull the gate shut behind me and start up the hill. It's still cold for May but the sun is not so low in the sky. Soon it will reach the valleys and push out the shadowy remnants of night. But for now it's dark down there and the houses have yellow squares of light in their windows and white plumes of smoke twirling from their chimneys. Morning has touched here first. The air is light and clean and the sun is almost warm on my face. In London I breathe in little shallow bursts trying not to poison the baby, but up here I take long deep breaths that clean us both out.

This was Nan's favourite time of day. Mine too. Though most days I don't crawl out of bed in time to see it. There's no point in London, surrounded by bricks and roads and stinking pollution. But in the Malverns it's different so I've made the effort. For Nan. And also for privacy. I don't want to bump into anyone while I've got Nan's urn tucked under my arm.

This morning my legs are heavy and tired, my neck is stiff and I yawn three times running. I'm exhausted. I've been painting through the day and long into each night, rushing to be ready for the exhibition. Max worries that working this hard can't be good for the baby. Or for me. But I'm using acrylics for now. They're safer than oils, and anyway, it feels so good to be painting again that I can't believe I'm doing any damage.

The two paintings I'm working on now mark the beginnings of something new. I'm moving away from minimalism. It's too early to know exactly where I'm going and that's exciting. It's a form of faith to let it happen like this, trusting the process to unfold as it should. Max loves the new paintings. He says there's a wildness in them that's fresh and exciting. They're portraits: one of Nan and one of Kita. Later I'll do Millie, maybe even Pop, though that will be hard. I've spent my life believing he was a kind and gentle man, a sane and nurturing force in our neurotic household... I loved Pop and I felt safe with him. Now I feel as if I should stop loving him, for Nan's sake, but somehow I can't. Loving isn't supposed to be conditional. The more I learn about human nature, the more complex it seems, though underneath everything I suspect it's fear that's the motivating force in most people, pulling their strings and keeping them unconscious. Something tells me this is a good thing to recognise and that once it's seeped through all the layers, my life might get a little bit more straightforward.

I pull the collar of my coat up around my neck, wishing I'd remembered to wear a scarf. And gloves, because my hands are turning red-blue and stiff with cold. It's only been a few weeks, but already I'm fading back to a sallow skin and a closed-up northern hemisphere face. I've almost forgotten the feel of the hot sun and the tingling sensual life it brings.

The heady light and heat and space of Australia is becoming an increasingly distant dream. Max and I shared the driving back down to Sydney, so Max could at least see something, and I could sell the van and pay off some of my monumental credit card bill. It was a strangely cold, post-battle journey, Max circling and wary, and me guilty and stunned. Both of us tending our wounds. Even so the vastness and beauty of the landscape seduced us and left us both impatient with this tiny cluttered country of ours. Australia is part of us all now and maybe one day we'll go back. One day I might visit Leo and ask him straight out if he's my father. Though I expect he'll say no. Even if he is. Leo's afraid too; he'll never put his perfect little world at risk. He didn't back then, and he wouldn't now. Anyway, I'm sick of having to rewrite my history again and again. I don't need a father or a mother. It's enough to have the baby coming, and Max.

I'm out of breath, puffing clouds of steam, my heart banging away in my chest as I climb towards Summer Hill. Robins and thrushes and darting swallows are busy working at their nests. The trees are covered with tight buds, poised to burst into blossom, there are bluebells everywhere. A rabbit flashes past, carrying leaves and grass to line its burrow. There's still a little frost in the shadowy places the sun hasn't found yet. But where the sun has reached, the grass is sparkling with wet dew and my feet leave a track of deep green prints.

When I find Nan's spot, I steady myself, letting my breath and my heart slow down again. There's nothing to show what happened here now, not even a scrap of the fluorescent orange police tape. Nothing but my memory and the word of the police to say she lay down here and died. I peer inside myself, treading gently just in case, but the anger has gone and the grief is changing to a gentle sadness. It's been nearly five months since Nan died, but I've stopped measuring time from her death. Instead I'm looking forward, to the birth of our baby. Max says that's a good sign. It means I've got it all out. But he's wrong. There's one more secret I'm not been brave enough to set free.

I tried so hard to be totally honest with Max. I've told the truth about David and a murdering father and every other sordid family secret. But I haven't been able to tell him about Pop. I've tried to get my mouth around the words, but I'm afraid it will be the last straw, that the weight of all the ugliness will drive Max away from me.

Nan was the keeper of all our secrets. She spent her life holding the darkness inside herself, trying to protect us all from the things she knew, but secrets have a way of passing down from one generation to the next, growing and deepening and poisoning, until eventually they erupt... It's better to tell secrets before they become powerful. It is better not to have secrets at all. I promise myself that I'll tell Max this morning, just as soon as I let Nan go. I won't make the same mistakes as Nan. I won't let secrets drive a wedge between me and the people I love.

I'm slowly coming to terms with the ordinariness of life. And people. All these years I've been yearning for something impossible, creating fairytale endings and heroic parents. Discovering the truth has left me with no excuses. The truth is ugly and I can't escape it. My mother was never heroic, just wild and messy and scared. And Bill seems as much a victim as a villain, his life destroyed by a single act of madness. Close-up, the drama of their lives seems pathetic and sad.

The baby is moving inside me, a gentle fluttering of butterfly wings. The midwife says it will get rougher later, with feet rippling across my belly and regular kicks in the kidneys. But for now it feels like little kisses. I put my hands on my belly. It's gently rounded now, the same rolling shape as these hills I love so much. This is my place, my anchor and my sail, and after twenty-eight and three quarter years that has finally stopped being a contradiction.

Looking out across Herefordshire I realise the yearning to return to the fairy tale land of my childhood has gone. For the first time, being here now encompasses all that. Kita was born here. Millie and Pop and Nan all died here. I grew up here. My baby will be born here. And our lives will encompass the hills and London and Australia and all the other places of my ancestors and Max's. I feel as if I've almost broken free of the thing that has tortured us for generations. The impossible tug that drove Millie crazy and imprisoned Nan and sent Kita on a wild and tragic journey. The curse that sent us all running, that made our men monsters, that forced us to live with secrets.

These days I sometimes feel a tantalising sense of optimism, which Max says is right out of character and probably won't last. He's pleased though and it's making us more at ease with each other. We're gradually letting down our defenses, doing things together instead of hiding. Though it will be a long time before he trusts me again. When I talked to Alison about it, she told me not to expect too much.

'When a rope has been cut,' she said, 'you can tie it back up again, but you'll always feel the knot.'

Maybe she's right, but I hope we can let go of the past. It takes courage to be honest. In a way I had to risk losing Max in order to find him. And now I feel closer to him than ever before.

Max is driving up to the cottage now, probably inching along the motorway from one traffic jam to another. I can imagine him in the car, his fingers rapping rhythms on the steering wheel, shifting between radio stations, listening to news hour and getting worked up about the state of the world. When he gets here he'll be full of it. Bursting to tell me all the things he's saved up, while he carries box after box down the stairs, clearing the way for us.

In the end I've enjoyed sorting out Nan's things. I asked Audrey if she'd help me and that took the sentimentality out of it, but not the feeling. It was a strange process, funny and tearful, like Nan's funeral should have been. The whole upstairs is full of boxes now and Max will have to make at least four or five trips to the charity shop. Then he'll pull out the carpets upstairs and I'll start washing the walls, ready for the first coat of paint. Bit by bit we're going to make this house our own.

It's time.

I throw the ashes into the air and feel a surge of joy as the breeze picks them up and plays with them in a perfectly choreographed dance. In death, Nan is finally free to be herself. And I feel lighter too, as if the last dark thing has lifted from inside me.

Somehow, in her portrait I will find a way to paint Nan's final dance.

A single ash has settled on the back of my hand. I lick it gently, letting its soft texture dissolve on my tongue.

'Good bye Nan,' I whisper. 'Lucky road.'

ACKNOWLEDGEMENTS

Firstly a big thank you to Teresita White for years of friendship, support and advice, but most of all for never wavering. Teresita, your feedback has been priceless.

Gathering Storm was originally published by Penguin Australia and I am still grateful to everyone there for getting behind this book so enthusiastically. I'm also immensely grateful for the timely financial assistance I received from the Australian Government through the Australia Council Literature Board, as well as assistance through Arts Tasmania. And thank you to Taswriters for providing a much needed residency as part of its Island of Residencies program.

Thanks to my beautiful children, Nikita, Freda and Harry who have provided inspiration and life lessons. And thanks to my husband, Tim, who has stood by me through the glorious peaks and the dismal troughs of a writing life.

Despite all the hard work in getting this story down on paper and shaping it into form, *Gathering Storm* was also a gift. My thanks, as always, to the giver.

FLIGHT

Some secrets will not stay buried...

Haunted by a chilling prophecy that foretold the death of her father, Fern was given up for adoption at birth by a mother desperate to protect them both. Now, twenty years later, Fern lives in Sydney, plagued by an unshakable sense of danger. Her family and friends think she is losing her mind but Fern is convinced someone is after her.

Seeking to unlock the mystery, Fern takes flight onto the streets of Sydney, where she meets unlikely allies in Cassie, a troubled clairvoyant cursed with second sight, and Adam, a tormented ex-soldier tormented by demons of his own. As danger looms, Fern and Adam embark on a journey which takes them far into the labyrinthine depths of the Tasmanian wilderness, where Fern is forced to confront not only the shadows of her past but the mysterious prophecy that has stalked her since birth.

With modern gothic overtones and interwoven with myth and metaphor, *Flight* is a metaphysical thriller and love story that weaves together psychological suspense and magical realism in a powerful tale of identity, fate, and self-discovery.

'An adventure story that encapsulates both a physical and spiritual journey... interesting and original with some startling contrasts between the ordinary and the extraordinary.'

Bookseller & Publisher

'A mesmerising tale of the real, unreal and surreal…'
Weekend Gold Coast Bulletin

'Dub writes evocatively about a beautiful landscape but, in the end it is the touching love story between Fern and Adam that truly compels.'
Sydney Morning Herald

'*Flight* contains all the elements of a Gothic romance: the villain the persecuted heroine, the damaged hero and the forbidding mansion. Dub has a firm handle on action and pacing but in the end the realistic details of this novel: the Tasmanian wilderness, the shambles of Fern's mother's house… enable *Flight* to take off on what proves to be an enjoyable voyage.'
The Sunday Australian

'The sharp depiction and the emotional force of the narrative are impressive. Still more striking is Dub's ability to maintain the reader's fondness for her eccentric characters… *Flight* is an effective, well-written and glimmering novel with well-drawn characters, a good sense of place and a satisfying number of twists along the way.'
Flinders Indaily.

'This tightly written contemporary gothic tale grips readers from the first page…'
Busselton Dunsborough Times

'*Flight* is propelled by passion and sincerity as well as the rapid trajectory of the story line. It's a novel that will speak particularly to those who find themselves troubled by a sense of powerlessness over their lives.'
Tasmanian Times

BETWEEN WORLDS

Some bonds are too powerful to be broken,
even by death...

Fern lives on Bruny Island in Tasmania, with her partner, Adam and their young daughter, Freya. Adam spends his time protecting the old-growth forests, while Fern is a herbalist who no longer heals. Instead, she's filled with a growing sense of foreboding.

When a stranger tells Fern she must resolve the divide between herself and Freya, she dismisses him, but in the wake of a tragedy, she's forced to reconsider his advice. Seeking answers, Fern and Freya travel to the home of a renowned past life therapist in the foothills of the French Pyrenees. There, in a haunted old villa nestled in the mountains, what begins as a search for healing soon becomes a descent into an historical drama that blurs the boundaries between past and present, life and death, and which threatens to possess Fern.

An unforgettable journey through the illusions of time and space that separate one life from another, *Between Worlds* is a compelling and atmospheric ghost story, as well as a profound meditation on grief, healing, and the complications of love between a mother and her daughter. It is at once a metaphysical story and a celebration of the magic of everyday life.

'A compelling and powerful story of how past lives can shape and shadow the present.'

Kate Forsyth

www.ingramcontent.com/pod-product-compliance
Lightning Source LLC
LaVergne TN
LVHW031536060526
838200LV00056B/4520